FALLING FOR YOU

This Large Print Book carries the
Seal of Approval of N.A.V.H.

A BRADFORD SISTERS ROMANCE

FALLING FOR YOU

BECKY WADE

THORNDIKE PRESS
A part of Gale, a Cengage Company

Farmington Hills, Mich • San Francisco • New York • Waterville, Maine
Meriden, Conn • Mason, Ohio • Chicago

Copyright © 2018 by Rebecca C. Wade.
Scripture quotations are from the *Holy Bible*, New Living Translation, copyright © 1996, 2004, 2015 by Tyndale House Foundation. Used by permission of Tyndale House Publishers, Inc., Carol Stream, Illinois 60188. All rights reserved.
Thorndike Press, a part of Gale, a Cengage Company.

LIBRARY OF CONGRESS CIP DATA ON FILE.
CATALOGUING IN PUBLICATION FOR THIS BOOK
IS AVAILABLE FROM THE LIBRARY OF CONGRESS

ISBN-13: 978-1-4328-5291-7 (hardcover)

Published in 2018 by arrangement with Bethany House Publishers, a division of Baker Publishing Group

Printed in Mexico
1 2 3 4 5 6 7 22 21 20 19 18

For my editor, Raela Schoenherr

You're easy to talk to, sincere, and enthusiastic. You have fabulous hair and admirable taste in fancy shoes. You're unfailingly gracious. You're wonderfully smart. And I'm very fortunate, because you've lent your wisdom to the editing of every one of my novels. I'm so grateful to have you in my corner.

Thank you!

CHAPTER ONE

"I discovered a secret."

Corbin Stewart looked sharply at twelve-year-old Charlotte Dixon. "What kind of a secret?"

"A family secret."

"A big secret or a little secret?"

"I think it's kind of big," she whispered. Her pale skin looked paler than usual against her long dark hair.

When Charlotte had appeared at his side just now, Corbin had been tugging on a resistance band with his injured right arm. Now he let the band drop and straddled the weight-lifting bench so that he faced her.

Charlotte was his cousin Mark's daughter, which technically made Charlotte his first cousin once removed. However, he both thought of Charlotte as his niece and called her his niece. Since Corbin was an only child and had only two first cousins — Mark and one who lived in Michigan with no kids — Charlotte was the closest thing to a niece he was ever going to get.

He lifted an eyebrow teasingly. "So? Spill the secret."

"I've decided not to tell you."

"Spill your secret, Charlotte. I'm stuck here doing rehab. I've got nothing better to do than listen to the yammerings of a middle schooler."

"Yammer? I don't yammer."

"Trust me. You yammer. Now tell me your secret."

Charlotte put on her drill sergeant face. "Get back to work with that resistance band, Uncle Corbin. Then we'll talk."

"Spill it."

"Resistance band," she insisted.

Charlotte wanted to be an orthopedic surgeon when she grew up and had made it her personal mission in life to "help" him rehabilitate his shoulder. For four months now she'd been meeting him for his physical therapy sessions at the Wallace Rehabilitation Center after she got out of school in the afternoons.

He picked up the resistance band and went back to work, watching her out of the corners of his eyes. "Spill it."

"Straighten your spine. That's better."

Back in early June, Corbin had left Dallas

8

and traveled to Seattle so that Dr. Wallace could perform Corbin's complex shoulder replacement surgery. It was the second surgery he'd had on the shoulder since his final game with the Mustangs last January. In the third quarter of that game, a defensive end had sacked him, crushing his shoulder against the helmet of a fallen player in the process.

Of the thousands of plays Corbin had run in his lifetime, none had impacted him as much as that one. The play had lasted only six seconds. Those six seconds had broken his humerus in five places, ended his football career, sent him on an emotional bender for six weeks, and doomed him to months of pain and one wicked scar.

After Corbin's second surgery, Dr. Wallace hadn't needed to pressure Corbin into rehabilitating his shoulder at the doctor's state-of-the-art facility in Shore Pine, Washington. Mark and his family lived in Shore Pine. Plus, Corbin needed a break from the intense media attention he endured in Dallas.

During June, July, August, and most of September, he'd undergone physical therapy. Neuromuscular massage. Electromagnetic pulse therapy. Cryotherapy.

Charlotte had talked the whole time.

She'd corrected his form. She'd told him about her love of Korean pop music and whales and science. She'd told him why her two younger brothers frustrated her and why her mom and dad didn't get her anymore. But this was the first time Charlotte had ever mentioned anything about a family secret.

Corbin was no stranger to family secrets. He'd carried a heavy one when he was her age. He didn't want that for sheltered, odd, sweet, sarcastic, smart Charlotte.

"I've been thinking about this for three days," Charlotte said, "and there's only one person I want to talk to about the secret."

Corbin's jaw hardened because he was afraid he could guess who she was referring to, and it wasn't either of her parents. "If you won't tell me, you should talk to your mom and dad about the secret."

She shook her head. "They're the ones who've been lying to me about the secret all my life. All my life! I can't trust them."

"On your feet," the physical therapist called. "Spider walk."

Corbin and Charlotte, both very familiar with all the shoulder exercises by this point, moved to an empty spot against the gym's wall. Corbin slowly spider-walked the fingers of his right hand up the wall until he'd extended his arm as far overhead as he could stand. Then he began again.

"Up until last night, I was planning to tell you the secret. But then I realized that I can't trust you, either."

He gave her a look of mock outrage. "Why can't you trust me? I'm the one who told you to keep an open mind about EXO's Sehun back when you liked Chen better. Later, you agreed with me. I was right about Sehun." It was all Charlotte's fault that he knew the members of at least three Korean girl bands and three boy bands by name. He'd been trying to wash the information from his memory, but it was sticking like graffiti.

"I can't trust you because you never told me that Willow Bradford was your girlfriend."

Shoot.

Charlotte glared at him suspiciously.

Corbin and Willow had a complicated history that had been sweet — very sweet — before it had turned bitter. Problem was, it had turned so bitter in the end that he had to grit his teeth and look away every time Charlotte started talking about Willow, which was often.

Willow had grown up in Shore Pine's nearby sister city of Merryweather. Char-

11

lotte was in awe of the woman who'd been raised practically in her backyard, then gone on to achieve worldwide success as a model. Charlotte believed her idol to be an angel sent from heaven to wear fashionable clothes, kiss babies, and perform miracles.

"I've talked to you about Willow so many times," Charlotte said. "*So* many."

He remained silent.

"Like, I've probably talked about her at least once every therapy session."

He said nothing.

"And you never said that you were her boyfriend." A scowl lined her forehead.

He sighed and let his arm fall to his side. "I didn't say anything to you about her because I knew you'd pump me for information."

"Well . . . *yeah.* I would have."

"My relationship with Willow didn't end well." Whenever he thought about Willow, a mixture of hurt, guilt, frustration, and desire cut through him. "So if you'd pumped me for information, I'd have had a hard time not saying anything bad about her to you. I was doing you a favor by keeping silent and letting you believe she's a saint. Actually, now that I think about it, I'm pretty impressed by my silence. I'm a hero."

"I was trying to find information on

12

Google last night about how I could, you know, meet Willow. To tell her my secret. I had a mint in my mouth and when I saw a picture of *you* with *her,* I was so shocked I spit it out. It was disgusting."

"The fact that I dated her or that you spit out the mint?"

"The fact that I spit out the mint. There's nothing disgusting about Willow Bradford. She's perfect."

He slitted one eye and growled softly. "See. Now that you know I know her, I can't let that slide. She's not perfect. She's human."

"Straight arm dumbbell lift," the physical therapist called.

Corbin gripped a weight in his right hand and slowly lifted his arm straight out in front.

"How long did you two, you know, date each other?" Charlotte asked.

"For seven months."

"How long ago?"

"Four years ago."

"Why'd you break up?"

"I don't want to go there."

"Did you love her?"

Yes. "I don't want to go there, either."

"Could you help me meet Willow?" Charlotte asked.

"No."

"Keep that arm straight, Uncle Corbin."

It infuriated him how difficult some of these simple exercises still were for him.

"My mom said she heard that Willow is running her mom's inn or hotel or whatever in Merryweather for a few months," Charlotte said. "Did you know that she's in Washington?"

"Yes," he said reluctantly. "I knew."

Her eyes rounded. "Have you *seen Willow Bradford* since you've been living in Shore Pine?"

"A few times." He remembered exactly how she'd looked the moment they'd come face to face with each other almost three months ago. Her long, graceful limbs had tensed. Her pale skin had flushed. Her blond hair had been slightly windblown, which made her look like she'd just been kissed by someone who knew how to kiss. The calendar had said July that night, but her green eyes had sparkled with winter anger.

"I saw her at a birthday party," he told Charlotte. "A birthday party I would never have gone to, by the way, if I'd known she was going to be there."

"You *could* help me meet Willow," Charlotte stated. "I know you could." She tested

14

a brave-but-pained expression on him. "I haven't been sleeping much because of this secret. I can't talk to my parents about it, and I can't talk to you."

He knew he was in trouble. He'd been a beast on the gridiron, but he was a marshmallow where Charlotte was concerned. "How about you talk to a school counselor?"

"No."

"The youth pastor at church?"

"No. I know in my heart that Willow Bradford can help me. She's really sweet and she loves kids because she volunteers for Benevolence Worldwide."

"Just because she's an ambassador for a charity doesn't mean she loves kids."

"Of course it does. Also, she and one of her sisters and her dad were interviewed on TV, and they talked about how they handled the family tragedy they went through when Willow's stepmom was killed. My secret is about a family tragedy, too."

Concern pulled his mouth into a frown. "It is?"

"Yes. So see? Willow and I have family tragedies in common."

He sighed.

"I know she'll help me. I think that *God Himself* wants her to help me." She spoke

15

with the kind of drama that belonged only to twelve-year-old girls.

Corbin recognized that she was working him over, but that didn't make him immune.

"Will you please, please, please help me meet her?" Charlotte asked.

Shoot.

Text message from Corbin to Willow fifteen days before their breakup:

Corbin
I miss you. It feels like forever since you left.

Willow
I just left Dallas yesterday.

Corbin
Exactly. Until I met you, I didn't know a day could feel like forever.

Willow
A day really can feel like forever, can't it? I miss you, too.

Corbin
Come back and see me this weekend.

16

Willow

I'd love to, but the people at Harper's Bazaar who hired me to do this shoot in Morocco might not be thrilled if I left. Come see me this weekend in Morocco.

Corbin

I might.

Willow

Except that you're playing the Eagles this weekend.

Corbin

Oh, right. Bummer.

Willow

As if you'd ever actually skip a game. You're crazy about football.

Corbin

I'm crazier about you.

Willow

Well, if you decide to stand up the Eagles this weekend, let me know. I'll make sure to have a cup of Morocco's famous mint tea waiting for you.

Corbin
I don't want tea. I just want you.

CHAPTER TWO

It was little wonder that pumpkin spice lattes were all the rage at this time of year. Willow took an appreciative sip of the homemade batch she'd whipped up for the inn. A little heavy on the cinnamon, perhaps, but undeniably delicious.

Willow's mom always served afternoon refreshments to her guests at the Inn at Bradfordwood. When summertime had recently bowed out to allow fall to sweep on stage, Willow had dutifully switched out the raspberry tea and lemon cookies for pumpkin spice lattes and almond shortbread cookies, as per the binder of instructions her mom had left for her.

The lattes had been a hit with today's arrivals: two sisters from Portland, one couple from Minnesota, one couple from San Francisco. Willow had checked them all in and given each group a tour before retreating to the inn's private kitchen to sample the leftovers.

She leaned against the kitchen counter, took a bite of cookie, and checked her phone. 5:02 p.m. She'd missed a call from her sister Nora, so she dialed her back.

Nora picked up on the second ring. "Hello?"

"Hey," Willow said. "Sorry I missed your call."

"No problem. I was calling because . . . Well, for a reason that you're not going to be thrilled about."

"Okay. What am I not going to be thrilled about?"

"The fact that it involves Corbin."

Willow winced, then concentrated on swallowing her bite of cookie. Nora was right. She wasn't thrilled.

Nora had recently acquired an excellent boyfriend named John Lawson. John's only fault, so far as Willow could tell, was his bad taste in friends. John, who'd been unaware of Corbin and Willow's past, had brought Corbin to Willow's grandmother's birthday party in July.

Since the party, Nora and John had been trying their best to keep Corbin separate from Willow. Ordinarily, Nora took pains not to breathe his name to Willow, despite that Willow knew that John and Nora hung

20

out with Corbin. Every time she found out that Nora had seen Corbin, Willow felt a little like a high school girl whose best friend was being stolen away by her archrival.

Willow only had two sisters, both younger. Corbin could have befriended the boyfriend of anyone else's sister in all of America. Anyone else! In all of America! Why had he insisted on befriending her sister's boyfriend?

She'd been waiting and waiting for Nora to tell her that Corbin had finished recovering from shoulder surgery and returned to Texas. So far, no such luck.

"I'm sorry to subject you to Corbin," Nora said. "My profuse apologies."

Willow stared out the window at a tree whose leaves were just beginning to turn gold. "It sounds like you're going to owe me Ben and Jerry's when you come to Bradfordwood tomorrow for dinner."

"I'm absolutely going to owe you Ben and Jerry's."

"I'm listening."

"Corbin has a favor to ask of you."

That's rich, Willow thought.

"His cousin's daughter is a huge fan of yours. Yesterday, this girl, whose name is Charlotte, told Corbin that she stumbled on a secret. But she's refusing to tell anyone about it other than you."

Willow straightened a stack of napkins imprinted with the inn's logo. "I see." Charlotte's determination to tell Willow her secret didn't surprise Willow, exactly. For years fans had told her strange things, asked strange things of her, or done strange things in her presence.

"Corbin's worried that the secret could be something heavy," Nora said. "Something she ought to talk to someone about. You know?"

"Yes."

"Corbin would like to bring her by to see you."

"When?"

"In about thirty minutes?"

Today? She'd rather have put it off. However, she'd lived long enough to understand that procrastinating things you dreaded provided no benefits. "All right, but now I'm insisting on Cherry Garcia Ben and Jerry's."

"Deal."

"Where does he want to meet me?" Willow asked.

"Are you at the inn?"

"Yes."

"Then I'll tell him to bring Charlotte there. Thank you so much!"

They disconnected, and Willow settled behind her mom's computer at the work alcove situated along a wall of shelves containing cookbooks, platters, cake stands, photos, and tea sets. She'd calm her mind by pulling up the inn's reservation system and browsing through the upcoming week's bookings to make sure the scheduled guests had received their confirmation emails.

Ten years ago her mom had leveraged a great deal of good taste, money, and hard work to turn what had once been Bradfordwood's dusty old dower house into an inn.

The two-hundred-acre plot of land that had been in their family for generations had been christened Bradfordwood long, long ago. In all that time, only two structures had been built on the family's acreage: the historic brick home Willow and her sisters had been raised in, and the flat-fronted, Colonial-style dower house with its glossy olive green door.

The five-bedroom dower house had been constructed of limestone in 1890 and nestled within deep woods adjacent a creek. This corner of the property was far enough away from the great house that the inn boasted its own separate entrance road.

When her parents decided to spend two years in Africa as missionaries, Willow had immediately volunteered to run the inn until the manager her mom had hired could relocate his family to Washington. She'd been in control of the inn from early May all the way through to today, September twenty-third, and would continue to manage the inn until Thanksgiving.

Her parents and sisters had been celebrating her for her generosity, but the truth was that she'd needed a break from the pressures of modeling. And she'd needed the inn.

Somehow, taking care of this place — making breakfast and afternoon cookies, interacting with the guests, overseeing the reservations and billing — had helped fill a portion of the yawning hole in her life . . . a hole that she'd been wanting and waiting and praying to one day fill with a family of her own.

Willow popped up from the chair and made her way to the bathroom to check her appearance. She had on her usual fall uniform of jeans and tall boots. Today she'd paired them with an ivory cashmere sweater and wide gold earrings. Peering into the mirror, she swiped a tiny dot of mascara from the skin below one eye. Yeesh, her hair looked flat. She finger-combed the loose waves that fell past her shoulders, then applied a fresh coat of sheer pink lip gloss. Makeup was armor, and if she had to face Corbin, she needed armor.

Within the inn's den, she switched on the automatic fireplace that anchored the space. Beams straddled the width of the ceiling, and muted rugs cozied up the ambiance. Four conversation areas filled the large space, two of which were currently occupied by guests.

In the years since her romance with Corbin, forgetting him had been challenging. Since she'd seen him at Grandma's party, forgetting him had been *excruciatingly* challenging. Memories of him intruded with torturous persistence, like bubbles from the bottom of an icy glass of Sprite.

She struck a match and was using it to light the candle that smelled like mulled cider when a knock sounded at the door. Defensiveness tightened like a fist around her torso.

She'd tune Corbin out. She'd tune him out and concentrate on the girl. Willow genuinely wanted to help the girl.

When she opened the inn's front door, she forced herself to meet Corbin's gaze. "Hello."

"Hello." His brown eyes were guarded. "I'd like to introduce you to my niece,

Charlotte Dixon. Charlotte, this is Willow Bradford."

"Hi, Charlotte. It's nice to meet you."

Charlotte gave a muffled squeak. "Wow. It really *is* you." She stared at Willow with a painful mix of fear and hope.

What must it be like to be young enough to wear those emotions like badges for everyone to see? Willow was thirty-one. She'd gone into modeling at the age of nineteen and hadn't worn an emotion like a badge since that day, except when in front of a photographer.

Charlotte, who was clasping a polished wooden box, looked very small next to Corbin's large frame, even though she was probably the same height and maybe slightly heavier than other girls her age. Her body appeared to be gathering mass in order to shoot her upward soon.

She had murky gray eyes and a soft rectangular face threatened by acne that, mercifully, hadn't yet decided to get serious. She wore a long-sleeved hoodie with the name of her church across the front and gray leggings stuck into Ugg boots. Her startlingly beautiful hair fell forward over one shoulder.

Willow led them inside. Almost immediately, the occupants of the den recognized Corbin. She could hear the proof of it in their quiet murmurs and feel it in the weight of their attention. Corbin Stewart drew attention the way light drew moths.

Corbin took the leather love seat near the window overlooking the front drive. Willow and Charlotte settled in the two overstuffed chairs directly opposite. Charlotte carefully positioned the box on her knees.

"Can I get you something to drink?" Willow asked.

"Yes — I mean . . ." Charlotte shook her head and giggled self-consciously, flashing a set of silver braces. "No. Please. I mean, thank you. Sorry! I'm a little nervous to . . . to be around you. I didn't think I would be. But I am."

"It's all right. Corbin? Can I get you anything?" *Arsenic perhaps?* Willow's attention flitted to him.

"No. Thank you." He wore a navy sweater and jeans. Blunt clothing.

Willow had seen him in person for the first time years before when he'd sauntered into a *Sports Illustrated* photo shoot featuring philanthropic pro athletes, models, actors, musicians, and business magnates. She'd been holding a to-go cup of coffee by its protective sleeve in that moment. Golden sunlight had bathed the studio. His legendary status had whisked around him like a spell.

He'd been very relaxed that day. His sense of humor, charm, and easy confidence had worked like a balm on all of them. He'd won over every person in the place, including cautious her. She'd had no idea then that the quarterback with the irresistible smile would become her downfall.

His face was leaner and more angular now than it had been then. He still wore his brown hair, which had a tinge of auburn to it, cut close to his scalp.

Corbin wasn't fairy-tale prince handsome. No, all six feet three inches of him was uncompromising veteran athlete handsome. He was thirty-five now, and the fact that he'd grown better-looking over the past four years struck her as grossly unfair.

Charlotte cleared her throat. "Thank you very much, Ms. Bradford, for letting me come over. It's really nice of you."

"You're welcome."

"Everyone in Merryweather and Shore Pine is really proud of you. I've followed your, you know, career for years and read everything about you I could find. I like how you've been a really good role model for kids."

"Thank you. That means a lot to me."

Guilt burned within her as she said the words because she was not as good a role model as she wished she were — as Charlotte, and even Willow's own family members, believed her to be.

Charlotte blushed. "Sure. It . . . it's so cool to know that someone who grew up around here went on to become, you know, famous. You're the first famous person I've ever met."

"The second," Corbin corrected.

Charlotte rolled her eyes. "Football players don't count."

"I agree," Willow said to Charlotte. "Why should football players achieve fame just for running around a field with a ball?"

"Exactly!" Charlotte said.

Corbin snorted.

"Is it okay with you if Uncle Corbin stays and listens?" Charlotte asked. "I didn't tell my mom what I want to talk to you about, but she knows Corbin brought me here to meet you. He's the reason I got to come and . . . Anyway!" She dashed a lock of hair behind her ear.

"I still think you should let a family member in on this, Charlotte," Corbin said.

Willow maintained eye contact with Charlotte. "It's up to you."

"I've decided that I'm cool with him

listening," Charlotte said. "He has good ideas sometimes."

"Am I allowed to talk or am I only allowed to listen?" he asked, amusement edging his voice.

Charlotte giggled. "You can talk a little. I guess."

"My sister told me that you've discovered a secret you want to tell me about," Willow said.

Charlotte nodded.

"Does the box have something to do with the secret?"

"Yes. My grandma and grandpa, my mom's parents, live in Shore Pine like we do. My brothers and I spend the night at their house sometimes. You know, like when my parents decide to go on a date or whatever."

Willow nodded.

"We spent the night with Grandma and Grandpa a few days ago. I couldn't fall asleep, so I got up and picked out a book. See, Grandma keeps books for me in the closet of the bedroom where I sleep. There was also a quilt on one of the shelves in the closet and I thought, 'Cool, I'll read with it in bed.' When I took down the quilt, I saw *this* on the shelf behind it." Charlotte rested a hand on top of the box. She'd painted her short nails pale blue. The polish on two of her nails was starting to chip. "I looked inside and saw that there were letters and pictures and stuff in it. So then I set it on the bed and looked through everything."

"And?" Willow asked.

"Everything inside this box is about a woman who disappeared in 1977. She was twenty-eight back then, and her name was Josephine Blake. She's my grandma's older sister. My grandma's the middle daughter. And then they have a younger sister. But see . . . my grandma and my mom and everyone else in my family have always told me that Josephine died."

Willow worked to get the family relationships Charlotte was describing aligned correctly in her mind.

"I've always known about Josephine," Charlotte continued. "They talk about her, and there are pictures of her around my grandma's house and stuff. But they said she was killed in a car wreck. Whenever I've asked about the car wreck, though, they get really awkward. They never want to talk about what happened to her." She scrunched up her nose. "I thought it was weird, and now I know why. They were lying. Josephine didn't die in a car wreck. She's missing."

31

"Is it possible that she died in a car wreck shortly after she went missing?" Willow asked gently.

"No. There are articles in this box from, like, the twenty-fifth anniversary of the day she disappeared that talk about how her case has never been solved."

"Ah."

"And here's what's really creepy." Charlotte's eyes pleaded with Willow to understand. "My name is Charlotte *Josephine*. And she looks just like me." Charlotte opened the box and handed Willow a black-and-white photo.

The photograph appeared to have been professionally taken, perhaps for Josephine's college graduation. The woman in the image wore an off-the-shoulder black shirt and pearl earrings. She'd parted her long, dark hair on the side and teased it up at the crown. Her eyes danced. Her wide smile spoke of adventure and confidence and optimism.

Just looking at this picture was drawing Willow in against her will. She had no connection to Josephine —

No, that wasn't quite true. Willow was also the oldest of three sisters, just as Josephine had been. They had that in common.

What had happened to this young, beautiful woman? Did Charlotte's mother and grandmother know the answer? Had they decided to keep Josephine's fate from Charlotte because it was too tragic to share with a child? Or had Josephine's disappearance remained unsolved for more than forty years, as Charlotte seemed to think?

Willow glanced at Charlotte. The girl was caught squarely in that tenuous tween stage. However, she could glimpse Charlotte's adult face playing hide and seek beneath the layers of youth. One day Charlotte would have strong, pretty features very much like those in the picture. Charlotte and Josephine had the same dark hair, the same nose, the same face shape.

"You're right." Willow passed back the picture. "I think you will look a lot like her when you grow up."

Charlotte extended the photo to Corbin. Willow deliberately avoided looking at him as the two made the exchange, though avoiding him didn't seem to be helping. He was taking up a disproportionate amount of the room's air and space and heat. She'd been talking with Charlotte and gazing at Charlotte, and still Willow was unbearably aware of his presence.

So much for her plan to tune him out.

"I'm, like, obsessed with all the stuff that's

in this box," Charlotte told Willow. "There are pictures and newspaper articles and letters. I've read and looked at everything in here about six hundred times."

"Have you talked to your grandmother about this?" Willow asked.

"No. I put the box in my sleepover bag and brought it home with me. I haven't even told her I have it yet."

"What about your mom and dad? Have you talked to them?"

Charlotte shook her head. "They've all been lying to me. I wanted to talk to you first. So you could give me your advice because I know that your family has, you know, been through something sad, too."

Willow's stepmother had been raped and murdered when Willow was only two. The Bradford family had been living with the reverberations of that ever since. "My family's experience has taught me that it's important to have all your questions answered, so that you can understand what happened and then move on from there. So my advice to you is to sit down with your mom and grandmother and have a long talk with them about Josephine. Your grandmother probably knows all there is to know about what happened to her older sister. How does that sound?"

"Kind of okay."

Willow waited. She could tell the girl was trying to work up the courage to say more.

"I've been thinking about it a lot, and I've decided that I'm going to find Josephine." Charlotte's words rang with the determination only people who've yet to be knocked around by life possess. "I wanted to ask you if you'd be willing . . . I know this is a lot to ask . . . but I wondered if you would help me, Ms. Bradford. Find Josephine."

Willow's heart sank. She didn't want to disappoint Charlotte, but that's exactly what she was going to have to do.

Willow was a caretaker at heart. Thoughtful and measured. Even back in elementary school, she'd been an old soul. Nowadays, she was more than mature enough to say no when necessary, to have forthright conversations, to deal with personal and professional disagreements, to set boundaries, and to make difficult choices. That didn't mean, however, that she enjoyed doing those things. She didn't.

She enjoyed harmony. She loved it when she could answer another person's request with an unqualified *yes.* "I don't have any experience at finding missing people," she said.

"That's okay. You don't need experience.

Um, I don't know a lot about missing people and disappearances and stuff like that, either. But I know that I'm supposed to find her, and when I saw the date that Josephine went missing, I knew for sure that God wanted you to help me."

"When did she go missing?"

"On April twelfth," Charlotte said. "Your birthday."

Goose bumps rose like a fated chill, like a tingling whisper, on Willow's skin.

Charlotte plucked the topmost newspaper article from the box. "There. Look at the date."

Shore Pine resident Josephine Howard Blake hasn't been seen since the morning of Saturday, April 12, Willow read. Josephine had indeed vanished on Willow's birthday, years before Willow's birth.

The yellowed newspaper clipping included a photo of Josephine wearing a strapless white terry cloth romper. She stood near a picnic table with a river and hills in the background. Her head was tilted slightly to the side and her lips rounded up at the edges. With her curvy body and lustrous hair, she looked like a poster child for good health.

Willow scanned the rest of the article. "I wish that I could help you with this, but I can't. I'm so sorry. I'm sure that the police, who are trained to handle cases like Josephine's, have already done everything that could be done to find her. I don't think there's anything I could add."

Charlotte's shoulders slumped.

"I'm only in Washington," Willow continued, "to run the inn for a few more months, I'm afraid. I'll be leaving right after Thanksgiving."

Charlotte peered at her with beseeching confusion.

Willow groaned inwardly. Devastating the hopes of a child had not been on today's agenda. Or any day's agenda.

"I understand," Charlotte said at length. "Do you think . . . Would it be all right if we — you and me — keep in touch? 'Cause what if I need to ask you a question or something?"

"Charlotte," Corbin warned.

"I'd be happy to give you my email address." Willow had three email addresses, all used for different purposes, all with varying levels of privacy attached. "Will that work?"

"Yes! Please. That would be great."

"I'll go to the kitchen and jot it down for you." Willow pressed to her feet.

Corbin immediately stood. "May I have a

37

word with you?" he asked.

No! Not a single word.

Charlotte, who'd remained seated, looked back and forth between them.

Willow inclined her head in acquiescence because she didn't want to shoot him down in front of Charlotte. No doubt Corbin had anticipated that, which is why he'd asked in front of the girl. Cad.

"Wait for us here?" Corbin asked Charlotte.

"Sure."

"You can do whatever it is girls your age do when they're alone for a few minutes. Play patty-cake?" he teased. "Jump rope?"

"We watch YouTube videos on our phones," she informed him.

"Bold choice, puppy. Way to be different."

Willow could *feel* Corbin behind her as he followed her down the inn's central hall to the kitchen. Once they reached the space, she steeled herself and faced him. An audience of modern appliances, granite countertops, and the scent of allspice surrounded them. The two yards or so of hardwood floor separating her position from his may as well have been a continent.

On their final night together before she'd left for assignment in Morocco, and then Germany, she'd brought Thai food to his house. The weather had been gorgeous, and they'd eaten and kissed and kissed and eaten in his backyard under the stars. He'd whispered velvet words into her ears, and she'd been filled with ecstatic intuition that he was the one. *Her* one.

Prior to him and after him, she'd dated guys for longer periods of time. But none of her other relationships had scarred her the way that her relationship with Corbin had because the only man she'd ever been wildly, stupidly, disastrously in love with — was him.

"Thank you for seeing Charlotte," he said.

She nodded stiffly and crossed her arms.

He assessed her as if they were opponents at chess. Coolly. Competitively.

She'd once pressed her lips to the small scar that faintly marked the skin below his bottom lip on the left side. She'd once touched her index finger to his slightly crooked incisor tooth on the right side and told him how his almost-but-not-quite perfect smile made her swoon. She'd once inhaled the piney scent of his soap when wrapped in his arms.

"John and Nora are happy together," he said.

"They are."

"Since we keep running into each other

because of them, do you think we should find a way to get along for their sake?"

"You asked for a word with me because you're wondering if we can get along for John and Nora's sake?"

"That, and to apologize."

Was he actually going to say he was sorry? He was more than welcome to grovel —

"I'm sure it's been hard for you to get over me." Cold humor glinted in his eyes. "I'm sorry you've had to suffer."

Anger shot heat through her bloodstream. "It hasn't been hard to get over you. And we didn't *run into* each other this afternoon. You asked me for a favor —"

"— on behalf of Charlotte."

"Which I foolishly granted. Because I let you bring her by, I've had to disappoint a very sweet girl. And now I find myself faced with you and your — your . . ." She couldn't find a word dire enough. "Nonsense."

He cocked his head. "Is that a no to getting along with me?"

"I'm waiting for you to go back to Texas so that we'll both be spared the effort of getting along."

"I'm not going back to Texas."

Everything inside her went still. "What do you mean? You live in Texas."

"I don't have to live in Texas," he said. "I

40

have four houses in different states, including the one I bought in Shore Pine a couple of months ago."

He'd purchased a house in her niche of Washington? *No!* The Great Bend region of the Hood Canal wasn't big enough for both of them. "Why did you buy a house in Shore Pine?"

He shrugged a muscular shoulder. "I have my reasons."

"Name one."

"The house needs a lot of work, and I need work to do. I'm renovating it."

Willow scowled at him as her dearly held hope that he'd soon leave toppled like a California freeway during an earthquake.

He studied her. "Four years have passed, and you still hate me," he said.

"I don't care enough about you to hate you."

"That's what your voice and your body language are saying. But your eyes are telling a different story."

She'd forgotten until now that he'd often told her — and many times proven — that he could read her feelings in her eyes. While he may have had that ability once, he didn't know her anymore. "Our relationship was a short-lived mistake," she said. "Ancient history. I don't hate you, but I'll always dislike you and distrust you because of the way things ended between us."

"I admitted to you at the time that I screwed up and asked you to forgive me. You wouldn't."

"I couldn't."

"So, technically, you were the one who ended our relationship."

"After you did what you did."

"You weren't exactly blameless."

She dropped her arms and gaped at him, astonished at his nerve.

"Derek Oliver," he said, by way of explanation.

She blanched.

"My point is that we both did things we shouldn't have," he said.

"Yes, but ninety-five percent of those things were things *you* did."

"Seventy-five percent," he counter-offered.

"Concussions have ruined your memory if you think you deserve just seventy-five percent of the blame."

"My memory of what happened between us is very, very clear. Make me an offer."

"You deserve at least ninety percent of the blame," she said.

"Eighty percent."

"Eight-five percent. That's my final offer."

"Fine. I'll take eighty-five percent of the blame." He took a step toward her. She could see banked anger in his dark eyes. He was goading her and enjoying it. "For the record, I dislike and distrust you, too."

She stepped abruptly back. "I feel the need to lay down some ground rules."

He gave her a grin underpinned with bitterness. "You always did love rules."

She was a rule follower, through and through. "Don't ask me for any more favors, Corbin. I don't owe you anything."

"According to you."

"Don't ask to speak to me in private again. There's no reason for us to be in a room alone together."

"I can think of a couple reasons —"

"Don't call me. Don't text me."

"Can I mail you a letter?"

"No."

"Can I toilet paper your house?"

"No. And that's another thing. Don't tease me. I realize that you think you're hilarious. But many of us don't share that opinion."

"Many of us? I dare you to come up with one other person who doesn't find me hilarious."

"If we do run into each other in the future because of John and Nora," she continued, "don't seek me out."

"Can I communicate with you from across the room using sign language?"

"You may not. And last but not least, do not flirt with me."

"Flirting is like breathing for me, Willow."

"Good. Then maybe when you stop, you'll suffocate."

Quiet reigned over the kitchen for the space of a few seconds. Then he threw back his head and laughed.

Willow frowned.

He met her eyes. "Huh," he finally said.

"Huh what?"

"Am I so dangerous that we need ground rules between us?"

"Yes," she answered emphatically. "You and the Ebola virus." She checked her watch. "Well! Look at the time." At her mom's desk, she scribbled her email address onto a piece of paper. Then she hurried in the direction of the den, eager to usher out the girl with the mysterious tale of a vanished relative and the man she'd long been desperate to forget.

Text message from Nora to Willow:

Nora
Look, here's a picture of me at Safeway buying Cherry Garcia. Take extra notice of

44

my sorrowful "forgive me, please" expression.

Shore Pine Gazette, April 15, 1977:

Shore Pine resident Josephine Howard Blake hasn't been seen since the morning of Saturday, April 12. Her husband of three years, Alan Blake, says that she left home at approximately 10:00 a.m. on Saturday after telling him that she had several errands to run.

When Mrs. Blake hadn't returned to the Blake home on Overlook Drive by that evening, Mr. Blake began phoning Mrs. Blake's family and friends. None knew her whereabouts, so Mr. Blake proceeded to drive around town in search of his wife.

He located her Chevrolet Impala parked on the edge of town, across the road from Penny's Diner and approximately seventy-five yards from the mouth of the Pacific Dogwood Hiking Trail. Inside her unlocked car, he found her purse with all contents intact. Her car keys were tucked beneath the driver-side car mat. There was no sign of a struggle. The police were notified and are conducting an investigation.

"At this time it would be premature to speculate about Mrs. Blake's whereabouts," said Police Chief Conrad. "We're hopeful that Mrs. Blake decided to take a spur of the moment trip and will soon contact her husband or family." However, when questioned further, Chief Conrad confirmed that the deputies seen dredging Lake Shore Pine on Sunday were indeed doing so in conjunction with the search for Mrs. Blake.

Mrs. Blake is the eldest daughter of longtime Shore Pine residents Frank and Helen Howard. After graduating from Washington State University, Mrs. Blake has been working as a counselor at the Summer Grove Treatment Center in Shore Pine.

The police have asked anyone who saw or spoke to Mrs. Blake on Saturday to call the station.

CHAPTER THREE

The one trait Corbin had never been able to resist in a woman? Calm confidence.

A pretty face and an attractive body were fine and good. Those things carried a degree of power. But calm confidence was his weakness.

And Willow Bradford had it in spades.

After his conversation with Willow yesterday afternoon at the inn, he'd dropped Charlotte off, then driven home. For the eighteen hours since — he was counting the hours when he'd been asleep because he'd dreamed about Willow — he'd been trying *not* to think about her. Without success.

Corbin ran an old, weathered plank of wood against his table saw, creating a clean new edge. His hands needed an outlet, and his brain needed something other than a green-eyed beauty to focus on, so he'd made his way to his garage, which he was currently using as a workshop.

He examined the plank and set it aside. Corbin's two brindle boxers sat near his feet, eyeballing him. He gave them both a scratch under the chin, then went to the stack of planks sitting outside the mouth of the garage. The wood had come from the two sheds on his property he'd torn down. He'd saved the wood, knowing he could re-purpose it inside his house. Before his shoulder injury, he would have been able to carry numerous planks in one trip. Now he was forced to carry just two at a time, and his left arm had to bear almost all of the weight.

Slowly, painfully, he moved the wood into the garage.

When he'd finally relocated a large pile, he paused, hands on hips, breathing hard.

Willow.

Willow Bradford had always been able to pass, outwardly, for a trust-fund baby. With her creamy skin and elegant clothes, she looked like someone who'd been raised with money and taste. Which, of course, she had been.

Back when they'd been together, though, she'd never acted like a trust-fund baby. She'd been easy to talk to. Down to earth. Patient. She had a good head on her shoul-ders. Unlike a lot of the women he'd dated, she wasn't moody. She didn't lose her temper easily.

The two of them had never said *I love you* to each other. Even so, he would have bet his house on the fact that she loved him.

If he'd taken that bet, he'd have lost his house.

The times he'd seen Willow since he'd come to Washington, including yesterday, she'd hit him with a double dose of trust-fund baby. Which only supported the conclusions he'd reached about her after their breakup: that she could be unforgiving when she wanted to be. That she hadn't felt the way about him that he thought she had. That he'd cared about her far more than she'd cared about him.

So why hadn't he been able to control himself better yesterday? Why hadn't he been able to feel as distant toward her as he'd wanted to?

He'd sat across from her in the inn's living room, watching her ignore him while interacting with Charlotte. She moved her hands gracefully when she talked. She listened. She spoke in that familiar voice that warmed him like liquor. Above all, she communicated her trademark calm confidence.

Willow had far more self-control than most women. Or men, for that matter.

49

He had a long memory, though. He knew her outward poise hid passion. Which only made her calm confidence that much more fascinating to him.

He tugged his work gloves into place, lowered his safety glasses, and fed another plank into the saw.

Since the fourth grade, he'd been a quarterback. Everything that had come to him through football had come on the strength of his right shoulder and arm.

For years now, he'd had it laid out in his mind how he wanted his exit from football to go. He'd planned to leave the game on his own terms, at a high point, playing his best.

Nothing about his retirement had gone the way he'd hoped.

In the dark days following his injury, his health tanked. The constant pain maddened him. Whenever he'd been sober, he'd been terrified that the mental illness that plagued his dad was coming for him, so he'd gotten un-sober as fast as possible.

For six gut-wrenching weeks, he'd been unable to accept the fact that the career that had meant everything to him had ended without his permission. No amount of logic or attempted gratitude had helped.

After a particularly brutal, sleepless night,

the Mustangs' chaplain, Pastor Mason, had visited him at his house.

Corbin had always considered himself to be a Christian. Not a *good* Christian. But still. He and his dad had gone to church when they'd visited his dad's family. Corbin's grandmother, his dad's mom, had taken him with her to church on Sundays and Wednesdays when he'd stayed with her for three weeks every summer.

When Pastor Mason had arrived at his door that morning late last February, a wave of relief had poured through Corbin. He'd known for some time that he couldn't continue the way he had been and live to tell about it. He'd also known he could trust Pastor Mason. Their relationship stretched back across the thirteen years Corbin had played for the Mustangs. The pastor, who'd played college football himself more than four decades before, had a good sense of humor and a laid-back personality.

Sitting across from Pastor Mason in his den, Corbin heard himself telling the truth and admitting just how far he'd fallen.

The pastor informed him that general belief in a religion, even the religion of Christianity, wasn't enough to save him. He'd said only Jesus could save him.

On that morning, Corbin had been desperate for saving. After the pastor explained what a prayer of salvation was and what it meant, Corbin had prayed one of his own.

He'd hoped that the prayer would fix what was broken inside him. Fix his life. Fix his shoulder. Fix his fears. He'd hoped it would make everything better and easier.

After the prayer, though, he hadn't felt like the new person the pastor had promised him he was. He'd mostly felt the same. Life had still been hard.

In the days that followed, however, Corbin's nose dive slowed. He started praying and stopped drinking. He focused on recovering.

Seven months had gone by since Pastor Mason's visit, and Corbin had no idea whether he was going about Christianity the right way or not. He was a veteran at every pleasure the world had to offer. But he was still a rookie Christian.

On Sundays he went to Bethel Church in Shore Pine and sat in the back. And he was almost finished listening to an audiobook of the Bible. Most days he still felt a lot like who he'd been before he'd prayed that prayer, except that he wasn't drunk or terrified or so angry he couldn't think anymore.

He was still mostly selfish. He continued to battle the same sins and weaknesses he'd always battled. He wasn't sure if he could trust God completely.

There were times when he wondered if he'd been crazy to think that a prayer he'd prayed silently in his house in Dallas could have made all the difference. It could be that he'd cleaned up his life himself through simple willpower.

He reached for another board.

This past spring and summer, through the loss of his job, two surgeries, two rehabs, and a move, his life had been like an endless brown winter field he'd been forced to walk across. He hadn't asked to walk across the field in the first place. But ever since he'd found himself there, he'd been putting one foot in front of the other in an attempt to reach the other side.

Sitting across from Willow yesterday hadn't been anything like walking across a brown winter field. For the first time in what felt like years, the world had seemed full of blazing color and interest again. He'd been filled with conflicting desires and strong emotions — both negative and positive — that he hadn't experienced for months.

She'd woken him up.

Even though he knew he should have kept his mouth shut and simply left with Charlotte after Willow said she wouldn't help, he hadn't been able to do what he'd known he should. Instead he'd forced Willow to confront him.

Why had he done that? Had he needed for her to give him her undivided attention? Why? Because he knew he couldn't have her? Because she'd been so determined to pretend that he didn't exist?

Corbin had no idea. Whatever the reason, he hadn't been able to make himself leave without talking to her first.

Over the course of his lifetime, he'd learned how to handle all types of women. Typically, he could smooth a woman's feathers in under a minute. But when he'd been in the kitchen with Willow, he hadn't wanted to smooth her feathers. He'd wanted to ruffle them.

Then she'd set down her ground rules and in response, his old competitive spirit had pounded within him like a thunderstorm. He'd never heard rules that were begging to be broken as much as those rules. She might as well have waved a red cape in front of a bull.

But just because a bull saw a red cape didn't mean it had to charge.

He had no business dreaming up ways to break Willow's ground rules. Only a fool would set himself up for heartbreak a second time. He wasn't going to go there with her again. It would be stupid to go there. . . .

Yet he felt more fierce determination at the idea of breaking Willow's rules and pushing her buttons than he'd felt about anything since January.

"Hi, neighbor!"

He looked up to see Macy walking toward him. He'd been so deep in thought that he hadn't noticed her car. He killed the saw's power. Straightening, he pulled off his safety glasses and faced her.

Macy, a divorced mom of three, was his nearest neighbor. His house sat in the center of seventy-five acres, which meant she had to drive over to visit, which she did a couple of times a week.

"The kids and I made pumpkin bread today." She lifted a foil-wrapped rectangle. She'd tied a bow around it. "I brought one over for you two."

"Thank you."

"You're welcome. I know how much you both like to eat."

"You're right. We do." He grinned. It was a grin he dialed in.

Unlike a certain professional model, Macy liked him.

Macy wasn't full of calm confidence, though.

Macy made him feel as though he were walking across a brown winter field.

"And that just about summarizes last night's craziness," Willow told Nora and Britt that night. She'd just brought them fully up to speed on her conversations with Charlotte and Corbin.

Both her sisters regarded her with arrested attention.

Nora, two years younger than Willow, had cinnamon-red hair, a bookish brain, and a proclivity for proving herself helpful. Willow had always loved Nora's look — her pale, heart-shaped face, medium height, intelligent eyes — because Willow had always loved Nora. But this past summer, when Nora's geeky tendencies had veered toward frumpiness, Willow had stepped in and very tactfully, with political correctness that would have stupefied Miss Manners, cajoled Nora into a makeover. Nowadays, Nora dressed like the stylish genealogist she was and wore the glow of a woman in love, thanks to John.

Britt was six years Willow's junior. With her expressive, finely boned features, light brown eyes, and mane of chestnut hair, Britt could have become a model, too . . . had she been two inches taller and even the slightest bit interested in Willow's profession.

The only profession Britt had ever been interested in was the one she'd achieved: chocolatier. She relished creativity, the pursuit of excellence at her art form, and adventure. Tonight she'd caught her hair back with a thin headband, then knotted it into a messy bun. She wore a plaid shirt, quilted vest, jeans, and duck boots that folded over at the upper rim to reveal a shearling interior.

The three sisters had carried bowls of ice cream, spoons, a thermos of decaf coffee, mugs, and three blankets to the dock that jutted out from the base of the lawn that rolled from the historic brick home's back terrace to the Hood Canal.

No boats were presently moored at the family dock, but the sturdy wooden structure did boast a portable fire pit and three chairs. Willow loved sitting on the dock, listening to the lapping lullaby of the water and taking in the view. Currently, she was the only resident of Bradfordwood, since her parents were overseas serving as missionaries and her sisters had homes of their own in Merryweather. She went to the dock on misty mornings, during golden afternoon hours, and at night, like now, well after darkness had fallen. At the moment, the orange-yellow flames in the fire pit cast a glow over Willow, her sisters, and the dark swells of the canal.

"So why do you *really* think Corbin asked to speak to you privately?" Britt asked Willow.

"Because he hates me and enjoys getting a rise out of me."

Nora opened her mouth, then, appearing to think better of it, closed it and studied Willow thoughtfully. Nora was likely tempted to defend Corbin. She wouldn't, though. Nora's first loyalty was to Willow, and she wouldn't risk hurting Willow by siding with Corbin.

"Corbin doesn't hate you." Britt wrapped both palms around her steaming mug. "The night of Grandma's birthday party there was *a lot* of something heavy between you two in the air —"

"Heavy loathing," Willow cut in.

"Nope." Britt gave her head a definitive shake. "You loathed-slash-loved him at Grandma's party. And he loathed-slash-loved you back, which is pretty much one step away from matrimony."

Nora snorted.

"It is not!" Willow said.

"Yes, it is," Britt insisted. "I know these things. I'm a romance guru."

Willow rolled her eyes, then ate a spoon-ful of ice cream, letting it melt over her tongue for a moment before chewing the cherry and chocolate pieces.

"You loved Corbin once," Britt stated.

"The operative word there is *once*," Willow said.

"But you did love him. And he loved you."

"He never told me he did."

Britt's eyes took on a shrewd cast. "I think that he did."

"He's a player," Willow said. "I don't think he's truly loved any of the women he's been with. He's never married. He's never even been engaged."

"Well, I think he loved you," Britt said. "A shared history like the one you have with him holds a lot of power."

"Power to irritate me. That's about it. I never should have let him get away with anything less than ninety-two and a half per-cent of the blame for our breakup." It wasn't exactly true that the power to irritate was the *only* power Corbin had over her. Since seeing him, she'd felt shaken at times. An-gry at times. Distracted by memories of the things he'd said during his visit to the inn.

59

"What exactly happened to break you two up?" Britt asked. "You were blissfully happy, and then you were done. All you said at the time was that he wasn't the man you thought he was."

"I don't want to go into it, to be honest." In large part because telling her sisters everything would mean incriminating herself.

"Have you forgotten about the TV interview Corbin gave on ESPN?" Nora asked Britt.

"Oh." Britt scrunched her forehead. "That's right. I had forgotten."

"Let's just say that I had good reasons to break up with him, and leave it at that," Willow said. "With any luck, I won't see him again. But if I do, I now have ground rules in place." She swirled her ice cream, then took two more bites. Their discussion of Corbin was blunting her enjoyment of her Cherry Garcia. Another black mark against him.

"What are you going to do about the girl?" Nora asked. "What did you say her name was?"

"Charlotte." Willow set her bowl aside. "She's adorable in an awkward, middle-school girl kind of way."

"Middle school was the worst!" Britt said.

"Terrible," Nora agreed.

"To answer your question," Willow said to Nora, "I'm not sure what I'm going to do about Charlotte. I've been feeling guilty ever since I told her I wouldn't help her." Charlotte had scored a direct hit to Willow's heart. The two of them, as Charlotte had pointed out, were both related to women who'd been struck by disaster.

It was more than that, though. Charlotte reminded Willow of Nora and Britt when they'd been that age. Willow was an oldest sister. Her identity as Helper of Younger Sisters had been hardwired into her since birth. It went against her role as oldest sister to turn down Charlotte's request for help.

Charlotte's not your little sister. Yet she'd definitely felt a sisterly protectiveness toward the girl.

"There's no possible way that I can solve a cold case involving a missing woman. Which is why I told Charlotte no." Willow gestured to Nora before reaching to refill her coffee mug. "You're a historian and a genealogist." Nora owned all of Merryweather Historical Village but took daily control of only its Library on the Green Museum. The other buildings she rented to vendors. "You're better equipped to help her than I am."

"Feel free to send her my way if she's interested."

"No offense, but I don't think she will be interested," Britt said to Nora.

"No offense taken." Nora buttoned the top button of her pea coat, then pulled her blanket up to her chin.

"It sounds like you're the one she trusts and looks up to," Britt said to Willow. "You're the one she wants help from."

"I, for one, am inclined to think that Charlotte chose the right sister," Nora said. "You listen, Willow. You care. You have an eye for detail. Who knows what you and Charlotte might be able to uncover together."

"True," Britt said. "The missing woman disappeared on your birthday, so maybe God *does* mean for you to join forces with this girl."

Clearly, her two sisters had been drinking the same Kool-Aid as Charlotte. "Charlotte's a fan of mine, which means she views me through rose-colored glasses. That's why she thinks that I have the power to unravel the mystery of Josephine Blake. But I'm just an ordinary person —"

"You're not *very* ordinary," Nora said.

"I'm not Sherlock Holmes," Willow said. Her sisters hadn't had years of experience with fans. They didn't comprehend how fans built their heroes up in their minds to be whatever the fan wanted them to be. Corbin would understand the fan dynamic, he had legions of fans —

Corbin was a scoundrel. Corbin was about as trustworthy as a toddler with a permanent marker.

"Charlotte needs to talk with her mom and grandma," Britt said. "They're going to have to tell her the truth so that she can understand exactly what went down."

"I agree," Willow said. "That's the advice I gave her."

"Are we sure that she's going to follow through, though?" Nora asked. "It's probably a little daunting for a twelve-year-old to confront her family about a lie they've been perpetuating."

Willow's guilt over Charlotte flared. "She has my email address. If she contacts me, I'll do what I can to encourage her."

Nora extended her booted feet closer to the fire. "If you and Charlotte need me to dig up historical research at any point along the line, all you have to do is ask."

"I told her no. Why are you talking as if Charlotte and I are already a crime-fighting team?"

"Because we can tell you're going to do

it," Britt said.

"I'm a model! You both seriously want me to look into the forty-year-old disappearance of Charlotte's great-aunt?"

"Yes," they answered in unison, smiling.

Email from Charlotte to Willow:

Ms. Bradford,
I just wanted to say thank you very much for meeting me. It was the best thing that's ever happened in my life.

I'd send you flowers or something if I had any money. But since I don't, here's a link to a lit song by BTS, one of the bands I love. Jungkook, from BTS, is one of my favorite singers.
                              Your friend, Charlotte

Charlotte,
You're welcome! It was my pleasure to meet you.

Have you had a chance to talk with your mother and grandmother about Josephine yet? If so, let me know how it went.

I enjoyed the music video. I especially

liked BTS's dancing and costumes. Back in the day, I was a fan of boy bands myself. I particularly loved *NSYNC.

— Willow

Ms. Bradford,
I watched the "Bye Bye Bye" video from *NSYNC. It wasn't bad. All the guys seem pretty talented except the blond one with the curly hair.

I haven't talked to my mom and grandma about it yet. I keep putting it off. The whole thing is sort of making me sick to my stomach.

Your friend, Charlotte

Charlotte,
I completely understand. It's sometimes easier to talk to perfect strangers about things that' matter than it is to talk openly about them with your own family members. Nonetheless, I think it's important for you to discuss this with them, so I encourage you to decide when and where you're going to ask your mother and grandmother about Jose-

phine, then say a prayer for bravery, then speak the words.

Keep me updated!

— Willow

Ms. Bradford,
When my mom told my grandma that I got to meet you, my grandma asked me to invite you to lunch at her house on Saturday. They want to get to know you and serve you some food. I'm sure you're really busy. But if you can come, then I've decided that I'm going to ask them about Josephine while we're all there together.

Can you come?

My grandma makes really good chicken salad sandwiches, which I usually don't like. But hers are really good.

I hope you can come.

Your friend, Charlotte

Charlotte,
Please thank your grandmother for inviting me to lunch.

I'd love to come.

— Willow

CHAPTER FOUR

Charlotte had not oversold the deliciousness of her grandmother's chicken salad sandwiches. They were amazing, indeed: studded with cranberries and walnuts, seasoned just the right amount, and served on brown bread with butter leaf lettuce and thin slices of tomato.

Willow had eaten every bite of her sandwich and her cup of vegetable soup, plus almost all of her chips and fruit salad. Charlotte's grandmother, Melinda, could *cook.*

"Thank you," Willow said sincerely as she passed her plate to Melinda and her bowl to Jill, Charlotte's mom.

"You're welcome."

Melinda and Jill collected the remaining dirty dishes, then sailed toward the kitchen to prepare dessert.

Willow, Melinda, and Jill had conversed easily during lunch, enjoying the meal on Melinda's back deck, which was surrounded by wooded hills. They chatted about the mild weather, the view, and local events. The only person who hadn't seemed to share in their enjoyment was Charlotte. She'd been quiet and skittish.

"Are you all right?" Willow asked once Melinda and Jill were out of earshot. She'd been waiting for Charlotte to broach the subject of Josephine, but so far, she hadn't.

"Sort of." She leaned toward Willow. "When should I say something about Josephine?" Charlotte's eyes reminded Willow of a rabbit in hiding.

"I think you should say something as soon as they come back."

"What do you think of . . . What if *you* asked them about Josephine? Then I could, you know, pretend to be shocked?"

Willow regarded the girl calmly. "The truth is the best policy. If what you found out about Josephine matters to you, and I think it does, then you need to be the one to ask your mother and grandmother about her."

Charlotte licked her lips.

"It'll be all right, Charlotte. They love you."

" 'Kay." Charlotte fidgeted with her dress.

"I've got your back."

"I know you already told me that you

can't help me find Josephine. But I just wondered if there's any chance that you've changed your mind." More words rushed out before Willow could answer. "I'll totally understand if you haven't changed your mind! But I'd just . . . really like your help."

Willow had to give the girl credit. Twelve years old and already full of persistence. Channeled well, that persistence would take Charlotte far later in life. "You know I'm only going to be in Washington for another two months."

Charlotte nodded.

"And like I told you at the inn, I don't know how to search for missing people."

Charlotte nodded again. Her eyebrows steepled in the center with anxious hope.

Over the years, charities and fundraisers and businesses had all requested Willow's support and endorsement. Hundreds of people had sent her letters and emails asking for money and sharing tragic stories of abuse or financial ruin or terminal illness.

Willow had responded to the flood of requests by choosing to focus her efforts on one particular cause. She'd teamed up with Benevolence Worldwide eight years ago as one of their ambassadors. Benevolence, a Christian non-profit foundation, provided food and education to impoverished chil-

70

dren across the globe. She loved the work she did with them and loved that serving as an ambassador for Benevolence often gave her a chance to share her faith in public ways.

How long had it been, though, since she'd invested in a young girl's life in a *personal* way?

Too long, perhaps.

She genuinely liked Charlotte and because of that she wanted to help her. She did. She only wished she could help her by giving a speech at Charlotte's school or taking the girl shopping. What Charlotte wanted was far harder. If she said yes to Charlotte's request, and if Charlotte's family gave her their blessing, then she'd be obligated to follow up her "yes" with time and commitment.

"Please?" Charlotte whispered.

Willow caved like an undercooked soufflé. "Okay."

"Really?"

"Yes."

"You'll work with me to find Josephine?"

"Yes. I'll do what I can."

"Thank you!"

Melinda, who was wearing a collared tennis shirt, a Nike power skirt, short socks, and purple ASICS, carried a chocolate

Bundt cake onto the deck. Charlotte's grandmother's short, light brown hair framed a face adorned with nothing more dramatic than mascara and peach lipstick. Her body was composed of lean muscle, sheathed in faintly saggy skin that had been freckled and tanned by the sun to the color of pecans.

Over their shared lunch, it had become clear to Willow that the older woman was controlling, direct, and organized enough to have become a CEO. Instead, she'd brought her talents to bear on her role of captain to her 3.5 doubles tennis team at Shore Pine Country Club.

Melinda's daughter Jill followed, bearing a platter loaded with a coffee carafe, cups and saucers, plates, and fresh silverware. Jill presented an interesting study in contrasts to her mother because Jill didn't appear to be particularly sporty, nor controlling, nor organized. She was soft-spoken and genuine, quick to laugh, and even quicker to happily announce her flaws. In talking with her, Willow had discovered that Jill was a jewelry designer, wife to Mark, and mom to not only Charlotte but two younger sons, as well. With her long dark blond hair, jeans, and trio of necklaces, she gave off a relaxed, creative vibe.

When coffee had been served and they were sectioning off slices of the rich, moist cake, Charlotte caught Willow's eye. *You go,* Charlotte mouthed.

No. You, Willow mouthed back and almost laughed because the exchange reminded her of herself and her sisters when they'd been little. You go! No, you! You!

Charlotte cleared her throat. She'd yet to sample a bite of cake. "Grandma?"

"Mmm?"

"When I spent the night at your house the last time, I found a — a wooden box . . . in the closet of the room where I sleep. Everything inside the box . . . pictures and newspaper articles and stuff . . . is about your sister, Josephine."

For a prolonged moment, Melinda and Jill seemed frozen.

"You said she died in a car accident. But she didn't, did she? She disappeared, and nobody knows what happened to her. Right?"

Carefully, Melinda set down her fork. "Right."

"Why didn't you tell me?" Charlotte swiveled in her chair. "Mom? Why didn't you tell me?"

"Oh, Char . . ." Jill's face dimpled with concern.

"Charlotte," Melinda said briskly, "we have company at the moment. This isn't the time to discuss a private family matter. We can talk about it later this afternoon."

"Actually," Charlotte said, "I asked about Josephine in front of Ms. Bradford because I . . ."

"You can call me Willow."

"I asked about Josephine in front of Willow because I've already told her about Josephine. I showed her the box and stuff."

Melinda and Jill's attention swung to Willow.

"The day we met, she brought the box with her," Willow explained. "My advice to her was to ask the two of you about Josephine."

"So why didn't you tell me about Josephine?" Charlotte asked.

Melinda and Jill exchanged a long look. Jill adjusted her chair so that she faced her daughter more fully. "I was born three months after Josephine disappeared," she said, in a voice that asked for understanding. "I never met her. Not once. But my entire childhood — my whole life, really — was overshadowed by speculation about Josephine. Reporters came to town on every anniversary of the day she went missing. Kids at school and their parents asked me about it. It was even worse when kids and parents didn't ask. In those cases, I'd see them pointing and whispering."

"You can't know, Charlotte, how much this affected our lives," Melinda said.

"We didn't want that for you." Jill's heavy hair slipped forward. "When I was pregnant with you, your dad and I, and Grandma and Grandpa, decided enough was enough. We wanted you to have a chance to grow up without this sad mystery hanging over your head. Do you understand?"

"Kinda."

"We stopped taking interviews," Melinda said. "We contacted the local papers and asked them to quit reporting on the story for the sake of our family's peace of mind."

"The time had come for us to simply move on with our lives," Jill said.

"And accept that the questions about Josephine would have to go unanswered," Melinda finished. "We invented the part about the car accident, we did. And I'm sorry about that. But it's most likely that Josephine *is* dead. That part is almost certainly true."

"But you don't know that for sure," Charlotte said. "I'm going to find out what happened to her."

"Honey," Jill breathed.

"I *am*. And Willow said she'd help me."

"You did?" Melinda asked Willow.

"Yes, but only if that's all right with both of you, of course."

Resignation settled into the grooves surrounding Melinda's eyes.

Charlotte ducked to pull a pen and notebook from the small backpack resting near the feet of her chair. "What can you tell me about Josephine —"

The doorbell sounded. "Excuse me," Melinda said, rising to answer it.

"Saved by the bell," Jill murmured to Willow, a self-deprecating curve on her lips.

Moments later Willow heard the rumble of a deep male voice approaching from the interior of the house. Ominous recognition drifted through her. *Oh, heavens, no.*

She looked up in time to see Melinda lead Corbin onto the deck.

Corbin. He had on jeans, a simple gray knit short-sleeved polo, and a baseball cap.

"Look who was able to join us," Melinda said. She grinned as though she'd just won a match 6–0, 6–0 and brandished both hands toward Corbin.

Willow sat stone still, a fake smile shellacked onto her face.

Jill rushed to her feet. "Welcome! I'm so glad you could stop by."

76

"Thanks for inviting me," he said.

"Of course!"

Why was he here? Willow couldn't fathom why Melinda or Jill would have invited him to their girly lunch. She'd been under the impression that *she* was the guest of honor. But based on Melinda's breathlessly smitten reaction, she wasn't.

"Sorry I couldn't make it until now," Corbin said.

He spoke as if a pressing concern had kept him away, when he had no pressing concerns that Willow was aware of other than laying tile or painting drywall at the house he'd bought in Shore Pine. He was retired.

"No problem," Jill assured him. "Did you meet Willow Bradford the other day, when you took Charlotte by the inn?"

"They've known each other a long time," Charlotte announced. "They used to be boyfriend and girlfriend."

A blush stung Willow's cheeks.

"Oh." Jill attempted a cheerful expression, but it was clear that the revelation had blindsided her. It seemed Mark hadn't kept her fully apprised of Corbin's dating life. Who could blame poor Mark? How was he to be expected to keep up?

"We have plenty of food left," Melinda said to Corbin. "It won't take me but a minute to fix you a plate."

"I appreciate that, but I already grabbed lunch."

"Dessert, then?" Jill asked. "We just sat down to eat my mom's chocolate cake."

"Yes, please. I love chocolate cake."

He was a very healthy eater except for his two vices: coffee and chocolate. Willow had gone out to dinner with him many, many times. In all those times, he'd never failed to order whichever dessert on the menu contained chocolate.

Jill pulled out a chair for him at the head of the table and dashed toward the kitchen for another place setting.

"Hello, puppy," he said to Charlotte as he removed his hat and settled easily into his chair.

"Greetings."

"Willow?" he asked.

"Yes?" The eye contact between them sparked like voltage.

He raised his hands and very deliberately moved them through a series of quick motions. Sign language.

Melinda was busy slicing off an enormous wedge of cake, but Charlotte was paying close attention. "What are you doing?" she asked him.

"Saying something to Willow in sign language."

"What are you saying?" Charlotte asked.

"Nice to see you again," he answered.

Not likewise. How did one say that in sign language?

"You know sign language?" Charlotte asked him.

"No. I learned a few words this morning, because I know Willow likes it."

When he'd jokingly asked her if he could communicate with her via sign language the other day, she very distinctly remembered telling him no. He'd broken a ground rule on purpose. He was *flouting* her ground rules! Worse, he appeared to be enjoying himself immensely. He looked to be on the verge of laughter.

"He's attempting to be funny," Willow said to Charlotte.

"He does that a lot," Charlotte said.

"I'm not *attempting* anything," he said. "I am funny."

Jill returned and provided Corbin with a napkin, silverware, a plate of cake, and a cup of coffee.

"Okay," Charlotte said loudly, calling them all back to order. "Uncle Corbin also knows about Josephine," she told Melinda and Jill. "And he's also agreed to help me

79

find out what happened to her."

Wait.

What!

Willow felt as though she'd swallowed a lemon. This was supposed to have been a project for two. Herself and Charlotte. Charlotte had refused to show the Josephine box to Corbin, or anyone else, until she'd shown it to her. Why had Charlotte changed course and welcomed him into the fold?

"What do you mean by he's *also* agreed?" Corbin asked Charlotte.

"A few minutes ago, Willow told me she'd work with me, too."

Corbin regarded Willow with unpleasant surprise. "You did?"

She nodded grimly.

She didn't want to see him on a frequent basis! It hurt too much. She wanted to see him on a when-hell-freezes-over basis.

Minutes ago, she'd been thinking that she couldn't take her "yes" to Charlotte lightly. But until now, she'd had no idea just how much that "yes" would cost.

Her brain spun, looking for honorable ways to step aside and let Corbin and Charlotte pursue Josephine together.

She didn't see any ethical ways out. None.

She'd been snared like a fish in a net.

Corbin watched the play of emotions in Willow's green eyes. Clearly, she hadn't known that he'd be involved in the search, too. If she had, she never would have agreed to take part. She was realizing that she'd been trapped. And she was looking for — and not finding — a graceful way out.

The uptight, ladylike way Willow was sitting right now reminded him of a queen. Even the dress was right — a pale green sundress with a full skirt. Her features revealed both strength and fragility; her legs were carefully crossed.

The only thing missing was a crown.

Just like when he'd seen her at the inn, her presence made his senses surge. His emotions were split between disliking her and liking her against his will. And his thoughts were swimming with all the ways he could tumble her off her throne.

"Willow," Charlotte said, "after I saw you that day at the inn, I asked Corbin if he'd look for Josephine with me."

"I was her backup plan," he said.

"And he said he would help. So . . ." Charlotte clapped twice. "Yay! Now the three of us are a team, which is like the best thing ever. I asked Mom and Grandma to invite Corbin," she said to Willow, "because I thought it would be good for him to hear what they have to say about Josephine, too."

"We didn't know that Charlotte had any ulterior motives," Melinda said.

"Right," Jill agreed. "Mom and I really did think this was just lunch."

"It *is* just lunch," Charlotte said defensively.

"We're going to have to talk later about springing things on people in front of others," Jill said. "It's not good manners."

Charlotte's face fell a little. "I'm sorry. It's just that I've been wanting to talk with you and Grandma about the box I found and decided I should do it here. With Willow and Corbin."

Corbin's respect for Charlotte's craftiness rose by a mile. Willow wasn't the only one who'd been trapped. Charlotte had trapped her unsuspecting mom and grandma, too. And she'd trapped him into working with Willow. His little rehab partner had a future as a CIA strategist.

"What can you tell us about Josephine?" Charlotte opened a notebook, held her pen above it, and peered at Melinda.

Melinda's gaze flicked uncomfortably from Willow to him to Charlotte. "What would you like to know?"

Charlotte lifted her thin shoulders. "Maybe start with what happened when she finished college?"

"Josephine graduated with a social work degree in 1971. She moved home to Shore Pine and got a job at a treatment center for substance abuse. Do you know what substance abuse means, Charlotte?"

"Substance abuse means taking drugs and drinking too much and stuff."

"Right," Melinda said. "Josephine was a counselor at the treatment center. She met with patients and provided support. She connected them to resources available through Child Protective Services, County Mental Health Services, and the like."

"Like a school counselor?"

"Somewhat." Melinda sipped her coffee, then set her cup carefully down. "She was a lot like you, Charlotte. Very determined. And passionate about many things. Education. Child welfare. Health care. She was known to carry signs in picket lines or participate in sit-in demonstrations. She was young and smart and involved."

Charlotte wrote furiously.

Josephine sounded to him like a 1970s hippie activist. Picket lines and sit-ins had never been his thing. He preferred to write checks. Corbin took a bite of cake and looked across the table at Willow, who was staring at Melinda as if her life depended on not glancing in his direction.

"Some of the articles in the box talked about Josephine's husband," Charlotte said.

"Alan was and is a music teacher at Shore Pine High School," Melinda said. "A friend introduced him to Josephine, and they married in 1974."

"Do you . . . think that Alan killed Josephine?" Charlotte asked.

"No one knows," Melinda answered. "There was a rumor circulating in town before Josephine's disappearance that she was having an affair."

"Mom," Jill warned. "Little ears."

"Not that little." Charlotte rolled her eyes. "I'm going to need the facts in order to solve this case."

"The rumored affair was just that, Char," Jill said. "A rumor."

"Who was Josephine supposedly having an affair with?" Willow asked.

The queen had spoken. During their relationship, they'd called each other every night when they'd been apart. He'd lain in bed night after night, missing her, holding his phone to his ear, listening to that voice before falling asleep.

"She was supposedly having an affair with a man named Keith," Melinda said. "Keith and his wife, Paula, were in the same Sunday school class at church as Josephine and Alan. The day Josephine disappeared, she left the house to meet Paula at the park and then run errands."

"And did she? Meet Paula?" Charlotte asked.

"Yes. In fact, Paula was the last person to see her alive. According to Paula, Paula arranged the meeting in order to ask Josephine about the rumor. Josephine told her the rumor wasn't true, that she and Keith definitely weren't having an affair. Paula got teary-eyed with relief, the women hugged, and even laughed. Then Josephine went on her way."

"Paula could have been lying about what happened," Corbin said.

"Maybe," Melinda said. "But there were two other women at the park who saw them together and they confirmed Paula's statement."

"Do the police know about this?" Charlotte asked.

"Yes, Charlotte," Melinda answered, with tired affection. "The police know everything. They interrogated Alan, Keith, and Paula because, of course, they were all suspects in Josephine's disappearance. So was one of Josephine's adult patients at the treatment center, who fancied himself in love with Josephine. So was a parent of one of her patients, who had a history of arrests for violent behavior."

"In the end," Jill said, "the police didn't have any evidence to tie any of the suspects to Josephine's disappearance."

"What do you think happened to Josephine?" Charlotte asked Melinda.

"She was my older sister. I'm just two years younger than Josephine, and Louise is just two years younger than me. We were all very close." Melinda pressed her lips together.

Everyone at the table waited in silence for her to finish.

"I think someone killed her," Melinda said. "The same day she vanished."

"Why do you think that?" Corbin asked.

"Her car was found near the base of the Pacific Dogwood Hiking Trail. Did you know that?"

Charlotte nodded.

"In 1981 a woman's remains were found near that same hiking trail. That's too big of a coincidence to ignore."

"Were the remains . . . like . . . studied?" Charlotte asked.

"Yes. The pathologist determined that they belonged to an early settler, but I don't think that pathologist could have told a turnip from a pumpkin."

"Where are those bones now?" Willow asked.

"I have no idea," Melinda answered. "In storage somewhere? Buried? I really don't know."

"DNA technology has come a long way," Corbin said. "Nowadays, I'm pretty sure they can identify bones by matching them to the DNA of living relatives."

"Even bones that were found long ago?" Melinda asked.

"I think so," he said.

"Have you ever provided the police with a DNA sample?" Willow asked Melinda.

"No. No one's ever asked me to. We really did walk away from all of this twelve years ago. I . . . Where would I go to give a sample?"

"I'm not sure," Willow answered. "But I can do some checking and find out." The breeze stirred through her hair and made Corbin remember a time when he'd had the right to run his hands through her hair and kiss her.

He was an idiot.

"I'll give my DNA," Charlotte offered.

87

"No," Melinda said. "If anyone's going to give it, it will be me. I have the closest genetic link to Josephine."

"Okay." Charlotte continued to write in the notebook. "We'll figure out how you can give DNA. And then we'll try to find out what happened to the bones that were found near the trail."

"It sounds like we have a plan," Corbin said.

Willow appeared dazed. She still wasn't looking at him. He'd have plenty of chances now to break all her rules. And she'd have plenty of chances to screw him up in the head.

Again.

"We have a plan," Charlotte said. She smiled widely at him and then at Willow. "Thank you guys so much. We have a plan!"

Birthday card inside wooden box:

Happy 26th, Jo!

I'm committed to being the best husband I can be. I don't want anything in this world as much as I want to make you happy. Have I told you how happy you make me often enough? I hope so. You make me extremely happy, Jo.

I wouldn't be able to live or breathe without you. You're my wife. My life.

Love, Alan

I wouldn't be able to live or breathe
without you. You're my wife. My life.
Love, Alan

CHAPTER FIVE

Willow had a slight compulsion.

Regarding the purchasing of housewares.

She told herself it was harmless enough. But it might even be considered a mini . . . addiction? Just a small one.

It was 3:02 p.m. She'd attended church with Grandma, then taken her to lunch at Flemings before returning to Bradfordwood to change into yoga pants and a sweat shirt. She'd spent time catching up with some of her modeling friends over the phone and had plans to see a movie with Nora, John, Britt, and Britt's boyfriend, Tristan, in a few hours. But for now, she was sitting at Bradfordwood's kitchen table, hair in a topknot, her computer open before her, clicking through page after page of Williams-Sonoma.com.

As she surveyed the site's autumn offerings, her stress level began to subside.

She added a set of dishes to her cart, as

well as one package of pumpkin bread and one package of harvest soup. Might as well throw in six dish towels stitched with pumpkins. And two fall wreaths — one for Bradfordwood's door and one for the inn's door.

She'd stewed with frustration yesterday afternoon and evening after lunch at Melinda's. Last night she'd read her Bible and prayed and tried to listen to God's guidance. Even so, she'd slept poorly because she'd been unable to rid her mind of Corbin.

Today? No different. All day she'd been doing her best to shove Corbin from her consciousness to a place so deep and dark that he'd never resurface. Which is pretty much how she'd been dealing with thoughts of him for the past four years.

But like the pea in the *Princess and the Pea* fairy tale, Corbin continued to bother her. He wouldn't go away. He wouldn't let her relax. The mattresses upon mattresses she'd stacked between her heart and his memory weren't doing the trick.

Look, a Thanksgiving platter painted with leaves and berries! Her emotions softened like caramel at the sight. One more item for her cart.

Chewing on her bottom lip, she considered her purchases thus far. They seemed incomplete. Not quite satisfying enough.

She rose and made her way into the pantry. As she swept a bag of chocolate-covered açaí berries from the shelf, she experienced a moment of déjà vu. How many times had she foraged in this pantry for snacks when she was growing up? Thousands? On the days when Mom fixed them lunch, she'd always been the one sent to the pantry to retrieve a bag of chips, more napkins, or an apple.

This was the thing about returning to live in the home of your childhood. Everywhere Willow looked, she saw sweet ghost-memories of herself, her sisters, her parents. If she listened hard enough, she could almost hear the squeals of their little-girl laughter echoing down Bradfordwood's hallways.

Willow carried the açaí berries from the pantry and leaned against the sink as she funneled a few into her mouth.

She could easily picture herself and her sisters when they'd all been small, sitting in a row at the old kitchen island. They'd sipped out of yellow Tupperware cups. They'd eaten peanut butter and jelly sandwiches, carrot sticks, and Cheetos off of plastic plates, which had probably been loaded with BPA.

Nora, with her brown eyes and big words, always insisted Mom cut the crust off her sandwich. Britt, with her petite face and daring spirit, often placed her carrots and Cheetos *inside* her sandwich.

As for Willow? Willow had eaten the crust. She'd kept her Cheetos and carrots carefully separate from her sandwich. She'd also said thank you, put her dish in the sink, and thrown her trash in the can.

Willow could confidently say that she'd been the best behaved and most dutiful Bradford daughter. After all, from the moment she'd comprehended that she was the product of a very brief, very passionate, and very much regretted love affair, she'd been cognizant of the fact that she had a lot to make up for.

Motherhood, the kind of motherhood that required day-to-day effort and sacrifice, hadn't suited Willow's biological mother, Sylvie Rolland. Sylvie was a tempestuous French artist given to traveling and parties and painting. What she wasn't given to? Changing diapers. She'd left Willow behind without a backward glance when Willow was four weeks old. Sylvie had never had another child. Nor had she married.

Sylvie's involvement in Willow's life had been like that of a benevolent, quirky, and surprisingly colorful international friend. Sylvie showed up out of the blue on rare occasions. She texted Willow pictures of her fabulous life. She sent outlandish presents.

Sylvie was astonishingly beautiful and interesting in the way that an exotic animal is interesting. But she wasn't someone Willow could trust.

Willow's dad had raised her. Nora's mom, Robin, had raised her for a while, too, after marrying her dad. But then Robin had died. Thus, Willow had gained and lost two mothers before her third birthday. Years later, when a few of the kids at school who'd been lucky enough to come from normal, nuclear families, had teased her because her father hadn't been married to her mother, Willow had understood herself to be twice abandoned and illegitimate, too.

She'd responded by flattening the more carefree aspects of herself beneath an overriding desire to be good. To be lovable. To be the sort of daughter her father would never want to leave. The responsible aspects of her personality magnified and became well-armed soldiers.

Her dad had never given her a reason to doubt his love.

Her dad's second wife, Kathleen — Britt's biological mom — had been a mother to all

94

three of them for well over two decades now. She'd never given Willow a reason to doubt her love.

Willow had become a Christian at the age of nine. God had never given her a reason to doubt His love.

Even so, her internal drive to be good — *be good, Willow* — had never relented.

Only once in her life, when she'd dated Corbin, had she shrugged out of her coat of goodness and set it aside. The lack of additional weight had at first felt exhilarating.

Then Corbin had given her a reason to doubt his love. At which time, the lack of her coat had made her feel vulnerable and unforgivably dumb.

Corbin Stewart was her biggest mistake.

She chewed chocolate-covered berries as she lowered back into her chair at the kitchen table. *Focus on housewares, Willow.*

She shopped when far away from home and lonely. As a way to fulfill her longing for family. When sad. To settle her mind and calm her nerves.

She absolutely needed to settle her mind and calm her nerves this afternoon, thanks to the fact that she'd committed herself to investigating Josephine Blake's disappearance alongside her biggest mistake.

Agitation tightened her shoulder muscles.

Don't think about him! Don't. Focus on housewares.

Willow contemplated her online cart. Already, she could anticipate how, where, and when she'd rotate her new purchases into use.

Bradfordwood and the inn didn't technically need any new items. And at this point, her house in LA was as charming as a house could possibly be . . . and had been for a long time.

Yet, over the past year and a half, she'd been shopping even more often than usual because she'd been battling a nagging case of modeling burnout.

There's no telling how much Corbin's re-entry into her life was going to add to her credit card bills when all was said and done.

Don't think about him!

With a deft click, she hit the purchase button.

"Jungkook just released a new photo today," Charlotte told Willow and Corbin on Tuesday afternoon. "Look how cute he is." She held up her phone to Corbin so he could see the photograph filling her screen.

"Cute as can be," Corbin said dryly.

"Uncle Corbin!" Charlotte reprimanded.

"As you already know, I'm the wrong per-

96

son to talk to when you're in the mood to go on and on about the cuteness of boys." He arched an eyebrow.

"Willow?" Charlotte asked hopefully, turning the phone's screen her direction.

"Cute," Willow said, though Jungkook looked young enough to be Willow's son and appeared to weigh ninety pounds. Ten of those pounds were courtesy of the product in his fashionably styled hair.

"Willow agrees!" Charlotte crowed to Corbin.

"*I* agreed," Corbin growled.

It had been decided that they'd meet on Tuesday and Thursday afternoons at the inn. Tuesdays, because Corbin could bring Charlotte over right after his PT session, which explained why he was dressed so casually today, in a white Mustangs T-shirt and track pants. Thursdays, because Charlotte didn't have orchestra practice or science club that day. The inn because Willow had to be at the inn almost every weekday to check in guests.

When Charlotte and Corbin had arrived at the inn five minutes ago for their first team meeting, Willow had led them to the antique French farm table that dominated the inn's kitchen. Here, they were sheltered from the star-struck attention her guests were likely to shovel in Corbin's direction.

She'd let Corbin and Charlotte pick their seats first, then chosen a chair that placed Charlotte between herself and Corbin.

"Cookies, anyone?" Willow asked. "Lattes?"

Corbin and Charlotte both helped themselves to the platter of almond shortbread cookies and the insulated pitcher she'd placed on the table. Corbin took a sip from his mug and screwed up his face. "What did you say this was?"

"It's a pumpkin spice latte. Have you never had one?"

"I'm from Detroit."

"And proud of it," Charlotte mumbled, while scrolling through images on her phone and chewing her cookie.

"Very proud. Detroit is where boys become men. I didn't go to sissy schools like you two."

Charlotte's head snapped up. "I go to public schools!"

"So did I," Willow said.

He remained unimpressed. "Yeah, but in Detroit, we didn't sip pumpkin spice lattes during recess."

"Don't mind him," Charlotte said to Willow.

"I'm trying not to." Which was the absolute truth.

"I think your pumpkin spice lattes are delicious, Willow."

"Thank you, Charlotte. I'm glad to see that one of you has good taste." Hopefully Jill wouldn't be too angry with her for pumping Charlotte full of afternoon caffeine. And hopefully Corbin would remain mostly silent during this meeting. That would enable her to look at him and interact with him as little as possible, which was her best shot of hanging on to her sanity between now and Thanksgiving.

Corbin's phone rang. When he checked his screen, seriousness settled over his features. "Excuse me. I need to take this." He exited through the back door.

He'd always had a streak of secretiveness running through him. Willow had never had the sense, back when they'd been dating, that he'd opened up to her fully.

He returned a few minutes later, and Charlotte flipped open the notebook she'd had with her at Saturday's lunch. "DNA test. That's the first thing I have written down on our to-do list."

"I did some checking," Willow said. "Melinda will need to contact the local police and set it up through them. After she has her cheek swabbed, her genetic information will be added to a nationwide database."

"Oh, cool! That sounds easy."

"The caveat is that there are a large number of Jane Does. . . . Are you familiar with that term?" she asked Charlotte.

Charlotte shook her head.

"Unidentified female remains are called Jane Doe," Corbin said.

"A large number of Jane Does have yet to be tested and included in the DNA database," Willow said. "So even if Josephine is a Jane Doe somewhere, if she hasn't been added to the database, then we won't get a hit when Melinda submits her DNA." Willow very much hoped that the young and pretty Josephine hadn't ended up as a Jane Doe, a skeleton without a name or funeral or headstone.

"I'll talk to Grandma and make sure she gives her DNA." Leaning over her notebook, Charlotte read, " 'Bones found near hiking trail in 1981.' That's the only other thing on my list." She lifted her face to Willow for direction, as if Willow was the lead investigator.

It struck Willow anew, the absurdity of herself as the lead investigator of a cold-case team comprised of a renowned NFL quarterback and a seventh grader. "I have no idea how we can find out what happened to bones discovered in 1981."

"Uncle Corbin?" Charlotte asked.

"I can tell you everything you ever wanted to know about the 4–3 defense, but I'm fresh out of knowledge about human remains."

"We could, like, call the police to ask about the remains," Charlotte suggested.

"When Melinda goes to the station to get her cheek swabbed, maybe she can tell the officers that they have her permission to talk with us about Josephine's case," Willow said. "I'm guessing they'll be hesitant to chat with us unless they're aware that Melinda has given us her blessing."

"Good point." Charlotte tapped her pen against the table's edge. "Once Grandma's talked with the police, then I think Corbin should be the one to call them about the bones found near the hiking trail."

"Why me?"

Charlotte turned to Willow. "A lot of people think he's awesome. Especially police-type guys."

"How come you said that like you're surprised people think I'm awesome?" Corbin stretched one arm languidly across the top of the empty chair next to him. He wasn't staying as silent as Willow had hoped.

"Because I *am* surprised," Charlotte said.

101

"I don't get why people are so excited about football. I think it's lame."

"Should people get excited about Korean pop stars and whales instead?" Corbin asked.

"Well, duh."

"America is the greatest country on earth, football is its greatest game, and I am its greatest player," Corbin told Charlotte. "They should be teaching you this in school."

"They teach us stuff like history and math and English."

"That's a shame." He hadn't shaved this morning, and auburn stubble covered his lean cheeks.

Willow remembered exactly how that stubble used to feel against her lips. Often, she'd cuddled with him when he was dressed in soft clothes like those he had on now. She'd lay her head on his shoulder. Then he'd tuck her in against his side and —

"Willow?" Charlotte asked.

"Sorry. Did you ask me something?"

"I asked whether you wanted to look through everything in the box now," Charlotte said. "Since we already talked about the stuff on the to-do list." Charlotte had brought the wooden box full of Josephine memorabilia to the inn. It sat in the center of the table like a small casket at a funeral service.

"Sure."

"How come Willow is the boss of this group?" Corbin asked. "I'm older than she is. I'm stronger. I'm richer. I'm better looking. And I'm more famous."

"Don't forget more humble," Willow said.

Corbin smiled wolfishly. His cheeks furrowed in a warm, roguish way.

Hastily, she looked away.

Charlotte reverently lifted the box's lid and separated the contents into three piles, one in front of each of them. "Once you finish going through your pile, tell me. And we'll switch."

"Should we switch to the right or the left?" Corbin asked Charlotte gravely.

A laugh slipped past Willow's guard.

"Did you just laugh at something I said?" he asked immediately.

"No."

"I've missed the sound of your laugh."

She pretended not to have heard those last words — *wished* she hadn't — and carefully went through her pile of Josephine artifacts. She read two newspaper articles, then examined a portrait of Josephine with her mother and father. Baby Josephine had a cap of dark hair and round cheeks. At some point in the 1950s, she'd sat for another portrait with her two younger sisters. In this image, Josephine wore short bangs, curls, and a starched dress with a wide skirt.

Inside a manila envelope, Willow discovered a silver bracelet with charms the size of Monopoly pieces. A sand dollar, a cross, the Liberty Bell, a heart lock, the Eiffel Tower, and many more. Thirteen in all. Not the luckiest of numbers.

Each charm likely represented something that had been important to Josephine. The bracelet testified that Josephine had traveled, pursued hobbies, collected accomplishments, cherished the people she loved, harbored dreams. She'd had a full life. She'd been a living and breathing daughter, wife, co-worker, friend.

Ask Melinda about the significance of the charms on the bracelet, Willow typed into the Notes app on her phone, then snapped a photo of the bracelet and set it aside.

Next, she studied a group of four Polaroid photos. Each shot captured a different interior view of the same car.

"Grandma told me that Josephine's husband, Alan, took those," Charlotte whispered to Willow, as if not wanting to disturb Corbin. "You know. When he found Josephine's car. After Josephine didn't come home."

In one picture a white sweater draped casually across the passenger seat. One showed a pair of sunglasses. One showed a tube of lipstick with a beige circle on its end. One showed a ring of keys partially tucked underneath a floor mat.

Ask Melinda why Alan would have brought a camera with him when he set out to look for Josephine. Ask if Josephine often left her keys under the floor mat.

Eeriness settled over Willow as she studied the pictures. They were retro, but still very crisp. It looked to her as if Josephine had stepped from her car with the intention of coming right back.

Then stayed gone for decades.

What in the world had happened to Josephine Blake?

Text message from Britt to Willow and Nora:

Britt

Zander sold his manuscript! He's been offered a big contract from one of the long-established New York publishers. I'm feeling very smug about this because I always knew he was a genius. Now the whole world is going to know what I know. Are

105

you free Thursday night? I'm planning on cooking a celebratory family dinner for him.

Willow
Go, Zander! I'm in for dinner.

Nora
I'm in for dinner, too. I'm so proud of Zander. Handsome, trustworthy, and creative to boot. He's a triple threat.

Britt
Please invite John, Nora. And I was thinking I'd include Valentina and Clint, too. If I do that, do I have to invite Grandma? We can count on her to bring down the atmosphere of the party like an anchor.

Willow
If you invite John, Valentina, and Clint, you have to invite Grandma. It's the law.

CHAPTER SIX

Corbin woke from a dream of Willow into darkness.

No. He didn't want consciousness. He wanted to go back to that. To her.

He closed his eyes, trying to recapture the dream. They'd been in a warm pool together at night. The lights set into the pool's sides below the water's surface glowed. Willow had been smiling as she'd swam toward him.

He'd wrapped her slender body in his arms, and there'd been no pain in his shoulder.

"I love you," he'd said.

"I love you," she'd said.

When he'd kissed her, adoration and desire had flooded him. So had a sense of rightness.

And none of it had been real. Not one second of it.

Desperately, he willed himself to return to the dream. Why couldn't he? He'd give a thousand dollars to return.

Two thousand.

Five.

It wasn't working. His contentment turned to stone.

Corbin rolled onto his back and let his hands fall above his head — only to have his shoulder remind him that his right arm couldn't fall above his head anymore. He returned his right arm to the mattress and tunneled his left hand into his hair, then gripped.

He'd dreamed of Willow a handful of times over the years. Since he'd taken Charlotte to meet Willow, he'd been dreaming of her almost nightly.

In his dreams, Willow wasn't defensive. She was laughing and soft. In his dreams, he was consumed with love for her and overwhelmed by his good fortune. In the real world, Willow didn't love him or even like him. She wasn't his. She hadn't been in his arms in a long, long time.

In the real world, his shoulder had been shattered. His playing days were done. And he was alone.

Corbin tossed his pillow aside and groaned as he rose to sit on the edge of his bed.

Willow had a hold on him he didn't un-

108

derstand. Even when they'd been together and he'd been in love with her, he'd been able to concentrate on other things. In those days, he'd experienced nothing but darkness when he slept.

But this time around, something had changed. Maybe his life was too empty? Could that be why thoughts of her filled his head when he was awake *and* when he slept?

All he knew for sure was that it was depressing as all get out to begin each day switching from dreams of her into reality.

Because of his promise to help Charlotte with her harebrained plan to find Josephine, he'd be seeing Willow often. He had no idea whether seeing her was the best thing for him or the worst. Being in the same room with Willow tied him in a knot because it reminded him of everything he'd lost. Being in the same room with Willow also had the power to make him feel like himself again . . . and nothing else he'd come across since January had that power.

Only her.

Why? Why her?

Willow glared at him while pretending to be polite, tensed every time he spoke, and looked away each time their eyes met. Which was probably for the best since he didn't want anything to do with her anyway.

A memory of how she'd smiled at him in the dream just now filled his head.

And his weather-beaten heart tightened with longing.

Just how many ounces would a slice of Britt's decadent cake add to my weight? Willow wondered. *And where, precisely, would those ounces adhere themselves?*

If only women could specify where they wanted the ounces to go. If she could specify, she'd definitely request that the ounces from Britt's cake go straight to her chest.

It was Thursday night, and Britt had just set out the finale of her three-course tour de force onto the center of Bradfordwood's formal dining room table. Britt's tall cake sat atop a white porcelain stand, its layers cloaked in seamlessly smooth chocolate ganache. Three slim sparkler candles protruded from the cake's top at artful angles.

"It's beautiful, Britt," Nora said.

"Since Zander's the man of the hour," Britt said, "I made his favorite."

"The top and bottom layer are dark chocolate cake," Zander told the group. "But the center layer is cheesecake flavored with orange zest. Then Britt covers the whole thing with chocolate buttercream and then ganache. It's ridiculously good."

"Why, thank you," Britt answered. "You're right as usual, Zander. It is ridiculously good."

"It's rude to compliment yourself," Grandma scolded.

Britt lit the sparklers, and they all sang, "Congratulations to you," to the tune of "Happy Birthday." Britt snapped pictures of Zander with his cake while the sparklers fizzed and shot sparks.

A smile curled Zander's serious lips. Willow couldn't tell if the smile was for the cake or for Britt. Britt, no doubt. He was looking straight past the tiny fireworks display to Willow's youngest sister.

Inwardly, Willow sighed. Zander had become Britt's best friend when he and Britt were both in the ninth grade. In those days, Zander had been as defiant and suspicious as he'd been dependable and smart.

Willow had understood many things about Zander the very first time she'd met him. His clothing told her that his family didn't have much money. His posture communicated pride. His blue eyes spoke of the furtiveness kids inherit when they haven't always been safe and haven't always been treated well. Most of all, she'd seen in Zander's every gesture, word, and expression that he loved Britt.

Willow understood something about her bravehearted little sister that Britt herself may not have fully grasped. Namely, that Britt had been extraordinarily fortunate to have received every advantage in life. Two biological parents who were dedicated to each other and to her. A great education. The careful fostering of her culinary talent. Time overseas to hone her craft. Money enough to open her own chocolate shop.

Zander, on the other hand, had been offered few advantages. He'd had to carve his future himself, like an artist chiseling a sculpture from granite.

In Zander and Britt's friendship, Zander was the underdog. Willow couldn't help but root for the underdog, for the hardscrabble boy who'd grown into a lean, austerely handsome man with dark hair and intricate tattoos running down both arms.

For a few years now, Willow had been not-so-patiently waiting for Britt to wake up and notice the true depth and breadth of the gift she'd been given in Zander. Willow couldn't *do* anything to force a happily-ever-after on them, however. If, by some miracle, Britt hadn't comprehended the fact that Zander loved her, Willow wouldn't be the one to spill Zander's secret and potentially hurt his chances.

The song and the sparklers snuffed out.

Britt lifted her glass. "To Zander and the publishing contract he's been offered for his brilliant book!"

They all clinked glasses and congratulated Zander. When Britt said his book was brilliant, she was only guessing, because Zander hadn't actually let any of them read his book. They only knew that he'd titled it *Geniuses,* that it was a psychological thriller, and that it starred two geniuses — one of whom was a serial killer and one of whom was brought in by the FBI to find the killer. According to Britt's insider information, the manuscript had sold via an auction that Zander's agent had arranged between three interested publishers.

Grandma leaned toward Willow as Britt sliced the cake. "That looks entirely too rich."

"It looks entirely too amazing. Just eat a little."

"A three-course meal of soup, black cod and vegetables, and now cake," Grandma said. "So expensive. There are people in this world who are starving. *Tsk.*" The air from the vent stirred the fur of Grandma's mink coat, aka Old Musty.

Grandma Margaret Burke, as usual, had

donned pearl earrings, brushed her white hair into a tidy coil, and set her lips in a disapproving curve.

"How's your Sunday school class going?" Willow asked.

"Not well. I have to correct the children in my class almost constantly on their spelling and their grammar."

"Ah."

"No Sunday school teacher should be expected to educate a young person, except in the things of the Spirit. It's terrible what's happened to public education in America. I can hardly sleep at night, for tossing and turning over it."

It seemed to Willow that the kids she met were exactly as bright and well spoken as they'd been in past generations. Maybe more so.

"We should *all* be tossing and turning over it," Grandma added.

"Mmm."

"The children in my class aren't well educated and, what's more, don't seem very grateful for my Christian leadership."

"No?" Willow asked with faux surprise. Poor kids.

"Kissing leadership?" Valentina asked Grandma. The forehead of Bradfordwood's

Russian housekeeper dimpled with confusion.

"Goodness, no! *Christian* leadership."

"Ah! Good miss. Kissing good."

"Kissing *is* good," Clint, Bradfordwood's groundskeeper and the inn's one-man cleaning crew, agreed.

Clint was in his late fifties. Since his early twenties, he'd made a career of being an *un*successful and *un*famous actor. Since unsuccess and unfame didn't pay very well, he'd supported himself during his decades in Hollywood by shirtlessly juggling silver rings at a knock-off, less good version of Cirque de Soleil.

Willow suspected he'd christened himself Clint Fletcher during his juggling days under the misassumption that women would find the name sexy.

Now that Clint lived in Washington and had grown a mite too old for shirtlessness, he paid his bills with his income from Bradfordwood while continuing to pursue every form of acting work Mason County provided.

He had long brown hair. Thin and straight, it didn't end in a horizontal line but instead came to a tapering point. He was never without his cowboy hat with the peacock feather in the front, tight Levis, and cowboy boots. He favored leather vests without anything underneath, except in truly cold weather.

"Two people can share the root essence of themselves through a kiss more fully than through the spoken word," Clint said. "Contact of lips is a metaphysical language all its own, you know?"

"No, I most certainly do not know," Grandma said sternly. "That's a load of balderdash, Clint Fletcher."

"Balder what?" Valentina asked.

Clint blushed, looked uncertain, then appeared to give himself a silent pep talk. "Kissing and dancing are both rhythmic conversations of the body. Beyond consciousness. Beyond intuition. They're conversations between the blue fire in one entity and the blue fire in another."

"I have no idea what you're talking about! Blue fire?" Grandma's mouth pruned. "I do know that I don't approve of dancing. It says in Ezekiel that we'll have to bear the consequences of lewdness, and much of what passes for dancing these days is lewd. It can lead to all manner of immoral urges."

"Oatmeal?" Valentina asked.

"Immoral," Willow said.

"I'll get some oatmeal at store for you, miss," Valentina assured Grandma. "Good

116

for your tummy."

"Cake, please!" Willow extended her hand to accept the plate of cake Britt handed her.

At the far end of the table, Nora and her boyfriend, John, bent their heads toward each other. Nora was saying something, and John was chewing cake and watching Nora with warm amusement in his eyes.

Willow sampled her own bite of cake. Dark chocolate melded with orange and cheesecake flavors. It was *to die for.* Fortunately for her, she was naturally thin and had never had to starve herself in order to model. That didn't mean she could eat anything and everything she wanted, however.

The ounces she'd gain from this cake? Worth it. They could go straight to her tummy for all she cared. She forked off another bite, watching Nora and John, trying to tune out the speech Grandma was laying on Valentina about the evils of dancing.

John had inspired a remarkable change in Nora. Under the lamp of his devotion, Nora had begun to see herself in a new light. She was perhaps finally recognizing in herself the qualities her friends and family had always seen: her kindness, her trustworthiness, her attractiveness. Nora had become more beautiful than even Willow had thought possible because she brimmed with burnished joy.

Nora was loved by a wonderful man. And it showed.

Jealousy curled inside Willow. She immediately squashed it like the poisonous snake that it was.

Unfortunately, ever since John and Nora had become an established couple, Willow had been forced to squash stabs of jealousy each time she was with the two of them. There was just so much dizzying affection between them. It was palpable. It was also something Willow wanted so very, very much for herself that she sometimes found it difficult to be in their presence.

She wished it wasn't so. She hated the miserable, slinking feeling of jealousy. Moreover, she knew it was awful of her to begrudge Nora anything. She should be *nothing* but happy for Nora. And she was! It's just that she was a little jealous, too. She'd been praying against her jealousy, asking the Lord to remove it from her heart.

John leaned over and whispered something in Nora's ear. The sight caused Willow to miss Corbin with a sudden sharp pang. It was the old Corbin she missed, the one who'd seemed to love her. . . . No, that wasn't entirely right. It was the new Corbin she missed, too. The handsome, joking lady's man she absolutely could not trust.

She refused to miss the new Corbin! Or the old. Goodness, if she let her guard down enough to miss him, even a little, she'd blink and find her whole life in shambles.

Hand trembling slightly, she took a sip of iced tea. She'd seen him and Charlotte for their second Operation Find Josephine meeting at the inn earlier today. They'd spent time researching missing persons cases that had been solved decades later in order to understand the methods that had worked in those cases. They'd learned that age-progression portraits were often an important tool, and Corbin had offered to pay to have one commissioned.

He'd been generous and great with Charlotte and intelligent and funny . . . and the entire meeting had been a brutal test of her fortitude. By the time he'd gone, she'd felt as exhausted as if she'd run for miles. Empty and deflated somehow, too.

She refocused on the conversation at the table in time to hear Britt say, "Tristan and I are going hiking tomorrow." Tristan, Britt's boyfriend-of-the-month, was a drummer in a Christian rock band on the weekends, a graphic designer on the weekdays, artsy all the time, and a lover of hiking and the environment.

Truth be told, Willow didn't like Tristan very much. Her sentiments had nothing to do with Tristan and everything to do with her loyalty to Zander.

"Where are you going hiking?" John asked.

Britt went into detail about the hike, then rhapsodized for a while about Tristan.

Zander's face turned into a defensive mask. His defensive mask looked pleasant enough at first glance, but it was entirely too still and controlled. The great liability of Zander's role as Britt's best friend was having to watch one man after another enter Britt's life and claim her affection.

I'm so sorry, Willow wanted to say to Zander. She fisted her linen napkin in her lap. This party was for Zander! They were all supposed to be making him feel happy. Conversation about Tristan wasn't allowed!

"So, Zander," Willow asked when a pause in the conversation gave her an opportunity. "Have you decided what you're going to do with the money you'll be receiving as an advance from your publisher?"

He leaned back in his chair, his eyes focused on Willow. "I'm going to quit my job and leave Washington."

"What?" Britt squawked.

"I'd like to travel," Zander said. "I've never had the time or the funds for it. But now I do."

'Atta boy, Zander.

"What?" Britt said again. "When did you decide this?"

"I don't know." He hefted a shoulder. "Today?"

"Today?" Britt asked.

Just now. He'd decided it just now, while Britt was going on and on about Tristan.

"I've been thinking through the ways I could spend the advance since I found out I was going to be offered this contract," Zander said. "I've decided traveling is the way to go. There are a lot of places I'd like to see, and writing is portable. I can take my laptop and work on my new manuscript when the mood strikes."

"Where do you think you'll go?" Nora asked. "What's at the top of your list?"

Britt appeared dazed. There weren't many secrets between Zander and Britt. The fact that Zander had told a table full of people about his decision before he'd talked it through with Britt had probably blindsided her youngest sister.

"Europe," Zander said. "England, Ireland, Switzerland."

"France isn't to be missed," Willow said. "Neither is Spain."

"Okay." Zander's lips twitched into a

smile. "Duly noted."

"What about Australia?" Nora asked.

"Sounds good."

"The Pacific Islands," Willow said.

"Will do."

"I'd love to go to China and Japan," Clint said. "The people there are all really awakened to karma."

"Karma is nonsense," Grandma said. "So is" — she made quote marks with her fingers — " 'the universe.' Every time I hear people talking about the universe and what it's given them or what it wants for them, I'm outraged. There's no such thing as the universe. There is no karma. There's only God."

"More cake?" Britt asked before Grandma could get her engines revving. "Or coffee? Would anyone like coffee?"

Oh dear. Willow was in deep trouble, and she hadn't even seen Corbin yet.

She turned off her ignition and sat, taking in the details of Corbin's barn. House. Barnhouse.

This was a setback. Because she really, really loved his barnhouse.

Charlotte had asked if they could hold this Operation Find Josephine meeting at Corbin's house on Tuesday morning instead of at the inn in the afternoon because Charlotte and her two younger brothers were enjoying a few days off for fall break. Her family had plans to spend the rest of the day on Bainbridge Island.

Willow had told Charlotte yes. But now that she'd arrived at Corbin's, the dangers of interacting with him on his home turf were suddenly revealing themselves. She was a woman who loved homes, who craved everything that *home* meant. She hadn't set foot outside her car, and already his home was seducing her the way cream seduced cats.

At ten fifteen on this cool, early October morning, swirls of pearly mist clung to the base of the structure and its surrounding trees. It looked like a place conjured out of dreams — *her* dreams — and served to her on a mystical platter.

The structure formed the letter *L.* An old-fashioned barn built in the classic shape formed one line of the *L.* The other line of the *L* was rectangular and two stories tall. Weathered, vertically-set wooden boards covered the exterior of both wings. Brown-red paint framed the windows. At least two charming porches tucked into the building at different points.

It whispered to her, this house. It spoke of

history, style, and spaces that waited for children.

Get your mitts off Corbin's house, Willow!

Corbin's Navigator sat next to a Mercedes sedan on the driveway. She hadn't realized Corbin had two cars with him in Washington. She saw no sign of Jill's car, likely because Jill had either already dropped Charlotte off or because Corbin had picked Charlotte up from her house this morning.

Still, she didn't want to risk arriving before Charlotte, so she waited until 10:20, five minutes past their scheduled start time, to make sure she'd be the last to arrive.

As mist does, it vanished as she neared, unveiling the stone pathway leading to the door.

Corbin answered her knock wearing tan carpenter's pants and a white T-shirt beneath a navy zippered sweat shirt. He met her eyes and for a pulse she couldn't find words. His chest looked especially broad in that sweat shirt. Which actually had nothing to do with his sweat shirt. The man had a broad chest. Was — wasn't he supposed to say something first?

He finally did. "Are you auditioning for the part of Little Red Riding Hood?"

Willow knotted the belt of her strawberry red wool coat. "If I am, then you know what that makes you, right?"

Corbin studied her, amusement creasing the skin beside his eyes. "The wolf."

"How appropriate."

"The wolf's my favorite character in that story."

"The wolf dies in the end."

"But he got in some good meals along the way."

"Before he died."

He held back the door for her to enter.

The threshold led into the barn section of the house, which stood empty.

"Can I take your coat?" he asked.

"No, thank you."

"Afraid I'll steal it?"

"No," she said tautly. "Being near you makes me cold."

He laughed.

She endeavored not to notice how blatantly handsome he was. Oh, how she wished that he'd returned to Dallas for rehab. Seeing him was like a dagger slicing against tender skin. Every time.

His dogs ran forward to greet her, tails wagging. She bent and rubbed each of their heads in turn. "Hi, Max." The boxers were brothers from the same litter. "Hi, Duke." They'd been friendly, loyal, rambunctious two-year-olds when she and Corbin had dated. She traveled too much to have a dog of her own, but she'd adored Max and Duke, and they'd always returned the favor.

"You're a lot happier to see them than you were me," Corbin observed.

"True." The dogs gave her panting, canine grins, then trotted at her heels as she followed Corbin. Portions of the barn's tall interior walls, which boasted numerous windows, awaited drywall and paint. An old stone fireplace climbed the full height of the wall that connected the barn to the rest of the floor plan. Corbin led her past the fireplace into a hallway. They passed an office and a dining room.

"Where's Charlotte?" Willow asked.

"She's running late."

Her gait faltered.

"You're not going to run back to your car, are you, Little Red Riding Hood?"

Should she? She came to a stop.

"I promise not to bite." Corbin continued around a doorway and out of sight. "Unless you want me to."

She didn't move.

Corbin stuck his head back into the hallway. "Are you scared of me?" he asked hopefully, as if the possibility flattered him.

Her pride prevented her from admitting that yes, yes, she was. "No," she said succinctly and continued into the kitchen. It smelled mildly like fresh paint and strongly like coffee. White walls. Gray concrete countertops. A backsplash of glistening white subway tile. Expensive appliances. Brand-new unpainted cabinetry.

Four huge panels of glass, the middle two of which were doors, took up most of the exterior wall. They overlooked yet another patio shaded by a rustic wooden portico.

The interior of Corbin's kitchen lacked much. It lacked a breakfast table, chairs, and every type of decorative touch that Willow excelled at providing. This house, this room, was begging for her attention.

Mitts off!

Corbin indicated the vintage metal stools that waited at the kitchen's island. Willow hooked the heel of one black boot over the stool's rung, crossed her legs, and did her best to project casual ease. She'd gained plenty of experience at conveying moods thanks to modeling. She could only hope that experience would pay dividends.

Max and Duke sat on their haunches, watching her with dark eyes.

"Coffee?" Corbin asked.

"Yes, please."

He poured her coffee into a ceramic mug, then went to the refrigerator and extracted the exact brand of vanilla creamer she'd used when they were dating and still used faithfully to this day.

Tenderness pricked her, a warm, deep nick. He'd remembered.

"Have you had anything to eat?" He slid her coffee to her, then filled a glass with ice water and passed that over, too.

"Not much," she admitted. The prospect of seeing him had rendered her too jumpy to eat a full breakfast this morning.

He glanced at her with an expression that gently chided her for not eating breakfast. He believed food was fuel. "KIND bar?" he asked, opening a cupboard.

"Sure."

"You like the fruit and nut flavor, right?"

"Right." She accepted the bar and un-wrapped it. "What year was this house built?"

"The barn was built in 1885."

"This is exactly the sort of building Nora used to acquire for Merryweather Historical Village. You're lucky she didn't get to it first."

"Very lucky." Though he didn't look the least bit threatened at the idea of a property competition between him and Willow's li-brarian sister.

Her granola bar tasted salty and nutty and

128

wonderful. "How did you find this house?"

He refilled his own coffee mug. "I came to Shore Pine to look at property before my second shoulder surgery. I wanted to rent something near Wallace Rehabilitation Center for a couple of months. This was on the market at the time."

"The rental market?"

"Yeah. Parts of the house had been badly renovated. Other parts hadn't been renovated it all. But when I saw it, I liked it." He shrugged. "So I called the owner and I asked if I could buy it from them."

"And the owner agreed."

"I offered a price that was hard to refuse. I moved in before the surgery, and I've been working on the house as much as my shoulder has allowed me to since then."

She sipped his delicious coffee, wishing she'd discovered this house when it was on the market. She'd have snapped it up and spent many happy years filling it with housewares. Instead, this craveable house had gone to the dark side.

From his position directly across the island from her, Corbin was communicating the brand of casual ease she'd been straining for. He crossed his arms. "Being alone with me breaks one of your ground rules, doesn't it?"

"Yes."

"Which is why you hesitated back in the hallway."

"Ground rules are meant to be followed."

"I know that's what you were thinking when you made up the rules. But all I could think then and now is how much I want to break them. All of them. So far I've only broken two, which is pretty disappointing. I'm off my game."

"You're off your rocker. The rules stand." She finished her KIND bar.

His attention trailed down to her chin, then back to her eyes. "Charlotte's not here, so —"

"It would be best if someone would notify me in the future if Charlotte's running late."

"I don't have your phone number. Want to give it to me? So I can notify you?"

"No."

"Like I was saying, Charlotte's not here. So this seems like a good time to talk about what happened between you and me."

Her posture went rigid. "There's no reason to talk about it."

"I think there is."

"Nope."

"Because it seems to me that you're carrying a lot of . . . hostility."

"That's because I *am* carrying a lot of

130

hostility. I don't want to discuss it further." She hated even thinking about the final days of their relationship, when she'd been so embarrassingly exposed and anxious.

"Your plan is to keep on giving me the cold shoulder every time we meet to discuss Josephine's case?" he asked.

"Every. Time."

He peered out the kitchen's wall of glass, his gaze appearing to trace the contours of his property. The murky light flowing into the room tipped every point along his profile. Masculine nose. Soft lips. Hard chin.

Corbin wasn't the Mustangs' quarterback anymore. A new player had taken over the role he'd held for so long. That circumstance had no doubt changed many things for Corbin, but it would never change the physical grace and command with which he carried himself. You could take the quarterback out of the game, but you could never take the game out of the quarterback.

He turned his head and looked at her. She could sense the dangerous beast called chemistry that still lurked between them. It was stirring. Its head was rising up from slumber and the beast was blinking at her with glowing eyes.

She braced, refusing to respond to his look in any way because she was afraid of what even a seemingly harmless response could lead to. She had no interest in being his friend . . . or . . . anything else.

"Hello?" Charlotte's voice carried from the front of the house.

"Come on back," Corbin called. "We're in the kitchen."

Charlotte bustled in, looking harried. The dogs sprang to their feet to greet her. "Sorry I'm so late. Liam and Brady were wrestling, and Brady hit his ankle on a chair. He cried and cried and everyone thought it might be broken, and then my dad gave him a popsicle and now he's fine." She shook her head and climbed onto the stool next to Willow's.

"KIND bar?" Corbin asked her.

"No, thank you." She opened her notebook. "I've been excited to hear what you found out about the bones near the Pacific Dogwood Trail."

"Well, first of all, let me just say that the Shore Pine police officers are a great group," Corbin said.

"Who like football?" Charlotte asked.

"Yes. That, and donuts. They were happy to hook me up with information." He poured Charlotte a glass of milk and set it before her. "After the bones were discovered by hikers, they were taken to a pathology lab. Like Melinda said, the pathologist

132

determined that they were historic. So they were sent to a college laboratory."

"Are they still there?" Charlotte asked.

"No. They sat there for twenty-eight years. Then, when the lab was reorganized and renovated, the college sent the remains back to the county. In 2012, the county sent them to the lab at the University of North Texas Health Science Center."

Charlotte scratched her jaw. "So does that mean the bones have been . . . studied or whatever? For their DNA?"

"Yes. They were entered into the nation-wide database, but no matches have been found. They're still unidentified."

"Are the bones really, really old? Like the pathology . . . or whatever guy said?" Charlotte asked.

"No. He got it wrong."

"So it's possible that they could have belonged to Josephine?"

"It's possible."

Charlotte's eyes rounded. She slanted toward Willow. "Grandma went to the station and gave her DNA last week."

"Which means," Willow said, "that we should find out soon if Melinda's DNA matches the bones discovered near the hiking trail."

"We're digging up the past," Charlotte said.

In more ways than one, Willow thought, her focus returning as if pulled unwillingly by a magnet . . . to Corbin.

Shore Pine Gazette, April 12, 1987:

One decade ago on this day, Josephine Blake disappeared from the streets of Shore Pine without a trace. Despite an extensive search by local authorities and the involvement of the American Coalition for the Discovery of Missing Persons, Josephine has never been found.

Three years ago Josephine's husband, Alan Blake, filed a petition to have Josephine declared "dead in absentia." Mr. Blake has subsequently remarried, and he and his wife are the parents of one young son. "I still think about Josephine every day," Mr. Blake said when contacted for a statement by this publication. "I pray that we'll one day know what happened to her."

CHAPTER SEVEN

The following Monday morning, the sound of Grandma's complaining greeted Willow as she entered the Inn at Bradfordwood.

Grandma's complaining was the anti-coffee. It made Willow want to turn around and crawl back into bed.

"You'll get a sunburn," Grandma was saying to Clint. "Not to mention that it's inappropriate for a man to show so much of his arms."

"Good morning." Willow hung her coat on the peg by the door.

"Good morning," Clint replied, looking deeply relieved to see her.

Grandma, who was stirring batter, had clearly put Clint to work. He gripped a pastry blender and was cutting butter into a cinnamon crumble.

"I stopped by to make my coffee cake." Grandma sniffed. "With what you're charging the guests per night —"

"With what Mom's charging," Willow corrected mildly.

"No matter who's charging it, it's highway robbery."

"Actually, the inn's prices are comparable to the other B&Bs in the area —"

"Anyway," Grandma said. "With what the guests here are paying, they have every right to expect homemade baked goods instead of the store-bought ones you and Kathleen serve."

Willow gave Grandma a peck on the cheek and refrained from pointing out that while she might not bake the pastries, she did whip up the main breakfast dish each morning.

"You're in early," Willow said to Clint as she set her mom's Egg in Hash Brown Nests recipe on the counter.

"The McKinnons in the Blakely Room left thirty minutes ago to catch a flight," Clint said. "I thought I'd work on their room now, before I mulch soil in the flower beds."

"I was telling Clint that it's unseemly to walk around with bare arms all the time," Grandma said.

"His vests are part of his personal style." Willow winked encouragement at Clint. "Right?" She donned an apron and went to the sink to wash her hands.

"You could say so, yes."

Grandma poured her batter into a casserole dish. "Jesus gave us an excellent example of how men ought to dress."

"In robes?" Willow asked.

"With decency. And self-respect. He certainly never went around half unclothed."

"What about at the Last Supper?" Willow set out the ingredients she'd need for her recipe. "When he washed the disciples' feet?"

"Clint is not washing the disciples' feet today! Are you, Clint?"

"Uh. Aren't all the disciples dead by now?" he asked.

"It's just appalling how people dress these days," Grandma continued. "Whatever happened to the virtue of modesty? Clint, please pass the cinnamon crumble topping."

He handed it over, and Grandma sprinkled it over her cake batter.

Clint edged toward the hallway and escape.

Grandma railed against the culture and the disastrous effects nonbelievers had had on the way Christians dressed while Willow worked. When Grandma finally left the inn to grace her women's Bible study with her negativity, Willow had the egg nests in the oven.

She sliced fruit, made coffee, and filled matching glass pitchers with ice water and orange juice. When the timer went off, she carefully lifted the egg nests onto the counter.

Since arriving in Merryweather, Willow had made each of her mom's fifteen breakfast recipes numerous times. The guests who'd come early in her stint as innkeeper had been subjected to her freshman attempts at baked French toast, egg sausage casserole, and the rest. The guests who'd come later had benefitted from all the baking practice she'd put in over the passing months.

Still wearing the white apron she always wore when serving breakfast, she made her way into the dining room and set the egg nests onto the warming tray beside the china plates, goblets, and sterling silver cutlery that were already arrayed on the enormous sideboard. She made trips to and from the kitchen until she'd added the fruit, the coffee cake, and the coffee urn.

"Good morning!" A middle-aged woman entered the dining room, followed by a man of around the same age and two college-aged kids.

"Good morning." This must be the Durant family from Oregon, who were staying for three nights. Willow hadn't met them previously, because Valentina had checked them in on Saturday. Three days a week, Valentina worked at Bradfordwood. On Saturdays and Sundays, Willow's days off, Valentina took over for her at the inn. "I'm Willow."

"Liz Durant," the woman replied. "This is my husband, Dale, and our kids, Cody and Madison."

"Nice to meet you all."

Madison wore her blond hair board straight, while her brother Cody wore his blond hair shaggy. It was somewhat unusual to host college kids at the inn. Most of the guests were either married couples further along in years or women enjoying a girl's trip.

Everyone in the family, except Liz, was dressed for golf. An early tee time probably explained why they'd arrived at the start of the B&B's 8:00–9:00 a.m. breakfast service window.

"What brought you to Merryweather?" Willow asked.

"The kids are both in school here in Washington," Liz answered. "They had a three-day weekend, so we decided to drive up and

139

spend it with them here. A friend of mine recommended the inn."

"Wonderful. Are you enjoying your stay so far?"

"We're having a great time," Dale said. "We've been playing a round or two every day."

"Everyone except me," Liz said. "I sit in the clubhouse and drink coffee and read books. They think they got the better end of the bargain, but they don't know what I know." Liz and Willow exchanged smiles.

The Durants made their way through the breakfast buffet line. A couple came down for breakfast next, followed by two sisters.

Willow replenished the juice, made sure everyone had butter within reach, and ran to fetch an additional set of salt and pepper shakers. The whole time she was aware of Cody Durant's gaze following her.

As she made her way around the table re-filling water goblets, Cody scooted his chair back slightly and looked up at her. "Are you Willow . . . *Bradford*? The model?"

Willow hesitated. The rest of the guests were talking about the weather. Cody had kept his question private by asking it in a low tone of voice. Still. This was the first time she'd been recognized by a guest since coming to work at the inn. She didn't want

him to pair her, the woman serving breakfast at the Inn at Bradfordwood, with the
much more public persona of Willow Bradford, model.

She bought time by leaning forward to
pour water into his glass.

These days, even the world's most successful models weren't household names.
Many of them wished they were and culti-
vated fame for fame's sake. They regularly
shared aspects of their lives with their hundreds of thousands of followers on Instagram or Twitter or Snapchat. They jostled
for chances to be interviewed. They did outrageous things to garner press. They hun-
gered for attention, and so they enjoyed it
when photographers tailed them because it
made them feel special.

Not Willow. She'd never courted that kind
of notoriety. Yes, she enjoyed receiving encouragement from girls like Charlotte. But
she wasn't a showman at heart. She didn't
crave the spotlight. She loved that no one
bothered her here in her hometown, that
she could still live a normal life, that her
freedom and independence were intact. The
only time she put herself out there was for
Benevolence Worldwide.

"I never imagined I'd run into Willow
Bradford here. But you look just like her,

and this place is called the Inn at *Bradford-wood*." Cody seemed social, like the type of college guy who had girlfriends and planned parties and talked his buddies into road trips. "Are you her?"

Sigh. "Yes."

"The model?"

"Yes."

He grinned. "Wow."

"I'm running my mom's inn while she's overseas, until the manager she hired arrives."

"Awesome."

"Listen, I'm trying to keep a low profile."

"Yeah?"

"So please don't mention my presence here to anyone. Okay?"

"Cool." His blue eyes turned soft. "Any chance I can . . . take you out while I'm in town? How about going out for drinks tonight?"

Was Cody past the legal drinking age? If so, barely. She felt a generation older than him. She had more in common with his mom. "It's nice of you to offer, but I never date guests." This was a brand-new rule. Since guests were usually over sixty, married, or female, she hadn't needed to institute this rule until now.

She pretended not to notice Cody's stare

as she poured water into his sister's goblet.

"I've been reading newspaper articles from the seventies online," Corbin told Willow and Charlotte the next afternoon. They were sitting in the inn's kitchen, which Charlotte had recently nicknamed League of Justice Headquarters.

In response to his statement, Willow avoided looking at him, as usual. Charlotte twirled a piece of her hair while staring at nothing.

Irritation needled him. Corbin was used to people giving him their full attention.

"Did you know that bowhead whales can live more than two hundred years?" Charlotte asked.

Corbin furrowed his forehead. "What do bowhead whales have to do with newspaper articles from the seventies?"

"Oh! Um. Nothing." Charlotte smiled. "I was just thinking about it and thought I'd tell you guys. Whale trivia. Do you like the game Trivial Pursuit?"

"What does Trivial Pursuit have to do with newspaper articles from the seventies?" Corbin asked.

"I don't really like Trivial Pursuit," Willow said. "I like Nertz way better, even though I'm not very good at it."

"I'd be happy to smoke you at Nertz anytime," Corbin said to Willow. "How about tonight?"

"I'm busy."

He'd known, of course, that she'd say no. But whenever he provoked her she tightened her lips, which made her look like a drop-dead gorgeous kindergarten teacher who was losing her patience. So provoking her was pretty much his favorite thing.

"Nertz? How do you play that?" Charlotte asked.

As Willow explained the game to Charlotte, Corbin watched Willow the way a mountain lion watches its prey.

What would it take to persuade her to kiss him with those kindergarten teacher lips? What would it feel like to have that mouth beneath his —

Stop it, Corbin.

Good grief, his mind was getting hard to control where she was concerned.

Willow had sat in his kitchen the other day in her red coat, every line of her elegant and untouchable and filled with that calm confidence thing that never failed to do him in. At first, all he'd been able to think was how good it was to have her in his house. He'd felt like a pirate who'd finally kid-

144

napped the one woman he'd always wanted most.

But then, when he'd tried to talk to her about their breakup, he'd been able to see in her eyes, her words, her body language just how much he'd injured her four years ago. His sense of victory over having her in his house had turned to ashes.

Both he and Willow were children of parents who'd abandoned them. It wasn't easy for either of them to invest themselves in someone who might desert them.

He hated that he'd been the one to break her trust.

His relationship with Willow had once been critically important to him. He'd never intended to risk it, but that's what he'd done, through carelessness. He hadn't been nearly as careful with Willow as he should have been. Maybe because he'd let down his guard. Maybe because he'd grown too sure of her.

And now he couldn't stop dreaming about her.

Clearly, too much time had passed since his last girlfriend. Which must be why he was losing his mind. Neither remorse nor recurring dreams were usually his style.

The girlfriend he'd had before his shoulder injury, he'd been unable to stand after his shoulder injury. He hadn't had a girl-friend since.

Finding a new girlfriend was easier for him than brushing his teeth. So he should go out and get a beautiful, friendly girlfriend who'd be star-struck and wouldn't ask any-thing of him. That's what he should do.

Willow wasn't friendly. In fact, she'd spent years hating him. She wasn't star-struck by him. Thousands of men would kill to date Willow, and she could have her pick of any of them. He definitely couldn't count on her not to ask anything of him. Chances were, she'd ask something of him. And he'd give it. And then he'd have the rug pulled out from under him as soon as he made a mistake because, just like the last time, she'd be unwilling to hear him out and give him a second chance.

She'd end up rejecting him. Again.

So no. He didn't want to date Willow.

But he did want to kiss her.

"As I was saying." Corbin broke into their conversation about Nertz. "I've been read-ing articles from the seventies online. About serial killers."

That last part got their attention.

Charlotte's eyebrows climbed upward. "Why serial killers?"

"Because it turns out that several of the

women who went missing in the seventies were victims of serial killers."

"How many serial killers were there in Washington in Josephine's era?" Willow asked.

"Several. Ted Bundy ring a bell? By the way, Charlotte, you're not allowed to look up anything about Ted Bundy or serial killers in general on your computer or phone. The information on those guys is disturbing."

"You think Josephine could have been one of their victims?" Charlotte asked.

"I think it's possible. Some of their victims have never been found."

Willow nibbled on the edge of her lip. Heat flared inside Corbin in response.

"Do we have any reason to think that Josephine may have been targeted by a serial killer?" Willow asked.

"She wasn't a runaway or a prostitute or a hitchhiker, which helps her chances of not being targeted by a serial killer," Corbin answered. "But she was young and pretty, which hurts her chances."

"How did the serial killers dispose of the bodies?" Willow asked.

"Most of them dumped the bodies in remote locations."

Charlotte wrinkled her nose. "Note to self.

Don't be a victim of a serial killer."

"If Josephine's body was dumped in a remote location," Willow said, "and hasn't turned up in the past forty years, I think we have zero chance of finding it now."

"I'll do more research," he said. "I'll look for similarities between Josephine and any of the serial killers' victims. And I'll look into more solved and unsolved missing persons cases from that time period."

"Great!" Charlotte wrote in her notebook. "Will you report back on that at the next meeting?"

"If that's okay with the boss here." Corbin gestured to Willow with a smile.

"The boss grants her permission," Willow stated.

Charlotte's phone rang. "It's my mom." As soon as Charlotte answered the call, Willow rose and carried the cookie plate and their mugs to the sink. No doubt she didn't want to be forced into a private conversation with him.

Her pale hair slid against her black sweater. She moved with easy grace.

Charlotte disconnected and began stuffing her things into her backpack. "My mom's here to get me because she's making me go to my brother's soccer game." Eye roll. "She says there's like three cars outside, Willow, with people in them. And a few more people standing near the front door."

"Hmm?"

Corbin's senses switched to alert. "Are you expecting more arrivals today?"

"No. All of tonight's guests have already checked in."

"Mom wanted me to tell you that she thinks it's weird," Charlotte said.

Immediately, Corbin went into motion. "Wait here, Charlotte. I'll go see what's going on. Then I'll walk you to your mom's car." He exited through the back door.

Willow watched Corbin vanish.

"Corbin's really cool, don't you think?" Charlotte studied Willow as she settled both backpack straps over her shoulders.

"Yep." Nope. Maybe *very, very appealing but not cool* was most accurate.

"How come you two broke up?"

Willow rinsed out the mugs and plate and loaded them into the dishwasher. "The reasons are complicated. I'd rather not drag you into it."

"I'm, like, usually the person who all my friends come to for advice. Just so you know."

Willow grinned at the girl.

She'd been hesitant at first about investing in Charlotte and her quest. It had turned out that her commitment to Charlotte *had* come with one big downside: having to see Corbin biweekly. However, knowing Charlotte was a joy. Willow hadn't realized she needed a Charlotte Dixon in her life until she'd had a Charlotte Dixon in her life.

"Do you think you'll ever date Corbin again?" Charlotte asked.

"No. I think we're good like we are."

"Bummer. If you change your mind, let me know, okay? Uncle Corbin and I are pretty close. I think I could help you out with him."

Corbin shouldered in through the back door. His mouth formed a flat line, and his eyes glowed with irritation. "The people out front are fans of yours, Willow. They found out that you're working here, and they're waiting to see you."

"What?" How in the world could they have found out . . . *"Oh."* Cody. She'd asked him not to mention her presence at the inn, and he'd agreed. But the temptation to broadcast her whereabouts must have proven too great.

"They saw on Twitter that you're here," Corbin said. "Some jerk posted a picture of

150

you. Who would have done that?"

"A college kid stayed here with his family for the past three nights. I know that he recognized me, so I'm guessing he's the one."

"Where is he?" Corbin asked. "I'll go strangle him."

"They checked out this morning." Her mind spun as she tried to sift through the ramifications of Cody's tweet.

"I told them that they were on private property and asked them to leave," Corbin said. "Some of them did, but two didn't. One of the two looks like he's twenty-five and weighs about three twenty. He had the nerve to tell me that I was on private property, too. He's not smart enough to understand that there's a difference between being invited and uninvited."

Willow could only imagine how fascinated her fans must have been to see Corbin Stewart emerge from the inn. His "help" had no doubt thrown fuel onto the fire of their interest.

Corbin pulled his phone from his pocket. "Do you want to call the police, or do you want me to do it?"

"I'll call." She didn't love the idea of involving Merryweather's small police force, but she liked the idea of strangers loitering outside the inn far less. Much of the time, her guests were here alone.

"Do you think the people out there are dangerous?" Charlotte asked.

"No," Willow answered firmly. "Merely pesky."

After Willow's brief conversation with the police, Corbin escorted Charlotte to her mom's car. Willow sat at the kitchen work alcove and ran a search on Twitter for her name. As suspected, Cody had been the culprit. He'd taken a photo of her without her knowledge at breakfast yesterday morning. The photo captured her in profile talking with one of the guests.

She heard Corbin return. He stopped near her shoulder to examine the tweet centered on the computer screen. "Is this what the college kid posted?" he asked.

"Yes."

"How long ago?"

"Last night."

"Can you ask him to delete it?"

"Yes. I have a phone number for his parents here somewhere." She pulled up contact information for the Durants and phoned the cell number listed. When Liz Durant answered, Willow explained the situation. Liz apologized profusely and assured Willow that she'd ask Cody to delete the tweet immediately.

152

After they hung up, Willow checked the reservation system. Her heart sank. "Every available room for the rest of the month has been filled since the tweet posted."

Corbin made a growling sound. "Can you put a freeze on new bookings between now and when the manager your mom hired arrives?"

Willow nodded.

"I think you're also going to need to cancel all the reservations that were made since last night. It's not safe for you to be here alone with people who made a reservation just because they want to be near you."

She thought it through. He had a point. She blew out an irritated breath. "The inn's revenue is going to take a hit."

"Maybe. But given a choice between revenue and your safety, your mom will choose your safety."

The doorbell rang. The two uniformed police officers, both male, broke into huge smiles when they saw Corbin. They thanked him again and again for bringing donuts by the station.

The officers explained that they'd escorted Willow's stubborn fans from the property and given them a warning. They assured Corbin that they'd add the inn to their patrol and swing by multiple times to make certain the trespassers didn't return and that no new fans of Willow's arrived. They encouraged Willow to call them if the problem persisted or if she had any questions.

"Those two were in awe of you," Willow said when the officers had gone and she and Corbin stood facing each other in a kitchen that all at once seemed too silent and private.

"Most people *are* in awe of me." Dimples marked his cheeks. It was the first glimpse of mirth she'd spotted in him since he'd learned of the people gathered outside the inn. "It would be nice if you were in awe of me."

"You can't have everything, O Famous Quarterback." She tossed her red coat over her arm and reached for her purse.

He held the back door open for her. "Bradfordwood is gated, right?"

"Right. And the house has a security system."

"Is anyone else staying there?"

"Only me." She locked the door behind them, and they walked side by side along the dirt path that wove through the trees for about fifty yards to the inn's gravel-covered parking lot.

"What do you think about staying with

one of your sisters for a few nights?" he asked.

"I think it's unnecessary. Like I said, gated. Security system."

She could feel reluctance flowing from him. But he didn't have the grounds to insist she stay with her sisters.

She had logic on her side, anyway. Fans who were avid enough to drive all the way to Merryweather on a weekday for a glimpse of her were a little strange, perhaps. But none of them, even the two who hadn't immediately left when Corbin had asked them to, had exhibited any kind of threatening behavior. It was highly unlikely that her fans wanted to do her harm. It was far, far more likely that they simply wanted photos with her, autographs, or a quick conversation.

"I'll follow you to your house," he said.

"Also unnecessary."

"I'll follow you."

She glanced at his Navigator several times in her rearview mirror as they covered the distance from the inn to Bradfordwood.

Willow was responsible. She was the one her parents, her sisters, her friends, and her business associates looked to for stability. The word *maturity* summed up her identity, her role in her family, her professional calling card in the world of modeling. Yet

155

Corbin was the one who had immediately handled the situation back at the inn.

She could have managed it. Would have. But for once, she hadn't needed to do the mature things and take the mature steps. He'd done that —

Great Scott! She would not soften to Corbin because he'd shooed off some fans and stuck around until the police arrived.

And walked her to her car.

And was now following her home.

Corbin was far more dangerous to her than any fan could ever be.

He drove past Bradfordwood's gate in order to tail her all the way to the garage. At no point, not even along the public roads, had she spotted any fans of hers lying in wait. Nonetheless, Corbin sat in his car, watching, as she made her way to the door that connected the garage to the interior of the house.

She lifted a hand in parting, hit the button to close the garage door, and escaped behind Bradfordwood's protective walls.

Willow let out a shriek that night around eight when her phone rang.

"It's just your phone, Willow," she whispered.

She'd done the right thing when she'd

shrugged off Corbin's suggestion that she stay the night with one of her sisters. Yet as darkness had fallen over the Hood Canal, Willow's imagination had turned jumpy. She'd switched on every light downstairs. She had the TV going. And she'd double-checked the security system and the locks on all the doors and windows.

When she saw an unfamiliar number listed on her phone's screen, she considered not answering. But chances were good that it might be one of the police officers calling.

"Hello?"

"I'm just checking on you. Everything okay?"

Corbin. Her heart stuttered with one part dismay and one part renegade pleasure. "Everything's fine." She muted the TV and settled cross-legged onto the den's sofa. "How did you get my number?"

"I stole it off Charlotte's phone a few days ago when she was in the bathroom."

"Ethical as usual. You're breaking another ground rule by calling me."

"I know. I'm pretty smug about it."

"I'll be hanging up now —"

"No sign of crazy stalker fans?"

"None."

"Good."

She'd forgotten how deliciously comforting his voice sounded over the phone. When they'd been far apart during the months they'd dated, she'd done her best to be ready for bed and snuggled under the covers in advance of his nightly call. While they'd talked, she'd let his voice pour into her. After their conversations, she'd closed her eyes and smiled herself to sleep.

"I'm sitting at my computer researching serial killers," he said. "Which isn't how I dreamed of spending my retirement from football."

"Sometimes dreams don't pan out."

"How come the boss isn't the one spending her evening researching serial killers?"

"Because she doesn't *enjoy* serial killers."

"Me either."

"But, see, you're just my lackey."

He laughed and the timbre of it warmed her. "What time will you be leaving Bradfordwood tomorrow morning?" he asked.

"Are you asking that because you're a serial killer?"

"No."

"A crazy stalker fan?"

"No."

She waited for him to say more. Silence. "I leave for the inn at 6:45 every weekday morning."

"I'll wait for you outside Bradfordwood

and follow you to the inn, just to make sure that your fans aren't there to greet you."

Stop it, she wanted to snap. *Stop being protective and thoughtful.* "No, you don't have to —"

"Good night, Willow."
Click.

Thank you card inside wooden box:

Josephine,

When I showed up at the treatment center, I was expecting to have to suffer through my time there. I was dreading it. Then I met you. You were the best part of my day, every day. I didn't end up hating my stay at the center. How could I? You were there.

Thank you for taking an interest in me and caring about me. You're not two-faced like a lot of beautiful women are. You're honest and loyal.

I left the treatment center because the doctors decided I'd gotten better. But if I did get better, it wasn't because of them. It was because of you.

I really miss you.

Jeremy

CHAPTER EIGHT

Corbin was waiting outside Bradfordwood's gate for Willow when she left for work the following morning, as promised.

"I was more comfortable with you when you were thoroughly evil," she murmured darkly as she drove past his Navigator.

When they arrived at the inn, everything was as it should be. Even so, Corbin insisted on staying while she prepared and served breakfast. He cleaned up after her in the kitchen while keeping an eye on the inn's parking lot through the window over the sink.

She was just about to put her foot down and demand he leave when more of her fans appeared. Corbin immediately called the police. Then he talked her into printing the inn's logo and each registered guest's last name onto blue pieces of paper that the guests could place on the dashboard of their cars. That way, he reasoned, they and the police could determine at a glance which of the cars in the inn's parking lot were legit and which were suspect.

Corbin Stewart was no stranger to fame. No stranger to protecting privacy.

"You're not my director of security," Willow said to him as he aligned the blue papers into a neat stack. She felt a little guilty for failing to inject sting into her words. Sting would be safest. She was letting herself down by failing to inject sting. Yet he was being so decent this morning that she couldn't quite manage it.

"You have no director of security," he said. "Which concerns me."

"The police are on it."

"The police aren't always nearby."

Once the inn had been put back to rights after breakfast service, Willow prepared to leave.

"I'd like to stay a little longer," Corbin said. He sat at the kitchen computer, one foot set on the opposite knee, his wide back leaning against the desk chair.

"I can't stay. I'm meeting Melinda for lunch."

"I'll stay without you."

"Oh. Ah . . ."

"Afraid I'll steal the silver?"

"Very afraid." If he was half as good at

stealing silver as he was at stealing hearts, then none of the inn's treasures were secure.

"I'll keep out of sight back here. I won't steal the silver, and I won't eat the leftover French toast. But I will call the police if I see any trespassers."

In the end, she let him stay. If he wanted to donate his time to watch over the inn, what was it to her? She wouldn't be here. And if she wasn't in proximity to him, she wasn't susceptible to his appeal.

"I'm interested in Josephine's charm bracelet," Willow said to Melinda.

The two of them were ensconced in Melinda's restaurant of choice, the dining room at her country club. Plates of salad and glasses of iced tea rested before them. Beyond the window adjacent to their table, rain fell steadily over outdoor tennis courts devoid of players.

"Josephine received that charm bracelet as a high school graduation gift from our mother's parents," Melinda said.

"Did she add each charm individually?"

Melinda nodded.

"Do you think you can tell me the significance of each charm?"

"I can try."

Willow consulted the photograph she'd taken of the bracelet. "Sand dollar."

"Our aunt and uncle have a beach house in California. Our family used to spend time there every summer. Josephine loved it. It was one of her favorite places."

Willow took notes on her phone. "Cross."

Melinda had just taken a bite of salad and held up a finger while she chewed. After swallowing, she dabbed her lips with her napkin. "Josephine became a Christian when she was around ten. There were times when she seemed strong in her faith and times when she seemed to drift. But, overall, her faith was important to her."

"The Liberty Bell."

"Hmm." Melinda appeared to think it over. "I don't know."

"Heart lock?"

"Perhaps Alan gave that to her as a gift at some point?"

"Eiffel Tower?"

"Josephine studied abroad in France one summer during college."

When they'd covered all the charms, Willow set her phone aside. "I wanted to ask you about the Polaroid pictures inside Josephine's box of the inside of Josephine's car. Charlotte said that Alan had taken them."

"Yes." Melinda zipped up her Nike jacket.

"When Josephine didn't come home in time for dinner the day she disappeared, Alan went out looking for her. He drove around town until he found her car, parked across from Penny's Diner. He went inside Penny's, expecting her to be there. But, of course, she wasn't."

"When we had lunch at your house, you said that Josephine met with Paula the morning of the day she vanished."

"Right."

"And they met because Josephine was rumored to have been having an affair with Paula's husband."

"Yes. They met at Columbine Park. Paula and Keith's son was around three at the time. I think Paula asked Josephine to meet her there because she didn't want Keith to know about the meeting, and she was hoping the playground equipment would occupy her son while she and Josephine talked."

"So at some point after Josephine left the park, she drove to Penny's Diner."

"That's right."

"And no one who worked at Penny's or near Penny's saw her that day?"

"No one."

"And no one knows why she parked there."

"No one knows. When Alan didn't find Josephine inside Penny's, he assumed she was shopping nearby. He couldn't find her, though, in any of the stores. So he decided to search the Pacific Dogwood Trail. Are you familiar with that trail?"

"No." Nora's mother had been killed while walking alone on a park trail. Her death had scarred Willow's dad, and for as long as Willow could remember, he'd been very protective of his daughters. He'd never allowed his girls to go hiking unless in a large group, which had been fine with Willow. After what had happened to Nora's mom, she'd never been eager to strike off solo down a wilderness path.

"There's an easy loop at the base of the Pacific Dogwood Trail," Melinda explained. "A few longer, more difficult hikes branch off from that, but it seemed unlikely to Alan that Josephine would have taken any of those, so he stuck to the loop."

"Why did it seem unlikely that she'd have branched off?"

"Because she'd left the house that morning wearing a casual dress and sandals that had a little bit of a heel to them."

It didn't sound as though Josephine had been planning on hiking. Willow jotted more notes. "Did Alan take the Polaroids after he completed the trail?"

"Yes. By the time he finished the trail, it was around seven thirty p.m. and the sun was starting to set. He was really worried, so he went home, got his camera, and raced back to her car to take pictures."

"Why did he want to take pictures?"

"I believe he wanted to show them to the police. After he took them, he drove to the police station."

"If he gave them to the police, then why aren't they still in the possession of the police?"

"I have no idea." Melinda scooted her plate a few inches away.

"In one of the Polaroids, I saw that Josephine's keys were tucked under the floor mat. Did she usually leave her keys in that spot?"

"Not that I can remember. She was a practical person, and leaving your keys in your car for anyone to find isn't practical."

Willow sampled some of her salad, thinking through everything Melinda had told her. "I read a thank-you card from Jeremy to Josephine. Who's Jeremy?"

"Do you remember me mentioning that one of Josephine's patients at the treatment center became a suspect in her disappearance?"

Willow nodded.

"That's Jeremy. He was a troubled young man a few years younger than Josephine." She made a shooing motion with her hand. "Yes, he was released a few weeks before Josephine disappeared. Yes, he had a crush on Josephine. But I never thought he had anything to do with what happened to my sister. He was with his mother on April twelfth. He had an alibi."

Mothers sometimes lied to protect their children. Willow set her fork aside carefully.

"I love Charlotte," Melinda said. "I'm glad to see her take initiative on something. . . . I just wish, I really wish, it wasn't this."

"I know," Willow said. And she did. She understood. "A science fair project about whales is probably more Charlotte's speed."

"Exactly. A science fair project on whales would be a lot less troubling and would give Charlotte a far greater chance at success."

"She's passionately focused on this case," Willow said.

Melinda rolled her lips inward. "That's just how Josephine used to get, too. *Passionately focused.* Once Josephine set her mind to something, no one could talk her out of it. She was as persistent as the day was long." She paused. "Which might have been her undoing."

167

Later in the day, when Willow returned to the Inn at Bradfordwood to make cookies and lattes and check in two new sets of guests, she found Corbin inside the inn's kitchen. He informed her that more of her fans had arrived during her absence and that he'd called the police.

Cody's tweet had been deleted less than twenty-four hours after it had gone up. Still, there was no chance of putting the cat back in the bag. Some of the people who'd seen Cody's tweet announcing her location had retweeted the information to their followers. And some of their followers had taken the news to other social media sites.

Her whereabouts were only of interest to a small group of her most rabid supporters. A much smaller subset of that group lived near Merryweather. And a much smaller subset of that group had taken the initiative to journey to the inn. Still, that final group was sizable enough to have created a recurring issue.

The next day, Thursday, followed an almost identical pattern. Corbin accompanied her to the inn that morning. Three of her supporters made an appearance during

168

the day. He called the station each time. The police responded quickly, and on every occasion, escorted her fans from the inn's property peacefully.

When she pulled out of Bradfordwood's gate on Friday morning, she found the street empty of Corbin. It appeared that he'd finally grown bored and come to the (justified) realization that he had better things to do with his time than keep an eye on her and her inn.

Several seconds passed as she looked both ways for a gray Navigator. Nope. He wasn't coming.

She turned her Range Rover onto the road and told herself she should be relieved that Corbin hadn't shown. Having him in her space at the inn, having to look at him every time she turned around, talk to him, smell his soap . . . it had muddled her head.

However, relief was not what she felt in response to his absence. Instead, she almost felt . . . sorry?

It dawned on her that she'd been looking forward to seeing him. She hadn't meant to! But the evidence was in the extra time she'd spent doing her hair and choosing today's long white top, scarf, leggings, boots, jacket.

She groaned.

What was she doing? Over the past few days, she'd allowed Corbin to involve himself in her fan situation. She'd allowed him to wash her breakfast dishes, joke with her, and call the police for her.

She needed her emotional soldiers, the ones who'd always protected her. She needed them back at their posts *immediately.* What was that term? Stat? *Stat, soldiers! Back at your posts!*

When she reached the inn's parking lot, she was encouraged to see that every car in the lot had a blue paper with the inn's logo printed on it lying on its dash.

She walked to the back of her SUV and was lifting the box of croissants she'd picked up at the Edge of the Woods bakery from her trunk when she heard the sound of tires crunching gravel.

Corbin? She leaned back to get a look at the approaching car.

Not Corbin.

The car appeared to be a Mitsubishi that had been souped-up. Its paint job was reminiscent of *The Fast and the Furious.* No blue paper on its dash.

She quickly closed her trunk and began walking along the path to the inn, carrying the box of croissants.

"Willow!" a man's voice called. "Willow

Bradford."

She glanced back.

A tall, heavy-set young guy — this must be the one Corbin had said weighed three twenty — hurried toward her. He had olive skin, a shaved head, a goatee, dark eyes. "Hold up a second," he shouted.

Willow's lungs tightened. "Sorry, this isn't a good time. I'm in a rush." She walked as rapidly as she could in her high-heeled boots. *Please, Lord, let him respond respectfully and leave.*

He didn't. Fast, heavy footsteps approached as he jogged in her direction. "I'm one of your biggest fans."

"Thanks, but I've got to get to work."

"It'll just take a minute."

The polite part of her chafed at the prospect of avoiding interaction with him. But the cautious, experienced part of her knew better. This guy hadn't left the property on Tuesday morning when Corbin had asked him to go. And now he'd returned to the inn even though the police had given him a warning when they'd ushered him off. He was stubborn, he was trespassing on her land, and he was three times her size.

He came to a stop a few yards in front of her on the path. His shortcut across the grounds had positioned him between her

171

and the inn.

He'd cut off her escape route.

Willow halted and tried to master the fear beginning to course through her.

"Willow, hey. I'm really glad to finally meet you." He was out of breath because of his sprint. "I've wanted to meet you for a long time. My name's Todd."

He had no sense of boundaries and was overly persistent, but those faults didn't have to mean he was dangerous. She straightened tall. "Todd, I really need to get to work inside."

"Yeah, yeah. I know. I won't keep you, I just . . . I'm a big fan. A huge fan. I really need a picture with you."

"Someone recently took a photo of me without my permission and posted it to social media. It's caused me and the Merryweather police quite a bit of difficulty. I don't want my presence in Merryweather to become a public thing."

"I get it. But this'll just take a second. I won't say anything on social media about where you are."

"If I allow you one picture will you go?"

"Yes."

"And you won't disclose my location?"

"No." One of his hands started to rattle nervously at his side.

172

Grimly, she nodded her permission. He leaned in and took a selfie of them.

"Now if you'll just let me pass by —"

"Willow, this one's not very good." He held up his cell phone. "Can we take a few more?"

"You agreed to one. Please let me pass."

He gave her a victimized look, as if she were the one who was out of line. "I'm not asking that much of you. I drove a long way to get here, and I've been waiting a couple of days for this, so let's try a few more." Rising determination underscored his words. "Some video footage would be good, too."

Anxiety seized Willow. She'd had to deal with people like Todd a few times over the years. No matter what you gave them, they wanted more.

She shot a glance over her shoulder toward her car. Should she run in that direction? Or should she try to make it to the inn? She was almost positive that he could outrun her before she could reach the safety of either place. She had pepper spray in her purse. If she dropped the croissant box and reached into her purse, would she be able to find her pepper spray quickly enough?

She looked him in the eye. "The answer's no," she said as confidently as she could.

"I'm going inside now."

Every trace of friendliness drained from Todd's face, revealing features stark with anger. He raised his phone and began videoing her. "You seem nice in interviews, Willow. Was that just an act? Are you nice? Be nice and let me take a few more pictures of us."

She walked around him toward the inn. As she did so, his hand shot out to grab her. Willow side-stepped, just escaping his reach. Panic burst through her and she ran —

He lunged and caught her forearm.

The box fell to the earth. She twisted her arm from his grasp and bolted toward her car. She thrust her hand into her purse for her pepper spray. Where was her pepper spray? The toe of her boot struck a root, and she went sprawling forward through empty air. She landed hard on her hands and knees, heartbeat hammering.

"I was just reaching out to position you for a picture," Todd spat. Distantly, she heard a car door slam. The crunching of twigs and leaves. "You didn't have to make me lose my temper." He leaned over her, reached down —

In the next instant, Todd was wrenched away. She looked up to see Corbin standing

174

in the gap between herself and Todd.

"Back off," Corbin growled.

Todd staggered back a few feet.

Corbin helped her — lifted her, really — to her feet. "Are you okay?" He scanned her face.

She couldn't remember ever being this glad to see someone familiar. "I'm okay."

Corbin released her and turned back to Todd.

"Who do you think you are?" Todd snarled at Corbin. His eyes roiled with adrenaline and wrath.

"I'm Corbin Stewart, you jerk. Get off Willow's property."

Todd advanced. "I just wanted a few pictures and some video with her."

"And you wouldn't take no for an answer?" Corbin asked.

"I wasn't asking for much —"

"Back off," Corbin warned. When Todd continued to approach, Corbin shoved him in the chest.

Todd came up swinging with both fists. Corbin arched out of the way, then threw a punch with his left hand. *Thud.* He connected squarely with Todd's jaw. Todd faltered, then ran at Corbin as if to tackle him. Corbin bent at the legs and stopped Todd's progress by burying his shoulder and upper

175

arm into Todd's midsection.

A sickening tearing sound rent the air.

Corbin drove Todd back until the younger man landed on the ground with a crash. Corbin stood, holding his own right shoulder, body taut with fury. "Get. Off. Willow's. Property."

He'd hurt his shoulder, Willow realized with dismay. Because of the angle at which Todd had barreled forward, Corbin had used his right side to stop him. That tearing sound had come from Corbin's healing shoulder.

Todd attempted to clamber up. Slipped back. Finally made it to standing. His chest heaved. "I'll sue you for that," he told Corbin.

"Be my guest. I have an excellent team of lawyers."

The two men faced off. *Please don't fight anymore. Please.* Too much damage had been done as it was. Corbin's shoulder had already been surgically repaired twice.

Todd stalked to his car, cursing with every step.

Corbin remained exactly where he was, attention trained on Todd. "Can you get a picture of his license plate?"

Willow just managed to capture a photo of Todd's car before it disappeared from sight. Then she faced Corbin, feeling disheveled and shaky. Numb and at the same time acutely sensitive. "You injured your shoulder."

He gave a curt nod.

"How badly?"

"I'm not sure. Did he hurt you?"

"No."

"What happened?"

She explained the exchange between herself and Todd. "He grabbed my arm, and I yanked it out of his grip. I was running to my car when I tripped. That's when you arrived."

"Let me see your arm."

With hands that weren't quite steady, she straightened her scarf and shirt.

"Let me see," he said.

She paused. Then pushed up her sleeve. An angry red ring encircled her forearm.

Corbin's tight countenance remained the same, except for his eyes. They turned positively murderous. He'd bent his right arm in, against his abdomen. He reached out with his left hand and turned her palm faceup. A few light scratches marred the skin. Gently, he brushed dirt from her palm with his thumb. He lifted her other hand and did the same.

She couldn't breathe. Her mind was a calamity.

To be touched by him again was delight. And torture. He wasn't trying to seduce her. He was simply brushing dirt off her hands. Yet the simple contact contained the force of a hurricane.

This is unsafe, her intuition murmured. The warning was sluggish, however. *This is unsafe,* she told herself more insistently and stepped back. She tried to push her hands into her pockets only to remember she was wearing leggings under her long shirt. She set her hands on her hips. "We need to get your shoulder taken care of."

"Probably."

"Should I call an ambulance?"

"No."

"Then where do I need to take you? The hospital?"

"The rehab center, if Dr. Wallace is there today. I'll call."

"I'm going to run inside the inn real quick. Then I'll meet you at my car."

Willow retrieved the box of croissants, which sat intact on the ground, lid closed, without even a dent. She deposited them on the inn's kitchen counter and called Britt to ask if she could take over breakfast duty at the inn. Britt said she'd be there within fifteen minutes.

"Dr. Wallace is on his way to the rehab center," Corbin told her as she neared her car. "They're expecting me."

An injury to the Super Bowl–winning body of Dr. Wallace's most famous patient? You better believe they'd be expecting him when he arrived.

"I also called the police," he said. "When you have time, they want to talk to you about what happened. You should press charges."

Willow opened the passenger door for him. He took a seat, his right arm still motionless against his side. She grabbed his seat belt and passed it to his left hand.

Willow started the engine and steered them toward the road. "Are you in pain?"

"Not much."

She peeked at him. His face was pale, and he was clenching his jaw. "I don't believe you."

"It's not bad." He gave a sardonic smile. "So long as I don't move."

"How long has it been since your first surgery?"

"Ten months. I had the first surgery back in Dallas in January."

"And the second surgery?"

"The beginning of June."

"Why did you need a second surgery?"

For a moment, no sound other than the hum of the engine filled the car. Corbin shifted in his seat, trying to adjust his large frame into a more comfortable position. "My orthopedic doctors in Dallas wanted to try to save the humerus bone and the shoulder socket, so they used a metal plate and twelve screws to piece it all back together."

Willow had yet to break a single bone.

"After the surgery, my right arm didn't heal like it should have. It ached all the time. I had limited range of motion. After four months of therapy, the doctors decided I needed a second surgery. This time, they wanted to cut the bone off here." With a flat palm, he indicated a mark halfway between his elbow and shoulder.

"They decided they couldn't save the bone, after all," Willow said.

"Right. They wanted to do something called a reverse total shoulder replacement."

"Were the doctors in Dallas wrong initially? To try to save the bone?"

"No, I don't think so. The theory is that it's best to try to save the bone if it can be saved. Ordinarily, the first surgery works."

"But yours didn't."

"Mine didn't. Then again, I've never been

180

ordinary."

"Don't feel obligated to joke with me while you're in pain, Corbin."

"I'm not trying to joke. I'm trying to flirt with you."

"As you well know, flirting's against the rules." A silver Honda pulled out in front of her. "Excuse me, Honda, but I'm *right here.*"

"Did you just talk to that car?"

"Did you call Dr. Wallace after you found out you needed the second surgery?"

"Yes. Dr. Wallace works on a lot of players. He's operated on a few of my buddies over the years with good results. So I came to Washington and, after the surgery, to Shore Pine."

"With a bionic shoulder."

He nodded.

It went unsaid that up until today, his recovery had been going well.

Willow steeled herself against a wave of regret. Corbin's confrontation with Todd had happened fast. She hadn't known what to say or do from the moment Corbin had pulled Todd away from her. Perhaps if she'd tried to reason with Todd or drawn Corbin away from him the outcome would have been different.

"I wish I'd been on time this morning,"

he said. "Something came up at home, and I was late getting to Bradfordwood to meet you."

"I assumed you weren't coming."

"I drove straight to the inn because I knew I was too late to meet you at Bradfordwood. I'm sorry I wasn't there when Todd showed up."

"I'm sorry about your shoulder."

"It's not your fault."

"Thank you for . . . defending me." The words sounded overly formal.

"You're welcome. That was the same guy I dealt with earlier in the week."

"I figured."

At a stoplight, she looked across at him. He'd tipped up his chin, the back of his skull against the headrest. His eyes were closed.

Her vision skimmed from his jaw to his collarbone. His neck looked both strong and, in that position, vulnerable.

"I have a favor to ask of you," Corbin said.

She refrained from pointing out that asking her for favors was a violation of the rules. "Okay."

"It involves my dad. He lives with me."

His dad? "When I came by your house the other day I didn't see anyone else," she said.

"He was at therapy that morning. I can't remember how much I told you about him when we were dating."

"Not much."

"I've never told anyone much about him."

The light turned green. As she continued in the direction of Shore Pine, she reached back in her memory for the information he'd given her about his father. "You told me that your dad worked at one of the auto plants in Detroit."

"Yes."

"I know that your mom left him when you were what? Six?"

"Five."

"I know that your dad was a single parent and that he faced some struggles. But I never could get you to go into detail about what he'd struggled with exactly."

"Bipolar disorder."

Willow's breath released gradually.

"I've always tried to protect his privacy." Corbin gave a muffled grunt as he tried again to find a comfortable position. If she had to guess, "comfortable" wasn't going to be an option for Corbin until someone gave him pain meds.

"The year I signed with the Mustangs," he said, "I moved my dad out of Detroit and bought him a house in his hometown

183

of South Haven, Michigan. I wanted him to relax and enjoy his retirement. For ten years, he did great. He felt good. He was surrounded by friends and family. He played golf every chance he got. He worked a few hours a week at the YMCA as a referee."

"What changed?"

"Three years ago, he was diagnosed with multiple myeloma. Have you heard of it?"

"Is it a form of cancer?"

"Yes. Cancer of the plasma cells in bone marrow. It's incurable, and the typical life span is around five years. Some patients live quite a bit longer than that, though. I wanted him to have access to the best doctors, so I moved him to Dallas to live with me."

"How's he doing?"

"Physically, he's doing okay, considering that he takes a few dozen pills every day and goes in for treatments once a month. He's tired a lot."

They were just minutes from Shore Pine. Since she couldn't see a single car in her rearview mirror, she twisted to face him at the next stop sign. "What's the favor you need me to do?"

He stared at her levelly across the close space between the seats. "My dad's expecting me back at the house soon, so I'm going to have to call him and tell him about my shoulder. When I do, he's going to want to come to the rehab center right away."

She dipped her chin.

"He doesn't drive. I had to take away his car keys a while back."

"Do you need for me to pick him up?"

"I do."

"All right."

"Do you remember how to get to my house?"

"I think so. If I get confused I'll pull up directions on my phone."

Solemnity settled into the contours of his face. "I'm not sure how he'll be, with you."

She could see that he hated that he'd had to tell her as much as he had, that he'd been forced to ask for her help. Corbin frowned. "Maybe this isn't the best idea. Maybe I could ask my neighbor —"

"Your house is just a few miles from the rehab center. As soon as I drop you off, I'll go get your dad. I'll bring him to the center. It'll be fine."

Several beats of silence.

"His name's Joe," Corbin said. "I'll tell him you're coming."

Excerpt from report filed by Child Protective

Services employee, April 18, 1992, Detroit, Michigan:

I responded to a phone call from a Mrs. Adele Carter regarding alleged neglect of her son's friend, Corbin Stewart, age nine.

Corbin banged on Mrs. Carter's door yesterday afternoon to tell her that his father was unconscious and to ask for her help. Upon arriving at the condo of Joe and Corbin Stewart, Mrs. Carter found Joe, age forty, unresponsive. Mrs. Carter called an ambulance, contacted Corbin's grandmother by phone, then drove Corbin to the hospital. It was later determined by hospital staff that Joe, who has a history of mental illness, had overdosed on benzodiazepines, which are typically prescribed for the treatment of anxiety and insomnia. Joe is expected to recover fully.

Mrs. Carter suspects that Joe is neglecting Corbin's care. The Stewart home is in fair condition and does not give evidence of neglect. I spoke with Joe, who assured me that he cares for his son, that this was an isolated event triggered by his bipolar disorder, and that he regrets it deeply. He has agreed to seek treatment.

I met with Corbin privately. He told me that his father meets his needs, and he in-sists on remaining with Joe.

I classify this case as low risk and will follow up with Joe Stewart in ten days.

CHAPTER NINE

Corbin's dad was standing outside the barnhouse, waiting for Willow, when she pulled up. She exited her car and approached.

Corbin had clearly inherited the auburn tint in his brown hair from Joe. Though Joe's still-thick hair had faded to a pale ginger color with age, he looked to her like a man who'd once had a full head of copper hair.

His fair skin was pinpricked with tiny freckles and a few age spots. Like Corbin, Joe's eyes were brown, though lighter in hue and faintly rheumy. She'd guess his height to be a few inches shorter than Corbin's. Maybe six one?

They were both brawny, big-boned men. But if Joe's body had once been as filled with strength and good health as Corbin's currently was, then his cancer or maybe his psychological health or both had sapped much of that strength from him. Joe's muscles hung on him. His thin frame held none of the latent, ropy power that characterized his son.

Unexpected fondness welled within Willow for Corbin's dad. Regardless of the challenges Joe had faced, he'd been exactly like her own dad in one critical way. *He'd stayed.* When her mom had left, her dad had raised her. When Joe's wife had left, Joe had raised Corbin.

For his part, Joe didn't appear to be experiencing a matching sense of fondness for her. He regarded her warily.

"I'm Willow Bradford." She extended her hand.

He shook it. "Joe Stewart."

"Nice to meet you."

"We should probably be getting on our way."

"Sure." For the second time in under an hour, she found herself driving a Stewart to the rehab center.

Joe wore sneakers, jeans, and a long-sleeved T-shirt with a graphic of the sun, ocean, palm trees, and the word *Hawaii*. He'd strapped a '90s-era Timex with a glowing electronic display around his wrist.

"Corbin mentioned that you're from South Haven, Michigan."

"Yes. Have you been there?"

189

"I'd like to. But no, I haven't."

"It's on the shore of Lake Michigan." He sat with his hands on his knees, face turned toward the side window. One of his knees bounced worriedly. "There's some good golfing around there. When the weather's nice." He spoke with a Midwestern accent. "Where are you from?"

"I'm from just down the road, Merryweather. My home base has been L.A. for more than ten years, though."

He rumbled assent.

Willow racked her brain for more to say. She could almost always keep conversation clicking along with people she'd just met, but Joe was proving to be a challenge. He was saying the right things, but he wasn't saying them naturally. It was as if he were a bad actor, woodenly speaking lines he'd been given.

"I think you missed the turn for Dr. Wallace's Center," he said.

Had she? She didn't think so, but then, she wasn't the one who lived in Shore Pine. She pulled to the curb and checked her phone. According to the GPS, she was right on track. "I think it's straight ahead, then left, then right."

His face swung toward her, his strawberry blond eyebrows drawn down as though he suspected her of kidnapping him. "It's back that way." He pointed behind them and to the side.

The rehab center was most assuredly *not* in that direction. "Let's just drive up here a little farther and see," she said smoothly. She had decades of experience dealing with Grandma, who often spoke and acted in direct opposition to everything Willow believed to be true. "I'm glad that Dr. Wallace is Corbin's doctor. I've heard he's excellent."

"Hmm?" he said distractedly.

Willow repeated herself.

"Yes," Joe answered. "Dr. Wallace has done a fine job. Not like those doctors who operated on Corbin the first time."

The Wallace Rehabilitation Center came into view. Willow pulled into a parking space.

"Thank you for the ride," Joe said gruffly.

"I'll come inside with you —"

"No, you've already done more than enough, what with driving us around."

"It's really no problem —"

"I'm sure you have a lot to do today. We don't want to keep you." He ducked his head in a gesture of parting and let himself out without giving her a chance to reply.

Willow scrambled from the car and locked

it behind her. "I'd like to see how Corbin's doing."

Joe responded with a frown. Inside the waiting area of the sleek, modern building, he approached the receptionist.

Willow took a seat and after a few minutes, Joe came to sit in the chair next to hers. He moved carefully, as if unsure of his balance. "They're running tests on him. X-rays and whatnot. They'll let me know when I can go back."

"Sounds good." The two of them stared straight ahead. "Magazine?" She pointed to the stack on the coffee table.

"No."

Most of the time people warmed to her. *Usually* people liked her. Only . . . not Joe. Willow didn't know if he disliked the majority of people or if he disliked her in particular. It could be the latter. After all, he no doubt remembered her from when she and Corbin had dated. There's no telling what Corbin had or hadn't said to his dad about their breakup. Plus, Joe might be blaming her for Corbin's screwed-up shoulder. Which wasn't altogether without merit.

In a bid to keep her mind occupied, Willow scrolled through email on her phone.

At last a young nurse in scrubs came to a stop before them. "Mr. Stewart? I'll take

192

you back to see Corbin now."

Willow began to rise, too, but Joe stayed her with a look. "I'd like to speak with my son privately."

"Of course." She remained where she was as Joe and the nurse walked out of sight.

Joe's shut-out stung. On the other hand, it wasn't as if she had a right to visit the patient. She wasn't a family member or a girlfriend or even a friend of Corbin's.

Which begged the question: Why *was* she determined to see her not-family member, not-boyfriend, not-friend Corbin before she returned to the inn?

He'd been injured protecting her. On her property. That's why. If she was harboring reasons beyond those, she didn't want to confront them.

"Miss Bradford?" The nurse had returned. "Corbin would like you to come back, too."

"He would?"

"Yes. And if you know him at all you know that he almost always gets what he wants." The nurse dimpled, and Willow could see that here was another of Corbin's groupies. Great.

Willow followed the woman down a few different hallways before entering a room that looked very much like every other doctor's exam room she'd entered in her life, with one very important distinction: This exam room contained a shirtless man.

Oh dear.

Even though she, Corbin, and Joe were the only occupants of the room at the moment, Willow edged against the wall next to the door in order to make herself unobtrusive and also to put as much space as possible between herself and Corbin.

He was reclining on the adjustable table wearing nothing but jeans. His upper half was raised to around a 45-degree angle, and they'd adhered ice packs to his shoulder with tape. His chest and abs were — heaven help her — even more beautiful than she'd remembered. Contoured muscles and sinew resting beneath bronze skin.

It seemed that sticking around to see him had been a tactical error on her part.

Her attention skittered to Joe, sitting in a chair by the window, looking disgruntled.

"You stayed." Though Corbin's face still showed evidence of pain, warmth lit his eyes.

"I just wanted to hear what the doctor had to say." *I didn't stick around because I wanted to see you shirtless or because I care.*

"It's a separated shoulder," Corbin told her. He was unashamedly masculine and not the least bit shy. "I've torn some ligaments, but that's all."

"Will it require another surgery?"

"No, thank God."

"What's the treatment plan?"

"Painkillers. Immobility of the shoulder. Ice."

"How long will it take to heal?"

"Four weeks."

She winced.

Joe glared at her.

Don't look at Corbin's chest. Don't look at his abs. If you have to look at him at all, look right into his eyes.

Willow smiled in the direction of the window. "Well! I'll leave you guys to it. See you later, Joe. Corbin." The heels of her boots rapped against the floor as she hurried down the hallway.

She tightly gripped the steering wheel as she drove back toward Merryweather. There'd been a time, right after their breakup, when she'd happily imagined all sorts of scenarios in which harm might befall Corbin. It had been a pastime of hers, dreaming up all the ways he could suffer. But just now, when she'd actually seen him suffering, her vindictiveness had left her.

It had left her in part because he'd seemed less . . . invincible than usual, there on the examining table with only his dad for support. If she'd been the one with a separated shoulder, her sisters, parents, Grandma, Valentina, and Zander all would have packed into her exam room.

Which served to highlight the differences between herself and Corbin.

She'd been raised in a quaint town in the Pacific Northwest. She had siblings and, from the age of five onward, both a dad and a mom. For well over a century and a half, the Bradford family had enjoyed the advantages of wealth and prestige. Opportunities had fallen into Willow's lap like ripe plums.

Corbin had been raised by a blue-collar father in a Midwestern city down on its luck. No mom. No siblings. He'd had to make his own opportunities.

She'd thought recently about how Zander was the underdog in his friendship with Britt. In many of the same ways, Corbin had begun life as an underdog, too. Willow had met him in his post-underdog days, after he'd achieved tremendous success, so it was easy to forget that he'd known difficulty. Corbin's toughness had been engraved into him early.

Willow had acquired her toughness gradually, first through the traumas she'd weathered early in life, then through the knocks the modeling world had dispensed.

She was composed and introspective.

He was charming and handy with his fists.

She was steady.

He was untrustworthy.

Willow chewed the edge of her lip. Except what she'd learned about Corbin today didn't square very well with the "untrustworthy" label she'd stamped on him long ago.

When she'd needed him this morning, he'd been there.

And he was taking care of his dad and had been for three years. Which probably explained why he'd been late for lunch on Melinda's back deck that day and why he sometimes had to leave the room during Operation Find Josephine meetings to take phone calls.

"That's not your lane, Mazda." She made a *tsking* sound and massaged one of her temples.

She didn't want to think that she could have been wrong about Corbin in any way.

Corbin woke the next morning from a dream of Willow to the familiar sensation of shoulder pain. He was beyond sick of it. Stupid shoulder pain.

He'd been trapped in a tunnel of grief over the loss of football and his shoulder's limitations for months. Even before he'd separated his shoulder, he'd been unable to find a way out of the tunnel, so this setback definitely wasn't going to help.

He rolled onto his side in bed to squint at his alarm clock.

He'd been late to meet Willow outside Bradfordwood's gates yesterday because his dad had been having a bad morning. Experience had taught him that his dad did best when he stuck to a daily schedule. Same wake-up time, meal times, exercise, bedtime. But yesterday his dad hadn't wanted to get out of bed. So Corbin had pulled him upright, brought him his medications, made him breakfast. All that had put Corbin behind by a few minutes.

When he'd finally reached the inn's parking lot and saw Willow being manhandled, white-hot rage had washed through him. It had blotted everything else out. He couldn't even remember exiting his car and running to her. He'd acted out of instinct.

Corbin let a groan escape as he pressed to standing. The blankets fell away.

It was Saturday. Willow didn't usually work at the inn on the weekends, but he'd drive by the Inn at Bradfordwood anyway to make sure Todd hadn't returned.

Pulling on his track pants one-handed was

an exercise in coordination. Or maybe humor. Zipping up a sweat shirt was an exercise in agony. Once he'd managed it, he settled his right arm into the sling Dr. Wallace had prescribed and slipped his feet into Adidas slides.

He found his dad in a kitchen that smelled of bacon and coffee, frying an egg. It looked like his dad was having a better morning today than he'd had yesterday, which was a relief.

"Hey," Corbin said.

"Morning." His dad's attention followed Corbin as he crossed to the coffeemaker and filled a travel mug. "Going out?"

"Yeah. Do you need anything at the store?"

"Not that I can think of. I . . . Are you going to drive with a separated shoulder?"

"I'll take the sling off when I get in the car and put it on when I get out." He'd strained and torn ligaments. It hurt to move the shoulder, but he could move it if he needed to while behind the wheel. There was no way he was going to be sidelined from driving like he'd been after his surgeries.

"Is the store the only place you're going?" his dad asked.

"No."

"You driving to Merryweather again?" His dad turned off the stove and used a spatula to move the egg onto a plate.

Corbin had become his dad's chaperon in recent years out of necessity. However, his dad was not *his* chaperon. Corbin was thirty-five years old. "Yes. I'm going to make sure Willow's fan hasn't come back." He stirred creamer into his coffee, screwed on the mug's lid, then faced his dad. Heat seeped through the travel mug into his palm.

"I don't trust that woman." His dad's frown sent grooves into a face that had once been handsome.

"Her name's Willow."

"I can tell that you still like her."

Where had he put his keys? Corbin lifted a stack of mail in search of them.

"I don't understand what you're thinking, son. Don't you remember how hard you took it when you guys split up?"

"I remember."

"So do I," his dad said flatly. "It was rough on you. Starting back up with her is a really bad idea."

Corbin walked along the counter, looking for his keys.

"Corbin."

He glanced up to see his dad nod toward the bowl they used as a catchall. His keys lay within. "Thanks. I'll be back in time to take you to your ten thirty group session." Corbin strode through the chilly morning, climbed into his Navigator using only his left arm, and drove toward the inn.

Willow had come back into his life through no wish of his own. But now that she was back and he was spending time with her on a regular basis, he could see the good in her.

His dad couldn't see the good because he was so tied to his memories of the bad. Four years ago his dad had been watching *Entertainment Tonight* when he'd seen coverage of Willow on the red carpet with Derek Oliver before Corbin had told his dad that he and Willow had broken up. His dad had called Corbin, irate, because it had looked to him like his son's girlfriend was cheating on his son.

Corbin wasn't in the habit of sharing the details of his relationships with his dad, but he'd tried to set things right back then. He'd explained his role in their breakup. Corbin had always understood just how much he was at fault for the end of his relationship with Willow. But his dad never had been able to understand. He'd picked sides while watching *Entertainment Tonight* and decided that Willow was the enemy.

The fact that Corbin had been miserable for months after their relationship ended hadn't helped Willow's standing in his dad's eyes. He'd blamed her for Corbin's heartbreak, in large part because he himself had faced a similar heartbreak when Corbin's mom had walked out on them thirty years before.

His dad's mental health had been shaky during Corbin's preschool years. But so long as Dawn Stewart had loved him and remained by his side, he'd been able to keep his life on course. When she'd jerked her love away, it had devastated his dad. His life headed into a ditch, and bipolar disorder took the upper hand.

His dad had been suspicious of women in general and beautiful women — like Dawn and Willow — in particular ever since.

Divorce hadn't been easy for his father.

Neither had parenting.

The honest truth was that it hadn't always been easy for Corbin to be his father's son, either. At times, it had been downright brutal for them both. But one thing Corbin knew — his dad had done his best. He'd earned money to feed and clothe Corbin. He'd sacrificed to make sure Corbin had every chance to learn and play the game of football. Whenever his work schedule had allowed, he'd shown up at Corbin's middle school and high school games. He'd driven him to every tournament.

His dad had supported Corbin when Corbin had needed it, and now it was Corbin's turn to support his dad. He'd made the choice to act as his dad's caregiver. He didn't regret it, and he didn't blame his dad for the fact that Corbin's professional life was currently in a holding pattern.

He wanted to be a football commentator one day, but there was no way he could pursue that at this point. Not with his dad's health the way it was. It wouldn't be possible for him to do everything he needed to do for his dad, plus work full time, plus travel for work.

The *City of Shore Pine, Population 6,220* sign slid past.

Their move to Washington had ended up serving several purposes, some of them unexpected. Until they'd come to Shore Pine, Corbin hadn't fully understood how beneficial it would be for his dad to see Mark, Jill, and their kids on an almost daily basis. The kids had brought something to his dad's life — and to his own — that had been missing.

It surprised Corbin how much his dad had taken to the Pacific Northwest. Here they were surrounded by green hills and blue water. The pace was slower. They could go watch a game at a bar or grab chicken wings for dinner, and no one would mob them.

The biggest surprise of all? Their house. Corbin hadn't planned, upon retirement from the NFL, on taking up construction. When he'd first seen the seventy-five acre property in Shore Pine that would soon become his, he'd planned to hire out the renovation. His dad, who'd taken shop class in school and been handy all his life, was the one who'd expressed an interest in working on the house. Thank goodness he had, because their joint project was what gave their days purpose.

When Corbin finally reached the Inn at Bradfordwood, everything was as it should be. No sign of trespassers. He looped back in the direction of Shore Pine.

Willow was safe.

Some of the worry he'd been carrying since Willow's fans had first appeared at the inn dissolved.

He'd been very concerned about the safety of the woman he had a lot of reasons not to care about. Even though he knew it would be best to follow his dad's example and hang on to his grudge against Willow, to go out and find himself a new girlfriend, he'd spent most of the past few days at the inn, keeping a lookout for idiots.

Corbin had come from a rough part of a rough city before going on to achieve just about everything he'd ever wanted. But here, in Washington State, he was realizing that there was still one thing — one person — left to want.

Voice mail from Melinda to Willow:

I'm calling to let you know that I've heard from Sheriff Raney. He told me that my DNA returned no matches. None of the Jane Does in the database share my DNA.

Letter from Corbin to Willow:

Willow,
I'm mailing you a letter. You know why.
— Corbin

CHAPTER TEN

Yes, she knew why he'd mailed her his two-sentence letter. Because mailing her a letter was against the rules.

Willow laughed.

She shouldn't be laughing. Only . . . his letter was just a little bit funny. Corbin was a little bit funny. Worse, his actions three days ago, when he'd protected her from Todd, had been just a little bit heroic.

She lifted her head and looked out the bank of windows that spanned Bradfordwood's den. She could not afford to soften toward Corbin.

She crumpled the letter, slam-dunked it into the nearest trash can, then fisted both hands in her hair.

Can. Not. Soften!

Yet she could feel it happening, deep within. Her best intentions were melting beneath the sun of Corbin's charm and his insistent humor and his willingness to defend her at cost to himself.

She made her way to the mudroom. She'd walk to Bradfordwood's inlet. Along the way, she'd do what she'd spent four years refusing to do.

She'd remember.

She'd remember every single thing about Corbin. She'd dig it all back up — each painful ounce of it — because remembering would replenish her ammunition against him.

Riding a fresh wave of determination, she slid on her rain boots, grabbed a light jacket, and let herself out. It had stormed earlier, but it was nearing lunchtime now, and bands of sun pierced the cloud cover. Dew tipped the grass, and the air held the clean, cool calling card of rain.

A well-established path led her into Bradfordwood's forest. Only a daughter of these woods, only a girl who'd grown up playing make-believe beneath these sheltering braches, would know how to locate the narrow path leading to the inlet. Locate it she did, despite that it was even more overgrown than usual. Willow pushed aside huge ferns and listened to the *drip drop* of moisture against leaves and fertile earth.

At length she reached the ridge above the inlet. Below, the curving course of the Hood

Canal formed a tiny, secluded beach ringed by cliffs and pine trees.

Her parents hadn't allowed her and her sisters to go swimming unsupervised in the inlet when they'd been growing up. Nor had they allowed them to swim immediately after a meal. Every now and then, though, when Willow's obedience to her parents in (almost) all things had mounted to such a high level that she'd felt more like a robot than a person with free will, she'd snuck down to the inlet and gone swimming. Completely, thrillingly alone.

She'd never gone after a meal because she hadn't been brave enough to break *two rules* simultaneously. Also, she hadn't actually wanted to drown.

Whenever she'd swum solo through the crystal cold waters of this inlet, she'd been hyper-aware of her solitude. She'd felt independent and free and courageous. This inlet was as close as she'd come to rebellion during her middle and high school years.

Then her small world had expanded in big ways when she'd left home to attend UCLA. Especially when, midway through her freshman year, she'd been approached by a modeling scout while shopping with friends at a flea market. She'd chatted with the scout, a stylish middle-aged woman, while surrounded by the flea market's haphazard treasures.

The scout had asked Willow if she'd ever done any modeling. Willow replied that she hadn't. The scout invited her to an interview the following week. Willow took the woman's expensive business card, even though she had no real intention of attending the interview. For one thing, she was a student pursuing a design degree. She couldn't envision herself as a model. For another thing, she was concerned that the scout was somehow trying to scam her for money.

Her friends were the ones who convinced her to go to the interview that had become the doorway to an entirely unexpected career and a whole new direction in life. Astonishingly, the scout who discovered her worked for the most prestigious international modeling agency in the world.

It dazed Willow each time she thought about how different her life might have been had she not visited that particular flea market on that particular morning.

From the start, Willow's modeling career had taken off in a way that couldn't be explained except by two words: *God's. Providence.* She'd dropped out of UCLA in order to keep up with her work schedule and enrolled in online courses instead. She'd weathered her parents' worries and moved into an apartment in LA with a chaperone and several other new girls who'd signed with the same agency. She'd lived there for a year and then in an apartment in Paris for two years.

Some of the girls she'd roomed with in those days, and so many others she'd met during the last twelve years, had been prettier than she was. Almost all had been skinnier. Many had been more talented at their craft.

But Willow had been the one who'd caught the eye of just the right designers and photographers and fashion magazine editors at exactly the right moments. Thus, her career, in the magical, hard-to-believe way of some rare things, had taken her to heights that she herself never would have predicted or even known how to imagine. Thanks to deals that had made her the face of a premier fragrance as well as a worldwide clothing company, she'd snuck onto the bottom of Forbes' annual Ten Highest Paid Models list four different times.

Modeling had brought her mountaintop moments. It had also plunged her into valleys. Every aspect of her appearance and behavior was fodder for public scrutiny. Fellow models who viewed her as a competitor said hurtful and untrue things about her. She'd been propositioned by more men than she could count, frequently in vulgar or downright creepy ways. Rich businessmen had offered her huge sums of money in exchange for a night in her bed.

She'd responded to the mountaintops and the valleys by working hard, praying hard, and conducting herself like a lady.

When she'd attained a bachelor's degree, her father had informed her that he wanted to give her a graduation gift that would help her make her way in the world. She'd known immediately what she wanted his gift to go toward: a house of her own. For months, she'd hunted the outskirts of Los Angeles for just the right property before unearthing, like a diamond from the wall of a cave, a 1930s cottage on a hillside plot dotted with trees. Since purchasing the cottage, she'd lovingly furnished, decorated, and stocked every square inch of it herself.

All those years ago, when she'd started modeling, it had seemed as though she had more than enough time to find the perfect husband. She'd been able to picture it so clearly. The two of them would move into her cottage and, after approximately two and a half years of newlywed bliss, start a family.

Modeling may have flung open the world's doors to her, but a family of her own had always been her highest, biggest dream. To that end, she'd chosen Christian boyfriends and behaved impeccably with each of them.

Then she'd met Corbin.

Pain made a grab for her heart. Slowly, she proceeded down the steep trail leading to the water.

Almost from the minute Willow and Corbin had started dating, she'd been certain that he was her future husband. His personality was the ideal complement to hers, and their chemistry was a rare and mighty force of nature. No, he wasn't a Christian, but he had so very, *very* many good qualities.

His entrance into her life had come at the perfect moment — right on schedule! — and she'd fallen for him like a sack of stones off the edge of a ten-story building.

She'd known that sleeping with him was a terrible idea.

Of course she'd known. But by the time they'd been together for three and a half months, the girl who'd dutifully eaten the crusts on her peanut butter and jelly sandwiches, who'd been virtuous for twenty-seven years straight, had wanted quite desperately to indulge herself in *that* particular way with *that* particular man.

Corbin had made it clear that he wanted her, but he hadn't pressured her. No, the bitter truth of it was that she'd let a mix of hormones and her own desperate love for him carry her away.

From when they'd started having sex to the end of their relationship had been the most volatile period of Willow's life. She'd been racked with guilt. She'd also been euphoric with happiness. She'd prayed on her knees for forgiveness. She'd been wildly in love. It had been electrifying. It had been horrible. It had been the most exciting thing she'd ever experienced. It had been a betrayal of her own beliefs.

Over and over she told herself that what they were doing had to stop. They needed to get married or break up or go back to drawing the line at kissing, like they had during the early part of their relationship. If they didn't repent, God would surely step in and separate them. Repeatedly, she determined to make a change.

Then Corbin would wrap her in his arms, grin at her, and kiss the side of her neck, and she'd want nothing more in the world than to make love to him again.

Before and after her affair with Corbin, she'd been good. To this day, the thing that scared her most was just how much she'd loved being bad with him.

He'd shown her how deep her sins ran and just how fallible she could be when confronted with the right set of temptations.

Having sex with Corbin had been to her adult self what swimming in the inlet had been to her teenage self. She'd managed to escape the consequences of swimming in the inlet. But one day the consequences of sex with Corbin had come calling. And when they'd come, they'd come armed with knives.

Seven months into their relationship, she'd been on assignment in Germany when her period had failed to arrive on schedule.

Willow reached the crescent of sand that formed the inlet's beach. With the kind of awareness that would have made a yoga teacher proud, she drew a few breaths right to the bottom of her lungs, filling them up. She clambered onto the flat-topped boulder where she, her sisters, and her parents had once set their beach bags and water bottles. Positioning her rain boots on the rock, she laced her arms around her bent knees.

Corbin hadn't broken her heart all at once. No, he'd broken it with three distinct blows. The first blow had been delivered in a German hotel room that she could still see with startling clarity in her mind's eye. The duvet cover. The sleek wooden furniture. The gray walls. The fashionable metal wall art that resembled a sun.

She'd said nothing to Corbin when her period was two days late. Then three. Then four. Instead, she kept willing it to arrive, while sleeping little and worrying much. No matter what activities she moved her body through during those days, her head was full of just one thought.

I might be pregnant.

Someone on the set would say, "Good morning, Willow," and she'd think, *I might be pregnant.*

A waitress would ask if she'd like broccoli or asparagus with her dinner, and she'd think, *I might be pregnant.*

The night she'd finally worked up the nerve to tell Corbin, the air inside that hotel room had been frigid with loneliness. The sky beyond her window black and pouring rain. She'd felt so sick to her stomach with anxiety that she'd stood in the bathroom for several minutes, eyeing the toilet, wondering if her dinner would stay down.

He'd answered her call with an affectionate "Hey" that had communicated the message that everything was right with the world.

Hearing the pitch of his familiar voice caused tears to well in Willow's eyes. All would be well. Why had she hesitated to share her fears with him? She could trust him with this, with anything. She could count on him. "How are you?"

"Good. I'm in the back of a limousine on the way to an interview with ESPN and I have you for a girlfriend, so all in all, my life couldn't get any better."

"I forgot about the interview. If this is a bad time, we can talk later."

"No, I'm glad you caught me. I'd have hated to miss your call. You're still in Germany, right? It must be late there."

"It is."

A brief pause. "Is something the matter, Willow? You sound sad."

"Not sad, exactly. More like . . . concerned." What a terrific understatement.

"About?"

The words stuck in her throat. A protective instinct within wanted to keep them unspoken.

"Willow? What are you worried about, sweetheart?"

"My period is late."

Yawning silence.

She could hear both the roar of rain outside her hotel and the hum of a radio station playing indie rock music inside his limo. "Are you there?" she asked quietly.

"I'm here. How late is your period?"

"Five days."

"We use protection."

"I know. I'm probably not pregnant," she hurried to say. "It's likely that I'm worrying about nothing. But I'm not usually late and this is, well, starting to consume my thoughts."

Another long stretch of quiet, during which Willow watched her pulse beat too fast in her inner wrist.

"I'm sorry," he said, but the words held none of the warmth she'd heard when he'd answered her call.

She bit her lip, hard. She needed much more from him than *I'm sorry.* She was *starving* for him to reassure her and to tell her not to be afraid and to acknowledge that now was not the perfect time for a baby — he'd never even said *I love you,* and she was waiting for him to say it first — but that he'd be thrilled for her to carry his child and, now that he thought about it, this was a huge blessing in disguise and they'd make it work and the only thing he really wanted in life was to marry her because he loved her like crazy.

I'm sorry didn't begin to cover it.

"And?" she asked.

"And what?"

"Is 'I'm sorry' all you have to say?"

"I don't know what to say! I'm racking my brain. You can't be pregnant."

Her anger flared. "Contraceptives aren't one hundred percent effective. The fact is that I *can* be pregnant."

Soft indie rock music answered. She wanted to claw through the space between them and hammer the power button on the limo's radio with her fist.

"I've wanted to be a mother all my life," she said unsteadily. It was hard to speak while her hopes were swerving downward. "I'd never do anything to stop any baby of mine from being born. But the possibility that I could be pregnant now, at this point, is scary, Corbin. I mean . . . my family. What will they think? And I'm an ambassador for a Christian charity. I talk about my faith all the time in interviews and from the podium at events that Benevolence Worldwide puts together. I'd be shunned by the Christian community if I got pregnant. Benevolence would fire me —"

"You volunteer for Benevolence. They

can't fire you."

"You know what I mean. Benevolence would let me go. And they'd be right to let me go. What kind of role model would I be?"

"You'd be the same role model you've always been."

"But a pregnancy would prove to the world that I haven't been practicing what I preach."

"Nobody's perfect, Willow."

Tears and hysteria pressed outward from her chest. "People think that I am."

"Who cares what people think?"

"I do. And you do, too. The two of us live in a fishbowl, Corbin." She hadn't wanted to explain herself or to argue with him. She'd just wanted to be comforted.

"It's crazy to stress about this. You're not pregnant."

"But what if I am? . . . Corbin?"

"I'm not ready for this."

"Not ready to be a father? Or not ready to discuss what we're going to do if I'm pregnant?"

"Both."

That one word connected with her midsection like a punch.

ESPN interview that aired two days before Corbin and Willow's breakup:

CORRESPONDENT: Are you in a relationship at the moment?

CORBIN: Yes. I'm in a serious relationship with the Dallas Mustangs.

CORRESPONDENT: [Chuckle] Let me rephrase. Are you in a dating relationship at the moment?

CORBIN: No, not at the moment.

CORRESPONDENT: I ask because you've been seen for months now with model Willow Bradford.

CORBIN: Willow's great. We're just having fun.

CORRESPONDENT: You're not ready to settle down?

CORBIN: I might be one day, when the right woman comes along. I'm in no hurry. Like I said, my relationship with the Mustangs is pretty serious. It doesn't leave room for much else.

Chapter Eleven

The afternoon after her visit to Bradford-wood's inlet, Willow sat alone at a table within the Edge of the Woods Bakery and Tearoom. The tearoom's peaceful interior — rustic pine floors, whitewashed walls, round tables supporting arrangements of pink peonies and tiny green berries — contrasted with the restless interior of Willow's mind.

She hadn't seen Corbin since she'd dashed out of the rehab center four days ago like a shopper toward a Black Friday sale. But any minute now, he and Charlotte would be arriving for today's Operation Find Josephine meeting. She'd be forced anew to confront the archvillain of her life. Who was the same person who'd injured himself on Friday protecting her.

Dredging up the past at the inlet had helped. As she'd hoped, it had stacked weight onto the Why Corbin Spells Disaster side of the scale right when the Why Corbin Might be Likable side had begun acquiring weight for the first time in years. She felt rejuvenated in her animosity.

As this meeting drew nearer, however, she'd also felt something that slightly resembled . . . anticipation? Almost as if she was looking forward to seeing him? She'd been *sternly* trying to talk herself out of the feeling.

With an agitated sigh, she pulled her phone from her purse and brought up CrateandBarrel.com. To distract herself, she scanned their Tabletop & Bar page.

All this angst over Corbin was pointless. It wasn't like she was going to *do* anything with him. She was leaving Washington in just six weeks. She lived in LA. Innkeeper was not her profession. Modeling was her profession.

When she'd taken this extended break from modeling, she'd assumed that she simply needed rest and a change of scenery in order to cure her case of burnout. She'd believed that the enthusiasm she'd once had for her career would return in time.

So far, it hadn't. In fact, somewhat the opposite had occurred during her five months in Merryweather. The more distance she'd gained from modeling, the more distance she'd enjoyed having and the less interested she was in returning. She still had faith, though, that when she showed up on the set of her first booking after her hiatus, her old enjoyment of modeling would greet her.

If that didn't happen, she'd need to re-evaluate. She had commitments on her calendar through January, and Willow Elizabeth Bradford did not break her work commitments. Ever. The jobs that were on her calendar, she would absolutely fulfill.

The door of the girly tearoom swung open to admit Corbin. The scale of his body made the furniture filling the space appear kid-sized.

Her breath jammed. He was a whole lot of . . . a lot.

He threaded his way through the space wearing a black sweater and jeans. In his left hand he carried an iPad. A navy blue sling encased his right arm.

At this hour, the high tea hour, the restaurant was filled without exception by women. Some of them hushed at the sight of Corbin. Some murmured to their friends. None of them was without a reaction and all of them tracked Corbin's progress.

"Good afternoon," Willow said, setting her phone aside.

"Good afternoon."

"Where's Charlotte?"

He placed his tablet on the table and took the seat opposite her. "It's Jill's birthday, so I dropped Charlotte off at home after PT. They have a celebration planned."

"But I suggested we meet here today instead of at the inn *for Charlotte.* I didn't have any guests checking in, and I thought she'd enjoy coming to the tearoom."

"And yet there's only me."

"You have my number now. Why didn't you let me know she wasn't coming?"

He raised a brow. "Why do you think?"

She swallowed.

"It's because I love tea," he said.

Humor tugged at her lips.

"Frankly, I'm glad for the chance to talk to you about Josephine without Charlotte present. Who are we kidding? The little K-pop lover is just slowing us real detectives down."

Willow laughed.

An employee set a glass of ice water in front of Corbin and handed him a tiny pink menu.

"You'll need to choose a tea flight," Willow said. "Once you do, they'll bring you three different types of tea to try."

"Sounds like today's my lucky day."

"More lucky than you realize because I'm paying."

He cocked his head. "I always pick up the tab. Remember?"

"I'm paying today to thank you for . . . the other morning." Maybe then they'd be even, and she wouldn't have to keep on feeling indebted.

"You're buying me a tea flight as a thank-you gift?" He appeared to be fighting back laughter.

"That and cucumber sandwiches, scones with clotted cream and jelly, and cookies."

"That sounds like a thank-you punishment."

"Just order, you ungrateful sod."

A waitress, aged approximately ninety, hobbled up to their table. Despite her years, she was not immune to Corbin's charms. She gawked at him like he was her Frank Sinatra.

Willow cleared her throat. "I'd like to order the decadent indulgence —"

"You betcha. Coming right up." Corbin placed his left palm on the table and rose halfway to standing. "Should we kiss here, or would you rather we take it outside?"

"Corbin!" She brandished her menu. "I was trying to order a food item."

"Oh," he said with false innocence.

Willow glanced at their waitress. The older lady was actually blushing. What was the correct protocol? Should she apologize for Corbin's inappropriate suggestion? Before Willow could formulate an apology, the waitress started to giggle.

Willow straightened in her seat. "As I was trying to say, I'd like to order the decadent indulgence high tea for two."

"What tea flight would you like, miss?" the older woman asked.

"The subtle and sweet flight, please."

"And you, sir?"

"Do you serve beer?" Corbin asked.

A fresh flurry of geriatric giggles erupted at his question.

"No," Willow said to him dryly. "They do not serve beer."

"In that case, I'll have tequila."

The waitress chortled. "I like you," she said to Corbin.

"I like you, too. How about you just choose a flight for me?"

"Certainly, sir." She ambled off.

"I can't take you anywhere," Willow said.

"You can take me outside for that kiss."

"Let's get down to business, shall we?"

Corbin eyed her. "Have you pressed charges yet against the guy who attacked you?"

It took Willow a second to adjust to his swift conversational tack change. "I met with the police about it. Going in, I wasn't sure if what occurred was enough to merit charges. But it turns out that it constitutes misdemeanor assault. So I pressed charges for that and also filed for a restraining order." She'd taken those steps, in part, because Nora and Britt had encouraged her to do so. Since the attack, Nora had been swinging by Bradfordwood to check on her, and Britt had been supplying her with extra chocolate.

"Good. You gave the police his license plate number?"

"I did. His name's Todd Hill, and he's from Olympia. The next steps will be the prosecutor's."

"Todd Hill from Olympia isn't one of my favorite people."

"Nor mine."

"If you see him anywhere, you'll call the police and me, right?"

"Yes." To the police. No to calling Corbin, though it was easier to leave that unsaid. She didn't want him wrecking his other shoulder, and she didn't want him doing anything that would give Todd a legitimate reason to sue him. "I'm really hoping the assault charge and the restraining order put

227

an end to it. How's your shoulder?"

"Improving."

"How long do you have to wear the sling?"

"A week total. So just a few more days now." A pause. "Do you ask because you're concerned about me?"

"I ask because I'm polite." She clasped her hands together on the table. "Let's talk about Josephine."

He went to work on his tablet. "Charlotte wouldn't part with her Josephine notebook, but she did let me take a picture of her to-do list from our last meeting."

They talked through the items listed. They'd both followed up on the things they said they'd do, but their efforts hadn't led to any promising new information.

"I heard from Melinda about the DNA she submitted," Willow said. "No hits."

He leaned back in his chair. "We know that DNA from the bones found near the hiking trail was logged into the system. So if Melinda's DNA turned up no hits, then the bones found near the hiking trail don't belong to Josephine."

"Exactly."

"Thanks to this shoulder injury I got while saving your life —"

"I don't remember you saving my life, precisely —"

"I haven't been able to work on my house the past few days. So I've been reading everything I can find online about people who went missing in Washington in the '70s."

"Did you find any similarities or connections to Josephine's case?"

"No. So then I searched for missing people in Idaho in the '70s. Then Oregon. Then Montana. Last night, I finally came across a lead."

Willow regarded him with surprise. An actual lead?

A server brought out cucumber sandwiches on fancy white china plates dotted with periwinkle flowers.

"Huh," Corbin said as he lifted one of the sandwiches. "I didn't know people made food this small. My sandwich is the size of a dog biscuit."

The server returned with teacups for each of them.

"About that lead," Willow prompted.

He ate his sandwich in two bites while opening the browser on his tablet. He clicked on a bookmarked website, then slid the tablet to Willow.

The website appeared to belong to a TV station in Montana. The title read, *Thompson Falls Resident Vanished Forty Years Ago Today.* A video of a news story that had run on the station was embedded below the title. It showed a still shot of a good-looking blond man dressed in '70s clothing. Willow scrolled to the article beneath the video.

"They say in the article the same things they say in the video," Corbin told her.

"When did this story run?"

"About a year and a half ago."

Willow bent her head to read.

Thompson Falls, Montana — Forty years have passed since businessman, rancher, and philanthropist Stan Markum vanished without a trace. Stan, the eldest son of multimillionaire businessman Charles Markum, was a famously private man. After Stan inherited his father's business and his 200,000-acre ranch in northwestern Montana, he quietly involved himself in numerous charities, Civil Rights causes, and the political campaigns of Foster Holt and Edward Russell, among others.

The thirty-nine-year-old father of two disappeared on the morning of April 12, 1977, after leaving home on his way to work.

Mr. Markum's case remains unsolved, and the vehicle he was driving the day he went missing has never been discovered.

Forty years later, Stan Markum's wife and children are left with far more questions than answers concerning the fate of their beloved husband and father.

If you have any information regarding the disappearance of Stan Markum, please call the Thompson Falls Police Department.

Willow lifted her gaze to Corbin. "This man disappeared on the exact same day as Josephine."

"Yes."

"What could possibly explain that?"

"Coincidence."

"Or . . . ?"

"Or a connection between Stan and Josephine of some kind," he said.

Willow rubbed the tip of her thumb against her plate, thinking. "What could connect a wealthy businessman from Montana to a social worker from Washington?"

Corbin ate another sandwich.

Willow looked back over the article. "It says here that Stan took part in the political campaigns of Foster Holt and Edward Russell. I'm not familiar with Edward Russell, but I'm very familiar with Foster Holt."

"Was he one of Washington's senators?"

"He was and *still is* one of Washington's senators. He lives in Redmond, and he's a legend in these parts. Very well respected.

He's one of the longest sitting senators in history. Back in 1977 he may have been serving his first term."

"Let's look it up." Corbin searched the senator's name. Both he and Willow bent over the results. "You're right," Corbin said. "Senator Holt was elected to his first term in 1976. But what does that have to do with Josephine?"

"Nothing."

Willow observed downtown Merryweather through the tearoom's windows. Beyond a neat row of storefronts and lampposts, she could just catch a glimpse of Nora's historical village.

Something tickled the back of her mind. A thought. About Senator Holt? Stan Markum? Josephine? She couldn't quite grab hold of it.

Their server returned, setting a three-tiered tray piled with scones on their table. Ramekins containing clotted cream and black currant jam, and their second cups of tea followed.

"More miniature food," Corbin said. "How am I supposed to eat this?"

Willow moved a scone onto her plate and split it in half. "You separate the scone like so. Then you spread cream on top of each piece. Then you add jelly."

Corbin followed her lead.

"You're doing exactly what I told you to do," Willow observed. "How refreshing."

He glanced up from the careful concentration he'd focused on spreading cream on his scone. Amusement glinted in the brown depths of his eyes, but seriousness defined the set of his lips. "I'll do anything you tell me to do. Always."

Her stomach lifted with joy. One second stretched into the next before she remembered the correct response. "It's more like you'll do anything I tell you *not* to do."

"How do I eat this? Tell me that. With a fork?"

"No. With your hands. Like a biscuit."

They both took a bite of their creations. While chewing, he kept his mouth closed and smiled at her simultaneously.

It was fun to introduce the quarterback who'd experienced everything to something entirely new. It was fun to eat a scone with cream and jelly while watching him eat one, too. It's possible that, in her organized and responsible life, she'd failed to schedule in enough time for things that were simply . . . fun.

"It's good," he said.

"It is. Especially with tea." She took a sip. Just as she was setting her teacup back into its saucer, the thought she'd been reaching for earlier came to her.

Josephine's charm bracelet. Something about the Stan Markum article had stirred a memory of Josephine's charm bracelet. What, though?

She opened the Notes app on her phone and found the page where she'd typed the information Melinda had provided about each of the charms the day they'd met for lunch at the country club. Sand dollar. Cross. Liberty Bell.

Liberty Bell. That was it. That's what she'd thought of when she'd read about Stan Markum's support of politicians. "Do you remember the charm bracelet that was inside the box of Josephine memorabilia?" she asked.

Corbin nodded.

"One of the charms on it is the Liberty Bell. Melinda couldn't tell me why Josephine had the Liberty Bell on her bracelet. Obviously, the Liberty Bell represents America. But it's possible that it might represent something more specific. Like our government. Our leaders? Politics?"

"It's possible. We know that Josephine was quick to support causes. Didn't Melinda tell us that she participated in picket lines?"

"Yes."

"It's not hard for me to imagine her volunteering for political campaigns."

"Me either. Senator Holt's campaign would have been mobilizing right in Josephine's backyard. It strikes me as strange that a Montana businessman took an interest in Senator Holt's election. But it's not that much of a stretch to imagine that Josephine might have been involved. I'll call Melinda."

Corbin finished his first scone and went to work doctoring another while Willow found Melinda in her list of phone contacts. When Corbin's attention wasn't on his scone, she could sense his gaze on her.

Melinda answered on the third ring. "Hello?"

"Hi, Melinda. It's Willow. I have a quick question for you if you're not too busy."

"Shoot."

"Do you happen to know if Josephine worked on the election campaign of Senator Foster Holt in 1976?"

A pause. "Goodness, I haven't thought about that in years. The answer is yes. She volunteered for his campaign. I can't remember if she made phone calls or knocked on doors or what."

Willow gave Corbin a thumbs-up signal. At last! Progress. Willow told Melinda about

235

Stan Markum.

"I've never heard of him."

"You didn't see news coverage about his disappearance near the time of Josephine's disappearance?"

"No, not that I remember."

Willow thanked Melinda and they disconnected.

"So Josephine and Stan both supported the senator's 1976 campaign?" Corbin asked.

"Yes."

"Which means they might have known each other."

"Or they might not have," Willow said. "Stan lived in Montana, so it could be that he was just a campaign donor. Josephine was a volunteer." She nibbled on her scone, then dabbed her lips with her napkin.

"I like how you fold your napkin before putting it back in your lap," Corbin said. "You're tidy."

"And proud of it." She wished he'd stop looking at her so intensely.

"Let's assume for a minute that Stan and Josephine knew each other," he said.

"All right. Elections are held in November. So what could have caused Stan and Josephine to disappear five months after the campaign ended?"

236

"I have no idea. But the fact that they vanished on the same day has me interested."

"Me too. What do you think we should do next?"

"I think we should have a conversation with Senator Holt."

Willow's eyes rounded. "You can't just call up a United States senator and schedule a meeting."

"Most normal human people can't. But I bet you a hundred bucks that Senator Holt will make time in his schedule for me."

Text message from Britt to Willow and Nora:

Britt
I'm completely bummed about Zander leaving. Did you know that he's planning to leave for London in TWO WEEKS, as soon as he fulfills the notice he gave his boss? Why the rush? He just came up with this idea!

Willow
You left to go and live in France for two years. Remember how supportive he was of you back then?

Britt
It was a lot less depressing when I was

the one setting off on the grand adventure. It stinks to be the one left behind.

Nora
Sorry I'm just now replying. I zoned out for an hour or two, staring blissfully at my boyfriend.

Britt
Bah humbug.

Willow
Bah humbug.

Nora
Think how great this trip will be for Zander, Britt. He's never traveled much, and now he can.

Britt
Outwardly, I'm saying and doing all the right, sweet, supportive things. It's just inwardly that I'm in despair. He's my best friend.

Voice mail to Joe Stewart:

Mr. Stewart, this is Lisa from Oncology Associates. I see here that you missed your scheduled appointment for a blood draw, and I was calling to reschedule. Please call me back at this number at your convenience. Thanks and have a great day.

and I was calling to reschedule. Please call me back at this number at your convenience. Thanks and have a great day.

CHAPTER TWELVE

Just because Willow wasn't impressed by Corbin didn't mean that other people weren't. And thank goodness for that. Doors opened for him every direction he turned, which was how he liked it.

Corbin had called his publicist from the tearoom on Tuesday. His publicist then contacted Senator Holt's people. Not only had the senator made time for Corbin, as Corbin had told Willow he would, but the senator had invited Corbin and Willow to visit him at his home in Redmond, Washington.

It was 10:53 on Friday morning. After a drive that had taken them less than two hours, they'd arrived seven minutes ahead of schedule at the stone fence surrounding Senator Holt's property.

Corbin could drive short distances with his injured shoulder, but long distances were harder. Willow had insisted on driving to Redmond, and as it turned out, sitting in

240

the passenger seat of her Range Rover came with one big advantage: the freedom to watch her.

She was wearing big round, black sunglasses that made her look like either a movie star or a spy. She had a habit of fidgeting with the stack of bracelets on her wrist. And whenever the cars around her did anything she didn't approve of, the skin between her brows would wrinkle, the kindergarten teacher in her would come out, and she'd talk to the cars as if they were people. She'd say "Hey, Volvo, why are you swerving?" Or, "It's not your turn, blue van."

Willow gave their names over the senator's intercom system, and the gates glided open. The drive eventually brought them to a new house pretending to be a mini castle from centuries before.

After they'd rung the doorbell, Corbin angled a look at Willow and found that she was already watching him. An earthquake went off within him, simply by meeting her eyes. It had always been like that for him, with her.

Immediately, she looked to the door.

"Were you just staring at me?" he asked.

"While thinking about how much I dislike you," she answered.

241

He chuckled. "You only wish you disliked me."

They'd both chosen fancier clothing for today's meeting than what they usually wore. He'd dressed in suit pants and a dress shirt and his sling. She had on a brown sweater, pants that molded to her knockout legs, and high-heeled ankle boots. There wasn't a single piece of dust or lint on her. Not one lock of her hair was out of place.

Which gave him the urge to mess up her hair, to tug her sweater off one shoulder, to kiss her. Just about everything about her made him want to kiss her lately. It had been like this at the tearoom, too, and during their meeting yesterday at the inn with Charlotte.

An elegant older woman answered the door and beckoned them into a marble foyer. She introduced herself as Marjorie Holt.

Corbin gave their names and went right to work making small talk with Marjorie.

He knew from the reading he'd done over the past two days in preparation for this meeting that Marjorie was Foster's wife. They had five children ranging in age from fifty-three to forty-three and fourteen grandchildren. The senator was the head of a large family and had himself come from a large family. He was the eldest of six, raised by wealthy parents here in Redmond. He'd pursued Ivy League undergrad and graduate degrees and hadn't looked back since. He was still going strong at the age of eighty.

Just as his wife murmured that she'd go and fetch Foster, the senator himself came around the corner wearing a white apron over khakis and a plaid button-down. Tall and lean, he moved with easy coordination. He had a strong, straight nose, a hard jaw, and a full head of white hair. Even with the white hair, he looked ten or fifteen years younger than he was.

"Welcome." He shook hands with Corbin. "I'm very glad to meet you, Corbin. I was fortunate to attend the second of your Super Bowls."

"Were you happy or sad when we won?"

"I'll have to call my lawyer to ask whether or not I can legally disclose that information without incriminating myself." He winked and faced Willow.

"This is Willow Bradford," Corbin said. "She's a model and an ambassador for Benevolence Worldwide."

"Ah." Senator Holt regarded her with growing recognition as he shook her hand. "Are you related to Garner Bradford?"

"Yes, he's my father."

"How lovely!" Marjorie said. "We've spent time with him and Kathleen on several occasions over the years."

"Indeed we have." The senator gestured to the hallway. "Right this way." He unlaced his apron and pulled it over his head as he led them deeper into the house. "I was in the kitchen just now, getting started on preparations for the dinner party Marjorie and I are hosting tonight. When I'm at home I always try to make time to cook."

"And I always make sure he *makes time* to cook," Marjorie told them. "He's very good at it." She took her husband's apron. "It was nice to meet you both. I'm on my way out the door to have lunch with a friend. See you in a few hours?" she asked the senator.

"See you then."

Willow and Corbin followed the senator into an office paneled with dark wood. Senator Holt took a seat below an iron chandelier and behind a desk that had to have been eight feet long. Corbin and Willow sat in the chairs opposite.

Most men, after being introduced to Corbin, wanted to talk football first. The senator was no different. Corbin had grown accustomed to answering questions he'd been asked a hundred times, to smiling over the mention of his career highlights as if he'd never smiled over them before, to giving out pieces of information about coaches or players or plays and making it sound like the words were coming out of his mouth for the first time.

Since he only had to use half his brain to talk football, Corbin used the other half to focus on Willow. She was sitting quietly, her hands in her lap.

Foster Holt broadcast good humor, but Corbin could tell that the man was no pushover. There was iron in his eyes, enough of it to have fueled decades of political battles.

"What can I do for you?" Senator Holt finally asked. "My aides mentioned that you had some questions for me."

"We do," Corbin answered. "We were hoping to talk with you about a woman who volunteered on your very first campaign."

"My first campaign?" The older man's expression took on a nostalgic quality. "What's the woman's name?"

"Josephine Blake."

"Ah," Foster murmured with surprise. "Is Josephine Blake the one who disappeared?"

"Yes," Willow answered. "She disappeared in April of 1977."

"It was awful, what happened to her. She was so young. I got to know a lot of the people who worked with me on that first campaign. If you'd come in and asked about any of the others, I probably would have had a hard time putting a name to a face all these years later. But I do remember Josephine Blake, in large part because of her disappearance. As far as I know, they never did figure out what happened to her. Is that right?"

"That's right," Willow replied. "There are still no answers."

"What a shame. Are either of you related to Josephine?"

"My niece, Charlotte, is related to her." Charlotte had lobbied to skip school and come with them today but Jill had held firm. "Charlotte's determined to find out what happened to Josephine. She talked Willow and me into helping her."

"I see."

"We recently came across information about a man named Stan Markum," Willow said, "who disappeared the same day that Josephine did. The article mentioned that Stan had been involved in a political campaign of yours. Since you only had one campaign before he vanished, it must have been the '76 campaign . . . the same one Josephine volunteered on."

"That's right. I remember Stan."

246

"Do you happen to know whether Stan and Josephine knew each another?" Willow asked.

"They did know each other, yes. Stan lived in Montana, so he wasn't a daily or weekly part of the 'boots on the ground' campaign team. However, he was one of our primary donors, and he also attended some of the campaign planning and strategy sessions. He'd had a hand in the election of Edward Russell, so he had insight and experience to share."

Foster leaned back in his chair, rubbed his jaw, then dropped his hands to his desk blotter. "Stan came to a few of the fundraising events we held in and around Seattle, including the gala ball. Josephine helped plan the fundraisers, so she was at those events, too." His eyes took on a faraway cast. "I think I even remember them dancing together at the gala because I recall thinking what a striking couple they made. They were good-looking, both of them."

"And both were married," Corbin said.

"Quite right."

"Do you remember hearing about Stan Markum's disappearance?" Willow asked.

"Absolutely. Once I learned of Josephine's disappearance, I began to suspect that something more than friendship may have existed between them."

"You think Josephine and Stan were having an affair?" Corbin asked.

"I didn't suspect that at all until they both vanished on the same day. The timing of it was what made me wonder if they'd run off together. Or, God forbid, whether something tragic had happened to them or between them."

"Did you share your suspicions with the police?" Corbin asked.

"I did. But nothing came of it. I can only suppose that there was no evidence to support my theory."

"What do you think about what Senator Holt told us?" Corbin asked Willow an hour later. The two of them were walking from her car to a taco joint in Redmond to have lunch.

He'd been trying to make sense of the information the senator had given them, to sort it out the way he'd once sorted what his eyes and instincts told him about a defense.

"I don't love the idea of Josephine having an affair," Willow said.

"Me neither."

"Especially after reading the letters from Alan to Josephine inside the box. But the senator's theory does makes sense. An affair between Stan and Josephine would explain why they disappeared at the same time."

"We know that Josephine was rumored to have been having an affair when she went missing," he said.

"And as far as we know, if she was having an affair, it wasn't with Keith, the poor guy from her Sunday school class."

"If I were a pretty twenty-eight-year-old woman who was considering having an affair, I'd choose the handsome multimillionaire from Montana over the Sunday school guy. Just saying." For once, the sky above them didn't contain a single cloud. Only sunshine. "What if they're both alive and living happily on a Caribbean island?"

"Then that means that they didn't care what kind of agony they put their families through. Which means neither of them are very nice people."

"The senator's other theory was that a tragedy had happened to them or between them," Corbin said.

"What do you think he meant by that? That their car could have run off the road into a lake or something?"

"Yes. Or that Stan could have murdered Josephine and then killed himself."

"If murder-suicide is on the table, then

shouldn't a double murder be on the table, too?" Willow adjusted her sunglasses as she looked across at him. "If Stan and Josephine were having an affair, then Josephine's husband, Alan, would have had motive to kill them both if he discovered them together."

"So would Stan's wife."

They walked in silence for a few yards. She was exactly the right height. Several inches shorter than he was, but not so short that he felt like he dwarfed her.

"What should we do next?" Willow asked.

"As of right now, Senator Holt is the only link we have between Josephine and Stan. So how about you research Senator Holt?"

"Agreed. But since I'm the CEO of our crime-fighting unit, I think it's only fair that you have a bigger homework assignment than me."

"Fine, boss lady. I'll research Stan." Corbin's attention narrowed on her feet. "Are you avoiding the sidewalk cracks?"

"What? No."

"Yes, you are." He felt a grin pull at his cheeks. He'd noticed that her strides weren't all the same length. Some were shorter and some longer — because she never set her boots on the seams between pieces of concrete. "You never step on cracks?"

"Not sidewalk cracks. I'm fine with tile

and stone and wood and the rest."

"Are you afraid it's bad luck?"

"Not afraid, exactly. Just careful. And a tiny bit superstitious."

"I'll protect you from bad luck."

"You *are* bad luck, Corbin."

He held the door of the taco restaurant open for her. They came to a stop at the counter and read the menu displayed on the wall behind the cash register.

"What are you going to order?" he asked.

"The brisket tacos."

"You've ordered brisket tacos at every taco restaurant you've eaten at in the last five years, haven't you?" She didn't need to answer. He knew her well enough to know that's exactly what she'd done.

"I like brisket tacos," she said defensively. "What are you getting?"

"I think I'm going to try the mahimahi *el Fuego* tacos."

"Those sound spicy."

"Spicy things are sometimes delicious." He spent the next five minutes waving new customers past them while he slowly talked her into trying the el Fuego tacos.

They sat at an outdoor table under a bright red umbrella and counted down before biting into their tacos at the same moment.

Their gazes locked in an unspoken challenge while they chewed. Tears rushed to Willow's eyes, but she straightened in her seat and stuck it out until she swallowed. After taking a sip of water, she smiled at him — a full smile without any walls between them. The green eyes he'd looked into so often in his dreams blazed with triumph.

And then, right then, Corbin knew that he had to win Willow back.

He had to.

There was nothing that could be done about it.

He'd been telling himself not to go there with her again. Not to set himself up for disappointment. Not to fall for her. But he couldn't support any of that anymore. Not for another day. He'd tried.

She was graceful and intelligent. Kind and independent. Calm, yet surprisingly strong. She was an adult, not a child, and she was exactly right for him in too many ways to name. In ways he didn't even understand.

He needed her to love him. And so he was going to make sure that she did.

He'd experienced this kind of single-minded drive before. When he'd decided to play college ball. When he'd decided to land a contract in the NFL. When he'd decided to win a Super Bowl. He was a focused man. Once he set his mind on something he only had one gear. Forward.

It wasn't going to be easy. She hadn't forgiven him for their breakup, and she'd probably rather climb Everest than take him back.

He'd need to play his cards exactly right. He'd have to stay one step ahead of her, and he'd have to be patient, which was fine. He wasn't scared of working hard to get what he wanted. And at this point in his life, Willow Bradford was what he wanted.

If he could convince her to eat el Fuego tacos, he could — *would* — convince her to give him another chance.

Later that afternoon, Willow and Corbin arrived back at the Inn at Bradfordwood. Willow parked her SUV, gratified to see that the inn's grounds were free of crazy stalker fans.

Corbin had met her here after she'd finished serving breakfast. They'd driven to Redmond and back. And now it was time for her to get busy baking cookies. Their road trip and time together had come to an end. She should feel gratified that the worst part of her day was behind her. Instead, she had the niggling sensation that the opposite was true. That the best part of her day was now behind her.

Corbin slanted his upper body to face her, his expression assessing. "Are you free to come over to my place this weekend? I'd like to cook dinner for you."

Was he . . . asking her out? A tingle of what might have been unmitigated pleasure or might have been outright panic slid down the back of her neck.

He'd protected her from Todd. He was caring for his dad. He was fantastic with Charlotte. She'd laughed more today than she'd laughed in the past twelve months combined. She could fall into a daydream just looking at him. Yet she *could not* allow any of that to melt her resolve. "You cook?"

"I cook a little. I'm not very good at it." One side of his lips curved with self-deprecation. "I didn't say I wanted to cook a delicious dinner for you. Just a dinner."

"I don't think dinner at your house is a good idea."

"My dad will be there as a chaperon, if you're worried about needing to protect yourself from me."

Yes, she needed protection from him all right. Heart protection. She climbed from the car.

He exited the car, too, and waited for her

near the front fender. "Come have dinner with me."

"Thanks for the offer, but no." She clicked her key fob to lock her car. Placing her purse strap over her shoulder, she took two steps in the direction of the inn.

"Please?" he said.

"No. We're helping Charlotte find Josephine, Corbin. That's it. Nothing more."

He didn't reply. He only studied her with an implacable gleam in his dark eyes. She recognized that look. It was the same look he'd once leveled on opposing football teams before mounting a fourth-quarter comeback.

Willow experienced a sudden and overwhelming urge to shop for housewares. To shop and shop and shop until she regained her steadiness and sense.

Caption beneath photo published on www .CelebrityGossipOnline.com the day of Corbin and Willow's breakup:

Just when things were starting to look promising for super couple Corbin Stewart and Willow Bradford, Corbin was spotted at one of Dallas's hottest nightclubs with this mystery woman. It seems that even the stunning Willow Bradford has failed to retain the affection of the NFL's most eligible bachelor.

Caption beneath photo published on www .PopNews.com two days after Corbin and Willow's breakup:

It's no surprise to see a beautiful woman on the arm of actor Derek Oliver. In this case, however, the identity of the beautiful woman is somewhat of a surprise. Model Willow Bradford, dazzling in a yellow chiffon Versace gown, has been linked in recent months with Mustangs quarterback Corbin Stewart.

Derek and Willow hit the red carpet for the premiere of Derek's new movie, *Until Sunset.* Does this appearance mean an end to Willow's romance with Corbin and an exciting new beginning with Derek?

Text message from Britt to Willow and Nora:

Britt
Willow, your ex-boyfriend just invited me, Tristan, and Zander over to his house for dinner Monday night.

Nora
He invited John and me, too! I wasn't go-

ing to mention it. My plan was to send John on Monday and stay home out of loyalty to you, Willow. But since he's invited Britt and her men, you must be coming, too, right? Are you and Corbin friends now?

Britt
Or is he still a snake? Should we tell Corbin to take his invitation and shove it?

Nora
I want to do whatever will cause Willow to keep me on her Christmas list.

Britt
I want to go. He said he'll have Monday Night Football playing on his big screen and T-bone steaks on the grill. Also, he's eye candy. And a famous football legend and all. He told me he's invited Charlotte's whole family, too.

Willow
He's a snake! He told me he wanted to cook dinner for me and I said no, so he went behind my back and invited every-one I'm close to except me.

Britt
Um . . . So can I say yes? I want a T-bone steak.

Text message from Willow to Corbin:

Willow
I hear you're planning a dinner party.

Corbin
Hello to you, too, boss lady.

Willow
Is this a ploy to get me to come to your place for dinner even though I already said I wouldn't?

Corbin
Not a ploy so much as a way for me to sweeten my offer.

Willow
I'll pass.

Corbin
Take pity on me, Willow. I invited your sisters and the Dixons and everyone else just so I could get one person to come. You.

Willow
What if everyone in my posse turns your invitation down?

Corbin

Why would they? Didn't you hear? I have T-bone steaks.

Willow

I heard.

Corbin

Do you not like T-bone steaks?

Willow

I'm not a fan of any meat that's still holding on to the bones of the animal it came from.

Corbin

What would you like to eat? Whatever it is, I'll buy it for you.

Willow

You really are hard to say no to, you know that?

Corbin

Filet mignon? Chicken? Pork? Cornish game hens? What?

Willow

Filet mignon will do very nicely.

Corbin

Perfect. See you Monday night.

CHAPTER THIRTEEN

The Dixon family arrived first for dinner on Monday.

Instead of making small talk like a normal person, Charlotte pulled straight the hem of her long-sleeved T-shirt and displayed the writing on it for Corbin to see.

" 'Eat. Sleep. K-pop. Repeat,' " he read. "Where can I order one of those for myself?"

She giggled, then said firmly to her younger brothers, "Quit shoving each other."

Lucky Charlotte. Corbin would have liked two younger brothers to order around. "C'mere, boys." Corbin pulled the nearest one in.

Corbin's dad hurried forward, eager for his own round of hugs.

As soon as Mark and Jill entered into a conversation with his dad and the boys headed in the direction of the backyard to

261

play with Max and Duke, Charlotte positioned herself before Corbin.

"Can we hold a quick Operation Find Josephine meeting when Willow gets here?"
she asked. "You guys went to Redmond
without me, which is, like, really rude since
Josephine is *my* great-aunt, and you
wouldn't even be looking for her if it weren't
for me."

"Hold your horses a second. We wanted
you to come to Redmond, but your mom
wouldn't let you miss school."

"Then you should have rescheduled!"

"Just so you know, puppy, if I'm given a
chance to see Willow, I won't reschedule."

The irritation vanished from Charlotte's
face. "Oh. Wait! Are you guys . . . . getting
back together?"

"Not yet."

"But you'd like to?"

"I would."

"I knew it!" She brightened at the juicy
bit of gossip. "You two are perfect for each
other. It's kinda gross that you're so old,
but it's also kinda nice —"

"Gross? *Old?*"

"I asked Willow if she thought you two
would ever date again, and she said no."

"Yeah, Willow's lack of interest in me is
confusing. Ninety-nine out of a hundred

women find me irresistible."

"Let me know what I can do. You know, to help things along."

"Will do." The day he'd need a twelve-year-old's help with women was the day he'd have no more reasons to live.

"So can we? Have a meeting when Willow gets here?"

"I guess."

The doorbell rang again.

It was Melinda and her husband, Walter, who was as quiet and patient as he was bald.

Corbin had been studying Josephine's case since he'd last seen Melinda. So when he looked at Melinda now, he recognized hints of Josephine's features — features that had looked back at him from yellowed newspaper articles and grainy Internet images — in Melinda's face. Which was sort of unsettling.

The doorbell.

It was Willow's sister Britt and her boyfriend, Tristan, who looked like he'd come straight off of a hiking trail.

Several minutes later, Zander arrived alone.

Where was Willow? Nothing against these people, but he hadn't held this party so he could spend time hanging out with Tristan and Melinda.

When he finally opened the door and saw Willow standing on the threshold, he stilled. She stood next to her sister Nora and Corbin's friend John. He barely registered Nora or John.

Willow's blond hair hung loose. She wore a soft gray knit sweater dress, small sparkly earrings, and the usual collection of bracelets around one slender wrist.

"Your sling is gone," Willow said.

"Yeah, I graduated out of it." He was having a hard time locating his train of thought. "Come on in. Hi, John." They shook hands. "Nora. Nice to see you again."

"Nice to see you, too." Nora hung her coat on the coatrack near the door. "I love your house."

"Thanks. My dad and I have been working on it. It's still not finished, but I hope it will be soon." He led them into the great room, where everyone had gathered in front of the huge flat screen showing the last of the Monday Night Football pre-game commentary. John and Nora made their way toward Britt.

"This space was empty the last time I was here," Willow said. "Now the walls are painted. There's furniture. Rugs. A TV."

"After I invited people over I decided I better have furniture."

"You bought all of this for this dinner party?"

"I was going to have to buy it eventually. This dinner party inspired me to buy it sooner rather than later."

Willow lifted one delicate eyebrow and motioned with her chin to the trays of appetizers spread on both the coffee table and the tall thin table that stood against the sofa's back. "Something tells me you didn't cook these appetizers."

"I know my limitations."

"You know your limitations?" She made a scoffing sound. "Since when?"

He laughed. It was like sun after days of clouds to have her in his house again. He took his first deep breath in what felt like a week. While she was here, his dad's condition couldn't drag him under, his shoulder wouldn't hurt, and he'd be okay with his status as an NFL has-been.

"When you invited me over, you said that you wanted to cook for me," she said.

"Right, but then you said you wouldn't come and forced me to invite all these people just to get you here. I can't cook for fifteen people."

"You said you were going to grill filet mignon for me." Her eyes shone with amusement.

"I said I was going to *buy* filet mignon for you. Subtle difference."

"You hired someone to cook all this." It wasn't a question.

"Yes. Easiest phone call I ever made —"

"Hi, Willow." Charlotte edged between them, and Corbin was forced to take a few steps back to make room for the girl.

Willow greeted Charlotte with a hug.

"Corbin said we could meet really quickly about Josephine," Charlotte said. She was carrying her notebook and a pen.

"Oh?"

Corbin shrugged. "She guilted me into it."

Jill leaned in their direction and asked, "Can Grandma and I join you?"

"No, Mom. Gosh!" Charlotte shot Willow and Corbin a long-suffering expression that said *parents are such a trial.*

Jill's laughter trailed them as Corbin led Willow and Charlotte to the downstairs room he'd made into his office. So far it held a desk, a chair, and several cardboard boxes he hadn't gotten around to unpacking. He offered the chair to Willow. He and Charlotte sat on top of boxes.

Charlotte turned pitiful gray eyes on Willow. "Can you fill me in on everything that's happened since I saw you last?"

266

Personally, Corbin thought she was laying the you-left-me-out-and-hurt-my-feelings thing on a little too thick. But, of course, Willow was compassionate, and Charlotte's shtick worked on her. Willow explained everything the senator had said during their meeting.

As she spoke, Corbin watched how she used her hands. How she gave Charlotte her full attention. He listened to the rise and fall of her voice. And he determined that he was going to have to convince her to talk to him about their breakup. He'd given it a lot of thought over the past few days. The only way forward for them was straight through their past. Not around.

Willow wasn't going to like it. She'd rather use her anger toward him to keep him at arm's length right up until she left Washington. For that reason, biding his time and trying to win her over gradually was never going to work.

Willow fell silent. Corbin waited until Charlotte had finished taking notes, then said, "I found some new information on Stan Markum yesterday."

"You did?" Charlotte asked.

"A couple of years before he disappeared, he was accused of extortion by a business-man who owned a company that was a competitor of Markum Industries."

"What does extortion mean?" Charlotte asked.

"It means using threats or force to get what you want," Corbin answered. "As best as I can figure, Stan and his lawyers settled out of court."

"Stan sounds like he might have been kind of mean," Charlotte said.

"The fact that Stan settled out of court suggests that he may have been guilty," Willow said.

"Maybe. Or maybe he was a rich guy who didn't want to be bothered, so he made the charge go away fast."

"Have you guys ever been accused of a crime?" Charlotte asked.

"Never," Willow answered.

"I plead the fifth," Corbin said.

"If Stan *was* guilty, then that means he wasn't afraid to dabble in illegal things." Willow's eyebrows pinched together as she thought it over. "I wonder if he or Josephine could have gotten involved in something illegal or dangerous and *that's* what ended up causing their disappearance."

Quiet fell as they weighed the possibility.

Charlotte wrote in her notebook. "Good thinking, Willow."

"I'm the one who found new information," Corbin said. "So what about 'Good work, Uncle Corbin'?"

"That too," Charlotte mumbled.

"I also found some new information." Willow gestured to his computer. "May I?"

"Sure."

She opened his Internet browser and went to work. "Stan isn't the only one with a few skeletons in his closet."

"Josephine had skeletons in her closet?" Charlotte asked.

"None that I've been able to find," Willow answered.

"Who are you talking about, then?"

"Senator Foster Holt." Willow rolled the desk chair to the side, revealing the computer screen. She'd pulled up a photo of a brunette with long hair and bangs. The woman in the picture was young, curvy, and attractive by early 1980's standards.

"When I told Britt that we'd met with Senator Holt, she asked if he was the one who'd been involved in a scandal with one of his staffers. I had no idea what she was talking about, so I looked it up. It turns out that Britt was right. This is the staffer." Willow considered the photo. "In 1982 she told a reporter that she'd had a . . . relationship with Senator Holt off and on for a year. The senator hotly denied it. Her history with men was a little on the shady side. So when Senator Holt said she was trying to discredit him for political reasons, people believed him and the whole thing went away."

Corbin frowned.

Willow turned back to the computer and started typing.

Corbin had gotten along well with the senator during their visit. He'd pegged Foster Holt as a man who'd become a public servant for the right reasons. That said, Corbin wasn't in the habit of discounting women who came forward to blow the whistle on famous men. All the biographies he'd read prevented him from allowing himself that knee-jerk reaction. For decades, it had been far too easy for men to say either, "It wasn't rape, it was consensual," or, "She's lying." Very often, the public would then make the woman the villain.

Willow moved away from the computer again. This time, the screen revealed a picture of a brunette with feathered hair. Attractive. Probably in her mid-twenties.

"I did some digging and discovered that three years after the staffer claimed a relationship with Senator Holt, this woman claimed a relationship with him. The senator and his wife had a full-time nanny, but they'd bring this woman in occasionally to help with their younger kids. She was their relief nanny."

"Let me guess," Corbin said. "Senator Holt hotly denied that they'd had a relationship."

"Hotly."

"And the whole thing went away."

"Exactly."

Charlotte was blinking and attempting to look as though she was used to discussing potential affairs involving married men.

Shortly after he'd signed on to help Charlotte search for Josephine, Corbin had talked with Mark and Jill about how they wanted him and Willow to handle the information in the Josephine box and any other information they might uncover. Charlotte was the one driving this whole thing. She was the one who desperately wanted to solve this mystery. Because she wanted it, Corbin wanted it. He just didn't like that this mystery meant exposing Charlotte to the heavy subjects of missing women and Jane Does and infidelity.

Mark and Jill had decided they were fine with Corbin and Willow telling Charlotte the truth, so long as they didn't go into graphic detail and didn't let her look at images that might give her nightmares. Corbin had also agreed to keep Mark and Jill updated on the things he and Willow discussed with Charlotte so they could follow up with conversations at home.

Still. There were times when he wished Charlotte had stuck to science homework, clarinet practice, and barking orders at him during his therapy appointments.

Willow maneuvered the photos of the two women so they lined up side by side. "Does anything jump out at you?"

A sense of unease sifted through Corbin. "Both women look like Josephine."

"Oh my gosh," Charlotte breathed. "They do. Oh my gosh."

"It seems that the senator may have a type," Corbin said.

Willow met his eyes. "I was thinking the same thing."

"So now we have another theory to consider." Corbin counted them off on his fingers. "One: Josephine and Stan ran away together. Two: Josephine and Stan died because of an accident or murder-suicide. Three: Josephine and Stan were murdered by a third party. Four: Josephine and Stan were involved in something dangerous and went missing because of it. Five: Josephine and Senator Holt were having an affair."

"That last theory doesn't explain why Stan disappeared on the same day as Josephine," Charlotte said.

"Not a bad observation," Corbin said.

"Thank you."

"For a puppy," he added.

Charlotte did one of her famous eye rolls. "What should we do next?" she asked Willow.

"Yes, boss lady." Corbin grinned. "Enlighten us."

"You're a handful, Corbin. You know that?"

"So I've been told."

"I'm wondering," Willow said, "if the businessman who charged Stan Markum with extortion is still alive. If so, we could contact him."

"He's dead," Corbin said. "He died fifteen years ago."

"Bummer." Charlotte pointed her pen at the computer. "What about these ladies? Are they dead?"

"No," Willow answered. "The first woman lives overseas now. But the second one, the nanny, still lives in Washington."

"What's her name?" Charlotte asked.

"Vickie Goff."

"Should we take Vickie out for coffee?" Corbin asked Willow.

"I'm thinking *I* should take Vickie out for coffee," Willow answered.

"What about me?" Charlotte asked.

"I really think I need to talk to Vickie alone," Willow said. "If she agrees to see me at all, it'll be because I'm coming alone and because I'm a fellow woman. Our conversation is going to be uncomfortable, no matter what. But less so if I go by myself."

Everyone other than Willow received a T-bone steak.

When Corbin handed Willow her plate, several of the guests remarked on her gorgeously seared filet mignon. Willow tried to laugh it off while battling an inner attack of sheepishness.

This filet marked her as the teacher's pet of the evening. She'd never wanted to be the teacher's pet, not in any class she'd ever been a part of. During her school years, she'd been a well-behaved A/B student. A good influence on classmates. However, she'd dreaded the attention and the dislike that came from the role of teacher's pet, so she'd mostly attempted to fly under the radar.

Tonight, maybe foolishly, she'd traded the chance to fly under the radar for six ounces of filet mignon.

Carrying her plate down the length of the island in Corbin's kitchen, she helped herself to the beautiful food. A bowl of green salad dotted with red tomatoes, cucumber, and feta. An urn of mashed potatoes. A platter of grilled asparagus, onion, carrots, and Brussels sprouts. There was even a pot of baked macaroni and cheese for the kids.

Food of this caliber did her homemaker's heart good. She tried to catch the eye of the caterer Corbin had hired, a plump woman with a severe ponytail. But the caterer — and the rest of the guests, for that matter — were preoccupied with Corbin. It seemed that Charlotte was the only person present carrying the flag of Team Willow.

She settled at the dining table. Unlike some of the other rooms in Corbin's barnhouse, the dining room was completely finished. It sat adjacent to the kitchen and, like the kitchen, boasted one wall mostly composed of windows. Outside, yard lights illuminated the trees. Inside, a modern trestle table large enough to seat twelve dominated the space. A card table covered with a white tablecloth had been set up in the room's corner for the kids. When Jill instructed Charlotte to join her brothers there, the preteen girl responded as though she'd been riddled with buckshot.

Corbin took his place at the head of the table and saved the seat beside him for his dad. As they ate, Corbin kept the conversation going by asking questions, joking, telling stories, and rising to refill glasses. He made dealing with a group of people, many of whom he didn't know well, look incredibly easy.

I'm not going to carry the flag of Team Corbin, Willow repeated over and over to herself while enjoying her amazing steak.

Unfortunately for her, though, three different factors were working together to erode her resistance to Corbin on this particular night.

One, his house. Willow couldn't fathom how he'd stumbled upon a house *so* perfect for her. With her help, it could become an absolute gem.

Two, Corbin's treatment of his dad. She'd watched Corbin bring his dad out of his shell by easing the older man into discussions with various guests. He'd carried his dad's drink and pulled out his dad's chair. Corbin had quietly corrected his dad when his dad had gotten Zander's name wrong. He'd slipped a few different medications onto his dad's napkin. Looking out for his dad almost seemed to be something Corbin did unconsciously, like it was second nature.

Which made her wonder . . . Just how long

had Corbin been looking out for Joe? For the last few years since Joe had come to live with him? Since Corbin started playing for the NFL? Since Corbin's teenage years? Since Corbin's childhood?

Three, Charlotte's family was eroding Willow's resistance. She'd spent a good part of her evening observing Jill and Mark with their kids. Mark had ginger coloring, stood a good five inches shorter than his cousin Corbin, and looked like a dad and an architect — and not at all like an NFL quarterback.

In addition to Charlotte, Mark and Jill had two sons. Liam, who was ten, and Brady, seven. The Dixons weren't a perfect family. For one thing, the boys appeared to have enough energy to power Seattle's electrical grid. Earlier, Brady had climbed onto an ottoman in Corbin's living room, taken a running jump off of it, landed in a karate roll, and come up with one sneaker against the wall, which had left a scuff mark. Jill had rushed to correct the boy, while Mark had obliviously continued his conversation with John.

Liam had been coughing and sniffing all evening.

And Charlotte had authority issues.

So, no, they weren't perfect. Their family

was real and authentic and messy and close-knit. The Dixons were everything Willow had ever wanted for herself and never been able to achieve. She wanted a son who did karate rolls and a son who had a cough and a daughter with authority issues and an oblivious husband of her own.

She always, always had.

Yet she was now thirty-one years old. She'd grown leery of men. She'd started to doubt whether she'd been dreaming the right dream in the first place. She knew very well that her deep longing for a family of her own had the potential to become a weakness. She might be tempted to settle for the wrong guy again, like she had with Corbin. Or veer away from God's plan for her if it turned out that His plan didn't include a husband or a family. . . . But if His plan didn't include a husband or a family, then why had He placed this particular desire in her heart in the first place?

Maybe He hadn't. Maybe it was her biological mom's departure from her life that had created this desire.

Willow took a bite of salad and looked up to see Zander watching Britt and Tristan while listening to something Nora was saying. Horizontal creases marred his forehead.

Zander had never avoided any of Britt's

boyfriends. If he'd stayed away from Britt during each of her relationships, he hardly ever would've seen her. So he'd found a way to coexist with Britt's boyfriends, which said a lot about Zander. It must have been torturous for him at times to befriend the guys who had caught the interest of the woman he loved. But he'd done it. Over and over.

Willow had been hoping that Britt might come to her senses about Zander before his departure for London. But with time running out, that possibility looked unlikely.

The guests finished dinner and reassembled in the great room to either watch, talk over, or ignore the Monday night game, depending on their interest in football.

When Corbin asked Willow if she'd lend him a hand with dessert, she followed him to the kitchen. He lifted a dish of cut strawberries out of the refrigerator and set it next to a cake frosted with swirls of white frosting.

"That looks incredible." She rested a hand on her already-full stomach and mentally tried to gauge how much room she had left for cake. "How are you planning to serve it? Did you want everyone to come in here to fill their plates? Or we can take it into the great room —"

"I didn't react well four years ago, when

279

you told me you were afraid you were pregnant." Corbin faced her, hip against the island, arms crossed.

Heat rushed to her cheeks. *What?*

Silence exploded around them.

She'd been thinking about cake. . . . But now the words he'd just spoken had snatched the thought away. She fought to keep her balance, because the ground beneath her feet suddenly seemed as unstable as the deck of a ship in a storm. "Was dessert just a ruse to get me in here?"

"Yes."

"Corbin," she chided.

"I know you don't want to talk about why we broke up."

"You're right. I don't."

"But I do," he said.

Avoid! "You know what? I'll just take this into the dining room —" She reached for the cake.

He placed a hand on the cake stand to anchor it in place.

Uncertainty stilled her. Great Scott, she did *not* want to talk about the conversation they'd had when she'd been in that hotel room in Germany or any of the rest of it. Should she turn and walk from the room?

"I get that you hate this subject," he said, his voice reasonable. "I get that." Gone was the easygoing irreverence that so often characterized him. He gazed at her with utter seriousness. No smokescreen. No shield. "It's important to me, though . . . really important to me that we talk about it. Every time I see you, what happened between us is the elephant in the room. I'm sick of it."

What was wrong with elephants? She had no problem with their elephant. In fact, she'd prefer to keep it between them as a buffer.

"I'm asking for five minutes of your time," he said. "Will you please talk to me about it for five minutes?"

Her conscience pricked, reminding her of the passage in the Bible that instructed her to leave her gift on the altar if she remembered that another had an issue with her. To reconcile. And then to return and offer the gift. It was easy to agree with that instruction during a Sunday school lesson. Much harder to put it into practice.

Her throat went tight. "Okay."

His big shoulders relaxed slightly. "Thank you." He pressed his fingers into the front pockets of his jeans. The austerity of his simple charcoal sweater suited the clean angles of his face and the auburn brown of his short hair. "Like I was saying, I didn't react well when you called to tell me you were afraid you were pregnant."

"That, I agree with," she said stiffly. "You *didn't* react well. You kept telling me I wasn't pregnant."

He waited for her to say more.

"I didn't confide in you that day because I wanted to argue with you about whether or not I was pregnant," she said. "I confided in you because I wanted you to comfort me."

"I hear you. I think . . ." His exhale held remorse. "I think I was trying to comfort us both the way that made sense to me in that moment, by telling you that you weren't pregnant."

"Were you trying to comfort me when you said you weren't ready? Because the last thing a woman who might be pregnant wants to hear from her boyfriend is that he's not ready."

"I don't have an excuse for anything I said during that conversation, Willow. Everything I said was just plain stupid." His brows formed a straight line. "When you called, I was in the back of a limo on the way to a TV interview."

"Yes, but right when you picked up, I told you we could talk another time."

"I know. I should have taken you up on it. When you mentioned pregnancy, it came

282

out of left field and it sort of knocked the wind out of me. I wish I'd taken time to think before I responded. I wish I'd asked you how you felt about it."

Up until that phone conversation, Willow had believed him to be someone she could trust. Despite his track record with women and the fact that her agent and one of her fellow model friends both had reservations about him, she'd been secure in his affection. His reaction over the phone that night had fractured a relationship that she'd perceived to be a solid rock.

"I'm guessing the pregnancy scare knocked the wind out of you, too," he said.

"You have no idea how much. Before you came along, I was certain that I hadn't inherited any of my mother's wildness. I was self-righteous about it, even. Then we started dating, and I realized that I'd been wrong before. I was susceptible to all of her weaknesses. When my period was late, it was like history was repeating itself."

He waited.

"My parents conceived me outside of marriage. And now I, of all people, had made the same mistake even though I'd spent my whole life wishing I wasn't illegitimate. I couldn't believe I'd been that foolish."

He studied her. "These would have been good things for me to know back then."

"You didn't ask."

"No. And then I gave the interview. Which didn't help matters."

"My memory is fuzzy. Is that when you denied being in a dating relationship?" she asked.

"Something like that."

"And then said you'd consider settling down some day. When the right woman came along?"

"Your memory doesn't seem all that fuzzy to me," he said wryly.

"No," she answered, the one word as sharp as an icicle.

The second blow to their romance, the interview, had aired the day after their doomed phone call. By then, she'd traveled to Frankfurt International Airport and was sitting inside a restaurant within the terminal, awaiting her flight home. When she'd first started streaming the interview on her computer, she'd felt shaky and angry. However, as she'd watched the interview unfold and listened to Corbin's voice through her earbuds, she'd begun to thaw. He answered the reporter's questions with intelligence and humor, and he looked fabulous while doing so. The quarterback onscreen was her

boyfriend and very likely her future husband, too. She started to tell herself that his
bad response over the phone didn't have to
spell disaster.

Then the interviewer had asked him about
her point blank and, in response, he'd dis-
carded their romance unequivocally.

The difference between her own private
hopes for their relationship and his public
answers could not have been more pro-
nounced. Sitting in that terminal — struggling to keep her body language neutral so
the travelers surrounding her wouldn't
know her world was coming apart — she'd
realized just how gullible she'd been.

A dozen more fractures had run through
the rock of their relationship —

"Willow?"

She let the memory of the Frankfurt airport and the computer screen and the disillusionment fall. Corbin, four years older
now than when she'd loved him but with
every bit of his magnetism intact, stood motionless before her. Old hurts and longings
simmered between them.

"In that interview, it appeared that you
didn't care about me at all," she said.

"I cared."

Over the thrum of her pulse in her ears,
she registered the whir of the refrigerator

and a cheer from those watching football in the den.

"I've always tried to keep my private life private," he said. "Especially when I was dating you. Especially with that reporter on that day."

She'd known he was private. He almost never said anything to reporters about his dad or his upbringing, for example. But that didn't mean, when given an opportunity to validate their relationship, that he had the right to throw her under the bus. "The reporter already knew about us. He asked you about me specifically. It wasn't as if keeping me secret was an option."

"I wanted you to be mine, Willow. Just mine." Intensity rolled from him. "Reporters and cameras watched everything I did on the field, and I was fine with that. But I didn't want to share you."

"That's how you spun it when we talked after the interview. But I've never believed that's the whole reason behind your interview answers. I think you denied dating me because when I told you I might be pregnant, your instinctive reaction was to distance yourself from me."

He scowled.

"Be honest," Willow said. "You don't have anything to lose or gain by telling me the

286

truth at this point. How much of what you said in the interview was motivated by a desire to distance yourself from me?"

"A little, maybe. Our phone call sent me reeling."

"Why? Why do you think it sent you reeling to the degree that it did?" She found she desperately wanted to know. Suddenly she understood why he'd insisted on dragging their past back out. He'd insisted because now that they were in each other's lives again, so was all this mess. What had happened between them wasn't gone. Here it still was — raw and tender and without closure.

"I guess it sent me reeling because my own parents weren't exactly . . . equipped to raise me," he said. "I didn't want to put a child through that."

She bristled. "I have a lot of flaws, but I'm not ill-equipped."

"No, you're not. And neither am I. I would have loved and supported you and the baby."

Yes, and the three of them would have lived in a house made out of sugar cubes next to a river of maple syrup. "But what you *actually* did was get drunk at a nightclub."

Two days after the TV interview, Willow

287

had woken in her own bed in LA heartsick and still racked with worry about the possibility of a pregnancy. By then, she'd been one week late, and she'd made up her mind to take a pregnancy test, no matter how much it scared her, and face the answer it gave.

Since before she'd left Germany, Corbin had been calling and texting her to ask for an update on the possible pregnancy and to apologize and to explain. She'd taken a few of his phone calls and replied to a few of his texts. The rest she'd left unanswered.

She'd been watching TV in her pajamas when the third blow to their relationship had been dealt. Her publicist had texted her a picture of Corbin exiting a Dallas nightclub.

The photographer had captured Corbin, who'd been wearing a shirt Willow had purchased for him, looking right at the camera with concern. A pretty, young, black-haired woman in a tiny dress had slung her arm around his neck. She was laughing up at him, a martini glass dangling from her manicured hand.

Willow's stomach had dropped when she'd seen that picture. Envy and betrayal had carved into her.

"A few of the guys from the team asked

me to go out with them that night," Corbin said.

"And you said yes because you were still reeling," Willow supplied. She remembered the version of events he'd given her over the phone the day the photograph had been published. "You made a mistake and had a few too many."

"Yes."

"You don't even remember the name of the woman who was hanging on you in the picture."

"No. I don't."

"And you didn't do anything with her."

"No."

"And yet you were leaving the club with her."

"I wasn't leaving the club with her. It was hot and loud inside. I was stepping outside to get some fresh air when she tossed her arm around me."

"See, I still have no idea if that's truly what happened or not."

"That's exactly what happened."

"Even if that's the case, your choices are still suspect. You decided to go out clubbing, to get drunk, and to let a woman hang on you."

"You're right."

"At that stage, it didn't even matter what

289

your intentions were toward that woman because I couldn't believe anything you said." The photograph sent so many more fractures through their relationship that there'd been nothing left to build on.

As soon as she saw that photo, she called him and told him they were through. She'd been very quick to fall in love with him, and he'd been very quick to let her down the minute they'd faced their first trial.

When a pregnancy test informed her that she wasn't pregnant, the rock of her romance with Corbin had already become dust. It was too late to salvage it. Corbin, though, had continued to try. He'd believed they could fix it. He'd wanted to do whatever it took to fix it. She'd remained furiously immovable in her resolve, even going so far as to accept Derek Oliver's invitation to his movie premiere.

Derek was gorgeous, well-behaved, and best of all, had no power whatsoever over her emotions. After the storm Corbin had put her through, it had been blissful to feel nothing more than indifference for Derek.

She'd let Corbin find out about Derek the way she'd found out about his nightclub photo — through others. When Corbin had reached her by phone the morning after the premiere, she'd told him that she regretted their entire relationship. Meeting him, sleeping with him, and every moment in between. She'd known her words had hurt him, and she'd been glad they had.

Then she'd lain on her bed and sobbed.

It had been their final conversation.

"Why couldn't you forgive me?" Corbin asked.

Because your actions were unforgivable. She held that response back because . . . was that really true? Had his actions been unforgivable?

"Be honest," he said, serving her own words from earlier back to her. "You don't have anything to lose or gain by telling me the truth at this point."

She reached back through time to recall where her head had been the day she'd broken up with him. "I knew it was wrong to have sex with you." She didn't like to think — and definitely didn't like to speak aloud — about the physical side of their romance. But he'd asked her to be honest. And this was her truth. "For months, I'd known we couldn't continue like we had been without God stepping in to separate us. When things started to unravel between us, it seemed to me that judgment had finally come. And it was nothing less than I — than we deserved."

He stared at her gravely.

"I realize that's probably hard for you to understand," she said, "because you're not a Christian."

"I am, actually."

"Hmm?"

"I'm a Christian."

"Excuse me."

"Since February."

She blinked at him.

"It's true. If they issued ID cards to Christians, I'd show you my ID card."

Corbin had aced secular living. He'd been born with more than his share of athletic ability, determination, charm, and good looks. He'd enjoyed every worldly benefit that had come to him because of those qualities. He . . . *Corbin* . . . was a Christian?

"I'm new at it," he said. "I'm a long way from figuring it out."

Surprise whitewashed her vocabulary.

"I screwed up four years ago," he said, looking into her eyes. "I want you to know that I regret it and that I'm sorry."

"Sorry that I've had to suffer because I've had a hard time getting over you?" she asked, reminding him of what he'd said to her in the inn's kitchen the day she'd met Charlotte.

He gave her a small, wickedly powerful smile.

Heat circled down her spine in response, leaving sparks.

"No," he said. "This time I'm just sorry. I'm trying to apologize. You probably can't tell because I don't do it often so I'm not very good at it."

"I'm surprised to hear you admit to being not very good at anything."

"That's because I'm good at almost everything." And just like that, the Corbin she was accustomed to returned.

Footsteps approached. Seconds later, Joe entered the kitchen. His progress faltered when he realized that he'd walked in on the two of them alone together.

"Dad, can you grab that tray there?" Corbin nodded to a tray the caterer had no doubt left behind. It was stocked with dessert plates, napkins, forks. "We're about to serve dessert." Corbin lifted the cake. Near the door, he stopped and looked back at her. "Coming?"

"Yes. I'll grab a knife and a spoon for the strawberries."

"Knives are in the block, spoons in the drawer next to the sink." As soon as Corbin left, the atmosphere in the room turned chilly. Joe eyed her with suspicion while she located the utensils.

"Are you hoping to start something back up with Corbin?" he asked.

She froze. No parent had ever inquired about her intentions toward their son. Not even when she'd been a teenager.

Beneath his ruddy complexion, Joe's pallor was off. Too pale. He'd set his jaw tightly, as if he were in pain.

She'd watched Joe with her sisters tonight. He seemed to like and accept them both, but he hadn't taken a liking to her at all. Even so, she couldn't help feeling a wave of tenderness toward him. He wore a long-sleeved polo shirt that boasted the logo of the Dallas Mustangs. Grandpa jeans. Sturdy tennis shoes with snowy white laces. His Timex watch.

"I don't think a relationship between you two is a good idea," Joe said. "Do you?"

She cleared her throat. "No."

"You and Corbin had your chance. Several years ago."

"That's true. We did." She set the knife on the tray Corbin had asked his dad to carry. "I haven't won you over yet, have I?"

"I'm sure you're a fine person."

"I actually am."

"If that's true, you'll leave Corbin be. He doesn't need any headaches over women right now."

She stuck the serving spoon into the strawberries. "You may need to have this conversation with your son."

"I already have," he said.

Facebook message from Willow to Vickie Goff:

Willow

Thanks for accepting my friend request! I'm reaching out to you because I've befriended a twelve-year-old girl named Charlotte Dixon. Charlotte has enlisted me to help her find out what happened to her great-aunt Josephine Blake, who went missing in 1977.

Five months before her disappearance, Josephine volunteered on Senator Foster Holt's first election campaign. It's possible that your experience with Senator Holt may give us a more complete picture of Josephine.

I'd love to take you out for coffee one day soon if you're willing to talk with me. I realize this is a lot to ask. I'm grateful for your consideration. Sincerely, Willow

■ ■ ■ ■

Facebook message from Vickie to Willow:

Vickie

It's a pleasure to "meet" you through Facebook, Willow. My mom is a huge fan of yours. Because you were born and raised in nearby Merryweather, she's followed you and your career closely.

I very rarely talk to anyone about Foster Holt. But for you and for Charlotte's sake, I'll make an exception. I can meet you at 11:15 on Wednesday morning at Common Grounds on the campus of University of Washington–Bothell.

CHAPTER FOURTEEN

Facebook was a faux detective's friend.

Willow had easily located Vickie Goff's Facebook profile because Vickie had remained in northwest Washington and because she'd never married and thus never changed her last name. From Facebook, Willow had learned that Vickie had two twenty-something daughters from a past relationship, a current boyfriend named Hank, and a fondness for dachshunds. Also thanks to Facebook, Willow recognized the older woman the moment Vickie entered the Common Grounds coffee shop on Wednesday morning.

Willow stood and raised a hand to catch Vickie's eye. Vickie nodded and made her way through the collection of students and staff members.

At the age of fifty-eight, Vickie's once-dark hair was now a golden brown highlighted with honey-colored strands. Her short hairstyle flattered her attractive features. She'd knotted a scarf patterned with shades of maroon and turquoise over a maroon blouse and slim, tailored pants.

Willow introduced herself, and they shook hands.

Vickie gave off a strong first impression of professionalism. Willow had learned — *thank you again, Facebook* — that Vickie was a professor of Global Studies here at UW–Bothell.

"What can I get you to drink?" Willow asked.

Vickie waved a dismissive hand. "Nothing. I've had my quota of coffee for the day." They settled into armchairs situated in a secluded corner facing the interior of the shop.

"I'm sorry that the circumstances of our meeting revolve around Foster Holt," Willow said.

"It's all right."

"I read that you met the senator when you took a job working for his family."

"Yes." Vickie tucked a strand of hair behind one ear. "I was putting myself through grad school at the time working as a waitress and for a baby-sitting agency. For about a year and a half the agency booked me to work for the Holts whenever Foster and Marjorie wanted an extra hand with their kids, which was relatively often. Between Marjorie's social schedule and Foster's work schedule, their calendar was elaborate."

"I can imagine."

"I was in my midtwenties and Foster was in his late forties when I worked for them. He was handsome. Confident. Powerful." Vickie wrinkled her brow. "There was always a great deal of physical attraction between Foster and me. Nothing came of it until I asked if I could interview him for a school assignment. He came by my apartment. We were alone together. And . . . that was the beginning of our affair."

Senator Holt had a reputation for being smart, mannerly, magnetic, and effective. He'd given hundreds of thousands of dollars to charities. Many credited the economic growth that Seattle and its surrounding cities had enjoyed to him. He, his wife, and his kids were widely regarded as upstanding.

If Vickie was to be believed, Foster wasn't as upstanding as he appeared. Of course, Willow knew she wasn't as upstanding as she appeared, either.

People often weren't what they seemed.

"Did you know that one of the senator's female staffers had come forward a few years prior to say that she'd had an affair with him?"

"Yes. When I asked him about her, he said that she made the whole thing up."

Willow took a sip of her cappuccino, then wrapped her hands around the cup. "How long did your affair with Senator Holt last?"

"Four months. When my roommate was gone, Foster and I met at my apartment. If my roommate was at home, we met at hotels. Either Don or I would check in under our names. We never used Foster's name."

"Don?"

"Foster's employee. He was like a henchman, bodyguard, and confidant all rolled into one. Basically, Don did whatever Foster needed doing because Don didn't mind getting his hands dirty."

"And Don knew about your affair?"

"Don knew everything. In fact, he was the one who was there at the end."

"The end?"

"I fancied myself in love with Foster." She sighed. "I was smart enough not to expect him to leave his wife and kids for me. But I stupidly imagined we were starting out on a long-term affair. I was stunned and devastated when he ended things with me."

"Did he give a reason?"

"He fed me some lines about wanting to make a fresh start with his wife and how the guilt had been eating him up inside. It was all lies. He'd simply grown tired of me." She squinted, as if focusing on something in the far distance. "When Foster wouldn't return my calls or my letters, I got angry. I called a reporter at the paper and told him about the affair. I imagined that Foster would be forced to resign or, at the very least, that he wouldn't be reelected."

Willow waited.

"None of that happened," Vickie said, meeting Willow's eyes. "Instead, I was the one who was very nearly derailed."

"In what way?"

"People immediately turned on me. I lost friends and received hate mail. My family was crushed." She frowned. "About a week after my accusations went public, Foster called me. He apologized and said that he'd been depressed since our breakup and that he was trying to figure out a way for the two of us to continue our relationship. He asked me to meet him at his vacation home in Laguna Beach, California, for a long weekend. I said that I would." Vickie bent to pull a bottled water from her bag, then took a few pensive sips.

Willow wished Corbin were here. He would have been a liability in this particular circumstance, yet it really was more satisfying to investigate Josephine's disappearance with him than without him. He saw things differently than she did, which was valuable. And he was arguably a better detective than she was, seeing as how he'd been the one to discover Stan Markum.

Lately, a renegade portion of her wanted to spend every free second thinking about Corbin. Wanted to see him. Wanted to ponder, for the thousandth time, the things he'd said to her in his kitchen on Monday night. *"I wanted you to be mine, Willow. Just mine. . . . I'm a Christian now. . . . I screwed up four years ago. . . . I'm sorry."*

Even here, on a college campus far from Merryweather, she could feel a physical pull toward him.

Insufferable!

She needed to be careful. She couldn't let the last of her anger toward him crumble in her hands like freeze-dried ice cream.

"It seems deluded to me now," Vickie continued, "but when Foster invited me to his beach house, I actually thought we were going to get back together. As if he ever could've gotten back together with a woman who'd claimed that she'd had an affair with him."

"You went to California?"

"Yes. A plane ticket showed up in my

mailbox just like Foster said it would. I flew down and waited several hours for him. But it wasn't Foster who arrived. It was Don. He told me that Foster had wanted to come and that he cared about me a great deal, but he'd decided at the last minute not to make the trip because he realized that our relationship had to end." She arched a brow. The coffee shop's espresso machine hissed.

"Don told me that Foster wanted me to use the beach house for the weekend," Vickie said, "to rest and relax and hopefully make my peace with the way things had turned out. Which seemed decent enough on the surface. But when I tried to leave the beach house to go for a walk alone, Don locked the door behind us and followed me. He didn't leave my side for the whole weekend."

Her fingertips tapped irritably against the chair's upholstery. "Don told me he was keeping an eye on me for my own protection, but it was for Foster's protection. Trapping me at that beach house was their way of isolating me, of making sure I didn't say anything to anyone else. They wanted to give me time to cool off and come around to their way of thinking."

Good gracious. "Did Don ever threaten you?"

"No, he was much too careful for that. He did talk at length about why remaining silent would be better for me and my career and my future. He didn't threaten me, though. And he never tried to buy my silence, either."

"Still, it sounds like you were a prisoner of sorts at the beach house."

"Exactly. And my jailer was terrifying. Don was tall and thin with cold, dark eyes. If I had to do it over again, I wouldn't have shut up and scuttled away. But back then? I considered myself sophisticated, but I was young and immature and thoroughly intimidated. Since that beach trip, every time a reporter has contacted me, I've refused to comment."

Willow regarded Vickie thoughtfully.

"You're wondering whether Josephine may have had an affair with Foster," Vickie said.

"Yes. She resembles you a little."

"That's not enough to connect her to Foster."

"I know. Unfortunately, we don't have any evidence, so we're having to speculate. If Josephine *did* have an affair with Foster, then I'm wondering whether he might have sent her off to his beach house like he did with you."

"It's a theory."

"Do you happen to know if he owned the beach house in 1977?"

"I'm afraid I don't."

"Do you think that harm would've come to you if you'd refused to stay silent about the affair?"

"I have no idea. His staffer is the only other woman who's admitted to the press that she had an affair with Foster. She never claimed that he threatened her in any way."

"It's possible that Josephine, and maybe other women, too, were silenced before they had a chance to speak out."

Vickie twisted her lips skeptically. "I don't think it's likely that Foster's left a string of dead and missing women behind him. That's the type of thing people tend to notice. And Foster's a very public man."

Willow stomped hard on her brake pedal the next morning as she was leaving Bradfordwood for the inn.

The entirety of Bradfordwood's massive front gate had been covered in zigzags of toilet paper.

Why would anyone . . .

Ah, of course. She knew why. And she knew who.

Another of her ground rules, broken.

Her jaw sagged as she considered Cor-

305

bin's handiwork. The gate was ten feet tall and composed of decorative wrought iron. He must've arrived here very early, because it had to have taken a long time to weave the strands of toilet paper through the bars in such a snug pattern. The pattern was so snug, she couldn't see through it to the road.

What was that red square? She narrowed her eyes. A piece of paper?

She hopped from her car, then plucked the red square, which was indeed a piece of paper, from where it had been tied to the toilet paper.

Willow,

I couldn't get to your house, so I toilet-papered your gate. You know why.

— Corbin

P.S. I'll come back later and clean it up.

A giggle bubbled from her. He was an inveterate rule breaker, which didn't suit her at all because she was a rule follower. But he did have nerve. A whole lot of nerve. She'd give him that.

After climbing back into her car, she sent him a text message. *I see you've vandalized my property. Am I going to have to file a re-*

straining order against you now?

Corbin replied: *Heck no. I only wanted to make you laugh.*

Willow was browning sausage at the inn Friday morning when she caught sight of Corbin walking toward the back door. Her heart executed the same type of expand-and-tingle thing it had done each time she'd caught sight of him from a distance back when they'd been together.

Shoot. The expand-and-tingle was an ominous sign.

She unlocked the back door, and he entered wearing a black tracksuit and white baseball cap, carrying a square box. He smelled like pine trees in winter and looked like temptation.

"No crazy stalker fans around?" he asked.

"You're the only one so far this morning."

He laughed. "Based on the cars in the lot, it seems to me like you still have plenty of guests, even after cancelling the reservations that were made following that college guy's tweet."

"Yes. Luckily, a lot of our guests made their travel plans far in advance. The inn won't be quite as full as usual between now and Thanksgiving, but my mom has assured me that she doesn't mind."

"Just like I knew she wouldn't." Looking self-satisfied, he pulled a stunning breakfast cake from the box. "The lady at The Griddle told me this is their most popular item. It's cranberry nut something or other. I was hoping your guests might like it."

"Thank you. I'm sure they will."

"You're actually going to accept something from me without a fight?" he asked teasingly.

"I almost never turn down breakfast pastries." Shiny glaze cascaded down the sides of the tall cake, which made the carrot muffins she'd purchased earlier look like poor relations in comparison.

She used a wooden spoon to break apart the sausage.

"What can I do to help?" Corbin asked.

She put him to work washing fruit. They'd fallen into a breakfast prep routine in the days leading up to her run-in with Todd, back when Corbin had spent much of his time at the inn. He hadn't returned for breakfast duty since, which made her wonder why he'd come today. She didn't think he'd come because he was worried about crazy stalker fans.

Buttery light from the window above the sink illuminated his forearms and the deft hands that had once been responsible for firing bullet-like passes. Those hands were currently washing blueberries and peaches and apples under a stream of glittering water.

He still had many of the same quirks he'd had before. He frequently couldn't find his keys. He had a sweet tooth for chocolate. He was wary of cats. He hated depressing movies, music, or TV, but liked depressing books. And he was doing chores for her that she suspected he hired other people to do for him at his own house. He used to wash her dishes for her when he visited her in LA.

"To what do I owe the pl—" She cut herself off.

"You were going to say pleasure of my company."

"Yes, but then I thought better of it. Let me amend my question. To what do I owe your company this morning?"

"I missed you."

"You just saw me yesterday afternoon at our Operation Find Josephine meeting," she said firmly.

"That was sixteen hours ago."

She scooped the sausage over the cubed bread that waited in the casserole dish. "The real reason you're here is . . . ?"

"It occurred to me after our conversation

on Monday that you never said whether or not you forgive me." He glanced across his shoulder at her.

"Mmm." She'd been thinking that she'd effectively sidestepped being trapped into a corner where she'd be forced to forgive. To be honest, she enjoyed her unforgiveness. She snuggled up with it the way she would a comforter whenever she was feeling down.

"So?" he asked. "Do you forgive me?"

She bit her lip, tilted her head, and whisked eggs with milk and seasonings as if whisking eggs was the most important thing in her universe. She poured the egg mixture over the bread and sausage, then sprinkled cut mushrooms and cheese on top while mentally replaying all the ways Corbin had hurt her four years before.

At length, when her silence had become her answer, and the fruit had all been washed, he shut off the faucet and faced her. "I listened to the audio version of the Bible this year."

"And?"

"And it's pretty clear that Jesus commands His people to forgive." He arched a brow at her challengingly.

Her biggest mistake, the man who'd caused her endless guilt and repentance, was lecturing her about the teachings of Jesus? "You've become a Bible expert, have you?" She deposited the egg casserole in the oven and set the timer.

"Nope. I didn't understand a lot of what I heard. But the whole forgiveness part? That I got."

He wasn't going to let her wiggle out of forgiving him, and really, she shouldn't be surprised. If Corbin Stewart wanted something, he went after it.

"Forgive me?" He tested a persuasive grin on her.

She shook her head.

"For. Give. Me." He stalked toward her, still grinning.

She squealed and dodged out of the way, putting the kitchen table between them.

"Forgive me," he growled as he feinted one way, then darted around the table.

She ran. The ties of her white apron flew out behind her as she dashed to the urn that held utensils. She grabbed the nearest one and found herself brandishing a spatula at him. "Come no closer!"

He approached relentlessly. "Or you'll flip me like a pancake?"

She laughed.

He took hold of the spatula and moved it slowly, very slowly, to the side. He was in her space now, and his face had turned just a little bit predatory. If he tried to steal a kiss from her, Willow was afraid that she might like it. A lot.

He came even closer.

"Fine!" she rushed to say. "I forgive you!"

His progress halted. He looked bemused. "You do?"

"Yes."

He set his hands on his lean hips. "Good."

She slotted the spatula back where it belonged and made her way to the industrial coffeemaker in an effort to put a few yards between them.

Corbin brought out a chopping board and began slicing the fruit he'd washed. "I've been thinking about the reason you gave for your inability to forgive me back in the day."

Fabulous. A conversation about their past sex life before 8:00 a.m. Was it too early to visit www.PotteryBarn.com?

"When we were together," he said, "I thought that the physical side of our relationship was . . . amazing. Can you explain why you felt that it was wrong?"

"If you listened to the Bible this year, you must have heard the verses about sexual purity, right?"

"Right."

"That's why I thought that it was wrong."

"But we both consented to it. We both enjoyed it. We didn't hurt anyone by it. So I'm still not clear on why it was harmful."

She took a deep breath, set the coffee-maker to brew, and angled toward him. "Our sex life harmed me because I felt conflicted and guilty the whole time we were together. I tried to explain that to you a few times, but trying to explain a faith position to someone who doesn't have faith is difficult. I had a hard time holding you to my standards, and I had a hard time maintaining my own standards when I was with you."

He watched her.

"The fact that we were intimate connected me to you more than two people who aren't married should be connected," she said. "Which made me feel insecure and uneasy, which I *hated* feeling, and which set me up to respond the way I did when things started to fall apart." It was painful to be this candid, yet the time had come to draw a line in the sand and explain why she was determined to stand on one side and why he had to remain on the other. "Can you understand that?"

"I'm trying. Even if I don't understand it fully, I can respect it." He lifted and re-settled his ball cap. "I'm realizing that I'm going to have to unlearn a lot of things I thought I knew."

"How was it that you became a Christian?" She'd been trying to imagine how the Corbin she'd known, who'd considered himself godly enough because he'd gone to church a handful of times as a kid, had been saved.

As they worked, he told her about the dark time after his shoulder injury, the hopelessness, and the chaplain who'd visited him at his lowest point.

"And how's it been going since then?" she asked.

"I'm not sure that I feel as different as I should. Sometimes the whole thing just seems . . . farfetched. It's hard for me to believe that I can trust this higher power that I can't see."

"God *is* farfetched," she said. "He's extreme."

"And abstract."

"Give Him time," Willow said. "The more you get to know Him, the more trustworthy He'll prove himself to be."

Corbin dried his hands on a dish towel and faced her. "If He's the one who caused you to break up with me, then I'm not sure I want to trust Him."

"You definitely *do* want to trust Him."

"I don't know, Willow. Life without you hasn't been easy for me."

314

As she filled a pitcher with juice, she could feel the heat of his full attention on her.

"I want one more chance with you," he said.

He'd spoken plainly. Without apology.

Her heart stuttered. Sweet, heavy longing tugged at her. Their awareness of each other had become a big, muscular presence in recent days. She'd sensed his interest in her sharpening and his initial bitterness toward her disintegrating. He'd invited a houseful of people to his home for dinner just so she'd agree to come. *But this?*

She steeled herself to look at him. "Our relationship has been over for a long time, Corbin."

"It doesn't have to be over."

"It does."

"Okay, then how about just one date?" He gestured to the cake. "How can you say no to the guy who brought you a cranberry nut cake?"

"Easily. That's how. If it had been a Ben and Jerry's ice cream cake, then the outcome might have been different."

"Are you free tomorrow night?"

"I'm booked."

"Sunday night?"

"Booked."

"Have you noticed lately how wealthy I

am, Willow?"

"No, but I've noticed how arrogant you are."

"I'm famous."

"You *were* famous."

"I'm handsome."

"Meh."

"I'm athletic."

"You have a separated shoulder."

"Which I got saving you. I'm destined for the Hall of Fame."

"That remains to be determined."

He looked at her like she was a jigsaw puzzle with missing pieces. "I'm devoted to you," he said.

And just like that, tenderness cracked open within her like a truffle spilling molten caramel.

"I'm getting closer, aren't I?" he asked.

She shrugged. "Not *that* close. The answer's still no."

Halloween arrived the following day in satisfyingly spooky fashion. Misty, overcast weather clung close to the earth, broken only by the ethereal orange and russet of the autumn leaves still stubbornly attached to their branches.

Every year Nora held a Halloween Spooktacular at Merryweather Historical Village.

Local moms and dads brought their kids to the village to trick-or-treat at each of the structures situated around the village's central green. It took all of the village's employees plus several volunteers to make the event happen.

Willow arrived for volunteer duty wearing a pale blue Cinderella-esque gown, long white gloves, and upswept hair.

Britt showed up as Amelia Earhart, complete with old-fashioned aviator goggles.

For approximately the tenth year in a row, Nora dressed as Hermione from *Harry Potter*.

John, who was a former Navy SEAL, covered his face with camouflage paint. He donned fatigues, lace-up military boots, and a field cap. His uniform ended up thrilling the heart of every preteen boy and adult woman present.

Zander wore a T-shirt, a hoodie with the hood up, and a plastic sword stuck into his leather belt. Since none of the kids could guess his identity, he eventually taped a sheet of paper to his chest that read *Percy Jackson*.

For three enjoyable hours, Willow handed out mini Butterfingers on the porch of the village building known as Doc Hubert's office. The whole time she tried *not* to picture how cute the housewares she'd bought during last night's online shopping binge would look in Corbin's barnhouse.

Corbin saw Willow before she saw him.

Warm pleasure washed over every inch of him as he watched her lock the inn's back door and make her way along the path to the parking lot. Spots of afternoon sun fought through the cover of trees to dot her hair and the shoulders of her red coat.

Little Red Riding Hood looped one hand around her purse strap. Afraid of pickpockets in the area? Her head was bent down slightly, as if concentrating on the path before her. Hoping to avoid stepping on cracks in the dirt?

When she finally caught sight of him, her steps slowed almost to a halt before she continued forward. He stayed right where he was, leaning against his Navigator, one ankle crossed over the other.

"You didn't look up until you were halfway here," he said when she'd drawn near enough to hear. "You should be more aware of your surroundings when you leave the inn."

"In case a man is lying in wait for me?" She gave him a meaningful look.

"In case Todd Hill is lying in wait for you.

You haven't seen him, even from a distance, since the day he attacked you, have you?"

"No, not even from a distance." The breeze gently mussed her hair.

"Would you tell me if you had seen him?"

She lifted her slim shoulders. "I'm pretty sure that you or the charges I filed or the restraining order did the trick and that Todd Hill is long gone."

He wished he could be as sure. Corbin had never been able to move past Willow; it was hard for him to accept that Todd would be able to.

"Did you come to talk to me about Todd?" she asked.

"No, I came to blackmail you."

She smiled, and the power of her smile connected with his torso. Good grief, she was beautiful.

"Blackmail?" she asked.

"Yes."

"How is it that I'm not even shocked?"

He pulled a check from his pocket and handed it to her. "If you will go on one date with me, I will send this check to Benevolence Worldwide."

She scrutinized the check for a long moment.

He scratched the side of his jaw. He was pretty sure he had her this time. Willow was devoted to Benevolence.

She handed back the check. "I strongly encourage you to send that check to Benevolence —"

"Will do. When can we go out?"

"— but a date with me cannot be bought."

He stared at her. "I'm asking for one date. In exchange for two hundred thousand dollars."

"A date with me cannot be bought," she repeated.

He held the check with both hands, right in the center, signaling to her that he planned to tear it in two. "You sure about that?"

"Corbin." She seemed caught between humor and indignation. "Benevolence will do wonderful things with that money."

"They definitely will. But only if you go on a date with me."

"You're a mercenary."

"For you," he spoke without a trace of guilt, "I absolutely am."

"My answer's no." She walked past him to her Range Rover.

Shoot. Willow's appearance could fool you into thinking she was made of sugar and spice and everything nice. The truth? She was as stubborn as they came and he couldn't help but admire her for it. He'd always appreciated a worthy opponent, and that's exactly what she was.

His determination heightened and heightened as he watched her drive out of sight.

He'd lost a lot lately. He refused to lose this particular fight. He *would* find a way back into Willow's heart. She had the power to erase both the grief and the pain he'd gone through this past year. If he had her, he'd have everything he needed. And so would she, because he'd dedicate himself to making her happy. This time around, he wouldn't let his guard down. He'd never be less than one hundred percent careful with her.

Willow didn't know it yet, but he was going to win her back.

"Corbin offered to donate two hundred thousand dollars to Benevolence Worldwide if you went on a date with him, and you turned him down?" Britt asked.

"You can bet he has accountants working for him and that he donates large sums of money every year for tax purposes. It's not like he was going to give anything to Benevolence that he wasn't already planning to spend on charitable causes." Willow could hear a note of uncertainty in her own voice.

The Bradford sisters had convened for a post-lunch dessert break at Britt's chocolate shop, Sweet Art. They were sitting on barstools that cozied up to a plank of wood mounted against the shop's interior walls. A view of Merryweather Historical Village filled the window before them.

"It may not mean much to Corbin to give to Benevolence," Nora said. "But think about what it would mean to Benevolence to receive that sum of money."

"Exactly!" Britt said. "Think of the orphans."

"I have been," Willow admitted. "Ever since I turned him down yesterday, I've been second-guessing myself."

"Eat chocolate." Britt scooted the plate, which once held nine chocolates and now held three, in Willow's direction. "Chocolate helps clarify thinking."

Willow selected a round milk chocolate capped with chocolate sprinkles.

"Why are you so reluctant to go on a date with Corbin?" Nora asked.

Willow turned her chocolate by degrees until it completed a full revolution. "In large part because I can't really . . . trust myself with him."

Nora and Britt considered her.

"Why?" Britt asked.

"I have a feeling that we don't know the whole story," Nora said slowly. "About your relationship with Corbin and your breakup."

Britt flattened her palms on the bar top and leaned forward. "Tell us the whole story! How are we supposed to discuss Corbin over chocolate if we don't know the whole story?"

Willow's pulse began to thud. "I'm ashamed of the full story."

Britt's eyes rounded. "Well, now you're definitely going to have to spill the beans."

"It's just us," Nora said gently. "You don't have anything to be ashamed of with us."

"I do, actually." Willow fussed with one of her bracelets, then the next, then the next. Why was it so hard to speak the things you regretted out loud? Pride, she supposed.

She liked that her younger sisters viewed her as infallible. At least she'd liked it back when she'd viewed herself as infallible, too. For the last four years, the gap between how her family saw her and reality had weighed on her.

Fake perfection was tiring. The mistakes you didn't confess accumulated more and more mass over time. No one ministered to you because you were busy broadcasting the fact that you didn't need ministering to.

She was done with fake perfection. She

was as fallible and sinful as anyone. "You both know about the TV interview Corbin gave and the photograph that was published of him with another woman at a nightclub."

They nodded. "That's why you broke up with him, right?" Britt asked.

"That's partly why I broke up with him." Willow twined her hands tightly in her lap to steady herself and told them the rest. The pregnancy scare. Her phone call to Corbin. Her remorse.

She braced herself to see disappointment on her sisters' faces. Or disillusionment. But she didn't. She only saw empathy. "Do you think less of me?" she asked when she'd related everything.

"No," Nora said at once, an ocean of kindness in the word. "We love you, and nothing could ever change that."

"I've messed up a bunch," Britt said. "You've shown me grace about a million times, Willow."

Both sisters stood to give her a hug. Willow kept tears at bay as she embraced each of them in turn. Nora and Britt felt so familiar; their arms, their hair. They still carried the sweet smell that had always belonged to each of them. Her sisters.

When they were all back on their bar stools, Willow realized that she felt emptied out inside, in a good way. As though she could breathe more deeply.

She ate her chocolate in two bites. Its rich, velvety texture flowed into her mouth like a cloud into the horizon. "So," she dabbed her lips with her napkin, "my problem with Corbin is twofold. I can't trust him. And I can't trust myself around him, either."

"The way I see it," Britt said, "he's asking for a date. A date doesn't have to include a kiss or hand-holding or any of it. Essentially, if you agree to a date, you'll just be agreeing to spend time with him. A date doesn't have to be catastrophic, does it?"

"It doesn't have to be," Willow answered. "I guess I'm just concerned about the path that one date could set us on."

"I think it's wise to be careful," Nora said.

Willow thought about the orphans.

"Have you two talked about what happened four years ago?" Nora asked.

"Yes."

"Has Corbin apologized?"

Willow nodded.

"And?" Britt prompted.

Willow took a sip of ice water. "And I told him I forgive him, but the truth is that I'm still working on it. Even if I can forgive him, that doesn't mean that I should trust him a second time. It's not like he's the one for me."

"Is it possible that he *is* the one for you, but the timing was just wrong the last time?" Britt asked.

"In my opinion the timing was perfect the last time," Willow answered.

"The timing might've been perfect for you," Britt said. "But maybe God needed more time to work on Corbin."

Willow had been certain that Corbin was the one for her, and then she'd been certain that he wasn't. After all that, was there any chance that he *was* the right man for her after all?

No.

He couldn't be the one. . . .

Could he?

"I'm leaving Merryweather in less than a month," Willow said. "Now is not the time to acquire a boyfriend."

Text message from Willow to Nora:

Willow
I just realized how you can help me, research-wise, with Operation Find Josephine. You game?

326

Nora
Yes, ma'am.

Willow
I'm wondering what vacation properties Senator Foster Holt owned in 1977. Is that information a matter of public record?

Nora
Yes. It'll take some digging, but that information can be found.

Willow
Thank you! I'm now the one who will owe YOU Ben & Jerry's.

Email from Willow's friend at Benevolence Worldwide to Willow:

Hi, Willow!

I hope you're still enjoying your stay in Washington and that the rainy weather there hasn't washed you away quite yet.

Listen, I heard that Corbin Stewart made a donation of two hundred thousand dollars to Benevolence and that he's pledged to give eight hundred thousand more over the next eighteen months. I remember that the two of you dated once, and I know he's living in Washington at the moment. So I'm dying to know . . . does this donation have anything to do with you?

If so, thank you! We're all thrilled. The entire office celebrated his donation yesterday with cinnamon rolls.

CHAPTER FIFTEEN

Willow groaned, squeezed her eyes shut, and rested her forehead on the upper tip of her laptop's screen after reading the email from her friend who worked for Benevolence. She clunked her forehead on the smooth metal a few more times for good measure.

She'd managed to withstand Corbin's attempt to blackmail her into a date with a donation to Benevolence. But now he'd gone and quietly donated to Benevolence anyway, plus pledged much more to the charity besides — without telling her. Without expecting anything in return. Which indicated that he might just be a redeemable human being, after all.

It would be churlish to refuse to go on a date with him now, considering the magnitude of what he'd just done for the organization she loved and had been pouring herself into for years.

It wasn't as if one date could put her chastity at risk. Was chastity even a term she could associate with herself at this point? Or had she spent all her chastity on Corbin way back when?

It seemed, suddenly, that she'd gone a little overboard with caution. If he could give a million dollars to Benevolence Worldwide, then she could go on a date with him.

Something that felt like relief smoothed the worry lines from her face. Relief? It couldn't be relief. But it *was* a strange sort of relief to know that for the next little while she wouldn't have to battle inwardly.

He'd finally given her a good reason to say what a dangerous part of her — the part that had motivated her to swim in the inlet — had been wanting to say.

Yes.

Any chance you've reconsidered my invitation to go on a date? Corbin texted Willow later that night.

He reclined on his sofa watching football, his phone on his chest, as he waited for her answer.

Fifteen minutes passed. Then forty-five. The longer his phone stayed silent, the more optimistic he became. When a full hour had passed, he sat up and dialed her number.

"Hello?" she said.

"You didn't immediately say no to my text. Which has made me hope that you might actually be reconsidering my invitation to go on a date."

"I heard a rumor, Corbin."

"What rumor?"

"A rumor that you didn't tear up that check for Benevolence. That you sent it in instead."

"You weren't supposed to know about that."

"But I do." A pause. "That was surprisingly decent of you."

"Maybe I should put that on my business cards. Corbin Stewart. Surprisingly Decent."

She gave a soft huff of laughter.

He moved to the sofa's front edge, sitting up straight, waiting. *C'mon, Willow. C'mon.*

"Thank you for donating. That money will make a big difference to a lot of kids."

"You're welcome. Are you finally willing to go out with me?" *C'mon.*

"Well, in light of your generosity, one date seems like the least the Benevolence Worldwide children and I can do."

"I'm happy for the Benevolence Worldwide children and all. But can you leave them at home when we go on our date?"

331

"If you insist."

"I do. I'll pick you up at noon on Saturday."

"Noon? I was expecting you to pick me up around seven p.m."

"You've only agreed to go on one date with me, so I'm planning a very, very long date."

"Heaven help me," she murmured.

"Don't eat before I pick you up. I'll feed you."

"You better."

"Dress casually."

"If you want me to dress casually because we're doing something outside, I feel inclined to warn you that the forecast calls for rain."

"It won't rain. It wouldn't dare."

When they hung up, he pushed to standing. He ran a hand through his hair, then did a fist pump with his good arm.

He gave a great deal of his money away every year. He cared about kids in need. He did. And he was glad that his donation was going to help them. But he hadn't donated to Benevolence because of the kids. He'd donated because he'd suspected that Willow would learn about it, and he knew her well enough to guess how she might react if she did. His strategy had paid off. And he didn't feel the least bit guilty.

Which could mean that he wasn't as good as he probably should be now that he was a Christian. On the other hand, he hadn't been prepared to stand around, behaving like a boy scout, while Willow slipped through his fingers.

He'd grown up in a hard neighborhood. He'd learned a person had to pursue their goals using the tools they had in order to have a shot at success.

One of the tools he had? Street smarts.

Willow spent the hour prior to her date with Corbin telling herself all the reasons why this date wasn't a big deal. She'd simply hold her heart in reserve. No problem.

However, as soon as she answered his knock and looked into his mischievous brown eyes, her confidence in her ability to hold her heart in reserve began to waver.

He'd dressed simply in jeans and a white athletic shirt. A day's growth of scruff marked his hard-planed face. "Hey," he said.

"Hey." She collected her tote bag. In addition to the skinny jeans, tall boots, blue shirt, and padded vest she had on, she'd packed a pair of sneakers, a light jacket, a down jacket, a hat, and a pair of gloves. "It would be helpful if I knew where we were going. That way, I could leave some of this behind."

"It's a surprise."

"Surprises are overrated."

"Surprises are fun." He held eye contact with her.

Great Scott. This attraction between them had suddenly become scary powerful.

She locked Bradfordwood's front door and climbed into his car. It was too late now for misgivings. She'd agreed to a date. They were going. The ship had sailed.

"A field?" she asked twenty minutes later when they arrived at their destination and he turned off the Navigator's ignition. "You're taking me to an empty field?"

"Yep," he said, looking pleased with himself.

Willow exited the car and stood in the tall grass alongside the rut marks that had passed for a road the last mile or so. Dense pine trees surrounded them on all sides. She couldn't fathom why Corbin had brought her to this high, remote spot in the middle of nowhere. Was he planning to abduct her? Perform science experiments on her?

Surely there wasn't a restaurant within a ten-mile radius — and her stomach was beginning to grumble. She'd eaten oatmeal and fruit this morning, but that seemed like ages ago.

Corbin opened his trunk. He wedged a rolled-up blanket underneath his good arm, then lifted a picnic basket in the fist of that same arm.

"We're going on a picnic?" she asked.

He led her down a barely discernible path. "We are."

That coaxed a smile from her. She loved picnics, even though she hadn't been on one in . . . years? "Was the food inside that basket prepared by your caterer?" she asked.

"Yes."

"Do you keep her on a retainer?"

"Sort of. She cooks five dinners a week for my dad and me and leaves them in the freezer for us to heat up. She's always happy to do extras, like that Monday Night Football dinner. Or romantic picnic lunches."

"Do you order a large number of romantic picnic lunches?"

"This is the first."

It had drizzled steadily all morning. Yet just as Corbin had predicted, the rain had swept to the side like curtains on a stage to make way for the production of Corbin's grand date.

Corbin didn't seem intimidated in the least by the pressure of planning a grand date. Come to think of it, he never seemed intimidated by pressure. He always rose to challenges. That facet of his character had been endlessly evident on the football field. He was renowned for playing with concentration and nerves of steel whenever the game was on the line. The bigger the stakes, the better he performed.

Commentators and reporters had speculated that Corbin had been born with the X factor that all truly great quarterbacks possessed — the ability to handle tremendous tension and expectation. The more Willow understood Corbin, though, the more she suspected that particular ability had also been forged in him by his childhood.

That's what she presumed, anyway. She didn't know that to be true for sure because he'd never trusted her with the details. "Corbin?"

"Yes, my darling?"

"That 'my darling' sounded mocking."

"I meant it to sound endearing."

Their footfalls crunched over pine needles as she followed him through air crisp with the fragrance of the forest. "You've never told me many details about your childhood."

"Where did that thought come from?"

"You're a public figure, but you're actually a very private person. Whenever anyone, including me, tries to ask you questions about your childhood that you don't want to answer, you counter with lots of charisma and humor. You keep people at a distance so skillfully that they end up laughing and liking you and hardly even noticing that you never revealed anything substantial about yourself. Am I right?"

"Well." He held a branch out of the way for her. They continued on. "You're not wrong. I don't like spilling my guts to everyone I meet."

"The problem is, you never spilled them to me, either. And I was your girlfriend for months. No one will ever be able to know you, Corbin, until you're willing to tell them things."

"So ask me something."

"What was it like for you, growing up with your dad?"

He groaned.

"See? You're like a three-year-old who refuses to eat his vegetables on this subject."

"If I answer your questions, will you answer mine?"

"Yes."

They stepped into a meadow that overlooked two distant hills sloping in a *V* to the lake they guarded. The sky resembled a masterwork impressionist painting in shades of blue and gray and cream. A trio of birds flew in quiet, lazy circles where the meadow rolled away, dropping off in elevation. Willow could see no evidence of civilization, only of God's workmanship.

"Our picnic spot?" she asked.

"Yes. Do you like it?"

"It's stunning. How did you find this place?" She'd grown up near here and never known of its existence.

"John told me about it."

Willow took the blanket from him and unfurled it onto the damp grass. Luckily, the blanket had plastic on one side and fabric on the other. They both sat and unpacked the contents of the basket. Ham, Swiss, and arugula sandwiches on crusty French bread. Dill pickles. Potato salad. Kettle chips.

"What's this?" Corbin held up a glass bottle filled with a burgundy liquid.

"Organic blackberry soda, apparently."

"Why would she have packed that?"

"Probably because it's delicious."

He pulled a face. "You're not allowed to take a picture of me drinking this girly drink. My reputation will be ruined."

"I have no intention of taking a picture of you, Football Star."

His caterer had thought of everything. Utensils, napkins, plates.

"So . . . about your dad," Willow said once they'd filled their plates and started on their meal.

"How about we talk about any other subject? Look at this setting." He gestured.

"It's a fabulous setting," she conceded. "I happen to think a fabulous setting is exactly the right backdrop for a difficult topic. Why did your mom leave?"

He leaned back on the blanket so that he was propped up on his good elbow. "I think she left because she couldn't deal with being responsible for both a young child and a husband who was battling bipolar disorder. I think she regretted pretty much every choice she'd made up until that time in her life and simply wanted to start over."

Willow took a bite of potato salad, tasting creamy mayonnaise, mustard, dill. She attempted not to notice how Corbin's shirt had hiked up when he'd levered himself back. Now his belt and an inch of golden skin were showing.

"Why did your mom leave?" Corbin asked.

"As you know, my parents weren't married when they had me. They met when my mom was traveling through the States on an around-the-world tour. They were both in their early twenties, and they'd only been dating for a short time when my mom got pregnant. I definitely wasn't planned. After I was born, she left me with my dad and continued on her tour. She'd never wanted to be a mother and definitely never wanted to be a conventional mother. How did your parents meet?"

"They met at a bar after my dad moved to Detroit in search of work. They were young, too, at the time. Neither went to college. Both liked to blow off steam by drinking heavily on the weekends. They fell in love and married six months later. I have no idea whether I was planned or not. Honestly, I'd be surprised if I was."

"How often did you see your mom after she left?"

"Almost never. She gave my dad full custody." He helped himself to another pickle. "A few years later, she married a rich guy twenty years older than she was who had two kids who were in college at the time. He and my mom never had children together. They're still married and they seem happy."

"Do you see her much?"

He shook his head. "Once every couple of years. I talk to her on the phone now and then. I just . . . . I don't feel toward her what sons feel toward mothers who raised them. I'm not obligated to her. There's not a lot of admiration or respect there." He plucked a blade of grass and tossed it. "I don't have many memories of her, and I don't want to make new ones. Is that how you feel about your biological mom?"

"Somewhat. Sylvie's been in my life more than your mom has been in yours. But I definitely don't feel toward her what daughters feel toward mothers who raised them."

They ate for a few minutes in silence. Willow had always imagined that children whose parents had been married and who'd desired a baby had it better than she'd had it. Corbin's parents had been married. But that hadn't translated into "better" for him. "What was the hardest moment you faced as a kid?" she asked.

He didn't answer right away, so she glanced at him and found him watching her with a somber expression. Wind blew a section of Willow's hair in front of her face. Before she could set aside either her plate or fork in order to dash the hair away, he reached up and brushed it aside with two blunt fingers.

Her lungs stilled as physical desire curled within her. She broke the moment by looking away and taking two careful bites of potato salad.

"The hardest moment came when I was

in the third grade," Corbin said, voice level. "My dad was going through a rough patch at the time. That's what he used to call them. He'd say, 'I'm sorry, son, I'm going through a rough patch.' "

"The rough patches were periods of depression?"

"Right. But I didn't know the term *depression* then. I just knew there were times when my dad seemed steady. And there were rough patches when he was down and sad and tired. And there were times when he was full of energy. He called his manic periods 'good patches.' When I was really young, I loved his good patches. We'd go to the park to throw a football in the evenings, then he'd take me out to dinner or to the movies or for ice cream. He'd laugh and joke and slap the back of everyone we came into contact with. He'd tell me about his plans to win the lottery and talk about the sports bar he was going to open. Sometimes we'd go on spur-of-the-moment trips to places like Atlantic City and Disney World."

Willow waited.

"As I got older, I realized I couldn't trust his good patches. They didn't last. And both the rough patches and the good patches were too extreme. I could only relax when he was in-between."

"What happened when you were in the third grade?"

"I'd been worried about him for a week or more. Several mornings in a row, I had to get him out of bed when my alarm went off. Even so, he missed a few days of work." He picked up a kettle chip, studied it, ate it. His attention settled on the lake. "One afternoon, I got off the bus and let myself into the condo just like I always did after school. When I walked in, I found him there, in the chair he sat in to watch TV, wearing the clothes he'd slept in." He pushed upward with a frustrated move.

Willow lowered her plate to the blanket and adjusted to face his profile.

"At first I thought he was asleep, but then I couldn't wake him no matter how hard I tried. He was white. And he wasn't moving. I was sure he was dead."

"What did you do?"

"I had a friend named Ryan who lived in our complex. I ran to his apartment and banged on the door. His mom came back to our place with me and she called 9-1-1."

"And?"

"He'd overdosed."

Willow exhaled gradually.

"They took him away in an ambulance. I stayed with my dad's mom, my grandmother, while he was in the hospital. Each day, we'd go to visit him. He was full of regret. He'd cry and apologize and tell me how much he loved me. But he'd just tried to kill himself. So I had to wonder how much he loved me if he was willing to do that and leave me behind. It was then that I decided to keep his attempted suicide and his condition secret from everyone in my life. I didn't want my friends to know."

"Did things change for your dad after his hospitalization?"

"Yes. My grandmother hadn't known the extent of his illness. Once she found out, she made sure that he went to doctor's appointments and therapy sessions and stayed current on his medicine. Until the attempted overdose, he'd been too stubborn to admit he needed treatment. It took the doctors a while to get him on the right medications at the right dosages, but once they did things leveled out. There were still plenty of bad times. But never as bad as that day again."

She couldn't imagine a child, any child, shouldering the weight of a sick parent by themselves. The stress of that had to have been crushing.

"I don't like to talk about the past because I want to protect my dad. But also because

I know that it sounds like I'm blaming him. I'm not blaming him." He set his jaw. "Should he have gotten treatment before he overdosed? Yes. But I don't blame him for the depression that led to the overdose. Or the manic periods. Or any of it. He didn't ask for bipolar."

"No. He didn't."

"He tried his best to be a good dad. He gave it all he had." An edge of emotion roughened his words. "I'm thankful to him."

Willow could say the same about her own father. He'd done his best. Her circumstance was different than Corbin's in big ways, though. Her dad hadn't dealt with mental illness. He'd married Kathleen when Willow was young, so she'd had the comforting influence of a mother for decades. She had sisters in her corner.

Corbin only had his dad.

"What was the hardest moment you faced as a kid?" he asked her.

She sipped blackberry soda through a straw. "Probably the day Nora's mother died. After my mom left, my dad married Robin and she became my mother. I don't remember the day she was killed. I was only two and a half. But my dad says that I walked around the house crying and calling for her for days afterward. I used to ask him when she was coming back. They say that early childhood trauma leaves a mark, and I believe it."

"What's been your hardest moment as an adult?" he asked.

"Maybe the day I saw a picture of you leaving a nightclub with another woman."

A hush blanketed the meadow. "The day I saw the picture of you and Derek Oliver was my worst adult day."

"The day of your shoulder injury was your worst day," she corrected.

"The shoulder injury was bad, but I felt like I might be able to find a way to live with it eventually. Losing you has never felt that way. It's never felt like something I could live with."

A tense silence ensued. "Why haven't you ever married?" Willow asked. He was one of America's most eligible bachelors. The subject of his love life had been much discussed on entertainment TV shows, in celebrity magazines, during interviews he'd given. Since their breakup he'd been linked with one pop singer, two actresses, and an Olympic athlete.

"Isn't it obvious why I haven't married?" he asked.

"No."

"Because none of the other women I

dated was you."

The words impacted her chest like a ball of starlight. Willow had to work to absorb them and then file them in their proper place. And also, not to swoon. "Corbin," she whispered. "Don't say things like that."

"Why haven't you married?" he asked, a dimple digging into his cheek.

"None of my boyfriends have been the one."

"You're half right. None of your *other* boyfriends were the one."

Corbin watched her blush. Emotion gathered in his chest, overpowering.

He loved her.

He loved both her feistiness and her peaceful spirit. She was the place he'd been wanting to rest his head all his life.

He'd come out of a blue-collar background. She'd come out of an American castle. Yet they were both levelheaded, responsible decision-makers. Both independent. Corbin had his life together, but so did she. She didn't need *anything* from him. She didn't require him to take care of her or to increase her fame or to pay her bills.

When he was with her, it was like a vacation, because he didn't have to be the dependable one. Here, they were both dependable. She was strong in her own right.

He leaned across the blanket to steal a kiss.

A conflicted groove notched the skin between her brows. She put out a hand to stop him.

Immediately, he stilled. Watched her.

Her face knit with concentration as she lifted a hand and ran a fingertip over his lips. Her thumb along his jaw. She caressed his ear lobe, then traced her touch down his neck. It was a focused, leisurely exploration, and it caused need to rock him.

Get yourself in hand, Corbin. Good grief. *She's just touching your face and neck.* So innocent.

His breath turned jagged.

Not innocent. Because this was Willow. The simplest thing she did had the power to tie him in a knot.

She pulled on his shirt to bring him closer to her. Stopped.

She met his eyes as if trying to weigh and measure what was in his heart. She neared so that their profiles were only two inches apart. Stopped again. He could feel the sigh of her exhale on his lips. Then she kissed him, slow.

It took extreme control to hold himself immobile. The kiss tasted wildly delicious.

Like the future. Like liquid passion.

She pulled back. "This isn't a good idea," she said breathlessly.

"It's a very good idea." He rose in one fast motion and reached down for her with his left hand. She put her fingers in his and he pulled her to her feet. Then he wove his hands into her hair and kissed her. He walked her backward, never breaking the kiss, until he'd settled her against the bare, low-reaching branch of a tree.

"This can . . . go no further . . . than kisses," she said. "Agreed."

He pressed her palm against his heart so she could feel the thunder of his pulse and kissed her with endless, drugging kisses. He kissed her like he meant it.

Because he did.

Willow functioned inside a sort of pink haze for the remainder of their date.

After the picnic, Corbin drove her to a zip-line course.

"Corbin," Willow said adamantly, craning to catch sight of the lines high above, "you can't go zip-lining with a separated shoulder."

"I've been before. The harness will support all my weight. I'll hold the brake with my left arm."

"This can't be sanctioned by Dr. Wallace."

"I won't tell him if you won't."

"Corbin."

There was no talking him out of it.

They met the two guides he'd booked. The lead guide gave them safety instructions as he outfitted them with equipment. Willow couldn't concentrate on a word he said. All she could think about were the kisses she and Corbin had just shared. It was as if she'd gotten drunk on them, even though she'd had nothing more potent than blackberry soda.

For the sake of their guides, she gave her best imitation of sobriety.

"Have you ever been zip-lining before?" Corbin asked her as their guide made final preparations on the first platform.

She strongly suspected that she looked ridiculous in her harness and safety helmet, but Corbin, of course, managed to look sexy in his. She giggled. See? Drunk. That question hadn't been funny. "No. I try to avoid pastimes that might involve me smashing my face into a tree. A smashed face would be bad for me professionally."

"I'm not going to let anything happen to your face," he said, utterly confident. "There will not be any smashing."

He went first, and then it was her turn.

Wind whistled against her cheeks as she sailed through the canopy of lush green. Was this fun? Or was this terrifying? It was both. Terrifying fun. The speed and height were thrilling. But what if the cable snapped? Then she'd hurtle to her death. Was the exhilaration worth the possibility of death?

If Corbin hadn't been with her, she might have informed the guides that one zip line was enough. However, Corbin had the ability to make daring things seem doable. Whether daring things — like kissing him — were actually *in* her best interest was a question to examine later.

By the time they'd completed the course, the weather had turned chilly. He drove them to a café packed with gleaming walnut surfaces and patrons in the mood to celebrate the advent of Saturday evening.

As soon as they stepped inside, the owner hurried over and showed them to a table situated next to a multi-paned window. They spent two hours nursing the mochas they ordered and enjoying talking to each other and to the townspeople. The sun slowly set on their grand date in a bonfire of orange and gold.

The entire time they were in the company of others while zip-lining and at the café, Willow battled an insistent yearning to kiss him or hold his hand. She knew he felt it, too, because the atmosphere sizzled with it. The fact that they couldn't act on the yearning because they were surrounded by witnesses only made it that much more delectable.

"It's almost time for dinner," Corbin said as he drove her home. "How about I buy us some food? We can take it to Bradfordwood, if you'd like. Maybe watch a movie."

"We've been together for six hours. I've been more than generous with the time I allotted you for our date."

"Yeah, but I don't want it to end."

She didn't want it to end, either. Sensibly, though, she knew she needed to give herself time to process what had happened without him in her space. His presence prevented reasonable thought. She wasn't going to let herself plunge into anything without plenty of reasonable thought, no matter how much she might want to.

He brought his SUV to a stop before Bradfordwood's front steps and shot her an expectant glance. "This is good-night?"

She nodded. She had self-control in excess.

"In that case . . ." He leaned across the center console and wrapped his hand gently around the back of her neck, drew her face toward his, and kissed her. Her self-control fled like a sprinter off the blocks.

"Thank you for going on a date with me," he whispered.

"You're welcome," she whispered back. Then she grabbed her tote and walked on what felt like clouds up into the house. When she reached the living room, she stopped. The walls of her childhood home and the tasteful, comfortable furniture her parents had chosen surrounded her. All of it seemed to be asking, *What are you going to do now?*

She'd agreed to go on one date with Corbin, and that's what she'd done. She wasn't beholden to him. She didn't *have* to go out with him again.

Yes, the landscape of their relationship had shifted in a mighty way today. He'd told her things about himself and his family that she'd be willing to bet he'd told to almost no one. His history and his honesty had softened her to him.

And then the kisses. *The kisses.* It was safe to say they'd softened her to him further.

It had gone straight to her head, the way he'd instantly stopped leaning toward her when she'd put out her hand to stay him, there on the picnic blanket. He'd restrained himself then and during the rest of their kisses.

And there had been a lot of kisses in that meadow.

She felt somewhat . . . concerned about the kisses. But not regretful, necessarily.

Great Scott. She was still surrounded by the pink haze.

Infatuation was one of the very best feelings in the world. She'd forgotten just how good it was. But she hadn't forgotten that infatuation could lead to one of the very worst feelings in the world. Heartbreak.

She walked aimlessly to the kitchen and, once there, wondered why she'd come. She washed an apple, sliced it, and peered toward the canal as she ate the crisp, sweet fruit.

Was dating Corbin a hideous idea?

All her risk-averse tendencies said yes in unison. But the rest of her remembered the things he'd said to her today. He'd said he hadn't married because none of the women he'd dated had been her. He'd said the day they'd broken up had been the worst of his adult life. And throughout their date, he'd looked at her with a slaying combination of heat and tenderness.

Here's what her past with Corbin had taught her: Corbin's superpower was his ability to say all the right things in such a way that she believed them. She'd swallowed down his words to her four years ago like they were the gospel truth.

In the end what mattered was a person's ability to back up their words over and over and over again with actions. That's where Corbin had failed the last time. She couldn't allow herself to think that Corbin had magically become trustworthy. If she decided to go on more dates with him, it would have to be with that clear understanding in the front of her mind. She could not invest her whole self in the things he said to her.

What to do, what to do?

Anxiously, she tugged on one of her bracelets.

She could cut things off right here, before they'd begun. Or she could try dating him. If she chose option B, they'd have to take things very slow. And they'd have to institute a strict nothing-more-than-kissing policy. Then she'd need to pray, hard, against getting swept away by her own desire the way she had the last time. If she and Corbin were both in agreement about the physical side of their dating life from the outset, then maybe — likely? — things would be fine.

It was as if she were a traveler holding a

map and trying to decide between two routes. One route was safe but dry and boring like a desert. The other route was frightening but potentially full of breathtaking beauty.

Willow, the careful sister, wanted to take the frightening, beautiful route.

Voice mail to Joe Stewart:

Hi, Mr. Stewart. It's Lisa from Oncology Associates calling. I haven't heard from you about rescheduling that appointment you missed, so I was hoping to catch you so that we could set up a time. Please return my call when you're able.

Text message from Nora to Willow:

Nora
In 1977, Foster Holt owned two vacation properties in addition to his residence in Redmond. He owned a condo in Breckenridge, Colorado. And he owned a house in Laguna Beach, California.

Condolence notes inside wooden box:

From Mexico:
I'm heartbroken to hear about your loss.

356

Que Dios les bendiga.

From Alaska:

I'm praying your daughter and sister and wife comes home to you safe and sound. Don't give up hope.

From Canada:

So very sorry. Thinking of you.

CHAPTER SIXTEEN

Britt Bradford had been dreading this day.

Today was the day of Zander's departure.

Ever since he'd given his two weeks' notice at work, he'd been moving the possessions he wanted to keep into storage, moving the clothes he wanted to take with him into a single suitcase, and selling the rest. Britt had helped him clear the last of his furniture out of his apartment yesterday. As depressing as it had been to stand in his familiar apartment that had become unfamiliar with its blank walls and stained carpeting, this day was worse.

She'd picked him up this morning at his aunt and uncle's. The couple lived in a modest house that had been Zander and his older brother's residence while they were in high school.

Zander had been living at his aunt and uncle's place for all of six weeks the day Britt had met him, their freshman year at

Merryweather High. At the time, he'd been withdrawn, furtive, hurting. His silence had bristled with hostility.

The fourteen-year-old girl Britt had been back then had liked him *instantly.*

He'd made her work to earn his friendship, which had been a first for her. During her childhood and adolescence, most of her peers had worked to earn *her* friendship.

She'd succeeded at winning Zander over through persistence and, she liked to think, charm. The weeks she'd invested in befriending Zander had paid incredible dividends because for the past eleven years he'd been one of her closest friends.

Once he'd said good-bye to his aunt and uncle, she'd driven him to Bradfordwood where Willow, Nora, Valentina, and Grandma had gathered to feed him a farewell breakfast.

Valentina, in typical Valentina fashion, had stuffed them all with Russian pancakes called *oladi,* plus sausage and fried eggs. It had been odd, the atmosphere at breakfast. It wasn't easy to feel celebratory over someone's departure. You wanted to be happy for them. At the same time, you couldn't help but feel sad for yourself.

Her sisters, Grandma, and Valentina had all done a better job of merrymaking than she had. But then, none of them loved Zander like she did. None of them were Zander's best friend like she was.

His flight departed in three hours, and they'd reach SeaTac in just minutes. She'd insisted on driving him to the airport, but man, what a gloomy duty this was. She felt like a coachman steering a horse-drawn hearse.

She cut a glance in Zander's direction. He looked over and met her eyes, his demeanor more subdued than usual.

"Is any part of you nervous about this big trip you're about to take?" she asked.

"No."

"What is it, then?"

"It's . . . hard to leave the people I love. That's all."

"It's not too late to change your mind, you know. I can say with complete selfishness that I'll support you fully if you decide to stay."

Asphalt hummed beneath them. She and Zander had become accustomed to quiet spaces between them years ago.

"I'm not going to change my mind," he said. He'd decided to explore England first, then Ireland, before traveling to the European mainland. After that, possibly Asia. Followed by Australia. He was leaving

360

Washington to have the time of his life. "I need to do this."

She didn't have to ask him why he needed to do this. She knew why. They'd talked and talked about his decision to quit his job and put the advance his publisher had given him for his upcoming book toward travel. Zander had seen almost nothing of the world, and he wanted to enlarge his boundaries. He also wanted to prove his independence and strength and creativity to himself.

She understood. It would be incredibly hypocritical of her to pretend she didn't understand, since she had lived overseas for two years. After she completed her degree at the Culinary Institute of America at Greystone, she'd gone straight to France to study under master chocolatiers. She'd loved her time abroad and was better for it, so she couldn't begrudge him the same experience.

Her dad had driven this same route the day he'd taken her to the airport to catch her flight to France. Her mom had sat in the passenger seat, and she and Zander had sat in the backseat, side by side. She'd been caught up in excitement and jitters that day. If she'd been distressed to part from them, or if they'd been distressed to part from her, she couldn't remember it.

"Just go ahead and pull up to the gate," he said as they drove onto airport property.

"I was planning to park and walk you in."

"No, it's okay."

"Boo."

"Just pull up to the gate, Britt."

Low-level panic began to swirl within her. She'd anticipated staying with him until he passed through the security checkpoint. But he didn't want her to do that, apparently. He'd never liked long, drawn-out good-byes.

She came to a stop in front of the terminal that housed his airline. The bright red curb and the signs loudly proclaimed *Loading and Unloading Only! No Parking at Any Time.* She helped him lift his suitcase and carry-on from her trunk.

He turned to her. She stilled.

Wind tipped with cold and car exhaust brushed past them. The conversations of nearby passengers mingled with the roar of a departing plane.

His blue eyes smoldered with seriousness. "Thank you."

He was thanking her for the ride, and the elbow grease she'd donated to his big move over the last few weeks. "You're welcome." In his expression, she saw that he was also, perhaps, thanking her for their long friendship.

Fear niggled inside her. It wasn't like this was the last time they'd ever see each other. They had many years of friendship still ahead of them, God willing. "Promise me that when you're done traveling, you'll come back," she said.

"I can't make that pr—"

"Promise me," she said sternly. "Otherwise, I'm not going to let you leave. I'll toss that suitcase and carry-on back into my trunk and push you in after them."

A tiny smile fractured his somber mood. "Is that a threat?"

"Yes. It absolutely is."

"I'd like to see you try to get my luggage and me into your car against my will."

She called his bluff by reaching for his carry-on. He caught her wrist and chuckled as he guided her back into a standing position.

"I'd rather promise to come back than fight you for my luggage," he said.

"That's what I thought." She sniffed. "Then go ahead. Promise." He'd never broken a promise to her.

He regarded her steadily. "I'll come back one day."

"Good. You know how much I like to get

363

my way." A passerby gave her empty car a worried look. It was sitting at the curb, idling, and she needed to return to it before someone either stole it or reported it to airport security. "I better go. . . ."

He nodded, and she stepped forward to hug him. His arms banded around her tightly. One second melted into two, then three. "Bye, Zander," she whispered. "Have fun on your big adventure." She straightened.

"I'll miss you." He looked like he wanted to say more. But he held the words back.

"I'll miss you, too. Now go." She tossed a false smile over her shoulder and strode toward her car.

Her lungs seemed to have both tightened and turned to fire. Once inside, she shifted into drive and pulled away. She watched him in her rearview mirror. He hadn't moved to grab his suitcase and carry-on. He stood motionless amid the hubbub, arms at his sides, watching her go.

Her days were going to be far blander and lonelier and less interesting until he returned.

Change was challenging.

Change hurt.

Willow excused herself in the middle of

Grandma's Sunday afternoon book club, ostensibly to visit the restroom. In actuality, she'd excused herself in order to seize a few minutes of vacation from Grandma's book club. And to text Corbin.

Nora unearthed information on two vacation properties that Foster Holt owned in 1977, she typed. Hitting send, she leaned against the inside of the bathroom door and soaked in the quiet.

Grandma had asked Willow to attend her book club meeting more than a week ago. *"When I learned you were coming to stay in Merryweather,"* Grandma had said, *"I'd so hoped that you and I would get to spend a great deal of time together. But it's seemed to me that you've been too busy for that. With Kathleen and Garner gone, this has been a difficult time for me."*

Grandma had explained that she felt obligated to attend her book club meeting this month because it was at Eleanor's house, and Eleanor was always so eager to please despite the fact that she had very little cooking talent and no inkling that linen napkins needed to be ironed. *"I need someone to come with me, Willow. To be on my side. I'm very much afraid the group won't feel the same way that I do about that awful book Eleanor picked for us to read."*

So here Willow was.

As it turned out, every single person, including Eleanor, felt the same way that Grandma did about the book. They all loathed it.

Willow had spent the last hour sitting on a folding chair in Eleanor's formal living room, daydreaming about Corbin and yesterday's grand date while the ladies called into question the author's morals, writing ability, and relationship with Jesus.

Corbin, take me away!

Her phone binged. *I think Nora's information calls for an emergency Operation Find Josephine meeting this afternoon,* Corbin's text read.

Nora's information isn't earth-shattering enough to merit an emergency meeting.

Of course it is. We can't rest until Josephine's mystery is solved.

His message wheedled a smile from her. *I'm with my grandmother at her book club. After this, I'll be taking her back to Bradfordwood, where she left her car.*

When?

An hour from now?

I'll see you there.

You'll bring Charlotte?

Who?

Charlotte, your relative, the girl who is the

366

reason for our involvement in Josephine's mystery.

Oh, right. Five feet tall? Bad taste in music? That's the one.

I'll call Jill to see if Charlotte's free.

Willow left the bathroom and returned to the book club's airing-of-grievances, fortified with the knowledge that she'd be seeing Corbin again soon. Less than twenty-four hours had passed since their date. It was probably unwise to see him today. It was probably unwise to look forward to seeing him as much as she was.

Probably. And yet, when she caught sight of Corbin's Navigator parked on the curb outside Bradfordwood's gate, she experienced an espresso-like energy rush.

"Who's that?" Grandma asked.

"Corbin Stewart and Charlotte Dixon."

"Do I know these people?"

"You met Corbin a few months ago." Corbin's car followed Willow's up the long drive to the house.

"Is he the handsome one?"

"Yes."

"Too handsome for his own good, as I recall. Who's Charlotte?"

"The girl I told you about who asked me to help her research her great-aunt's disappearance. That's what we're meeting about today."

Willow helped Grandma down from the Range Rover. They made their way toward Corbin and Charlotte, who were already walking in their direction.

Corbin wore battered jeans and a waffle-knit shirt he'd pushed up at the forearms. He looked effortlessly casual and just a little bit rumpled, and Willow could all but hear his legions of female fans sighing.

She performed introductions.

"It's a pleasure to meet you," Corbin said to Grandma.

"Likewise." Grandma employed the tone one would use to say *scoundrel.* "What do you do for a living?"

"At the moment I'm renovating my house."

Grandma's nostrils flared with displeasure. She'd never earned a paycheck in her life. She'd gone straight from the care of her mother and father to the care of her husband. When he'd died young, Grandma's father-in-law had provided for her luxuriously during his lifetime and to this day via a trust fund. Grandma had no right to judge Corbin. However, having no right to judge had never acted as a speed bump for her in the past.

"Corbin's retired," Charlotte said.

"Retired?" Grandma asked.

"He used to play football," Charlotte said. "He's sort of rich."

Grandma would go into anaphylactic shock if she had any idea of Corbin's net worth.

"And some people think he's famous." Charlotte shrugged in a way that communicated *there's no accounting for taste.*

"What football team did you play on?" Grandma asked Corbin.

"What football team do you like, Mrs. Burke?"

"My husband used to support the Washington State Cougars."

"That's the team I played for."

"Corbin!" Willow laughed. "No it's not." To Grandma she said, "He played for an NFL team called the Mustangs."

"I'm sorry that I never had a chance to play for the team your husband supported, Mrs. Burke," Corbin said. "I'd have liked to have met him. If he was married to you, then he must've been a wonderful man."

That was completely over the top. Grandma's face creased with condemnation, and Willow waited for her to lash Corbin with the sharp side of her tongue.

Instead, inexplicably, the older lady

smiled. "You're an ornery rascal. I can tell."

"Yes," Corbin admitted.

"He's not to be trusted, Willow." Affection marked Grandma's usually sour expression.

"No," Willow said. "He's not to be trusted."

"Where can I appeal this decision?" Corbin asked.

"Grandma doesn't grant appeals." Willow walked Grandma to her Oldsmobile, waved her off, then escorted Charlotte and Corbin to Bradfordwood's den, which opened to the kitchen and overlooked the emerald swath of grass leading down to the dock.

"Can I get you anything to eat or drink?" Willow asked. The pink haze of infatuation she'd existed in yesterday had returned, though she tried not to let it show. Charlotte had the eyes and ears of a fox.

For his part, Corbin was not being terribly subtle. Since his arrival, he'd been following her with his gaze and giving her a small, knowing smile every time she peeked in his direction.

"I can offer you popcorn," Willow continued. "Fruit? Almonds?"

"No thanks," Corbin said. "I'm not here for the food."

The timbre of his voice assured her he wasn't here to work on Josephine's case, either. *Don't look at him, Willow.* She could feel a blush threatening.

"Well, I *am* here partly for the food," Charlotte announced. "Popcorn sounds great."

"Coming right up." Willow popped a bag of microwave popcorn, dumped it into a ceramic bowl, and set it on the coffee table.

Charlotte grabbed a handful of popcorn and ate it while looking back and forth between them. "Why are you smiling at Willow like that?" she asked Corbin.

"No reason."

The girl frowned at him doubtfully, then opened her notebook and clicked her pen. "What's happened that's so important that you called an emergency meeting?"

Corbin made a lazy, enlighten-the-child hand gesture from Willow to Charlotte.

"After I met with Vickie Goff, I asked my sister Nora to find out whether or not the senator owned any vacation properties at the time of Josephine's disappearance. And, if so, where they were located." Willow crossed her legs and bobbed the toe of her ankle boot. Trying to focus on Charlotte while Corbin was nearby was like trying to ignore the blazing heat of the sun. "It turns out that Senator Holt owned the same beach house in California the year that Josephine went missing that he did when he was connected to Vickie. He also owned a condominium in Breckenridge, Colorado."

"What do you think we should do with this information?" Charlotte asked Willow.

"We could —" Corbin started.

"Shhh," Charlotte said jokingly to him. "Willow and I are trying to have a conversation here."

"You knew me first! I'm your rehab project. I'm the one who drives you places."

"Yes," Charlotte acknowledged patiently. She gestured to Willow. "But she's *the* Willow Bradford."

Corbin regarded the girl with a slit-eyed stare. "Your smack-talking skills are coming along thanks to me, *the* Corbin Stewart."

"What are you thinking we should do with the information your sister found, Willow?" Charlotte asked.

"I already ran searches in Laguna Beach and Breckenridge for residents named Josephine Blake. No luck. So I'm thinking that this might be a good time to contact the American Coalition for the Discovery of Missing Persons and forward them the age-progression portrait of Josephine that we had made."

"That *I* had made," Corbin corrected.

"If Foster Holt did have a relationship

372

with Josephine like the one he had with Vickie," Willow said, "then it's possible he may have sent Josephine to one of his vacation properties when their relationship started to go south, just like he did with Vickie."

"If the Coalition circulates the age-progression portrait of Josephine around Laguna Beach and Breckenridge," Corbin said to Charlotte, "then we may get a few tips."

"But what are the chances someone in those towns would remember Josephine from so long ago?" Charlotte asked.

"Slim," Corbin said.

"We said from the beginning that it was unlikely that we'd find her," Willow said gently to Charlotte.

"I know."

"Okay. I just wanted to make sure you remember that, because I'm leaving soon, and I don't want you to be upset if we haven't solved the case when I go."

"I won't be upset. It's just . . . I really want to solve this case."

"I understand. After I go, you'll still have *the* Corbin Stewart here to help you." Willow looked him full in the face for the first time since they'd entered the house. The impact of it went off like a bliss grenade.

"What else do we have to talk about?" Charlotte reached for more popcorn.

"I tried to get my hands on more information about the extortion charge against Stan Markum, but I couldn't dig anything else up," Corbin said. "I think that's a dead end."

"Willow?" Charlotte asked.

"I don't have anything else."

"You called an emergency meeting just to talk about Senator Holt's vacation houses?" Charlotte asked Corbin.

"Yep."

Charlotte's face revealed both suspicion and confusion.

Corbin bobbed his chin toward the terrace. "How about you take that popcorn and go play outside for a few minutes?"

"I'm twelve. I don't play, and I definitely don't play outside."

"Then how about you take your phone into the front room so I can talk privately with Willow?"

"Why?"

"Grown-up reasons. Go."

She peered at them with open curiosity. "Did something happen between you two?"

"I wouldn't tell you if it had," Corbin answered.

"How about I play Jungkook's new song

374

for you guys? It's super romantic."

"If you'll go hang out in the study for ten minutes, I'll listen to Jungkook's song on the drive back to your house. Deal?"

"Deal." She collected her phone and the popcorn, then sailed down the hall.

"Good riddance," Corbin whispered. He tugged Willow to standing and kissed the spot where her palm met her inner wrist.

A thrill of sensation ran all the way up Willow's arm.

"Can I see you tonight?" he asked.

"I don't know."

"What don't you know?"

"Whether or not another date, so soon after the first, is a good idea."

"It's an excellent idea."

"What did you have in mind?"

"You love sushi, right? How about we go to that Japanese place in Shore Pine? Maybe we can go out on the lake after with John and Nora on John's boat."

"Yes to the sushi. No to the boat. I haven't told my sisters about yesterday's date yet." As soon as she told them, they'd ask questions she had no answers for.

"You're keeping me a secret?" His dark eyes glimmered with amusement. "I like being your secret."

"I'm keeping you secret for a few days,

just until I figure out what to do with you."

"Marry me."

Her throat went dry. "I'll go on a few dates with you before I leave, but that doesn't mean that we're *together.* All right?"

He didn't look daunted. "Not ready to make it exclusive?"

"I'm keeping my options open."

He moved his body in close, so close he had to tilt his head down to keep their gazes locked. So close she could smell his soap. "Waiting for a better man to come along?"

"Exactly."

"I can be a better man." He intertwined both his hands with both of hers, then kissed her. Slow and intimate.

That night, they ate sushi.

The next night, he bought her a kite and they flew it at Bradfordwood on the bank of the Hood Canal.

The next day he came over at eleven a.m. after she'd finished her morning duties at the inn. They watched a Will Ferrell movie and ate nachos for lunch. Once upon a time, they'd loved eating nachos while watching movies. It felt decadent to watch a movie with him in the middle of a weekday. She'd never tasted more delicious nachos.

"This doesn't mean we're together," she

said to him each day.

"I know," he said lightly every time. Then he'd ask her when he could see her again.

On Wednesday, Corbin found his dad in the upstairs guest bedroom, painting the walls the color they'd chosen, a gray so pale it was one shade darker than white. "I just got off the phone with the woman from Oncology Associates," Corbin said. "She told me that you missed your appointment three weeks ago and haven't called her back to reschedule."

The wet sound of the paint roller answered. "I don't know why she would've called you. No sense in bothering you about this," his dad grumbled.

"She called me because my name and number are on your paper work."

His dad said nothing.

"I scheduled an appointment for you with them for this afternoon, so we'll need to leave in about an hour."

"Cancel it. I'm not going."

"Why not?" Corbin had checked the desk calendar they both used, and his dad hadn't written anything under today's date.

Silence.

"Dad? Why can't you go to today's appointment?"

"Because I don't want them telling me what I already know." He worked the paint into a new section of drywall. "The cancer has gotten worse."

Fear punched Corbin square in the gut. He stared at his dad's back, struggling to order his thoughts. "You're saying you missed your appointment on purpose and didn't return the office's calls on purpose. Because you didn't want to hear what they had to say?"

"Because I don't want *and* don't need to hear what they have to say."

"You might be completely wrong about the cancer, which is why we have to go in and have tests run. That's the only accurate way to determine what's going on."

"I've been living with multiple myeloma for years now."

"So have I."

"But I'm the one who's been living with it inside my body, Corbin. I don't need tests to determine what's going on."

The roller brush began to run dry, leaving weak, uneven tracks in its wake.

His father had once been a ten-foot-tall giant in Corbin's eyes.

When Corbin was small, the two of them would wrestle on the patch of old brown carpet in front of the TV in their living room. His dad had been able to pin Corbin without even trying, as if Corbin had been a stuffed animal.

At bedtime his dad had sometimes tossed Corbin over his shoulder on the way to Corbin's room. "Sack of potatoes for sale! Ten dollars! Any takers?" his dad had called. Then he'd tickled Corbin's ribs. "No takers? This is one good sack of potatoes. I guess I'll have to eat them myself."

At Pee-Wee football practices, his dad had thrown the football what seemed like a mile.

Whenever his dad had been in a good patch or a steady patch, he'd shown up for Corbin's parent–teacher conferences at school wearing a tie, his thick red hair combed and shiny.

When Corbin was in the fourth grade, his dad brought three store-bought cakes for the class Valentine's Day party. He'd carried them into the classroom without breaking a sweat, grinning.

The passing of years gave gifts. But the passing of years also stole things from you.

Corbin was now the one in the prime of his life. He was the strong one. The tall one. If needed, he was the one who could throw his dad over his shoulder. Corbin was the provider. He paid the mortgage and drove them places and made his dad eat vegetables.

His dad set the brush into the paint pan and leaned the handle against the wall. He turned and slowly faced Corbin.

As far as Corbin could tell, his dad looked much the same as he'd looked for the past three years. He may have lost a few pounds in recent weeks, but if so, it was hardly noticeable. His face held the same amount of color that it usually did. The only difference Corbin could see, now that he was looking closely, was in his dad's eyes. They were lit with resignation. Stubbornness. And something else. Something that might be pain. Or grief.

"I'm dying," his dad said.

The fear that had socked Corbin earlier drew in on itself, tightening. He opened his mouth, but his dad held up a hand to stop him from speaking.

"I've been dying for years. To tell the truth, I'm surprised I've lived with cancer as long as I have. I'm lucky that I've had these extra years with you. I'm glad I got to see the last few seasons of your football career. I'm glad I got to work on this house with you, and I'm glad that I'm going to be able to finish the renovations on this place." He gave a sad smile. "It's good that the house is almost done. Because I'm almost done."

It was one of the most honest and emotional speeches his dad had ever given. What Corbin felt in response to it? Denial and a boatload of anger. "You're not almost done."

"I'm sorry, son, but I am. I don't have the heart for more chemotherapy, more treatments, more doctors and hospitals. I just want to live in peace for however long I have left. I'm sick of fighting."

"Well, I'm not. I've just *started* fighting, and I'm definitely not willing to quit without tests, without proof. We're going to that appointment, and we're leaving in an hour."

His dad shook his head.

"We're going," Corbin vowed.

He stalked from the house. When drizzle hit him in the face, he slanted his steps toward the garage, still in use as their workshop, and came to a stop just inside the mouth of the garage door. His vision fixed on his property. His mind fixed on the things his dad had just told him.

He refused to accept his father's self-diagnosis. It wasn't uncommon for his dad to have harebrained ideas that had no basis in fact. It didn't make sense to worry at this point. He'd remain calm — which had always been the best policy in the face of his dad's ups and downs — and wait for test results.

Later, at the appointment, Corbin stayed at his dad's side in order to ensure that his dad told the doctors everything that he'd communicated to Corbin.

His dad was sunk deep in a bad mood. But he said to the doctor what needed to be said and he submitted to the tests.

This isn't the time for worry, Corbin reminded himself several times. He'd wait for test results.

Even so, worry thudded through his veins. And wouldn't leave.

Phone call from Dr. Benton to Corbin:

Dr. Benton: I just finished talking with your father, and he asked me to call you and discuss his test results with you personally.

Corbin: Thank you. I appreciate it.

Dr. Benton: Since he became our patient in June, his numbers have been stable. In the seven weeks since his last rounds of tests, that's changed. We're seeing an overgrowth of plasma cells in your father's bone marrow. His hemoglobin is low. And the blood chemistry labs we ran show that his kidney and liver are not functioning as well as they have in the past.

Corbin: So my dad was right. The cancer's gotten worse.

Dr. Benton: I'm afraid so. I've seen this many times in my career. Some patients can sense when they're recovering. Others can sense when their condition has grown more serious. I wish that your dad had been in the former category.

Corbin: He . . . I — I'm . . . What treatments do you recommend we pursue at this point?

Dr. Benton: Your father made it clear two days ago when you were both in my office that he doesn't want to pursue additional treatments.

Corbin: I'd like to know what the options are so that I can sit down with him and talk through everything.

Dr. Benton: There's not a precedent, Corbin, that suggests that aggressive treatment would be beneficial to a patient with your dad's prognosis.

Corbin: Money is not a factor. There must be something we can try. Something we can do.

Dr. Benton: There are two clinical trials being conducted. They accept applicants based on age, diagnosis, and previous treatments, among other things.

Corbin: Can you please send me the information about those two trials?

Dr. Benton: Certainly.

Text message from Corbin to Willow:

Corbin
Would it be all right if I came by Bradfordwood? The news about my dad isn't good.

Willow
Yes, of course.

CHAPTER SEVENTEEN

Willow was waiting outside for Corbin when he pulled up at Bradfordwood.

Darkness had fallen, yet he could see her well in the glow cast by the mansion's exterior lights. She was standing on the bricks that paved the driveway, wearing a puffy silver coat. Corbin shut his car door and closed the distance between them.

Willow's face, a face that had been captured in a thousand photographs, regarded him with compassion as he approached. She was a listener and naturally sympathetic. Many people were too blinded by their own emotions to understand the emotions of others. Not Willow.

He wrapped her tightly in his arms, bent his head, and pressed a kiss against her temple. Her arms banded around him. She rested the side of her face against his chest.

Slowly, as he concentrated on the sensation of holding her in his arms and he lost himself in his fierce love for her, the dark chaos that had been drowning him since the doctor's call began to still. He filled his lungs with her clean, fresh scent, and eventually his world stopped spinning too fast.

He almost wanted to cry, which was ridiculous. He never cried.

She threaded her fingers through his and guided him toward the line of trees next to the house.

"You're taking me into the woods?" he asked.

"I am. Tell me what the doctor said."

As they walked, he related his conversation with the doctor in a flat, emotionless voice.

She drew him to a stop. He squinted, but it was so black that he could only make out a faint shadow stretching between two tree trunks.

Willow let go of his hand and bent. Moments later he heard the rasp of a lighter. She touched the flame to a thick, white candle set inside a lantern, then closed the lantern's glass door.

The patch of forest that surrounded them came into focus. Towering trees, a carpet of leaves. The shadow he'd seen was a hammock.

"When I was growing up, this is where I

used to come on bad days," she said. "I'd rock and think and pray . . . and look up at the trees. It seemed to help." She climbed onto the hammock first. "Be very careful of your shoulder," she warned as he climbed on after her.

His heavy weight tipped the thing so suddenly that it almost bounced her off. His hand shot out to steady her. "You okay?"

She giggled. "Yes."

It required a few moves a contortionist would have been proud of, but they got themselves straightened out and balanced in the center of the hammock. His whole side, from shoulder to calf, pressed against her side. The line of contact glowed.

"After I got off the phone with the doctor, I talked with my dad. I can't understand why he won't even consider one of the clinical trials."

Her hand found his again. "What would being a part of one of the trials involve?"

"Relocating, for starters, since one is being held in Chicago and the other in Boston. Beyond that, he'd have to submit to new treatments and medicines. New doctors. Tests."

"What part of that does he object to?"

"All of it. He refuses to move. And he refuses to go through any more treatments.

I'm going to talk with him about it again. And again, if I have to, until I can get him to see it my way." He waited for her response. When none came he said, "Go on. Tell me what you're not saying."

"I'm just wondering whether you're willing to spend the final stage of your dad's life fighting with him."

"I only expect to spend the next few days fighting with him until I can convince him to apply for a trial." He gave the ground a push and set them into motion. "This doesn't have to be the final stage of my dad's life."

"And if you can't convince him to participate in a trial?"

"I'm not ready to think about that yet."

"This is all very new. I mean, you just got the call. Over the next few days, though, maybe you should at least consider what your dad's saying. It's possible that the route your dad wants to take might be what's best for him."

"Dying? How can dying be best for him?" He gave the ground another push. "When I was eleven and the Lions were playing the Packers in the playoffs, I was on my feet the whole second half, yelling at the TV."

"Yelling what?"

"That they better not give up. And also,

telling them what they needed to do to have a chance at winning. I couldn't accept that they were going to lose. Even after the game, for days, I couldn't accept that they'd lost. I'm nothing like those people who leave before the fourth quarter is over. No fight is ever over until it's over."

"Which is probably one of the reasons why your dad has done as well as he has for the past three years. I'm just wondering out loud whether your competitiveness is something that's beneficial to you or your dad at this *particular point.*"

She sounded reasonable, but she was flat-out crazy. After the conversation he'd just had with his dad, he had to wonder if he was the only sane person. "If I was the one with multiple myeloma, I'd be on a plane to Chicago. I can't accept any less for my dad. I'm responsible for him. I can't lose him, Willow. He's the only immediate family I have."

"I know," she said simply.

After some time had passed with no sound between them but the creaking of the hammock, she said, "My door is open anytime you want to talk about it."

He supposed he should feel grateful for her offer. But he didn't want Willow to be available to him in the way that she meant.

As a friend. A supporter.

She'd said over and over that they weren't together. She was determined to keep a wall between them. So much so, that he felt fortunate to have gotten their relationship to the place it was currently.

That said, he wanted much, much more.

It was not going to be okay, her leaving after Thanksgiving. He needed to be near her. Here. Or wherever she was going.

"How old is your dad?" she asked.

"Sixty-six. People live till eighty-five or ninety all the time. I'm going to be mad if I don't get eighty-five years out of him, at least."

"He's had a serious form of cancer for years. I'm guessing a lot of people with his condition don't get as many years as he's already received."

"I can't lose him," Corbin repeated with conviction. He just couldn't . . .

He couldn't lose his dad.

He twisted on the hammock to face her. Willow turned to him, and they stared at each other. Powerful desire existed between them. But so did things that were a lot more rare. So rare they'd only happened to him with her.

Love. Fate. Devotion.

Looking into her eyes on a hammock surrounded by dark woods with stars watching over them, he knew with certainty that she was the one for him.

The two of them were meant to be.

He couldn't lose his dad, and he couldn't lose Willow.

"I come bearing borscht." Willow staggered into Nora's Bookish Cottage the next evening carrying a huge pot.

Valentina's borscht-cooking binges always left Willow feeling two ways. One, comforted, because she loved borscht. Valentina had been making the hearty Russian stew for the Bradford family for as long as Willow could remember. Two, anxious, because Willow hated to waste food and she was, at present, the only resident of Bradfordwood. Even at the best of times she had what could be classified as a moderate appetite. Thus, when she'd caught a telltale whiff of vegetables and bacon in the air earlier today, she'd texted Nora and Britt and made plans to meet them at Nora's as soon as they got off work.

"Did she make enough to feed twenty, as usual?" Britt asked.

"Yep."

Nora helped lift the pot onto her stove top, then lit the burner beneath.

Britt studied Willow with interest. "We ordinarily hear from you a lot during the week."

"That's because I'm living alone and doing a part-time job that only takes up five hours of my day."

"So how come you've been unusually quiet this week?" Britt asked.

"You heard from me today. I'm the one who invited you to eat borscht." She was stalling.

"She's stalling," Britt said. "Can you see it on her face, Nora?"

"Yes, indeed."

Oh, good gracious. She was not going to push nervously at her cuticles like she had the urge to do. She'd given up pushing her cuticles when she started modeling.

"Is there something you'd like to tell us?" Britt asked with a shrewd smile.

"Fine. I've been quieter than usual this past week because Corbin and I have been out on a few — not many — dates. Just for fun."

Nora and Britt waited expectantly for more information.

"After I turned him down for a date, I found out that he went and donated the check to Benevolence plus a lot more. Then he asked me out again and knowing what I knew about his donation, it seemed really petty to say no. So I said yes."

"Let's discuss this further over appetizers." Nora opened her fridge and extracted a platter bearing three kinds of cheese, a selection of raw veggies, and a bowl of French onion sour cream dip. She handed the platter to Britt. Willow filled glasses with sparkling water, and Nora carried napkins and baskets of tortilla chips and crackers into her living room.

Nora's already small house was made tinier by all the books it contained. Despite its diminutive size, every time Willow walked in the front door she felt at home.

They arranged the food on the ottoman and the drinks on side tables. Nora took the chair she sat in when watching her beloved BBC historical dramas. Willow chose the remaining chair, Britt the floor.

"Well?" Britt said. "How did your first date with him go?"

"It went very well."

"Too vague," Britt said. "I'm going to need *a lot* more information. Where did you guys go on your first date?"

"And on the subsequent dates?" Nora asked.

Willow filled them in on their past week's itinerary.

"Wow." Britt cocked her head speculatively. "Picnics overlooking the lake. Sushi. Kite flying. Sounds to me like he's bringing his A game."

"Corbin only has an A game."

"When we talked about him last, you were concerned about going on a date with him because you didn't trust him or yourself," Nora said.

Willow nibbled a baby carrot. "That hasn't changed. I still feel very wary."

"Yet you agreed to more dates," Britt said.

"I did, because I had a wonderful time on our first date."

"You were afraid of the path that one date might set you on," Nora said. "But it sounds to me like the path that your first date set you on has turned out to be a good thing."

Willow nodded. "That's true, so far. It has."

"I assume these dates have included kisses?" Britt asked.

"Britt!" Nora squawked. "That's none of our business."

"Not technically, no. But in case you've forgotten, that's never stopped me from asking questions before." She winked at Nora and popped a square of cheese in her mouth.

"The dates have included kisses," Willow

said carefully.

"A-game kisses?" Britt asked.

"A-game kisses," Willow verified. "But respectful A-game kisses." That made the kisses sound as boring as cardboard when they were *anything* but. Willow balanced a slice of cheese in the center of her cracker, then took a bite. Sharp cheese. Crispy, salty cracker. "What is this?" she asked once she'd swallowed. "It's delicious."

"Manchego," Britt replied, even though Nora was the one who'd assembled the appetizers. Her youngest sister recognized the cheese by taste because Britt was a food savant. Even as a child she'd been able to concoct delicacies armed with nothing more than their family kitchen, a whisk, and a bowl.

Nora dragged the corner of a tortilla chip through the dip. "Do you think you'll continue to go out with Corbin until you leave in a few weeks?"

"I think so."

"Then what will happen between you two?" Britt asked.

"I've made it clear to him that we're not a couple in any serious kind of way, so maybe nothing."

"Nothing?" Nora asked.

"I have bookings on my calendar I committed to months ago. One's in New York. Another's in St. Barts. Another's in Paris. And he can't leave here because his dad's health is shaky. It wouldn't be smart for either of us to expect our relationship to progress after I go."

"You could give long-distance dating a try," Britt said.

"Long-distance dating is tough." The last time around, she and Corbin had maintained their romance while living in two different cities and traveling for work. They'd done their best to deal with the logistical challenges, but it had been a struggle. She'd missed him every day they were apart. The travel to and from Dallas had drained her. The phone calls never seemed like enough. Even their reunions had been tinged with desperation because she'd always known the next departure was looming. "Anyway." Willow gave an industrious sigh. "Corbin and I are keeping things very casual. Very."

"Uh-huh." Britt's tone indicated that she wasn't convinced.

"The topic of my love life is giving me a headache," Willow said.

"Really? It's curing my headache," Britt stated. "I'm loving this conversation."

"Easy there," Nora said to Britt. "We have to be nice to Willow. She brought us borscht." She tucked her feet under her on the chair. "How's the search for Josephine coming?"

Willow balanced her glass on the arm of her chair. "The age-progression portrait of Josephine that Corbin commissioned has been posted in Laguna Beach and in Breckenridge. A few tips have come in, but none of them have led to anything. We're out of ideas. We don't know what else to do."

"You've already searched for articles that mention Josephine or Stan Markum or Senator Holt, right?" Nora asked.

"Right."

"Online?"

"Yes. We've read everything we were able to find online, and we've read the clippings that were inside the wooden box of mementos that Josephine's sister, Melinda, kept."

"Many of the articles and newspaper stories written in the '70s," Nora said, "especially for local papers or small publications, have never been digitized, so there's no way you'd be able to find them online. They're only available on microfiche or through physical copies stored in local libraries, that kind of thing. If you'd like, I can do some additional digging for you in those places to see if I can come up with anything new."

"Thank you, that would be great."

"My pleasure."

Willow angled toward Britt. "What have you heard from Zander lately?"

"He emailed a few days ago. He's doing well — and, Nora, you'll be pleased to know he's developed an appreciation for tea."

"I knew travel would be good for him," Nora said.

"Good for *him*, yes," Britt said. "Sad for me. His absence is even worse than I expected. I'm irritated with him for leaving, but I'm keeping that secret because I'm an unselfish person."

"You're not doing a terribly good job of keeping it a secret," Willow said wryly.

"Tristan's still here," Nora pointed out.

"The things I found appealing about Tristan are beginning to get on my nerves."

Willow and Nora exchanged a look.

"I don't want to break up with him or anything," Britt hurried to say. "I like Tristan. It's just that he's sort of . . . replaceable. You know? Zander's not."

Text message from Corbin to Willow:

Corbin
What're you up to?

Willow
I just returned home after dinner with my sisters at Nora's house.

Corbin
Want to meet me at Fleming's for dessert?

Willow
Yes and no.

Corbin
?

Willow
Yes, I'd like to meet you. No, I don't want to meet you at Fleming's for dessert. I'm stuffed.

Corbin
Where can I meet you, then?

Willow
Here at Bradfordwood. Since you're in the market for dessert, I'll make you brownies.

CHAPTER EIGHTEEN

"Good afternoon."

Willow jumped at the sound of Joe's voice. She'd been approaching the front door of the barnhouse, chin tilted down, because there was no reason to inadvertently step on a crack out of sheer carelessness.

She spotted Joe as he rose from a chair situated on the patio tucked against the house.

"Good afternoon." She pointed her steps in his direction. She'd interacted with Joe several times since the Monday Night Football dinner, but this was the first time he'd initiated a conversation with her. That he had was a hopeful sign. A pleasant surprise.

"Care to have a seat?" He indicated the wooden chair next to his own.

"Sure." They both sat.

"Corbin's inside. He mentioned that the two of you had plans." He spoke brusquely.

"Yes." When Corbin had been at Brad-

400

fordwood last night, eating the brownies she'd baked for him, he'd sweet-talked her into going hiking with him today.

"Well, I don't want to keep you, but I wondered if I might have a word."

"Of course." She placed her purse on the patio's stone floor and slanted toward him.

Joe sat stiffly, hands braced on his knees.

Corbin was affable, easygoing, and confident with friends and strangers alike. His father couldn't have been more different. The two adjectives that seemed to suit Joe best were *agitated* and *irritable.*

According to Corbin, Joe had been friendly in his younger days. It seemed to Willow that Joe's friendliness had been wrung out of him over time. Or maybe there was still friendliness in Joe for other people, just not for her. If so, that was a shame, because she genuinely admired him for providing for Corbin.

"I'm guessing Corbin has told you . . . about my health?" he asked.

"He has."

He focused his gaze on the stunning foliage before them. Cottony pearl-gray clouds separated just enough to allow the afternoon sunlight to bathe the trees. The light seemed to make the deep crimson and yellow autumn leaves glow.

"And you probably know that he's been trying to talk me into some fool clinical trial."

"Yes."

"Well, that's not going to happen. There's only a few things I want, and one of them is to stay right here. We're close to finishing the renovation, you know."

She nodded.

"It's important to me for the house to be done . . . when I go. It's something he can remember me by. Something we did together."

Compassion pricked her. "I understand."

"Do you?" He cut his attention to her.

"Yes."

He seemed to be taking her measure. "One of the other things I want concerns you." Beneath his lax skin, his jaw firmed. "I've expressed to Corbin my concerns about his relationship with you, but he's set on ignoring me. He thinks I'm wrong and won't see sense."

Her heart gave a sick lurch at Joe's words. So much for thinking his interest in talking to her privately might be a hopeful sign. She waited while he collected himself.

Shortly after she'd started modeling, she'd learned that it was unrealistic to expect everyone to like her. She had plenty of critics who enjoyed saying ugly things about her online. She'd done her best to make her peace with that. She'd accepted that detractors came with her career, and she'd attempted to let their animosity roll off her back.

But this was Corbin's dad, someone she knew personally. She couldn't seem to let his dislike of her roll off her back.

"It's my belief that if two people are both determined to stay together, then they will." His lips twisted. "But that's not what happened between you and Corbin the last time you dated, was it? He was determined that you two would stay together. But you were determined to break up. So you broke up."

"Has Corbin told you the reasons for our breakup?"

He jerked his chin in assent.

She smarted at the unfairness of it. *What about what Corbin did? He's more at fault than I am!* The words she wanted to say in defense of herself lined up in her mind. But as she studied Joe, she opted to hold her tongue.

He wouldn't thank her for casting blame on his son. Worse, she could see that his mind was already made up. Worse still, he wasn't wrong. In the end, she was the one who'd ended things even though Corbin had badly wanted to make things work.

Corbin had told her that his mom's departure from their lives had nearly devastated Joe. If Joe couldn't forgive Dawn for leaving him, then why would Joe forgive her for leaving Corbin?

"You have no idea what your breakup did to him," Joe said. "He wasn't himself for months afterward. He lost interest in football for a whole season, which wasn't like him. Before and after that, he's always loved football."

After she and Corbin had gone their separate ways, it had looked to her like he was having the time of his life. Partying. Dating stunning women. Smiling at the cameras that followed him. Winning football games. "I didn't know that he struggled."

"Because you weren't around to see it. I was, and let me tell you I was worried about him. Up until that time, I'd never had a reason to think that my son had inherited my . . . weaknesses. Of everything in my life, that was one of the things I was most grateful for. I never wanted him to deal with the things I've dealt with. For a while there, it looked to me like he was going to deal with them after all. It frightened me."

It sounded like Joe blamed her for sending Corbin into a depressive episode. Joe, who fathomed the bleakness and despair of a depressive episode with clarity. He understood what her actions had cost Corbin in ways that she couldn't.

Until this moment, she'd been fixated on what Corbin's actions had cost her. She'd felt justified in her decision to break up with him, and so long as she was justified, she hadn't cared how the ramifications of her decision affected Corbin. Except to hope, vengefully, that the ramifications would be dire.

Based on what Joe was telling her, it appeared that she'd gotten her wish. The ramifications of their breakup *had* been dire for Corbin.

She experienced a wrench of regret.

"I don't think anything good can come of a relationship between you and Corbin," Joe said.

She wanted him to be wrong, yet she herself was half convinced he was right.

His knee began to bounce. "Corbin's had a hard go of it lately, what with his shoulder and the end of football. On top of all that, I just . . . I can't have him sad because of you."

His eyes were as hard as caramel-colored marbles. In them, she could see the urgent truth of his statement. He was dying, and he could not stand for her to cause Corbin added grief.

He gestured to the barn. "We have a house to finish." Confusion tweaked his expression. He appeared to be unsure as to whether he'd mentioned the house to her.

"I don't want to cause Corbin sadness," she said. It was true. The silver-tongued former quarterback with the multimillion-dollar skill had far more than his share of sadness coming for him as it was.

Joe grunted to indicate he'd heard. "You're leaving soon, aren't you?"

"Yes, the Monday after Thanksgiving." *Two weeks.*

"We don't know each other well, but I have a request to make of you all the same."

"Okay."

"Could you . . . I don't know . . . ." He shifted uncomfortably. Color stained his cheeks. "Keep things from getting serious between you and Corbin?"

"I've been trying to keep things from getting serious. I'll continue to try."

"When you go, will you stay away?" he asked.

She hesitated, adjusting to the hurt his question brought. She tried to think. Just last night she'd told her sisters that she didn't expect much from her dating relationship with Corbin after she went away. So why should she be reluctant to agree to Joe's request? This was, after all, the request of a dying man.

"My family lives in Merryweather," she said. "How long would you want me to stay away?"

"At least until I'm gone." She saw desolation in Joe. "Will you stay away that long?"

She swallowed. The consequences of her actions and Corbin's actions all those years ago were *still* cropping up. "Yes." Her heart tripped painfully.

"And you won't ask Corbin to come to you?"

"No."

"You'll end things?"

"I think my best play is to switch us into friend mode once I leave. If I were to end things completely when I go, I think he might be furious and suspicious."

"I don't want him to be suspicious," Joe said.

"No," she agreed.

"You won't tell Corbin that I talked to you about this, will you? I don't want him knowing I had anything to do with this."

"I won't tell him."

"You promise?"

"I promise."

"Good, then." His craggy face revealed his relief. "Thank you —"

"Hey," Corbin called.

The sound of Corbin's voice went through Willow like a painful electrical current. She turned to watch him approach. "I saw your car through the window," he said. He wore cargo pants and a Windbreaker. His stride communicated easy athleticism. Max and Duke trotted on either side of him. The light that had graced the leaves now graced him in a way that indicated that he was Michigan's, Texas's, football's *and* sunshine's favorite son.

He grinned at her, and she had to clench her muscles against a bolt of longing.

"What are you two doing out here?" he asked.

"Talking," Willow answered. "Enjoying the view."

"Well, good. It's nice to see you two getting along."

Joe stood. "I'll be going in now. Goodbye, Willow."

"See you, Joe."

Once his dad had disappeared indoors, Corbin gathered her against him. "Was my dad nice to you?"

"He was." In order to keep her promises to Joe, it occurred to her that she was going to have to lie to Corbin. How many lies was she going to have to tell? Quite a few, most likely. Just the idea of that made her nauseous.

Corbin's attention swept slowly down her face, hesitated on her lips, then returned to her eyes. "I missed you."

He often told her he'd missed her. It was a luxury, to be cared about so much that she was missed even after a short time apart. "You just saw me last night. Brownies, remember?"

He pulled a perplexed face and shook his head. "The chocolate chunk brownies that were so gooey I had to eat them with a fork?"

"The very same."

"You must be mistaken. That can't have been last night," he whispered as his mouth neared hers. "I haven't seen you for a month at least." He kissed her. "Where have you been, Willow?" He kissed her again and again, a string of breathless, gentle kisses. "I've really missed you."

Such a piquant mixture of joy and sorrow overcame her that she couldn't locate a suitably flirtatious reply. Her fingers trembled as she interlaced them behind his neck. Was she being traitorous to Joe by interlacing her fingers behind Corbin's neck? Was this "keeping things from getting serious"? Was Joe watching from inside the house?

Corbin swept his thumb along her chin. "Everything okay?"

"Yes," she lied.

"Ready to go?"

She nodded, and he wove his fingers with hers as they walked toward his car. Just before they reached the driveway, a Volvo XC90 came into view, driving in their direction.

An attractive thirty-something brunette brought the car to a stop and rolled her window down. The woman's smile sagged a few degrees as she took in the sight of the two of them holding hands.

Another of Corbin's groupies. Willow freed her fingers from his.

"Sorry to disturb you guys. It looks like you're on your way out," the brunette said. "Corbin, I made a pot of white chicken chili earlier for the kids, and I thought you and your dad might like some. I just dropped by to deliver it."

Corbin introduced Willow to the visitor, whose name was Macy. Both Willow and Macy reacted to the other with obligatory and patently false enthusiasm.

"How did you know that my dad and I

love white chicken chili?" Corbin asked Macy.

"I must have ESP." She laughed.

Answering dimples marked the planes of Corbin's cheeks and Willow knew — knew exactly — the effect that those dimples were having on Macy.

Willow's field of vision tinted red. She did not want Corbin giving those dimples away so easily to other women. Until this moment she wouldn't have thought herself capable of the ferocious possessiveness that submerged her. She'd just finished promising Joe that she'd leave and not come back! Yet she wanted to tell Macy in no uncertain terms that Corbin was hers.

My boyfriend. My husband. My children's father. My soul mate.

Not yours, Macy of the white chicken chili.

Macy walked around the hood of her car and lifted a Crock-Pot from her passenger seat. She passed it to Corbin with what seemed like an inordinate amount of hand contact as control of the handles passed from her to him.

"Thank you," Corbin said. "I'll clean this out and return it to you tomorrow."

"Perfect! Have a nice day."

"You too," Willow said. *You can have your Crock-Pot back, but you cannot have Corbin.*

411

Would Joe find Macy suitable for his son? Probably so, seeing as how she'd apparently been finding her way into the guys' hearts in the tried-and-true fashion — through their stomachs.

Willow waited inside Corbin's car while he ferried the chili to the kitchen. She chewed the inside of her bottom lip, annoyed and so jealous she felt cross-eyed with it. Compulsively, she pulled out her phone, surfed to Nordstrom.com, and scrolled through housewares.

When Corbin returned, he twisted to look over his shoulder to reverse the SUV from the driveway.

"Nice food delivery service you have there." Willow had firmly decided to say nothing about Macy. The statement had slipped out without her permission.

"Yeah. Macy's crush on me has worked out really well for my diet."

"It would seem so."

"Are you jealous?" he asked hopefully, shooting her a glance as he paused to shift the car into drive.

"No."

"Not even a little bit?"

"No." Oh, the lies. Lies upon lies.

"You should be a little bit jealous, Willow, because *a lot* of women like me. Almost all women, actually."

She crinkled her nose. "I don't think I'm supposed to be jealous of the fact that a lot of women like you. It's who *you* like that matters. I'm supposed to be jealous of the women who you like more than me."

"Spoilsport. Because in that case, I don't have a hope of making you jealous." He reached for her hand. She provided it, and he kissed one of her knuckles as they drove. "There are no women I like more than you."

Willow had been to plenty of concerts. Professional, expensive, impressive concerts. But none of them had charmed her half so much as the off-key, amateur concert before her now.

She and Corbin sat next to each other inside Shore Pine Middle School's auditorium. The structure boasted quintessential 1980s architecture, and the air held the faint tang of a bygone spaghetti lunch.

They'd come in support of Charlotte and her fellow seventh and eighth grade orchestra members. The Dixon family flanked Willow and Corbin on both sides, including Charlotte's two brothers, who looked like they'd rather be tarred and feathered than sit through another minute of the recital.

It was Wednesday evening. Three days had

413

passed since Joe had asked Willow to keep her relationship with Corbin light and not to come back once she left. She'd been telling herself that the promises she'd made to Joe hadn't changed much of anything.

However, ever since she'd made the promises, her circumstance felt fully different. The roadblocks preventing her from falling in love with Corbin weren't solely ones she'd built herself. Some of them had now been built by Joe.

Corbin was well and truly off-limits.

And perversely, that fact bothered her.

Now that she couldn't have him, his good qualities were glaringly obvious. He made her laugh. He lightened her sometimes too-serious side. He seemed to be under the impression that she'd hung the moon. His treatment of his father had proved him to be more responsible and sacrificial than she'd understood him to be four years before.

Corbin's shoulder nudged hers. He leaned his mouth near her ear. "Is the dark-haired kid in the bow tie playing the violin or is he having a seizure?"

Her lips twitched. "Hard to tell."

"I may call an ambulance. If paramedics arrive, they could not only help the kid but put a stop to this early."

"I don't want them to put a stop to this. I'm loving it."

"What?"

"It's adorable to watch the kids play."

"Kittens are adorable. Rookie pre-teen musicians aren't."

"Yes, they are."

"You're a softie."

"For some things?" Anything that had to do with kids and families? "Yes."

The musical piece came to an end, and the audience applauded. "I bet you played an instrument when you were in the seventh grade," Corbin said to her over the din.

"I did."

"Let me guess. The flute?"

"No. I was a percussionist." At his look of astonishment she said, "For a fleeting moment in middle school I imagined that I might like to play drums in a girl band."

He laughed.

"Did you play an instrument?" she asked.

"Do I look like I played an instrument?"

"No."

"Thank you."

"It wasn't a compliment."

He chuckled. "I'm going to kiss you senseless for that later."

At the performance's end, Charlotte's brothers burst from their chairs like rockets.

Willow and Corbin chatted with the Dixon family in the school's foyer until Charlotte joined them. When she did, Corbin handed her the bouquet of roses he'd brought.

Charlotte's cheeks turned pink with delight.

Don't fall in love with him, Willow! You can't. Quit it!

Once Charlotte had put in time visiting with her cheering section, Corbin and Willow bundled her into Corbin's car and set off for The Pie Emporium.

Earlier in the day, Nora had contacted Willow to let her know that she'd found and printed out some articles concerning Josephine's case. Willow had swung by and picked up the stack of pages. Now she, Corbin, and Charlotte were off to celebrate Charlotte's recital with pie while combing through Nora's papers.

The Pie Emporium was one of more than a dozen buildings located within Merryweather Historical Village. Warmth greeted them as they passed from the misty night into the clapboard building's cozy interior.

Willow ordered a slice of pecan pie crowned by a dollop of whipped cream. Corbin ordered apple a la mode. Charlotte went with chocolate cream.

Charlotte set the wooden box containing

Josephine paraphernalia on one of the shop's round tables. "I decided to bring the box after my mom told me you had new articles and stuff to put inside it," Charlotte said to Willow.

"Nice to see you again, box." Corbin gave it an affectionate pat. "You're looking good."

Willow divided Nora's research evenly between them.

"You know, Willow," Charlotte said, "if you want to take the box home with you until the next meeting, I'll let you."

"You will?" Charlotte's offer was akin to a teacher offering to let a student take home the prized class hamster for the weekend.

"Yes."

"Then sure. I'd love to."

"What about me? Can I take the box home?" Corbin asked.

"Um . . ." Charlotte giggled. "Probably not."

Corbin gave the twelve-year-old a look of mock outrage, which goaded her into fresh giggles.

An assortment of decorative pie plates and signs bearing quotes about pie looked down at them from the walls as they ate and read the articles one by one.

"Here's something," Corbin said after a time.

Willow and Charlotte instantly raised their faces.

"This is from an interview with a television actor that ran in the *Seattle Post-Intelligencer* in 1979. The reporter asked the actor if he finds time to relax with his busy shooting schedule. The actor answered," Corbin began to read, " 'I do find time, yes. In fact, I just came back from a week at Senator Foster Holt's cabin on the Fraser River.' " He met Willow's gaze. "It sounds like the senator may have had one more vacation property we didn't know about."

"Where's the Fraser River?" Charlotte asked.

Corbin went to work on his phone. Within a few seconds, he showed them a map that revealed the Fraser River snaking through British Columbia.

"When I asked Nora to search for the senator's properties, she searched for properties here in America," Willow said.

"How far away is this river by car from where Senator Holt lives in Redmond?" Corbin asked.

"Some points along that river are probably less than a three-hour drive from Redmond," Willow answered.

"Then of the three vacation properties the senator owned in the late '70s, this cabin would have been the closest, distance-wise, to his house," Corbin said.

"Yes."

"Which would have been convenient for him if he'd needed to get someone out of the way quicker than the way he did with Vickie Goff."

Charlotte clicked her pen over and over in rapid succession. "Are you thinking we should ask to have Josephine's age-progression portrait put up near the Senator's cabin?"

"It couldn't hurt," Corbin answered.

"It looks like the Fraser River is, um, pretty long," Charlotte said. "How are we supposed to figure out where his cabin is? Or was? It's probably not still there, right? Because it's super old?"

"I don't know how to find out where the cabin was located," Willow said. "But now that we know what we're looking for and have a general idea of where to look, I'll bet you a K-pop T-shirt that my sister Nora will know what to do."

"No deal." Charlotte's smile glinted with metal braces. "I can't risk any of my K-pop T-shirts."

Corbin's eyes met Willow's. The smokiness in their depths informed her of two things.

419

He'd come to care about her. A lot.
He'd promised earlier to kiss her senseless.

Note left by Josephine's husband, Alan, on their kitchen table, April 22, 1977, ten days after Josephine's disappearance:

I have to return to work today. If you come home and find this, drive immediately to Shore Pine High to find me. I love you, sweetheart. I've been out of my mind with worry and grief and nightmares.

Every day, I've waited for you to walk in the door. Now that I'm about to walk out that same door to go to work, I'm sick with the thought that you'll come home and find the house empty.

If you do, come to me. I'm desperate for you.

CHAPTER NINETEEN

Willow was sitting cross-legged on her bed at Bradfordwood, folding clean laundry, when her phone rang near noon the following day. "Hi, Nora."

"Hi. I've located the title to Foster Holt's fishing cabin on the Fraser River," her sister said proudly.

"Already?"

"I found it through tax records."

"You're amazing! Thank you."

"I'll text you the cabin's exact address."

Moments later, Nora's text arrived. Willow lifted her laptop from her bedside table, set it before her on the mattress, and mapped the location of the cabin.

A long segment of the Fraser River meandered horizontally through southern British Columbia. The cabin appeared to be located in a remote stretch of that segment, far from civilization.

Shoot. Josephine's age-progression poster

421

would need to be seen by a large number of people to have any hope of creating even one good lead. The two towns nearest the cabin were both tiny. In a radius outward from them, numerous other small towns dotted the map. The population appeared to be thinly spread through the whole area.

From the starting point of the cabin, where might Josephine have gone?

Willow had no idea.

She tucked her cell phone in the back pocket of her jeans and carried her computer downstairs. Last night when she'd returned from The Pie Emporium, she'd placed the wooden Josephine box on the dining room table.

Bradfordwood's dining room stood adjacent to the foyer and overlooked the home's front drive. At the moment, the sky beyond its windows hung low, streaming rain.

The Pacific Northwest was famous for its rain, and with good reason. The movie *Sleepless in Seattle,* for one. The fact that it really did rain a lot, another.

Of all twelve months of the year, November was the rainiest. Willow hadn't spent a whole November here since she'd left for UCLA and had forgotten the reality of a Merryweather November. It had rained more days than not so far this month. Even when it wasn't raining, sunbeams only reached the ground a third of the time.

She thoroughly enjoyed the rain. It was beautiful. Moody. And since she was a homebody at heart, snuggling up at home with a fire, a mug of coffee, and a book was no hardship. Yet even she was beginning to crave the sun. Perhaps she needed to start taking Vitamin D supplements.

Willow flipped the switch to light the room's chandelier, then set her computer on the glossy table. She carefully opened the lid of the box that held everything Melinda had left of her sister Josephine.

Willow's mind spun with a kaleidoscope of memories of all that she'd shared with her sisters. Afternoons playing make-believe in the woods. Weekend mornings sailing on the Hood Canal with their dad. Birthday parties. Fights over clothes. The camaraderie and trust and friendship of their adult years. Her sisters were inextricably linked to her. Their histories were intertwined more tightly than any braid.

Like Josephine, Willow was the eldest of the three. She couldn't imagine having one of her sisters vanish. Just the thought of it chilled her. Nor could she imagine, four decades later, having nothing more to show for that sister than a wooden box and a host of haunting questions.

What happened to you, Josephine?

She wanted to find the woman who'd disappeared on the day of the year that would become Willow's birthday. Josephine, the smiling brunette in the terry-cloth one-piece. Josephine, who'd been smart and determined and idealistic enough to involve herself in politics and social work.

Had Josephine's husband killed her? Had the man from church she'd been rumored to be having an affair with kill her? Or his wife? Why had Stan Markum disappeared the same day? Did Senator Holt, with his affinity for curvy, dark-haired women, have anything to do with it? Or had Josephine's disappearance been the result of terrible chance? Had a vicious man, like the man who'd killed Nora's mother, come upon her at exactly the wrong moment? Or had Josephine's disappearance been purposeful? Had Josephine decided to walk off the stage of her own life either through suicide or through a carefully crafted escape?

Lord, grant me wisdom.

She spent the next forty-five minutes removing every item from the box and aligning them in chronological order across the table. When she stepped back, the display created a timeline of sorts depicting Josephine's life.

Photos and mementos from her girlhood. Her graduation portrait and diploma. The charm bracelet. A photograph from her wedding. And numerous other items.

And then came April 12, 1977. That day was the line of demarcation. After that, the keepsakes were mostly comprised of articles and sympathy cards. No photographs except for the Polaroids taken by Alan of the interior of Josephine's eerily empty car. No belongings that had been personal to Josephine in any way.

Willow scanned the articles. The back of her neck tingled with . . . what? A warning? A reminder?

Had she forgotten something she should have remembered about the articles? Frowning, she considered the timeline. Many of the articles had been published by the *Shore Pine Gazette* in the two weeks directly following Josephine's disappearance. Others had run at later dates, including the five-year, ten-year, and twenty-year anniversaries of the day Josephine went missing.

Willow had read every one of the articles in the past, but now she studied each one again in turn. Two of the articles were stapled to handwritten notes. These were part of a small grouping that had been sent to the Blake family from strangers or friends living in faraway places.

Willow fingered the edge of the first one, which had been sent from Mexico, along with a card that had a picture of flowers on its front.

The second had arrived from Alaska. The brief article, which included a grainy picture of Josephine, had been stapled to a piece of pink stationery.

The third article hadn't been stapled to anything because the sender's short sentiment was written vertically onto the margin of the article. *So very sorry. Thinking of you.* Willow squinted to read the article.

It summarized the basic facts of Josephine's case. Nothing about the article was unique, except that it had run at the top of its newspaper page, thus the date and the name of the newspaper were displayed in small print across the uppermost portion of the clipping.

The Mission Tribune
April 26, 1977

Wait. Something about that was ringing a bell. . . .

Mission. She'd heard of it before. Where was Mission located? Willow opened her computer and ran a search for Mission within Google Maps. The website gave her a menu of options.

Mission TX
Mission Viejo CA
Mission KS
Mission Tejas State Park
Mission Beach San Diego

She shook her head. Only three of those were towns, and only two were towns named Mission. Mission, Texas? Mission, Kansas? No. Neither seemed right.

She navigated to Google and typed in *City of Mission.* Almost immediately search results populated.

City of Mission TX
City of Mission BC
City of Mission Viejo

There. The second listing, Mission, B.C. Goose bumps rose on Willow's skin because B.C. stood for British Columbia. That's the Mission she'd heard of.

Willow enlarged a map of southern British Columbia until it filled her computer screen. Narrowing her eyes, she hunted for Mission.

There. Situated in a crook of the Fraser River, east of Vancouver.

She snatched up the article and scrutinized it, front and back.

So very sorry. Thinking of you had been written in messy, awkward block letters. It looked like the person who'd written it had done so painstakingly. Either because they were very old. Shaky. Or writing with their non-dominant hand.

To disguise their penmanship?

Was there any chance . . . Could this article have been sent to the Blake family by Josephine herself?

So very sorry. Thinking of you was something Josephine might have wanted to say to the people she'd left behind. Logically, it was also something a kindly stranger or an acquaintance of the family might have wanted to say.

Like all the paper artifacts stored in the wooden box, this paper showed signs of age. It had yellowed. One corner had tattered. Willow held it up to the light. A few circular stains marked it, very faintly. She set it down and ran the pad of her index finger over those spots. They were a tiny bit stiffer, more crinkly, than the rest . . . as though water had dropped on this article at some point, then dried.

Tearstains?

They could as easily have been spots of rain. Or tea. Or soda. But their circular pattern did seem to indicate droplets of some kind.

Willow conjured a vision in her imagination. A young Josephine, who'd traveled to the senator's fishing cabin either by choice or by force, reading this article about her own disappearance. Carefully cutting it out. Crying over it. Writing the note with her opposite hand. Then mailing it to her family anonymously.

The envelopes that had carried the articles from Mexico, Alaska, and Canada hadn't been saved. Thus, there was no way to check any of those envelopes for a return address.

Willow read Mission's Wikipedia profile. Nestled in the central Fraser Valley in the shade of Mount Robie Reid, the town of under forty thousand had been founded in 1868 and named Mission for its nearness to St. Mary's Mission.

She ran a search for address and telephone information on Josephine Blake, resident of Mission, British Columbia. No hits.

Undaunted, she used the address Nora had given her for the fishing cabin and researched the distance between the cabin and the town of Mission.

Just 25.02 miles.

She dialed Melinda.

"Hello, Willow."

"Hi, Melinda. Sorry to disturb you. I was just looking through your box of Josephine mementos and came back across an article written after Josephine's disappearance that ran in a newspaper in the town of Mission, British Columbia. The words 'So very sorry. Thinking of you' are written in the margin."

"Mmm hmm. Yes. I think I know which one you're talking about."

"Do you know who sent this? Did your family have friends or relatives in Mission?"

"No, not that I can remember."

"Did it come directly to your house or to your parents' house? Or was it sent to the city of Shore Pine or the police of Shore Pine and passed to your family?"

"I have no idea. What is it about that article that's caught your interest?"

Willow relayed the information about the fishing cabin.

"Interesting," Melinda said.

"Do you think there's any possibility that Josephine herself might have sent this?"

"Why? As a kind of clue?"

"Not necessarily, since she took pains to disguise her handwriting. Perhaps she sent it because she wanted to say that she was

430

sorry and that she was thinking of you."

"If she had the ability to write and send letters and if she wanted to say she was sorry, then she could have written a letter to us explaining what had occurred. Why wouldn't she have done that?"

"I don't know," Willow answered.

"Do I think there's a possibility that Josephine sent that article? No," Melinda said with her trademark pragmatism. "I don't. I've always believed that she died the day she went missing or shortly thereafter, Willow."

"I understand." Not for the first time, Willow wondered if she was doing Melinda a disservice by digging up the past. Asking questions about Josephine. Forcing Melinda to dwell on the painful topic of her missing sister. Stirring up hope when it might be more humane to let Melinda's long-gone hope stay dead.

"What do you plan to do?" Melinda asked. "With this information about the fishing cabin and Mission?"

"I plan to ask the American Coalition for the Discovery of Missing Persons to circulate posters of Josephine in Mission, British Columbia."

Corbin watched the teeth of his miter saw

bite cleanly through a strip of beechwood. He'd been working in his garage most of the day. Physically, he'd been cutting crown moulding. Mentally, he'd been thinking about Willow.

He and Willow spent time together every day. She let him take her places. She let him kiss her. He knew that she liked him in a general sense. But he was not making the kind of progress with her that he needed to make. Willow didn't want to talk about the future or even about the present of their relationship. She kept insisting that they were having fun but that they weren't together. And reminding him that she was leaving soon.

He was a speeding train and Willow's departure from Washington was a granite mountain. The train tracks ended at the mountain's face, which meant the coming crash was drawing nearer every day.

He had to find a way to soften her heart toward him before she left. He had to.

Worry that he'd fail at that, that she'd leave him like she'd left him before, had begun to greet him every morning and stay with him until he stretched out in bed at night.

He couldn't fail, and yet he might soon have to admit to himself that he didn't know how to succeed with Willow. He'd been racking his brain, struggling to understand the combination of words and actions that might break apart her distrust of him.

His dad approached, carrying several more lengths of wood. Corbin acknowledged him with a dip of his chin.

He'd been lobbying his dad for a week now about enrolling in one of the clinical trials. He'd stayed up late each night researching treatments. Holistic approaches. Middle eastern medicines. South American remedies that claimed success. And every other thing the Internet had to offer. He'd read it all, and he'd talked to his dad about the less-crazy choices.

Corbin was a forceful person used to getting his way, but so far his dad was flat-out refusing to consider any of the options.

He hated that he was the only person, other than his father, involved in this decision. Corbin had no siblings. His dad had no wife. Corbin was it, his father's closest family member. As heavy as that responsibility had seemed at other points in Corbin's life, it had never seemed heavier than it did now.

His dad handed him a fresh piece of moulding, and Corbin positioned it beneath the saw's blade. As they worked, Corbin

433

launched into another speech aimed at convincing his dad to try one of the trials.

His dad stood at the end of the workbench, saying nothing, passing Corbin piece after piece of wood. When Corbin finished, he switched off the machine, tugged free his gloves, and removed his safety goggles. "So, how about it? I'll handle everything that's needed for the trial. I'll get everything in place. You won't have to do anything but show up for appointments."

His father set his shoulders defensively. "I've heard everything you've had to say, and I know that it's coming from a good place. I know that you have my best interests at heart, just like I hope you know I've always had your best interests at heart." He waited, expectant.

"Yes."

"In this case, your idea of what's best for me and my idea of what's best for me are different. But the thing is, we're talking about *my* life here. I know that my life affects yours. I understand that. But I've lived my life my way all this time. That's been my right and my freedom. Now I want to die my way. I want you to give me the freedom and the right to do that."

"Dad —"

"My mind's made up," his dad said.

Corbin couldn't speak through the pain.

"My mind's made up," he repeated.

What Corbin hadn't seen or been willing to see until now was that time had already run out on this particular battle. His father had decided how he wanted to spend the final stage of his life, long before Corbin had even realized that cancer had taken the upper hand.

"I don't want to argue about this with you," his dad said. "I don't want you staying up till all hours on the computer because that's just wasted time right there. What I want is for us to get along, same as we've always gotten along. And I want to finish this house."

Corbin clamped his jaw shut to keep his opinions from spilling out.

"I'm not afraid of dying, but I can't take any more talking about multiple myeloma treatments," his dad said.

Silence.

"Son?"

Mentally, Corbin forced himself to lay down his hope that medicine might save his dad's life. As soon as he did, a new priority rose. If he couldn't save his dad's life, then he needed to do what he could to secure his dad's afterlife. Right?

Is that what it had come down to now?

His dad was going to die, and maybe soon. Which meant there was only one thing left that Corbin could do to impact his dad's future. "I'll make you a deal. I'll stop talking about multiple myeloma treatments if you'll start going to church with me on Sundays and if you'll let me schedule a meeting between you and the pastor."

His dad screwed up his face. "Why would I want to see a pastor?"

Corbin gave him a pointed look.

His dad's ruddy skin turned red, something it often did when he got riled. "You — you want me to talk to him about heaven and all that?"

"Exactly."

"There's no need for me to talk with some fool pastor."

Corbin and his dad had entered churches more often for funerals and weddings than they ever had for Sunday services when Corbin was young.

"The alternative is to talk to me about it," Corbin said.

"You just started believing earlier this year. How much do you know about it all?"

"Not enough. Which is why I'd rather you talk to someone who's more educated about it than I am."

"I'm not talking to a pastor."

436

Great. Now his dad's care *and* his dad's salvation rested on Corbin's shoulders. He didn't feel near worthy enough to talk to anyone about God. "You're stuck with me, then."

"I have been for thirty-five years," his dad quipped, amusement cracking through the stubbornness stamped on his face. "If we talk about God, you'll stop nagging me about those idiot treatments that won't work?"

"Yes."

"Deal." He began to move away.

"Dad."

The older man paused.

"I'm sorry if I've added to your stress this last week," Corbin said.

"It's all right." Joe opened his arms. "C'mere."

Corbin gave him a hug complete with the two usual back slaps.

Soon, Corbin wouldn't be able to hug his father, hear his voice, look into the face that was more familiar to Corbin than any other face in the world. His first supporter, the one who'd always loved him, the one who'd never left, was dying.

He wanted to scream, *No!* That he couldn't made him feel as if he were hyperventilating. He wished he could give his dad his own strength and health. He wished he could beat the cancer, the one opponent he most wanted to conquer. He wished he could unload some of his own powerful will to fight into his father. He wished he'd managed to convince his dad to attempt a trial or an experimental treatment.

But none of those wishes were going to come true.

His dad's mind was made up.

Phone call from Roger from the American Coalition for the Discovery of Missing Persons to Willow:

Roger: I'm calling to let you know that we distributed the posters of Josephine in Mission two days ago. Since then, we've received three phone calls from people who say that they know the woman in the picture.

Willow: Three calls?

Roger: We've actually received far more calls than three, thanks to the posters. What's promising about the calls I mentioned is that all three people said that the woman's name is Felicia Richmond. Apparently Felicia owns a small but popular plant nursery called Haven Gardens on the outskirts of town.

438

Willow: Felicia Richmond?

Roger: Yes. Whenever we receive corroborating accounts from multiple callers, we sit up and take notice.

Willow: Oh my goodness. . . . Do you think that Felicia might be Josephine?

Roger: It's possible, but I feel compelled to caution you. It could be a coincidence that the age-progression portrait of Josephine resembles Felicia. Felicia might not be connected to Josephine in any way.

CHAPTER TWENTY

Willow sat in her Range Rover in the parking lot of the Wallace Rehabilitation Center, her attention trained on the building's front door. Her heater chugged against the forty-five degree temperature outside. Dark gray fringed the canopy of a sky that looked to be considering the merits of turning stormy.

The moment she'd finished talking with Roger about Felicia Richmond, she'd checked her watch. It was Tuesday, and on Tuesday afternoons Charlotte coached Corbin through his PT sessions before the two of them drove to the inn, aka League of Justice Headquarters, for their meetings.

Since the news Roger had given Willow was too momentous to keep to herself until their meeting, Willow had decided to intercept them here instead —

The automatic sliding doors zoomed open, and Corbin strode out. Her breath caught with pleasure at the sight of him.

She turned off the ignition, grabbed her red coat, and cinched its sash as she waited for him near her front bumper. Chilly air that smelled of fir, rain, and ocean enveloped her.

Corbin hadn't yet seen her, so she took advantage of the chance to study him without his knowledge. He wore a black waterproof jacket over his workout clothes. He held his keys in one muscular hand. He walked purposefully, head bent, rugged features troubled.

No doubt, he was thinking about his dad. She fisted her hands against an instinctive need to comfort him. To love him.

You can't love him!

Loving him would not be good for her.

Not good at all.

Thanksgiving was the day after tomorrow. Her flight left Monday, just six days from now. The manager her mom had hired to run the inn had arrived. She'd been training him and — no surprise — he was more than accomplished. More than ready to take over.

Corbin lifted his chin and caught sight of her. As soon as he did, a crooked grin overtook his face.

She didn't need Vitamin D. That smile was sunlight to her.

All at once Willow wanted to cry. Because she was leaving. Because she was scared to let herself love him. Because of the promises she'd made to Joe. How in the world was she going to say good-bye to Corbin without telling him about the promises she'd made to his dad?

He walked to her, took her face in his hands, and kissed her. "This is a nice surprise."

"You're not worried I'm stalking you?"

"I don't think I'm lucky enough to have you as a stalker. Speaking of stalkers, have you seen yours around lately?"

"Nope."

He kissed her again and, in response, delight swirled at the backs of her knees. Almost three weeks had passed since their first kiss. They'd spent time together every day since then and, impossibly, every kiss was somehow sweeter than the last.

"Corbin?"

"Yes?"

"You're kissing me in the parking lot of the Wallace Rehabilitation Center."

"This is rehabilitating me, that's for sure."

"We're in a parking lot."

He pulled back a few inches. "Would you rather we go inside the center and kiss there?"

"Charlotte will see us!"

He rested his hands on the side of her neck. "I couldn't care less if Charlotte sees."

"Where is she?"

"In the restroom. I came out ahead of her so I could warm up the car —"

"I knew it!" Charlotte called from far away, voice ringing with triumph.

"I think she saw us," he whispered.

They stepped apart.

Charlotte rushed to them, eyes glittering. The faux fur on the hood of her parka encircled her face. "I knew you guys were together!"

"How'd you know?" Corbin asked.

"Because you're always staring at Willow like you're in love with her."

"No!" he protested.

"And you're always staring at Corbin like you're in love with him."

"No!" Willow squeaked, alarmed.

"Yes," Charlotte said, planting her hands on her hips. "How long has this been going on?"

"Just a little while," Corbin said.

"Why didn't you tell me?"

"We just did," Corbin said.

Willow clapped her hands together once to command their attention. "Enough about that. I drove here so that I could tell you

443

both, in person, that we might have a break in our case." She related the call from Roger. "I ran a phone and address search for Felicia Richmond. No phone records came up. But look . . ." She extracted a small sheet of paper from her coat pocket and held it out so they could see what she'd written. "An address did come up."

Charlotte covered her mouth with her hands. *"We've found Josephine?"*

"The answer to that is maybe. I don't know if we have. But . . . maybe?" Willow extended her cell phone to the girl. "I thought you should be the one to call your grandma and tell her about our lead."

"Yeah. Sure! Oh my gosh."

Charlotte turned and took a few steps away to have her conversation.

"We couldn't have found Josephine," Corbin said to Willow. "Could we?"

"I would have bet against it. Until today."

"No one who met me when I was a kid would have bet on me playing in the NFL one day."

"She wants to talk to you," Charlotte said to Willow, offering her the phone.

Willow took it. "Hello?"

"Do you think that this Felicia Richmond could be Josephine?"

"It's possible. Felicia owns a nursery. Was

444

Josephine a gardener?"

"No, she wasn't." A space of quiet. "In order to settle this, we'll need to go and meet Felicia for ourselves."

"If you'd rather call, I can look up the number for the nursery. I'm sure you could get her on the phone that way."

"And give her another chance to disappear before I can see her? I need to be able to see her with my own eyes. That's the only way I'll know for sure if it's her."

"What do you suggest?"

"That we all drive to Mission on Friday. You, me, Charlotte, and Corbin. Charlotte said you have an address."

"I do."

"Then we'll drive to her address. And we'll knock on her door. And then we'll see."

So far Corbin's discussions with his father about faith were going about as well as the Exxon Valdez voyage.

"Praying a prayer seems too easy, Corbin." They were sitting across from each other at the breakfast table.

"I know."

"You just say a prayer, and then you go to heaven when you die?"

"If you believed what you were saying, then yes."

His dad's face puckered. "I've never been one for praying out loud."

"You can pray silently."

"If I do this, are you going to expect me to pray out loud before meals and such?"

"No."

"Nobody better try to hold my hand while *they* pray out loud, either."

Corbin took a desperate sip of coffee.

"And I don't like hymns," Joe stated. "You're not going to make me listen to hymns, are you?"

"I don't like hymns, either, Dad. In case you forgot, I didn't grow up in church singing church music. Praying out loud and hymns are things that religious people do, but they're not the main thing. The way I understand it, the main things are believing and asking for forgiveness."

His dad ran a hand over his scruffy cheek, then shook his head. "I just don't buy it, Corbin. Christianity seems like something people invented to make themselves feel better about death."

One of the necessities of autumn in the Pacific Northwest? A good bathrobe.

Willow stepped from the shower at 5:15 p.m., dried off, then wrapped herself in her favorite pink velour robe. She combed out

446

her wet hair, donned slippers, and hurried downstairs to retrieve her phone. She'd left it in her purse and wanted to stay up-to-date with the text conversation she, Nora, and Britt had been having about the "last supper" her sisters were hosting for her the night before her flight to New York.

She scooped up her phone. No hurry. She still had a full hour before Corbin was scheduled to pick her up for tonight's date. They were attending a black-tie fundraiser in Tacoma benefitting the NFL Foundation. Willow had brought only one fancy dress with her to Washington, a navy confection with a beaded halter-style top and a voluminous skirt. She was delighted to finally have a reason to wear it. And she couldn't wait to see Corbin in a tuxedo.

She was turning back in the direction of the staircase when she caught sight of movement beyond the den's windows. She stopped and tried to make out what she'd seen, but the sun set early in November. The familiar view was a study in shades of charcoal and black.

All manner of wild creatures visited Bradfordwood. It wasn't uncommon to spot them on the lawn. She went to the light switches next to the French doors and flipped on the outdoor floodlights.

They illuminated a man's figure, running out of sight around the corner of the house.

Willow's heart contracted. She'd only had one long glimpse of him before he'd disappeared, but it had been enough. She recognized his heavy build. The olive skin. Shaved head.

Todd Hill. Todd Hill had snuck inside Bradfordwood's protective gates. He'd no doubt been watching her just now, in her robe. Fear squeezed her consciousness, threatening her ability to move, to think.

Valentina and Clint, the only two people who were sometimes on the property with her, had both gone home. She was the only one here.

Corbin. She should call Corbin. He would help her —

What? No. He was too far away.

She scrambled toward the alarm keypad. She'd armed it earlier, hadn't she? Yes. It was still armed. She kicked off her slippers — bare feet were faster — and flew to each of the downstairs doors to make certain they were locked. They were.

She dashed inside the hallway powder room, locked the door behind her, and dialed the Merryweather police. An officer informed her that a squad car was on its way. Using her phone, she remotely opened

Bradfordwood's gate so that the police would be able to drive all the way to the house.

Thud thud thud. Todd knocked on the front door.

Willow flinched against the ominous sound.

"Willow!" he yelled from outside. "I just want the chance to talk to you. Things went wrong the last time, but I know if you'd let me explain myself you'd see that I don't mean you any harm."

"You jumped my fence and violated a restraining order," she whispered, voice shaking.

More insistent knocking. "Willow!" A moment of silence. More knocking. "Willow, I promise I won't hurt you. I just want to talk to you. That's all." The front door rattled on its hinges. "Can you open up?"

Not going to happen.

Her breath came fast and jagged. She felt all wrong. Too faint. Her fingers weren't working as well as they normally did, either, because it took two tries to pull up Corbin's contact details. She hit Call.

"Hello?"

Hearing his voice gave her a shot of courage. Her eyes briefly sank closed. "Todd is here."

449

"What."

"Todd is here, at Bradfordwood. I came downstairs and noticed movement outside, so I switched on the lights and saw him. The security system is on, and I've called the police. They're sending officers who should be here soon." The words tumbled out in a rush.

"I'm on my way." His tone rang with forceful reassurance. With those four words he communicated *You're going to be fine* and *I'm going to kill him* and *You can count on me.* She heard rustling in the background of the call. Then static caused by wind. He was running. "Stay on the line with me."

"Okay."

"Where are you inside the house?"

"The downstairs hall bathroom. There are no windows in here, so I can't see what's going on but I can hear him at the front door. He's knocking and saying he wants a chance to talk with me."

"Do you have a weapon with you?"

"I only have my phone with me."

"Is there a baseball bat in the house?"

"I don't think so."

"Golf clubs?"

"Yes, but my dad keeps them in the garage and the garage feels far away."

450

"What about a poker? For the fire?"

"Yes. In the den."

"Go get it."

She bit her lip and had to force herself to unlock the bathroom door. But really, the simple doorknob lock on the bathroom door wasn't going to protect her if Todd was able to get past the far stronger locks at the front of the house. If he did get past them, she'd rather be holding a fire poker.

She ran to the den. Grabbed the poker and returned to the bathroom. Re-locked the door. "Got it."

"Good."

A surge of ferocity went through her as she gripped the long strip of metal with white knuckles. Now she wasn't defenseless.

Corbin asked for updates on Todd. She told him that Todd was still calling for her. Still occasionally banging on and rattling the door.

He explained to her where and how to hit Todd with the poker if it came to that. When he guaranteed her that she was strong enough and brave enough to bring Todd down, she believed him.

All at once, the noise Todd had been making ceased. Willow didn't know whether to take that as a terrible sign or a good sign. Where were the police? It felt as though a great deal of time had passed since she'd called them, but that was probably wrong. Anxiety made every minute into a marathon.

Corbin remained with her over the phone. A lifeline. A comfort.

"I hear sirens," she finally said.

He released an exhale, as if he'd been holding his breath.

She refused to let her guard down, so she remained where she was, listening to Corbin, holding the fire poker as the sirens drew nearer.

Her phone beeped to let her know she had an incoming call. "The police are trying to contact me."

"Okay. I'll be there in a minute."

She clicked over. They informed her that they were pulling up to her residence. She crept out of the bathroom, pulled the lapels of her robe more tightly closed, and opened the door for them. After she'd explained what had happened, they searched the house. Todd was nowhere within.

Another squad car arrived and two of the officers remained with her while the others set out to find Todd on Bradfordwood's grounds.

She was jittery and a robe wasn't the clothing she'd have chosen to wear in the company of intruders and policemen. But all in all, it could have been so much worse. Todd had frightened her, but he hadn't injured her.

She filled the teakettle and set it over a burner. She'd grab a mug of chamomile and take it upstairs to sip on while she changed.

She was watching steam wisp up from the teakettle's spout, idly listening to the officer in the den as he talked to his colleague at the station, when she heard the front door open and shut. She looked up in time to see Corbin fill the dining room doorway.

He was dressed in tuxedo pants and a tuxedo shirt opened at the throat. He looked pale, shaken, and coldly furious. His dark eyes were seething. But when he crossed to her and took her in his arms, his embrace expressed nothing but tenderness and protection.

"Are you all right?" he asked roughly.

"I'm fine."

He examined her face to verify the truth of her statement for himself.

"He never came inside," she said.

He guided her head against his chest, and she soaked in the power and heat flowing from him. She worked to memorize the feel of him, the nuances of his solidity. To be held by Corbin Stewart was sheer bliss.

Complete security. Which was ironic, considering that she'd long considered him to be the greatest threat to her security. "After I drink some tea and finish getting ready for our night out, I should be back to normal," she said. She didn't believe that fully, but she wanted to sound as daring as he thought her to be.

"We don't have to go to the fundraiser, Willow."

"There's no way we're not going. I'm determined to wear the dress I brought."

"I'll do whatever you want to do. I just don't want you to feel pressured to go."

"Did I mention that my dress has a taffeta and organza skirt?"

"No."

"And that I'm wearing coral shoes? And long gold earrings?"

"No."

"Well, I am. I've been looking forward to this. I wouldn't miss it."

The answering kiss he pressed against the crown of her head assured her he'd take her wherever she wanted to go.

In that instant, standing barefoot in the kitchen, with a teakettle beginning to whistle and a police officer pretending not to notice what was going on between them, Willow forgave Corbin.

She'd told him that she'd forgiven him a while back, but now she really did. She forgave him for the mistakes he'd made four years ago. She forgave him for breaking her heart. It seemed possible that the things he'd told her about the events that led to their breakup might all be true. And if so, it was feasible that she'd been wrong not to give him the second chance he'd so badly wanted at the time. It could be that she deserved more than fifteen percent of the blame for their split.

Regardless of who deserved what percent of the blame, she forgave him for his share. And it felt like freedom to let the last of the accusation and hurt melt away.

Late that night, Willow lay in bed, eyes closed, replaying and replaying the evening's events. Unable to sleep.

At the fundraiser Corbin had put in an admirable amount of time socializing with her at his side. The rest of the evening, he'd been focused solely on her. They'd discussed what happened with Todd at length. They'd both recounted the times over the years when fans had overstepped boundaries. She had a few stories. He had many. It had helped to talk it out.

The police had found and arrested Todd.

He'd rented a boat a few miles down the canal. Run it up onto the sand of the inlet. Then hiked to the main house.

He'd told the authorities that he'd never breached Bradfordwood's acres before. Willow decided to accept that as fact because the alternative, Todd watching her on prior occasions, was too creepy to stomach.

When she and Corbin returned to Bradfordwood near one in the morning, Nora and Britt had been there to meet them. They'd brought their overnight bags and insisted on staying.

Good sisters. Willow had brought them up well.

After Corbin had gone home, the three sisters had talked and snacked on chocolate-covered açaí berries before settling into the bedrooms that had belonged to each of them when they'd been young. They'd left their doors open to the shared hall, where one light remained on. Just like the old days.

Willow opened her eyes and contemplated the ceiling.

When terror had been racing through her earlier, it hadn't been Nora or Britt that she'd called. Even John would have been a logical option. He was former military and, no doubt, handy with trespassers.

Instead, she'd called Corbin. Now, hours

456

later, the fact that she'd done so somewhat surprised her. But there it was. Her fear had stripped away her misgivings about him, and of all people, he was the one she'd called.

Four years ago his actions had given her cause to doubt him. But today, when it had mattered, his actions had been as dependable as concrete. She'd faced a trial, and he'd come through for her.

And she might just . . . love him a little for it.

Oh no.

Oh yes.

She loved him.

She'd fallen in love with Corbin Stewart for the second time.

Love was an intensely powerful emotion, but it wasn't always the smartest of entities. Was it possible to control whom you loved? Perhaps in part. But not fully. Sometimes, you just loved. Love didn't always take direction well.

How she responded to her feelings for Corbin — that part, she could control. She wasn't ready to jump headlong into anything with him at this point. She'd promised Joe she wouldn't. But even if she set her promises to Joe aside, jumping headlong was still ill-advised. She wasn't staying.

Nor was she ready to place *all* her trust in Corbin. She'd forgiven him, but that didn't mean she had to be dumb.

Today had gone a long way toward restoring her battered hopes in him. But the idea of investing herself in him further worried her. Was his relationship with God as strong as she needed it to be? They'd had some great conversations — transparent conversations — about faith recently. He was coming along. But could she count on him to value what she valued? To help her keep their physical intimacy in check? To be faithful to her even though the majority of the female population of America would sell their mothers for a chance to be with him?

She didn't know.

Wearily, she sighed.

There was a chance that things might end happily for the two of them.

However, she was also painfully aware of the flip side of that coin. Things might also end very, very badly for the two of them.

She loved Corbin. But she had no idea whether her love for him would result in joy or heartbreak.

■ ■ ■ ■

Text message from Corbin to Willow:

Corbin
Still awake?

Willow
Yes.

Corbin
Upset over what happened earlier with Todd?

Willow
A little.

Corbin
I can't sleep because I'm still fuming about it.

Willow
You looked a wee bit worried when you rushed into my kitchen.

Corbin
I was the most worried I've ever been in my life. I didn't want to trust a fire poker with your safety.

Willow

I have a feeling I might have been ferocious with that fire poker, if needed.

Corbin

Would it be all right with you if I borrow
the fire poker, hunt Todd down, and stab
him with it?

Willow

No, sir. Todd's going to get what's coming
to him. I don't mind him ending up behind
bars, but I'm determined to keep you out
of jail.

CHAPTER TWENTY-ONE

The Bradford family tradition had always been to celebrate Thanksgiving with one side of the family one year and with the other side of their family the next year. This year, the sisters were spending Thanksgiving with their mom's side of the family, the Burke side.

Their mom, Kathleen, had one older brother. Uncle Shane was a confirmed bachelor with a very expensive mid-century modern house and a welcoming spirit. He'd good-naturedly opened his doors, and aunts, uncles, cousins, and second cousins descended on him like ants into an anthill.

As soon as Grandma entered Shane's house, she asked her granddaughters whether it was cold inside. They replied that it wasn't. She wore her coat indoors for the rest of the day to call attention to the fact that they'd been gravely mistaken about the indoor temperature.

Whenever anyone asked if she was chilly, she icily replied, "No, not at all."

Britt was one of the few Burke family members with cooking chops. The sublime turkey she'd cooked appeared to be insulted by its surrounding dishes, which had all originated from cans and boxes.

The Burke family talked and laughed while sitting around Uncle Shane's metal and concrete table. They ate their Thanksgiving feast off extraordinarily masculine place settings and sipped from sleek, modern glasses.

After the meal Willow dropped her sisters off at their homes, then drove the night-dark streets toward Bradfordwood. Ordinarily, she enjoyed a sense of peace and gratitude on Thanksgiving Day. She'd behaved all day as if she'd felt those things but — in all honesty — hadn't quite been able to grasp them.

She was tired from too little sleep and still a bit rattled by Todd's appearance yesterday. The prospect of returning to a dark and empty Bradfordwood seemed more frightening than soothing.

Plus, she missed Corbin.

Corbin and Joe had spent their Thanksgiving with the Dixons, so they'd been in very good hands. She should be pleased that they had a wonderful family to spend the holiday with. And she was. It's just that the hours of her day had been longer and dimmer without Corbin in any of them. They'd texted back and forth as recently as thirty minutes ago, when she'd let him know they were headed back to Merryweather. But it wasn't the same as seeing him.

Today would be their first full day apart since the kissing picnic.

What does it matter? It was ridiculous to care about going a day without seeing him, when in just a few days, she wouldn't get to see him anymore at all.

Which was why she wanted to see him now.

She groaned and bumped her fist against the steering wheel.

She'd already slowed to enter the gates to Bradfordwood when she spotted Corbin's car, parked on the curb.

He was here.

Thank you, God!

She was grinning with surprise when she pulled up beside him.

"I didn't want to break our streak," he said.

"What streak?"

He lifted an eyebrow. "Our streak of seeing each other every day."

"Oh."

"You know exactly what streak I'm talking about. You don't want to break it either."

"I don't?"

"No," he assured her.

"Fine. I don't want to break it either," she permitted herself to say. "Even though we're not —"

"Together? Yeah, yeah. I know." Humor lurked in his eyes, but so did determination. She suspected he was saying one thing to placate her while resolutely and absolutely believing something different.

He followed her along the drive, then into the mansion's kitchen. She'd just set her purse on the counter when he came up behind her and kissed the side of her neck. "Happy Thanksgiving, Willow."

She turned. "Happy Thanksgiving, Corbin."

"I don't want to spend another Thanksgiving without you," he said.

Elation rushed from the tip of her head to her toes. She should correct him. She didn't want to, but she should put down the same firm boundary she'd been putting down —

"Here." He pulled a wrapped present from his jacket pocket, gave it a small toss, and caught it on the flat of his palm. It was square, short, and covered half his hand.

"What's this?"

"A Thanksgiving present."

"Thanksgiving isn't a gift-giving holiday."

"It is now."

Reverentially, she took the package and pulled off its bow and paper. "Did you wrap this yourself?"

"Do I look like someone who could wrap a gift that well?"

"No."

"Thank you."

"It wasn't a compliment."

He laughed. That particular exchange was becoming an inside joke between them. She removed the box's lid. A bracelet nestled within. She released an awed breath as she plucked free the piece of jewelry.

The bangle-style bracelet had been fashioned of platinum. One small, round charm imprinted with a cursive *W* swayed from it. It was exquisite. Tasteful. Costly, but not so costly that she'd have to refuse it.

"I love it," she said. "It's exactly my style."

"Good." He looked more pleased than if he'd been the one on the receiving end of the gift. "I know that you like bracelets."

"They're my favorite kind of jewelry. And this is my new favorite of all the bracelets I own." She placed it on her wrist. "Thank you."

"You're welcome."

"I wish I had something for you."

"I didn't expect —"

"Oh. That's right. I *do* have something for you." Shooting him a mischievous look, she slid the platter decorated with acorns and autumn leaves (thank you, Williams-Sonoma) closer to them. She'd baked an almond cake this morning for her family's Thanksgiving. With the leftover batter, she'd created a second almond cake just big enough for two. In case their streak went unbroken.

Astonishment flared in his face. "You made this for me?"

She shrugged. "I spent the morning baking." *And I was thinking about you.* "And I know you aren't a fan of pumpkin pie. So I made you a Thanksgiving almond cake. It's full of butter and I serve it with caramel sauce, so how bad could it be?"

"Nothing I eat with you could ever be bad." He gazed at her steadily.

When asked what qualities they wanted in a boyfriend, no woman ever said, *I'd like him to pay attention.* But they should. Because that was the thing that slayed her the most.

Corbin saw her. And not just the outward part of her that everyone else saw. He saw her sense of humor, which usually went un-

466

noticed. He saw the scars that her mother's abandonment had left. He saw her idiosyncrasies and her strengths and her weaknesses and seemed to find beauty in the whole.

He grabbed a fork and sectioned off some cake without bothering to cut a slice. He held the fork out to her, offering her the first bite.

She took it and chewed. Subtle, rich flavors of butter, vanilla, almond.

He lifted the cake platter with his good arm. "Let's move this party to the sofa. I'm tired." He snagged some napkins and another fork.

"Can't stand the pace?"

"I'm not in Thanksgiving shape, apparently."

She fed him some of her bites of cake and he fed her some of his. They laughed and joked while her beloved Alison Krauss bluegrass played over the sound system and her new bracelet sparkled on her wrist.

Leftover concerns about Todd Hill could not coexist with Corbin. It wasn't scientifically possible because Corbin's larger-than-life presence filled every corner of the home.

When nothing was left of her almond cake but one tilting morsel, she snuggled against him and laid her head on his shoulder.

Quiet surrounded them like a blessing. She massaged one of his hands. Then trailed her fingertips along his injured arm and across his collarbone. Up and around one ear. Down his neck.

She was endlessly fascinated with the masterpiece that was his body. The sturdiness of it. The labyrinth of muscles and veins. Its lines.

He spun her suddenly and she landed half-propped against him with a gasp of laughter. Her face hovered inches above his.

She waited, staring into his eyes, watching as they clouded with need and his smile faded. Her love for him expanded through her chest like rays of sunlight.

Then slowly, the torture of it sweet, she lowered to kiss him.

Within minutes, her body had become a mass of sensation and pleasure. Dark temptation began to pull at her. She wanted more. Of him. Of this. Would it be terrible to go just a little further? Dimly, she knew the right answer. And yet this felt *excruciatingly* good. Very nearly irresistibly good. Her body's needs were demanding and loud. Her principles were distant and quiet —

Gently, Corbin set her about a foot away from him. He held her gaze for a searing space of time, his breath hitching unevenly.

Then he groaned as his head flopped against the sofa's back. He covered his eyes with his elbow. "You're killing me."

Willow realized she'd been tugging the hem of his shirt. She began to regain her senses. Not fully. Just enough to smooth his shirt back into place after getting an eyeful of his ribs.

Drawing on the small amount of willpower she had left, she moved another few inches away so that no part of her was touching him. She tucked her feet beneath her.

Great Scott.

She felt dazed. Her blood was rushing, her skin was flushed. Later, when he wasn't sitting so close and looking so kissable, she'd probably be very glad they'd ended the kiss when they had. But as of this moment? She yearned to return to him for more.

Strain tightened Corbin's jaw. He was having to work at it, but he had himself under control. He'd been the one who'd found the strength she'd been unable to summon just now to break the kiss before it could spiral into more. Shame mixed with a dash of embarrassment knotted her stomach.

"That wasn't easy for me," he said in a low voice, arm still covering his eyes. "I'm not in the habit of denying myself something I want as much as I want you."

"You did the right thing."

"And yet I'm not feeling too happy about it at the moment."

Alison Krauss's sweet, clear voice continued to quietly hum from the speakers.

"You did the right thing," Willow repeated.

At length, he straightened and extended his arm along the sofa. He skimmed a fingertip from the edge of her shoulder to her collarbone and back, watching its progress.

When his eyes finally met hers, the banked fire there stole her breath.

"I'm starting to want your standards for myself," he said. "But I can promise you that I didn't stop for my sake just then. I stopped for you."

She nodded. "We — or I, as the case may be, came close to crossing a line."

"But we didn't. I want you, Willow. Badly. Whatever attraction you feel toward me, I feel twice that for you. But here's what I need for you to know." He concentrated on her intently. "I'm determined to keep a handle on it this time around because I'm not going to do anything that might mess up my chances with you."

She longed to believe him. But did she dare?

"I won't be careless," he said. "I won't do anything to risk you."

She took a deep, tremulous breath.

"Doesn't it hurt your knees to sit like that?" he asked.

"Not really."

"It's hurting *my* knees for you to sit like that."

Smiling, she adjusted one of the sofa cushions so that it acted like a back rest for her, then straightened her legs and set her crossed feet on his thigh. "I'm feeling sort of . . . chagrined. I can't believe I just tried to pull off your shirt after feeling guilty for *years* over the things we did the last time we dated."

"Why all the guilt? The way the chaplain explained it to me, once we ask God for forgiveness, we're forgiven. Right?"

"No . . . ah . . . I mean, yes." She picked at a seam in the upholstery.

"Have you asked forgiveness for the things we did the last time?"

"Yes."

"Then how come you're still carrying guilt around?"

His question struck her like a splash of water. "I . . ."

"The mistakes you've made are forgiven, Willow."

"I wish it were that simple."

"It is. Isn't it?"

"Not for me." She wished she could wipe away the regret that dogged her and the unworthiness she felt whenever people called her a role model. Wholeheartedly, she wished that.

But what was that saying about wishes? Ah, yes. She remembered it.

If wishes were horses, beggars would ride.

Letter from Jill, age nine, to Josephine:

Aunt Josephine,

Mom has been sad all day today. When I walked into the kitchen a while ago, she was crying. So I asked her what was the matter, and she said that today's your birthday.

You went away right before I was born, so you've been gone a really long time now. We still don't know what happened to you. Sometimes people from TV or the newspaper ask Mom questions about you. Sometimes people call to say they think they might know where you are. But they never do.

Please come back, Aunt Josephine.

We'll make you cake and have ice cream and give you a birthday party.

I'm going to tear up this letter and spread it over the fireplace, so it can go up the chimney to you just like the letter in Mary Poppins.

I love you, Jill

CHAPTER TWENTY-TWO

"So, Melinda," Corbin said the next afternoon. "If Felicia Richmond turns and runs when she sees you, do I have your permission to tackle her?"

"Yes," Melinda answered with a rusty chuckle.

"No," Willow said. "No tackling for you. Think of your shoulder."

"I'll have to tackle her with my left shoulder, Melinda. Is that cool with you?"

"Yes, Corbin."

They'd made the drive from northern Washington to southern British Columbia in four hours, Melinda sitting in the passenger seat of Corbin's Navigator, Charlotte and Willow occupying the captain's chairs in the second row.

The atmosphere had started out relaxed. The adults had talked. Charlotte had watched a movie. They'd stopped for a quick lunch and continued on. As they'd begun to near Mission, though, tension crept into the car.

Now they were only a few miles from Haven Gardens, the nursery run by Felicia Richmond, the woman who looked a great deal like the age-progression portrait of Josephine Blake.

At this point, Corbin appeared to be the only one in the SUV unaffected by their nearness to their destination. In order to loosen everyone up, he'd begun firing humorous questions at Melinda.

"Is it okay with you if I whip out Josephine's wanted poster and hold it up next to Felicia's face?" he asked.

"Unnecessary," Melinda said. "I'll know if it's her."

"What do you think about us stopping to get some ink?"

"Ink?" Melinda asked.

"That I can use on her fingers," Corbin said. "Then I'll force her fingers onto paper and — boom — we'll have her fingerprints."

"The idea has merit."

"We should be able to see the nursery soon," Willow said. She'd served as the trip's navigator. "It's coming up in half a mile on the left."

Charlotte snapped to attention. "There!" She pointed. "Is that it?"

Willow leaned to the side to see. "Yes. I think that might be it."

Corbin slowed.

"It is!" Charlotte said. "Look at the sign. *Haven Gardens.*"

Corbin pulled into the small parking lot situated in front of the shop.

Back in Washington, when they'd compared Felicia Richmond's address to the address of Haven Gardens, they'd realized that the two were one and the same. Felicia both lived and worked on this property.

Silence descended over the car as the four occupants drank in the details of the place. The nursery occupied land a few miles outside of Mission. The only evidence of the nearby city was the well-traveled road curving into the distance.

A metal roof topped the clapboard-sided shop. To one side of it, bordered by a split-rail fence, stood rows upon rows of plants and flowers in buckets of all sizes. Shoppers browsed the merchandise. A large greenhouse hunkered on the shop's other side. Beyond the nursery, a gardening plot bristled with growing trees and shrubs. Past that, three hundred yards or so in the distance and facing a small lake, sat a house.

"Grandma?" Charlotte asked. "How do you want to . . . do this?"

476

"Let's go inside and see if Felicia's there. If she isn't, we'll speak with the employee who is."

Melinda had called earlier to make sure the shop was open. When she'd asked the young man who'd answered the phone whether Felicia was in today, he'd said that she was, so they had every reason to hope that they'd have the chance to meet her face-to-face.

Stress burrowed into the grooves of Melinda's profile. Willow was painfully aware that these next few moments might be filled with abject disappointment should Felicia turn out to be a stranger.

Or these next few moments might bring Melinda into the presence of her long-lost sister, and in so doing, illuminate a situation that had been filled with darkness for forty years.

The shop's door creaked cheerfully as they entered. It occurred to Willow that she was holding her breath, so she made herself inhale air scented with cloves, lemon, and dirt.

No sign of Felicia.

A college-aged kid as skinny as a scarecrow stood behind the counter. "Welcome." He smiled widely. "How can I help you?"

"I was hoping to speak with Felicia Richmond," Melinda said.

477

"Oh, sure." He looked around as if checking to make sure Felicia wasn't standing behind one of the potted plants. "I think she said she was going to work on the plot out back. Head through the back door, and the pathway should take you right to her."

They thanked him. Corbin held the door as Melinda, Charlotte, and Willow filed out. Momentary sun had broken through the hazy day, making the fifty-five degree temperature feel warmer than it was. Greenery bowed and murmured in the light wind as Melinda led them along the path.

Willow couldn't see anyone.

Maybe the employee in the shop had been wrong —

But, wait. There. Off to the side, a figure dressed in loose pants, rain boots, a canvas jacket, and a floppy straw hat knelt between lines of bushes. The woman's back was to them. She appeared to be pulling weeds and tossing them into the basket near her feet.

Melinda faltered.

Air bunched up in Willow's chest. *Could it be?*

Melinda squared her shoulders and continued forward. As they drew close, Felicia turned and lifted her face to them. Her features were framed by her hat, her body framed by the scene of the garden and the more remote backdrop of the lake. She held herself completely still for several seconds.

Then, slowly, she rose. Her face smoothed with shock. Her lips parted, as if she was on the verge of speaking, but she said nothing. Her eyes roamed Melinda's face.

Melinda came to a stop a few feet from Felicia. The two women, very much matched in height and build, faced each other. The wind ebbed away.

"Josephine," Melinda said in an emotion-roughened tone.

Moisture pooled in Felicia's eyes. "Melinda."

Melinda nodded and opened her arms. Both women began to cry, shoulders shaking as they clung to each other.

The tiny hairs blanketing Willow's skin stood up as a chill ran through her. This woman in the gardening hat and rain boots, here on this verdant piece of earth on the shoulder of a lake in southern British Columbia, was Josephine Blake?

It was a miracle that she was alive.

It was a miracle that they'd found her.

She and Corbin had gone on this missing persons hunt for Charlotte's sake, because Charlotte had truly *believed* that they could solve this case. Willow had been convinced they couldn't. Just like she'd been convinced that she and Corbin could never work out.

Charlotte had been right, and she'd been wrong. Perhaps she'd been so bent on protecting herself from the improbable that, somewhere along the line, she'd stopped believing in the miraculous.

Corbin took hold of her hand. She looked across at him, and he gave her the same unadulterated grin that he'd once worn in the moments following a Super Bowl victory. That time, the grin had been snapped by a photographer and immortalized on the cover of *Sports Illustrated.* This time, the grin pierced her heart.

Willow intertwined her free hand with Charlotte's so that they formed a chain, the three of them. The Operation Find Josephine detectives.

"That's *Josephine,* " Charlotte stage-whispered.

"It better be," Corbin said. "We'll have to take Melinda to a mental institution if this is how she greets all gardeners."

"We found her," Charlotte said to Willow. "I think we did."

"I'm, like, in shock right now," Charlotte said.

Melinda and Josephine walked toward them arm in arm, supporting each other.

Their faces were splotchy from crying. Despite that, an angelic glow emanated from them both.

"This is my granddaughter, Charlotte," Melinda said.

"Hello, Charlotte."

"This is Willow Bradford and Corbin Stewart," Melinda continued. "They're friends of Charlotte's. When Charlotte asked them to help her look for you, they said yes."

"Nice to meet you," Josephine said.

"Likewise," Corbin said just as Willow said, "It's nice to meet you, too."

"This," Melinda said, patting Josephine's forearm, "is my sister Josephine."

Josephine was now a mature woman in her sixties. Nonetheless, she very much resembled the photographs of her twenty-something self. Her body was softer than it had once been, but sturdy and healthy-looking. She'd protected her skin from the sun, so while Melinda's skin was tanned and crepey, Josephine's was much paler. Wrinkles delved beneath her eyes, bracketed her lips, and lined her forehead. Her hair, once long and mahogany, had lightened to a mellower shade of brown shot through with gray. She'd bobbed it above her shoulders in a straight line.

"Come with me," Josephine said, turning to guide them down the path that continued toward the lakeside house.

Charlotte scampered ahead to walk next to her grandmother and great-aunt. Willow and Corbin followed, still holding hands.

Josephine's house came into crisp focus as they approached. The rectangular structure had been built of aged bricks. Ivy covered large swaths of the exterior. Pale blue shutters framed gleaming, multi-paned windows. Its steeply pitched slate roof made it look like an illustration from a fairy-tale picture book.

Indoors, Josephine had furnished her home in farmhouse style. Off-white sofas. An abundance of honey-colored wood. Pottery. A sisal rug.

"Please, have a seat," Josephine said. "I'll put on a pot of coffee."

When Josephine disappeared around a corner into her kitchen, Melinda, Willow, Corbin, and Charlotte eyed one another with disbelief.

I'm shaking, Melinda mouthed, holding out her hands to show them. It was quite an admission, coming from the usually stalwart Melinda.

Charlotte laughed and rubbed her grandmother's hands between her smaller ones.

Corbin and Willow took seats on one of Josephine's sofas. Corbin put his arm around her and idly ran a fingertip up and down a patch of her upper arm. Willow's thoughts whirled with the magnitude of the reunion that had just occurred, while her senses focused on the motion of his finger — up and down, up and down — and its warm wake of sensation.

The gasp of a drip coffeemaker coming to life interrupted the quiet. Then Josephine arrived with a plate of Pepperidge Farm Mint Milano cookies.

Willow felt too keyed up to eat, but Charlotte and Corbin could, as always, be counted upon to eat cookies.

Josephine lowered into the delicate armchair near the brick fireplace. "The coffee will be ready soon." She'd taken off her hat while in the kitchen and finger-combed her hair. She wore side bangs and her bob was slightly layered, Willow could now see.

Josephine Blake was what she'd always been. A beauty.

Josephine didn't lean back into the armchair but sat upright in the center of the seat, legs together. She had the look of a witness testifying at a trial. "I'm amazed that you're here at Haven Gardens." She laid a hand on her chest. "To look up and

483

see you there," she said to Melinda. "What a shock."

"It was a shock for me, too," Melinda said.

"You'll have to tell me how you found me. But I'm sure you have a hundred questions for me first."

"More like a thousand," Melinda said wryly.

Josephine nodded and sorrow stole over her features for the first time.

"Why did you disappear?" Melinda asked.

"To answer that, I'll need to start well before the day of my disappearance. Do you remember that I worked on Foster Holt's election campaign in the fall of 1976?"

"Yes."

"I'd volunteered on a few other political campaigns prior to that, but in those cases, my volunteer jobs were small. Foster's campaign manager must've seen something in me because he gave me a lot of responsibility. I met Foster relatively early in the campaign and, over time, I got to know him well. He was an extraordinarily charismatic man. Handsome. Smart. Everything he wanted for the country was exactly what I wanted for the country. I believed in the things he believed in. I had . . . stars in my eyes," she said bitterly. "I think I was already in love with him when he began showing a romantic interest in me."

The revelation that Josephine had loved Foster Holt did not deeply surprise Willow, seeing as how they'd found Josephine less than thirty miles from Foster's fishing cabin.

She thought back to the weeks she and Corbin and Charlotte had spent sifting through data and pursuing leads. They'd had no idea which piece of information would unlock Josephine's whereabouts. In the end, Foster Holt had been the key.

"But you were married," Charlotte said. "And so was the senator."

Josephine inclined her head. "Yes. At the time, Foster was married and the father of five young kids. I'm not at all proud of what I did, Charlotte. In fact, I'm very ashamed of it. And, as you'll hear, I've paid dearly for what happened between Foster and me. But back then, the fact that Foster was forbidden made our relationship seem all the more exciting." She gave Charlotte a level, apologetic look.

"How long did your relationship with the senator last?" Corbin asked.

"Five months. We almost always met at hotels. There were only a few occasions when I saw him at his office and once when he came to my house when Alan was gone for the weekend. I both liked and loved

Alan. But I fancied myself wildly *in love* with Foster." She paused.

The motion of Corbin's fingertip against Willow's arm stopped. Then resumed.

"I was willing to divorce Alan," Josephine said. "I started asking Foster whether he was willing to divorce his wife. I was determined and naive enough to think I could pressure him into doing what I wanted." Her lips pursed. "In case you can't tell, I'm not fond of the woman I was in those days. I was either too foolish or too self-absorbed to realize that a United States senator in the opening months of his first term would never, ever leave his wife and kids."

Charlotte reached for another mint Milano.

Melinda looked both shell-shocked and grave. She was no doubt thinking about the pain that Josephine's disappearance had caused her, their parents, their sister Louise, and Alan.

Josephine's poor husband. For seven years after Josephine had vanished, he'd been married to a missing woman and his life had been locked in suspended animation. Once he'd finally had Josephine declared dead, he'd remarried. And, by all accounts, he'd gone on to find companionship and a measure of peace. However, no one who'd loved Josephine had escaped from her disappearance without indelible scars.

"What happened between you and Foster?" Willow asked. It felt presumptuous to ask someone she'd just met questions about the intimate details of her history. However, Charlotte was too young to be expected to ask questions, and Melinda didn't look capable of it at the moment.

"On April twelfth, 1977, I left the house to meet Paula, a friend from our Sunday school class. She'd heard a rumor that I was having an affair with her husband, Keith. When I learned about the rumor, it frightened me, because even though they'd gotten the man wrong, they'd gotten the affair part right. I wanted to move quickly to stop the rumor, so Paula and I had a nice conversation and then I got in my car and drove to a hotel in Lakewood."

"You left the meeting with Paula around ten thirty in the morning," Charlotte said. "You went to a hotel at ten thirty a.m.?"

"I did," Josephine answered. "Foster and I met at the Cornerstone Hotel fairly often because it was halfway between Shore Pine, where I lived, and Redmond, where Foster lived. Don, Foster's employee, would always book the room under his own name or under aliases, let Foster in through a side door, and hand him the hotel room key. When I reached the room that day, Foster was already there. Lunch was spread out on top of the dresser. Apples, bread, deli meat, cheese. The roasted peanuts Foster ate all the time. A bottle of wine. We ate and talked and laughed and then we did . . . what we did. We spent two hours there together."

Overall, Josephine was speaking calmly. The signs of her emotion were subtle — in the stiffness of her hands, the muscle flexing in her jaw, the vertical line between her brows.

"When it came time for him to go," she continued, "he kissed me, told me he loved me, and left. Once he was gone, I did what I always used to do after our meetings. I took a long shower." Josephine seemed to lose herself in thought for a moment. "When I came out of the bathroom, there were two men in the hotel room. Neither one of them was Foster."

"Two men?" Charlotte asked.

Josephine nodded. "One of them was Don. I'll never forget the way he was standing. He was casually leaning against the window, curtains drawn, with his arms crossed. He was wearing leather gloves, and he was looking at me with an expression that was just completely . . . blank. The other man was Stan Markum. I'd gotten to know him during the campaign because he was one of Foster's biggest money donors. He was lying on a tarp on the floor, dead."

"Jill's going to have my head when she finds out I let Charlotte listen in on this conversation," Melinda said under her breath.

"No, she won't," Charlotte replied. "I'll stick up for you, Grandma."

"How had Stan Markum died?" Corbin asked.

Josephine moved her attention to him. "He'd been stabbed while I was in the shower with the knife I'd used to cut the apples and the bread and the cheese. I hadn't thought anything of it at the time, but Foster hadn't touched the knife once. My fingerprints were all over it. Only mine." She moved her focus to Melinda. "Do you remember the monogram necklace I used to wear?"

"Yes."

"The chain of that necklace had been ripped as if there'd been a struggle and it was lying in some of Stan's blood. Also, Don had collected every single article of my clothing. My shoes and my dress. My undergarments. I could see my things, sitting inside a bag near his feet. Don had killed

Stan. But he and Foster had set me up as Stan's murderer."

Corbin made a low whistling sound. "Why would Foster have wanted Stan Markum dead?"

"All these years later I'm not one hundred percent sure. Here's what I do know: Stan Markum had plenty of good qualities, but he could also be ruthless when it came to getting what he wanted. He'd been raised with great wealth, and he wasn't afraid to spend huge sums of money. Once he spent that money, though, he expected to get exactly what he'd requested in return. I suspect that Stan donated to Foster's campaign in exchange for promises Foster made to him about how he would vote once he was elected. When Foster didn't follow through on those promises, Stan must've been furious." She paused. "I think he may have tried to blackmail Foster into doing his bidding. You see, Foster was never the clean-cut family man he seemed to be. If Stan hired an investigator, it probably wouldn't have been hard to dig up incriminating evidence against Foster."

"We found out that a businessman once charged Stan Markum with extortion," Corbin said.

"So Foster may not have been the first

person Stan tried to blackmail. But he was the last."

"Why would Stan have come to the hotel room?" Willow asked.

"I think Foster and Stan had arranged to meet there. But by the time Stan arrived, Foster was long gone."

"What did you do?" Charlotte asked. "When you came out of the bathroom and saw the dead guy?"

"I just stood there, appalled, trying to make sense of what I was seeing. A few minutes before, I'd been in the shower, humming and washing my hair. And then I came out to find . . . that. I'd never seen a dead body before. Certainly not one that had been murdered. I'd never seen that much blood."

"What did Don say?" Melinda asked.

"He said, 'Don't scream and don't run. I'll let you live if you don't scream and you don't run.' I was terrified. I didn't scream and I didn't run."

Corbin leaned forward, setting his elbows on his knees and watching Josephine beneath lowered brows. Willow had sensed his anger building as the story unfolded.

"Foster and Don's plan was both elegant and simple," Josephine said. "What happened that day took care of two birds with one stone. They got Stan out of the picture. And they got me, the woman who'd been pressuring Foster to get a divorce, out of the picture, too."

"I can't believe they got away with it," Corbin said.

"The perfect murder," Josephine said quietly. "Don explained that not one piece of evidence would point to himself or to Foster, and that if I didn't do exactly what he said, that he'd call the police and tell them there was a dead man in my hotel room. He'd booked the room in my name."

"Oh my gosh," Charlotte whispered.

"Don had a new set of clothes for me to change into. I put them on and he made me leave everything else behind, including my purse. He locked the door on Stan and hung a *Do Not Disturb* sign on the door handle. Then we got in his car, and he drove me to Foster's fishing cabin here in British Columbia."

"How did your car end up in a parking space next to the Pacific Dogwood Trail?" Corbin asked.

"Foster must've driven my car there when he left the hotel."

"The police didn't find his fingerprints in your car," Corbin said.

"Foster and Don were nothing if not careful. And intelligent." She rose. "Let me get the coffee."

"I'll help," Melinda said.

Corbin pushed to his feet and started to pace.

Minutes later, the sisters returned bearing coffee. Willow accepted the cup she was passed and took a dainty sip. Corbin accepted a cup, too, and remained standing as he drank it. The cup looked like a toy in his large grip, which reminded her of the day they'd visited the tearoom together and he'd good-naturedly drunk tea out of girly china cups.

"What happened once you reached the fishing cabin?" Corbin asked.

Josephine hadn't returned to her chair. Instead, she stood near the fireplace, cradling her steaming cup and saucer. "Don asked me what I wanted my new name to be. I made up the name Felicia Richmond. Then he locked me in the basement for three days while he waited for the forged documents I'd need in order to apply for Canadian citizenship to come through."

Josephine tested her coffee before returning her cup to the saucer with a *clink*. "I was frantic because I knew what Alan and the rest of my family must've been going through." Her eyes met Melinda's. "I had no way to reach any of you. On the fourth day, Don let me out. The paper work was ready, and he'd bought me another set of clothes. I showered. I put the documents and the wallet he gave me filled with two hundred dollars into a new purse. On the drive to Vancouver, he told me that he'd buried Stan, the knife, my necklace, and my clothes in a remote location known only to himself and Foster. He said that if I ever tried to contact any of my family members or if I ever returned to the United States, that they'd alert the police to Stan's burial site. Then he dropped me off on a street corner and drove away."

"Did you ever think about coming home and telling us what had happened?" Melinda asked.

"I thought about it all the time for years. But I knew that the evidence against me was overwhelming. The hotel room was in my name, which would have made it look as though Stan's murder was either premeditated or an act of passion because Stan and I were having an affair. No one would have believed that Foster and Don had been behind it, especially because I had no way to prove my relationship with Foster. He never wrote me letters or allowed me to take pictures. He was widely admired then, and still is. I just . . . I couldn't risk it. I'd seen firsthand what Don was capable of. When he told me what he'd do if I tried to contact my family or if I came back to America, I absolutely believed him." Her fingers encircled her coffee cup's base, as if instinctively seeking its reassuring warmth.

"Why do you think Foster let you live?" Corbin asked.

She sighed. "I'd never tried to blackmail him like Stan had. The worst thing I'd done to Foster was attempt to love him more than he wanted me to love him. Perhaps Foster knew me well enough to know that I'd go along with everything Don said from the moment I stepped out of that shower."

"How did you end up here?" Willow asked.

"I had the documents I needed to apply for citizenship, but the actual process of getting citizenship takes time. No one who was aboveboard would hire me because I was an illegal alien at that point. I quickly realized that Vancouver was not the best place for me to search for a job, that I'd likely have more luck farther out in the country, maybe with someone who needed hourly laborers to work on their property. I hitchhiked from Vancouver to Mission, then hitchhiked again from Mission. The car I was riding in drove down the road that runs in front of this place." She gestured. "As soon as I spotted the nursery through the window, something about it felt . . . safe and right to me. Nothing had felt safe or right for days, and I was down to my last ten dollars. I asked the driver to let me off. When I came into the shop, I met Haven's owner. His name was Bill, and he looked a little bit like Santa Claus. He was sixty-five at the time, and an incredibly softhearted man. I reminded him of his daughter, so he hired me."

"And now this nursery belongs to you," Melinda said.

"It does." Josephine took another sip of coffee. "Bill taught me everything he knew about gardening and about the nursery business. When he retired, I took over his responsibilities. He died twenty years ago, and I still miss him every day. He left his money to his kids, but he left this place to me, and I've been taking care of it ever since. I've found a kind of peace here, I suppose, working with the plants."

"Did you read an article about your disappearance in the *Mission Tribune*? Then mail it to your family?" Willow asked.

Josephine inclined her head. "Yes. I read that article shortly after I arrived here at

Haven. It was strange and awful to read about myself in the paper. It brought home everything that was going on back in Washington. I was terrified to send anything home, but I found that I needed to say that I was sorry. So I wrote on the article and sent it home even though I never expected anyone to be able to forgive me."

"I can forgive you," Melinda said.

"So can I," Charlotte said.

Josephine regarded them as if they'd taken her completely unawares.

"Does that surprise you?" Melinda asked.

"It does because . . . I've certainly never been able to forgive myself."

Willow experienced a pang of kinship with Josephine. She understood that sentiment well. "The article you sent is what eventually led us to search for you here in Mission."

"I'm glad that you're here, Melinda. That you're all here. At the same time, I'm worried. If Foster learns that you found me . . ."

"No one followed us on the drive here," Corbin said.

"We'll have to figure out a way to communicate in secret," Melinda suggested. "Were you ever planning to . . . come back to us?"

"Yes, as soon as Foster died. But of

course, he's still very much alive."

"Are you married? Do you have children?" Melinda asked.

Josephine shook her head. "I've never wanted to subject anyone else to the shadow I live under."

A pause opened.

"We can't let Foster Holt go on about his life without paying for what he did," Corbin stated flatly.

"There's no evidence linking Foster to Stan's death," Josephine said.

"I don't think we have a chance of pinning Stan's death on Foster," Corbin admitted. "But we know that he's had at least three affairs and that he was an accessory to Stan's murder. We suspect that he made false promises to Stan in exchange for campaign donations. And that's just the stuff we're aware of. Think about all the illegal things he's probably *actually* done. I'm going to hire an investigator."

"An investigator?" Josephine asked.

"More like a whole team of investigators to look into every aspect of the senator's life. Personal. Financial. Political. I'm certain we'll find something. And when we do, we'll tip off a reporter or the police and let them take it from there."

Willow, Josephine, Melinda, and Charlotte

all stared at him.

"A rat's a rat," he said. "Now that I know Senator Holt's a rat, I'm going to bring him down."

How was she going to give Corbin up?

She wanted to keep him. She wanted desperately to keep him.

Written by Josephine in her journal that night:

Friday, November 27th

Today. Today has changed everything. Today Melinda, her granddaughter, Charlotte, and their friends found me.

To look into my sister's face again after so long was pure joy and regretful sadness all mixed up together. She's still exactly who she always was . . . yet the years, the years have marked her just as they've marked me. We've lost decades of sisterhood. We are familiar strangers, and it will take time, perhaps a great deal of time, to build a new relationship.

To look into Charlotte's face was to see the past rushing up to meet me, because she looks just like I did at that same age. Every decision and heartbreak and thrill of life is still before her. I can only pray that she takes better paths than I did.

Family.

It's been so long since I've spent time with people who are related to me. I'm filled with a hundred emotions tonight, but most of all, I'm filled with gratitude. God allowed Melinda and Charlotte to find me. Regardless of what I've done, He took mercy on me. And He allowed my family to find a way back to me.

I'm unspeakably grateful.

Chapter Twenty-Three

"I've already asked a few people for advice on how to set up a team of investigators," Corbin told Willow the next day. It was Saturday, and they'd spent the past few hours with John and Nora at John's house on Lake Shore Pine. The four of them had donned hats and gloves over their athletic gear, gone on a short hike, then explored the nearby inlets by kayak.

At the moment, John and Nora were making their way up the trail to John's house to start dinner. They'd insisted they didn't need help, so Corbin and Willow had stayed behind on John's dock. They sat on the planks, their shoulders leaning into one another.

"It'll probably take quite a while to compile evidence against Foster Holt," she said. "He seems to be very good at covering his tracks."

"I can be patient."

"There's also Don to consider."

"I know. And even when Foster's put in prison —"

"I like your positive thinking."

"— he and Don will still have the ability to leak the location of Stan's grave. So until both Foster and Don are dead, I don't see a way for Josephine to come home or openly visit with her family."

"Me neither." Actions had consequences. Sometimes the consequences turned out to be far more long-lasting and terrible than one initially imagined. The consequences of Josephine's affair with Foster Holt had changed the course of Josephine's life. "At least now Melinda's family has answers. Charlotte's mystery is solved. And if they're careful, Josephine can keep in touch with her relatives secretly. We did what we set out to do. We found Josephine."

"We found Josephine," he repeated.

This was their second to last day together. The sunset was painting the sky with brushstrokes of mauve and plum.

And Willow's heart was breaking.

Her departure had seemed distant enough to bear, right up until this morning when she'd hauled out her suitcases and stared at them as though they were tarantulas. *I'm leaving. This is happening,* she'd thought over and over.

While in Corbin's presence, she'd been working to act as though nothing was wrong, which was like trying to dance in the ballroom of the Titanic while it was sinking.

She injected lightness into her tone. "You know, you remind me a little of Stan Markum. Like him, you're determined and rich."

"Right, but I don't buy or blackmail politicians. I'm not above buying or blackmailing you, however. Name your price, and I'll pay it if you'll stay in Washington."

"Not going to happen."

"Blackmail it is, then," he said.

She rested her head near his collarbone. "You've already tried to blackmail me once. With the Benevolence Worldwide check. It didn't work."

"That doesn't mean my evil plans won't be successful this time. Let's see . . . What can I blackmail you with?"

"Not much. My past is squeaky clean. I'm nauseatingly respectable on the surface."

When he noticed her rubbing her hands together, trying to warm them, he unzipped his jacket and opened it to her. She scooted in closer and he hugged her against the hard contours of his dri-fit shirt. Heat enfolded her.

"If you don't stay in Washington, then I'll tell everyone that you binge shop for housewares," he said.

She giggled.

"I'll tell them that you talk to cars when you're driving."

"Ooh. Scandalous."

"I'll tell them that you like terrible movies."

"Romantic comedies aren't terrible!"

"I'll tell them you eat more ice cream than a thin person should be able to eat. That'll make them really mad."

She lifted her head. "Blackmailer," she accused affectionately.

He held her gaze and she could see how he felt about her in his eyes — the depth and the breadth and the commitment of it. "Willow . . ."

She placed a finger on his lips to stop him, because if he said, "I love you" — if he went that far, and she was scared he would because he wasn't shy and he wasn't fearful — then she couldn't imagine how she'd be able to keep her promises to Joe.

She'd given her word to Joe, and she couldn't allow her love for Corbin to wreck her honor a second time. She needed to keep the thin walls remaining between them in place. If she didn't, their separation would just be that much harder to bear.

She set her forehead against his.

They stayed that way for a long moment. Then he kissed her, showing her that he had ways of telling her he loved her that didn't require words.

"I take offense to the whole suggestion that I need God," Joe said.

Corbin was up on a ladder, hammering one of the pieces of crown moulding into place.

"I haven't needed Him yet," Joe said.

"Really? You don't think God's help might have come in handy along the way? From where I was sitting, it didn't look like your life was a picnic." Corbin sighed. He felt about as qualified to explain the reasons why his dad needed God in his life as he was to give a lecture on quantum physics.

"No, but I got through the hard times by depending on myself and through hard work."

Corbin drove another nail home, moved the ladder, and accepted a fresh piece of moulding from his dad. "I'm not saying that self-dependence and hard work aren't good values. They are. It's just that they're not . . .

enough."

"Enough for what?"

"To save you from what I hear is a very fiery hell."

"You know I don't believe in heaven and hell. I believe that when you die that's just *it*. Lights out. The end."

Corbin sent the hammer barreling forward with more force than needed. "I can tell you that self-dependence and hard work weren't enough to save me after my shoulder injury. If it weren't for God, I might still be in Dallas, drinking myself stupid."

His dad frowned. "It wasn't necessarily God who helped you last winter, Corbin. It could be that time is what healed you."

"I wasn't sure at first whether or not it was God who helped me. But looking back on it now, it's pretty clear."

"Your recovery could have been due to any number of things," his dad said stubbornly.

"It could have been," Corbin replied with equal stubbornness. "But it wasn't."

To Corbin's everlasting frustration, none of the guests who showed up for dinner at Bradfordwood to say good-bye to Willow seemed to be in a hurry to leave.

Nora and Britt had served everyone appetizers, followed by a dinner of lasagna and salad. They'd eaten dessert an hour ago, and now it was time for *every one of these people to go away* so he could have Willow to himself. Tomorrow she was flying from Washington to a photo shoot in New York.

At the moment Willow was standing at the edge of the den talking to Tristan. Since Tristan was Britt's boyfriend, Corbin had no idea why he was looking at Willow the way die-hard female Mustangs fans looked at him. He watched the two of them through narrowed eyes.

Nora, Britt, Jill, and Charlotte had walked down to the canal. John and Mark were standing next to him, watching the fourth quarter of the Vikings–Saints matchup. Corbin was faking interest in the game. He couldn't drum up any actual interest, not even for the league he'd been playing in this time last year.

A year ago the NFL had been his complete focus. All he could think about tonight was resisting the urge to scream, *Get out!* Every time he looked at his watch and saw the minutes ticking down to Willow's departure, he felt a sick sense of powerlessness in his gut.

Most of the people here had known and loved Willow a lot longer than he had. Of course they wanted to spend time with her on her last night in Merryweather. Thing was, no one loved her as intensely as he did, and no one wanted to spend time with her as badly.

Get out. *Get out.*

Willow's grandmother, Clint, and Valentina made their way toward Corbin. "I'm sorry that your father couldn't make it tonight," Margaret said.

"Yeah. Me too." Nora and Britt had invited his dad to join them. His dad had boycotted in order to underscore his disapproval of Willow.

Whatever. At the moment, Corbin didn't have the energy to be irritated with his dad. All his energy was going toward being upset about Willow's departure.

"What kind of work did your father do before his retirement?" Margaret asked.

"He worked for GM in Detroit."

"Ah!" Her eyes lit with passion. "I remember the heyday of American automobile manufacturing. American cars were the absolute best of the best. Then overseas car companies pushed their way in, and many Americans turned their backs on our own wonderful cars and began buying cheap, poorly made vehicles. It's criminal."

Not exactly criminal.

"I still drive an Oldsmobile," she said. "I understand what it means to be loyal."

"Royal?" Valentina asked, grinning. "Yes, miss. You Queen Margaret of this family."

"In a few years, cars as we know them won't exist," Clint said, looking proud of the prediction. "We'll all be riding around in computer-driven pods."

"Pies?" Valentina asked with confusion.

"That doesn't make a bit of sense, Clint Fletcher." Margaret looked outraged. "What a thing to say."

John caught Corbin's eye and gave him an amused tip of the chin.

"I've read about it in —" Clint said.

"No. Pods. Gracious me. Certainly not." Margaret continued preaching about American cars.

Clint shifted on his feet. The guy had to be at least fifty-five, but he looked like a kid who'd been scolded.

"Well, this seems like a fun conversation," Britt said, putting an arm around her grandmother and cutting off the older woman's speech. "But I'm ready to call it a night. Tristan and I will give you a ride home, Grandma."

God bless Britt.

Everyone finally began gathering their things and filing out. Corbin helped the women find their coats and purses. He shook hands with the men.

Get. Out.

Charlotte and Jill were the last to leave.

"Thank you," Charlotte said, when they were all standing near the door.

"You're welcome," Willow said to the girl. "I loved getting to know you, and I'm so glad that you asked me to find Josephine with you, because it was a privilege for me to work with you on her case."

Tears gathered in Charlotte's gray eyes.

Corbin's spirits dipped even lower. He couldn't stand to see Charlotte cry.

"It was really nice of you to help me," Charlotte said to Willow.

"It really was," Jill said.

"The pleasure was all mine. If I had it to do over, I'd say yes again in a heartbeat. Will you keep in touch?"

"I promise I will," Charlotte answered.

"Good, because you're my source for whale trivia."

Charlotte smiled. "And pictures of Jungkook."

"Yes! How could I forget?"

Willow hugged Charlotte, then Jill.

Charlotte waved, then pulled her mom onto the front steps. Corbin shut the door behind them.

510

Finally, he and Willow were alone. "I thought they'd never leave."

He prowled toward her.

Playfully, she backed away.

He continued his offensive.

"Uh-oh." Willow smiled.

"Uh-oh what?"

"You look like a quarterback on a drive."

"That's exactly what I am."

Her shoulder blades came up against the smooth wall of the hallway. He took her mouth in a hard, fast kiss. Their hands intertwined. He trailed his lips along her jaw, then slowly down her neck.

"That dinner," she said weakly, "seemed to take a really long time."

"It felt like it took ten hours." He spoke between kisses. "I'm not a good person because I don't want to share you. Even with them."

She gasped when he found a sensitive spot on her neck. "You had me convinced for a long time that you weren't a good person. But now I suspect the opposite to be true."

He straightened, tilting down his chin so he could look at her directly. "I'm good, am I?"

"Yes."

His heartbeat thudded in his ears, his wrists. It was ridiculous, the power she had over him. Scary. Wonderful. Unchangeable. "Am I good enough for you to keep? After tomorrow?"

Pain moved across her face like shade from a passing cloud. She'd always been careful to keep a separation between them, which he hated. If he could crush that separation, he would. Only, he'd never known how. He loved her, and he wanted her to love him back, but he couldn't figure out how to convince her to keep him. He didn't want to shame himself by pleading, but he was afraid he might.

She regarded him now through piercing green eyes that turned gray around the rim of the irises. Her nose was narrow. Her lips smooth. Her cheeks glowing. She was grace and beauty and calm. He was none of those things, and he loved her for being what he wasn't. For being so unlike him and so perfect for him at the same time.

She turned her head and pressed a kiss to his wrist. He groaned and gently tilted her face to him. *Keep me,* he said through their kiss.

She wrapped her arms around his neck and made a quiet sound of answering pleasure.

She was leaving . . . and he couldn't survive without her. *Don't pressure her,* he told himself. Whenever he was in his right mind, he was convinced that no good could come of pressuring her. But he wasn't in his right mind. Frustration had been carving him up all night while he'd watched her eat lasagna, talk with her family, collect dessert bowls, and carry them to the sink. He was fuming with it now. He couldn't let her go until he knew where he stood and what he could expect over the next few months.

"We need to talk," he said.

Panic flared in her features. "Sure!" She ducked away from him and walked in the direction of the den. "How about we talk about all the reasons why Britt and Tristan are not perfect for each other and how much I want Zander to come home so Britt can realize that he's the love of her life."

"Willow."

"Let's sit. I feel like I've been standing for hours."

He softly caught her wrist, stopping her. She regarded him with concern, and an alarm went off within him. It told him to stop. Not to say anything else. To turn back.

Only, nothing important in his life had ever come to him from stopping, from not saying anything, from turning back. "We need to talk about us." He released her wrist.

She stuck her fingers into the pockets of her jeans. She wore a pale pink shirt. Short boots. "I'd rather we didn't talk about us, Corbin. I don't want to spoil this . . . thing we have at the eleventh hour by trying to define it."

She was trying to let him down gently, which both frustrated and worried him. He wasn't a client she had to carefully manage. "I don't want to spoil anything, but I do need for us to define it. What's going to happen after you leave tomorrow?"

She hesitated. "We'll stay in touch. We'll talk. We'll send text messages and pictures."

"I talk to and send texts and pictures to my friend Gray. The way I feel about him is nothing like the way that I feel about you. I'll come and see you in New York."

Her skin paled. "You can't come see me in New York. You can't leave your dad, not for any reason. He needs you here."

He knew she was right, yet claustrophobia choked him at the thought of remaining in Shore Pine without her. "I can get away for a few days."

"No," she insisted. "You can't get away for a few days. You would never forgive yourself if something were to happen to your dad while you were gone, and at this point something could happen to him at

514

any time. He's your priority." Her expression begged him to agree.

"You're my priority, too. How am I supposed to do a good job taking care of my dad if I can't see you? If I can't be with you?"

She didn't answer.

"If I can't travel to see you, then how soon can you get away to visit me here?" he asked.

She swallowed. "I'm not sure. I'm going to be really busy for the next several weeks."

She was hedging. "But you *are* planning to come back?"

She looked down at her feet for a long moment, then up at him. "I really don't know. I'm sorry, but that's the best answer I have at the moment."

The air left his lungs.

"Corbin." She spoke kindly, persuasively. "Every day I've told you that we weren't together."

He interlaced his hands behind his head.

She gestured him forward. "Come sit down with me. Let's not fight on our last night together, okay? I can get you some more ice cream since the portions that Nora dished up were small, and I'm sure you're probably still hungry. Let's eat ice cream and make out." She attempted a coaxing smile.

He took a step back from her.

"Corbin," she whispered.

He continued to press his hands into his skull in order to hold himself together.

They were still standing inside Bradfordwood's foyer. Which was perfect, wasn't it? She'd never let their relationship take them anywhere. They'd always been stuck in a place that was just an entrance to something better. And now the foyer of their relationship had become an exit to something worse. "Let me get this straight." He kept his voice ruthlessly level. His arms lowered. "I can't see you and you don't have any plans to come back here to see me."

"I really am sorry. I can't express to you how thankful I am for the time we've had together."

"I don't want your gratitude."

She flinched but kept her chin up. "I don't know when we'll see each other again, but we can talk every day on the phone —"

"I love you," he said. Subtle fury edged the words.

He'd been ruined by her abandonment the last time. Even so, he'd given her the power to ruin him a second time. He was furious with himself and furious with her for refusing to trust him, for refusing to love him back. He wanted her to fight for them, to hang on to what they had. But he could see in every inch of her that — just like his dad — she'd decided not to fight. She wasn't going to hang on.

"You are everything to me, Willow. I'll do anything in the world for you. I want to marry you. I want to have a shot at taking care of you and loving you and making love to you every day for as long as I live. There never has been and there never will be another woman for me. You're it."

She moved toward him, and he could tell by her expression that she meant to throw her arms around him. To kiss him and comfort him. And then abandon him tomorrow.

Just like he didn't want her gratitude, he didn't want her comfort.

He held up a staying hand. Her steps immediately stopped.

"Do you love me?" he asked bluntly.

"I . . ." That one sound. It was just one syllable, and yet it was enough to damn all of his hopes.

He waited.

Tension vibrated through the space between them.

He waited.

He gave her more than enough time. Too much time.

One second slid into the next, but she

didn't say anything more. What more proof did he need? She'd made herself very, very clear.

He spun on his heel and slammed Bradfordwood's door behind him.

Involuntarily, Willow lifted both hands to cover the lower half of her face. During their exchange just now, her lungs had tightened as if she were being physically wounded, and her breath had wanted to stop off in her throat. She stood unmoving on Bradfordwood's polished hardwood floor, struggling to comprehend what had just happened. Things had fallen apart so quickly and so completely.

Just minutes ago, her family and friends had been here, and she'd been having a lovely time. Just seconds ago, she'd been in Corbin's arms.

And now this.

If only she'd responded better to the things he'd said to her. If only she'd been able to find the words that would have placated him. Instead, she'd been limited to an inadequate handful of words because of the promises she'd made to Joe.

She felt like the mother in the fairy tale Rumpelstiltskin, who'd promised the little man her firstborn child and later come to regret her promise. Except in Willow's case, knowing the word *Rumpelstiltskin* wasn't going to save her.

Back when she and Joe had their discussion, she'd had no idea that her promises would prove so hard to keep. She hadn't fully anticipated the power of Hurricane Corbin. She hadn't understood then that he had the ability to change a day from bad to good with a smile, to make her feel as though she'd finally found home, to revolutionize her heart with his acceptance of her.

He'd said he loved her.

A wave of dizziness rolled over her.

He'd said he'd do anything for her. That he wanted to marry her. That she was the only woman for him. He'd spoken with unvarnished honesty and vulnerability.

Numbly, she walked toward the sitting room at the front of the house. Perhaps he hadn't driven away. Maybe he was still parked out front, rethinking things. If so, then it was possible that he'd come back inside and spend more time with her on her very last night. She'd completed all her packing earlier in the day so that she'd be able to focus entirely on him when the others left.

The view out the sitting room's window revealed empty driveway. He was gone.

519

She needed to make it right.

She couldn't make it right. For now, she had to leave it the way that it was.

She must have seemed like the coldest, meanest woman alive just now.

Willow lowered into a nearby chair and wrapped her arms around her middle. For months now, she'd been the only occupant of her childhood home. But for much, much longer than that, she'd been encased in aloneness. Since she'd left home for college? Since she'd set out to pursue modeling? The girl whose big dream had been to be a part of a loving family of her own had been living with a sense of aloneness for so long now that she couldn't put a start date on it.

She'd wanted to tell Corbin that she loved him, too. To assure him that she'd come back to see him. Soon.

Did you really think your relationship with Corbin would end happily? a taunting voice within her asked. *After what you did in the past with him? You're not good enough to deserve a happy ending.*

Another thought rose up in defense: *But I'm doing this — honoring his dad's request — to prove that I'm trustworthy. To prove I'm not that same girl, riddled with mistakes.*

She sprang up from the chair and went

straight to the mudroom. She couldn't stay inside, alone, with these thoughts. Not tonight, during the hours she'd planned to spend with Corbin.

She exchanged her ankle boots for rain boots, then donned her coat and a pair of gloves. Flicking on a flashlight, she struck out in the direction of the inlet.

She wanted to clench her fists and scream at the sky. She wanted to bawl.

She did neither.

She was the best behaved sister because she was the sister who'd been a mistake. She was the sister who'd been left behind by her mother. She'd never wanted to give anyone a reason to look at her and shake their head and say, "That's the unwanted Bradford daughter, you know."

You are not a mistake.

Unlike the voice she'd heard earlier, this one was not taunting. It was not malicious. It was as quiet as intuition, as steady as time.

She *had* been a mistake, though. The facts of her birth testified to that.

I planned you, Willow. I knit you together. You were never a mistake.

I was.

I don't make mistakes.

She drew in an aching breath and thought back through her family's history. Her father's affair with her biological mother, Sylvie. His subsequent marriage to Nora's mom, who'd died tragically. For years after, her dad had poured everything he had into caring for her and Nora, and into his work. Emotionally, he'd closed himself off from everyone else inside a shell of grief and blame.

But, in time, the Lord had brought healing. After all the heartache her dad had endured, funny, smart, feisty Kathleen had come into his life. Her dad had been determined not to love Kathleen, but in the end, he'd been unable to stop himself. And thank goodness for that. If her dad hadn't married Kathleen, Britt wouldn't have been born. Her dad wouldn't have experienced the joy and peace he'd found in his long marriage to Kathleen. And his three daughters wouldn't have had a mother.

When Willow took the long view of her dad's story, she could see plainly how God had taken her dad's failures and sorrows and created something beautiful out of them.

Why was it so hard for her to accept that God could do the same for her?

Was her faith too small? Or was her regret too big?

Perhaps her regret was so big that it had

kept her faith small these past four years.

"How come you're still carrying guilt around?" Corbin had asked her a few nights ago.

She'd had no answer then. Why couldn't she receive forgiveness and move on the way Corbin had?

Because it seemed to her that her holy God would and should expect more perfection of her than she expected of herself.

That was wrong theology. She'd never had any perfection of her own to offer. Even before her affair with Corbin. That was right theology.

Yet . . . she'd believed there for a while that she *did* have something of her own to bring to the table and that her worthiness might inspire God to love her. When she'd lost her worthiness, she'd concluded that God no longer had as many reasons to love her.

Following the beam of her flashlight, she reached the cliff above the inlet. This place, this cove, was a symbol of all the rules she'd broken. She'd let those broken rules trip her up, like ropes around her ankles.

But Jesus.

Jesus was the antidote to broken rules.

She was finally ready to accept that and to embrace His forgiveness because she flat out *couldn't* deal with the alternative any longer. She couldn't continue to carry the guilt.

"I never had any goodness of my own," she whispered. She said it several times, allowing the stark truth of it to penetrate. "You were always the only good one. I have nothing to bring to you but faith."

Please, please forgive me. I love you.

A sense of full acceptance and all-consuming, all-forgiving, unconditional love swept through her. For long minutes she simply stood, unmoving and praying, letting herself feel God's love. His love wasn't narrow, the way she'd tried to make it. It was the widest and deepest love there was.

"You love me," she breathed. And instantly, she could feel His answer in the wind, the air, the life beating through her veins.

He loved her without reservations. Without keeping a record of her wrongs. As far as the east is from the west, that's how far He'd removed her sins from her.

He loved her. And He forgave her.

She scooped up a handful of dirt in one gloved hand and extended it in front of her. Deliberately, she let the dirt fall between her fingers, over the side of the cliff. With it, she worked to let go of the shame. She worked to forgive herself.

By the time no dirt remained in her hand, she felt clean inside.

He, in His grace, was giving her a new beginning.

A rivulet of tears ran down her cheek.

She prayed earnestly for Corbin and for herself. She prayed that God would somehow take their failures and do for the two of them what He'd once done for her father.

Lord God, make something beautiful out of our mistakes, in your time.

Text messages written by Willow and deleted before sending:

Willow
Corbin, please forgive me, I'm so sorry.

Willow
I know I might have come across as unfeeling earlier, but I'm not. At all. I've had a lot of practice at covering my emotions. At the slightest sign of risk, I put up barricades and hide behind them. But that doesn't mean that I don't feel. I care about you, deeply.

Willow
Please keep on loving me. Despite the

way that things look. I can't tell you why I did what I did tonight. Will you love me and believe in me, anyway?

Willow
Is it okay if I drive over to your place? We can't leave it like this between us. I want to see you one more time before I go.

Willow
I love you.

CHAPTER TWENTY-FOUR

Britt Bradford hated good-byes.

The schmaltzy sentiment. The gloomy parting hugs. But also, she just plain didn't like to say good-bye to the people she cared about most. She'd been off her game ever since Zander had gone. Now Willow was leaving, too, which was making the ten o'clock hour of this overcast, misty Monday morning all the more depressing.

She'd filled Sweet Art with several sources of bright, happy light. Still. Depressing. "Here." Britt handed Willow a box containing milk chocolate caramel truffles, her favorite. "A little something for the plane."

"Thank you." Willow tucked the box into her purse. During these past months in Merryweather, Britt's oldest sister had dressed in a style that was, for her, fairly casual. Today, she'd switched back into her modeling persona. She wore a scarf over a designer shirt, skinny pants, heels, and a chic gray leather jacket. Her big round sunglasses had been over her eyes a moment ago, when she and Nora had entered Sweet Art, but were now propped on top of her head. She looked like the high-powered, fashionable woman she was.

"It's not fair to vie for the title of Best Sister by giving Willow chocolate," Nora said to Britt. Then, to Willow, "I can offer you a stack of historical documents to read on the plane."

"I'll pass," Willow said. "Britt's clearly my best sister."

"You stink, Britt," Nora said.

"I have no sympathy for you, my vanquished foe."

Nora laughed and Willow tried to join in, but something about Willow's manner was off. It was as though she was providing them with an imitation of herself. Her makeup had been applied meticulously. Beneath it, though, her skin was a touch too white. She seemed fragile. If she were to stumble and fall, Britt worried she'd break. "I can tell that something's wrong," Britt said to Willow. "What is it?"

"Nothing."

"It's not nothing." Nora set her hands on her hips and cocked her head. "I agree, something's bothering you."

Willow massaged her temples.

"Yikes, she's doing that massage-the-temples thing," Britt said.

"Things didn't go well between Corbin and me last night." Willow dropped her hands. "After you guys left."

"Oh no," Nora murmured.

"What happened?" Britt asked. Maddie was helping a customer at the counter, and an older woman was sitting off to the side, making her way through a piece of dark chocolate pistachio bark and a coffee. Here, standing in a sisterly huddle in the middle of Sweet Art's floor space, they had a small buffer between themselves and eavesdroppers.

"I don't want to go into it because I want to respect Corbin's privacy," Willow said.

Tactful Willow. "Privacy's overrated between sisters," Britt said.

"Let's just say that he wanted more from me than I could give. I can't come back here anytime soon, and he can't leave because of his dad's health."

"But . . ." Britt said. "There's this cool thing they've invented called FaceTime. Maybe you've heard of it."

"Be kind." Nora nudged Britt's upper arm. "Be kind" was the refrain their mom had used on the three of them whenever

529

they'd gotten into arguments.

"I don't think we're getting the whole story," Britt said.

"I don't either," Nora said.

A flush lit Willow's cheeks. "And you're not going to get the whole story."

"Fine," Britt said grumpily.

Britt met Nora's eyes.

"You two aren't allowed to exchange meaningful glances about me in front of me." Willow's stab at teasing fell flat.

"I don't understand why *you're* not engaged to John," Britt said to Nora. "And why *you* aren't willing to try dating Corbin long-distance," she said to Willow. "These men aren't ordinary, run-of-the-mill men, you realize. They're once-in-a-lifetime men, in my opinion. So if you aren't going to snag them, I can only assume it's because you're staying single out of solidarity with me. Which is nice and all, but I can assure you, it's also unnecessary. I'm six years and four years younger than you two grandmas. I haven't even reached my prime."

Willow gave her a droll look. "Did you just call us grandmas?"

"I'll have you know that I'm definitely not staying single out of solidarity with you," Nora said to Britt. "John and I just started dating in July. If and when he proposes, I'm going to say yes before he finishes his sentence."

"You go through a boyfriend every season of the year, Britt," Willow said. "Why would you want us to settle down?"

Britt adjusted the apron she wore. "I want you to settle down because your boyfriends are great. I switch my boyfriends every season because none of them have been great in the way that John and Corbin are great. You two are weird."

"You're weirder," Nora said to her.

"You're weirdest," Willow said to Nora.

They shared a smile of complete accord. They had different personalities, but the ties that bound them together were far stronger than their differences. They were the best thing any little girl can be to another little girl and any woman can be to another woman. *They were sisters.*

Britt held her arms open to Willow. The time had come for the gloomy parting hug. Willow always drove herself to Sea-Tac in her own car, which she then left in long-term storage until her next arrival. She didn't need Britt or Nora to give her a ride to the airport, so this was good-bye. "Stay safe and come back to see us soon," Britt whispered.

"Love you," Willow said.

"Love you, too."

"I promised Nikki you'd drop by at the library to say good-bye," Nora said.

"Okay, will do." Willow took a step toward the door, then stopped. "Would you guys keep an eye on Joe and Corbin for me? It's just —" She set her lips together a fraction too tightly. "Joe has the Dixons, but I don't think he has many other friends in Shore Pine. He likes both of you, and it might be nice for him and Corbin to have visitors."

"Of course," Britt and Nora said in unison.

"Jinx!" they said in unison.

Then Willow and Nora were gone, and Britt had officially lost the proximity of one of her sisters.

"I heard the speech you gave about how John and Corbin are once-in-a-lifetime men" came a voice from behind Britt.

She swiveled to see her longtime friend, Maddie, resting her crossed forearms on top of the chocolate display case. Maddie's messy bob, darker at the crown and streaked with a few caramel-colored strands at the bottom, gleamed. A smear of sugar crystals marked one of her cheeks. Maddie was spunky, sweet, and had a fondness for Instagram and potato chips. She was also Britt's primary employee. While Britt worked in the kitchen, Maddie saw to everything else that made Sweet Art run.

Britt came to stand directly across the display case from Maddie. "I was thinking that we were protected from eavesdroppers."

"The only part of your conversation loud enough to hear was your once-in-a-lifetime men speech. It was a good speech."

"Thank you."

"And it got me thinking. I know a once-in-a-lifetime man who you, my friend, are not snagging."

"Zander?" Every so often Maddie floated the idea that Britt and Zander should become a couple. Which was ridiculous.

Maddie nodded. "He's not an" — she did air quotes — " 'ordinary, run-of-the-mill man.' "

"No. He's my friend. My very good friend."

"Wouldn't it be nice to fall in love with someone who's also your very good friend?"

"No, it would just be strange."

"He's handsome, in case you haven't noticed lately."

"I haven't noticed lately because he's gone. But even if he were here, I wouldn't notice because he's *my friend*." Britt cinched the tie on her apron tighter. "By the way, you're not really one to be giving out dating advice seeing as how you've been in love with Leo Donnelly for years without ever mentioning it to him."

"Leo," she said dreamily. Britt had known bringing up Leo would divert Maddie the same way throwing a tennis ball diverted a dog. "I can't mention it to him because he's Olivia's husband."

"He was Olivia's husband until she died. Now he's *your* future husband."

"He thinks of me as nothing more than a friend. Kind of like the way you think of Zander."

"Yes." Britt blinked. "Wait, no. It's not the same at all, because Zander doesn't have romantic feelings for me like you do for Leo." Flustered for some reason that made no sense to her, Britt headed toward her sanctuary in the rear of the shop to continue work on a batch of white chocolate macadamia popcorn. "Get back to work, employee of mine."

"I am working! You pay me to loan you my wisdom."

"I pay you to sell chocolate, smarty-pants."

Willow exited Nora's Library on the Green, then paused to extend her umbrella. When she had it up, she took one last look at Merryweather Historical Village. Half a dozen

534

people, bundled into rain gear, hurried along the village paths with their heads down. Only one figure was still —

Recognition clanged within her.

Corbin sat on one of the benches lining the village's ribbon of grass. He was leaning forward, elbows planted on his knees, looking directly at her beneath the brim of a black baseball cap. He'd dressed in a jacket and track pants. No umbrella. He must be soaked.

She walked toward him on wobbly legs, her pulse thrumming fast. *Thank you, Lord.* It must be a good sign that he'd come here. Surely? Or maybe not? Maybe he was here to let her have it for hurting him.

He stood, his hands thrust into his pockets.

She stopped near him, but not too near. Certainly not as near as she'd have stopped yesterday before their fight. The relatively small distance between them felt big and unnavigable.

He hadn't shaved. His face was grave. His eyes, red and haggard.

Her mood, already bleak today, took a spiraling journey toward her toes. She couldn't stand it. She loved him, and she needed to tell him. She needed to kiss him and whisper to him how sorry she was for letting him down.

Instead, she stretched out her arm so that her umbrella covered him instead of her. She was dry and warm, but he must be cold and wet, and she refused to watch the rain saturate him further.

His lips quirked up sadly. "You keep it." He moved the umbrella's stem back in her direction. "I knew you'd come by the village this morning to say good-bye to your sisters."

"You were right. I . . . didn't see you sitting here earlier."

"I was waiting inside The Pie Emporium until a few minutes ago. I saw you and Nora go into the library."

"I see." This was terrible! She knew him incredibly well. Why did she feel so tongue-tied? Because this meeting meant so much, that's why. These were her last moments with him.

"I wanted to see you," he said, "because I can't leave things between us the way I left them last night."

Hope flickered to life within Willow. "I can't, either." It was a relief to say one thing that was wholly true.

"I have to know if I've been reading you wrong all this time, Willow. Was I way off base to think you cared about me?"

536

"No. I do care about you. A great deal." *I love you, in fact.* "I know it seems like I don't. But I do."

He scowled, and she knew he was wondering why, in that case, she'd insisted on suspending their relationship. No doubt he'd been battling anger and confusion all night. She knew for sure that she'd lacerated his pride. Yet here he was, working to build a bridge between them this morning.

"I guess we're going to have to agree to disagree on where our relationship should go from here." A network of tendons flickered along his jaw. "I can stomach disagreeing with you. But I can't stomach not being able to communicate with you after today."

"Neither can I."

"I can't handle my dad's situation. Or finish construction on my house. Or bring down Foster Holt if I have to do those things without you. . . . Without at least talking to you. I can't do it."

Tears hazed her eyes. She moved to him and hugged him tightly, the umbrella's handle trapped between her chest and his. His arms came around her, and she felt his face press near her ear.

"I'm sorry I can't be here in person." Her voice broke. "I'm incredibly sorry for that and for everything else." She knew that talking on the phone probably sounded to him like a lousy consolation prize. But . . . "I'll take talking to you on the phone, Corbin, because it's so much better than nothing."

"Don't forget that we're also going to text and send pictures," he said.

"Yes." She laughed, sorrow clutching her.

"What about emails?"

"Yes."

"Facebook messages?"

"Neither of us likes Facebook."

"Oh, right."

They stayed there, clinging to each other, as surrounded by pain as they were by rain, the circle of the umbrella their only protection.

"I'll miss you," she whispered.

"I'll miss you." He spoke in a sandpaper tone, as if his throat was sore. "Come back when you can."

"I will." She looked into his face, committing every detail of it to memory. Telling him, *You didn't read me wrong,* without words.

He gave her one feather-light kiss. It was a respectful kiss. Safe. He'd retreated from her behind a new fortress of his own. "Good-bye, Willow." He released his hold.

She walked backward a few paces.

He remained frozen in place. His big body

was full of power. Speed. Strength. Yet standing there alone, he looked both proud and bereft.

She was certain in that moment, positively certain, that he was the one for her.

She nodded once, then turned and walked to her car.

Text message from Willow's agent, Blythe, to Willow:

Blythe
Congratulations on your first day back on the job! I'm so happy for you, Willow. I hope the break in Washington was everything you hoped it would be and that you're feeling refreshed. In addition to the bookings already on your calendar, I have several more opportunities to discuss with you. Some big players are rabidly interested in signing you. Call me when you get a chance, and we'll discuss!

CHAPTER TWENTY-FIVE

"I've never understood why Christians are so determined to make everyone feel bad about themselves with all that talk about sin and sinners. *Sin and sinners.*" Joe grunted with disgust. "They go on and on about it."

Why had Corbin imagined that talking to his dad about faith was a good idea? At the moment, he'd trade one of his Super Bowl rings for the chance to avoid this conversation and lay tile alone in this bathroom he no longer cared about in this town he no longer cared about now that Willow wasn't in it.

She'd left two days ago. That he'd found a way to go on shocked him.

He and his dad were both wearing knee-pads and hunching over to place spacers between slabs of tile. "Christians go on and on about sin," Corbin said, "because they know that God can't do anything with a person until that person can admit their sins. Problem is, most of us would rather ignore our mistakes. We want to view ourselves as good at any cost."

"Most of the people I know *are* good."

"How good are they, though, in comparison to God?" They worked for a few minutes in silence. "There's something that the people who want to see themselves as good don't understand," Corbin said.

"Which is?"

"There's freedom in admitting that you're not good, in being accepted for who you actually are. It was a relief for me when I got to that place."

His dad positioned another tile on the grout.

Man, he missed Willow.

A huge distance separated them now. He had no idea when he'd get to see her again, and the idea that it might be months worsened his already rotten mood.

When his dad let the discussion drop, Corbin didn't try to resurrect it. He wasn't in the right frame of mind to talk about God.

He wasn't in the right frame of mind for anything.

Willow remained perfectly still as the stylist adjusted her hair. She was stretched out on a low-slung white cement sculpture in front of miles of aqua Caribbean sea.

She'd worked with this photographer several times in the past. He was talented and professional. The location was stunning. Even so, her thoughts were thousands of miles away in a little town called Shore Pine with an ex-pro football player and his dad.

During her months in Merryweather and over the three weeks that had passed since she'd left Washington, she'd given herself several work-related pep talks along the lines of, *Your enjoyment of modeling is sure to come back. This burnout will pass. Be patient with yourself.*

But, so far, Willow hadn't felt positively enough about the opportunities her agent had presented to her to commit to any of them. Her halfhearted response baffled Blythe.

Willow understood why. The idea of walking away from a successful career was, on its surface, baffling. Willow herself had some reservations about it.

One, she didn't know what God was calling her to next, so leaving modeling felt a little like letting go of a trapeze bar to fall into nothingness. The state of her finances did provide her with a type of net. (Because she had not, thank goodness, frittered away all her income on housewares.) Even so.

Two, she worried that her distress over Corbin might be unfairly slanting her objectivity. Everything felt drab and boring without him. Had her pining for him made the modeling seem unbearable, even though it wasn't?

Three, if she quit modeling, would she regret it later? At the age of thirty-one, she didn't have many years of modeling ahead of her anyway. Would she be upset with herself twenty years from now if she quit at this point?

Across three continents in three weeks, Willow had been thinking about and praying through these issues. Gradually, she'd come to accept that her discontent with modeling was *not* a phase.

She'd always be grateful for all that modeling had given her. She'd traveled the world, and in so doing, seen and experienced a treasure trove of things she never would have otherwise. She'd met scores of interesting people. She'd been given a platform to help Benevolence Worldwide. For a long time, the exciting job of professional model had suited her. However, Willow's modeling life was no longer, for her, the model life.

God had called her to modeling all those

years ago. She firmly believed that. And she'd seen how He'd been able to use her profession for His glory. She'd felt satisfaction in her work and peace concerning her direction.

God had removed her satisfaction and peace some time ago. She'd been blundering along without Him ever since, for longer than she cared to admit. Just because God started you on one path didn't mean He intended to keep you on that path all your life.

If God wasn't calling her to modeling anymore, and she really didn't think He was, then she had no business continuing in this profession. Her doubts about quitting needed to step to the side and get *out of her way* because she didn't want to go where God wasn't leading.

He was the one who'd sustained her these past three weeks, who'd traveled with her, who'd doggedly comforted her when she'd been desolate without Corbin. She was determined to live her life in sync with God from now on. So if God was ready to do a new thing in her life, then she needed to collect her bravery and embrace change.

The hair stylist scampered off. The makeup artist brushed more highlighter onto her cheekbones. The photographer's assistant modified the lighting. The photographer called out instructions. Willow dutifully obeyed.

"Yes," the photographer said. "Yes!"

No, thought Willow. *No.*

I'm really done.

What she wanted most in the world at this particular moment, sitting by the sea, was to be with Corbin. Grief gathered into a hot ball behind her rib cage.

Great Scott! *Get ahold of yourself.*

It had taken scheduling gymnastics to talk to him each day across time zones and her shooting schedule. But he'd never complained. Nor had he blamed her for leaving. Nor had he said he loved her again. He was somewhat guarded with her now. He hadn't once asked when she was coming back.

In addition to the updates she received from Corbin, her sisters had been supplying her with insider information. Nora, Britt, or Grandma had been stopping by Corbin and Joe's barnhouse every few days. According to her sisters, Joe was slowing down and growing thinner, but still working alongside Corbin on the renovation.

Willow fervently wished that she could be there. What kind of person showed their love by remaining distant when their loved one's closest family member was dying? It was a person's stubborn determination to stick by another when things got hard, in the very worst moments, that defined love.

"Can you brighten that smile by a few degrees?" the photographer asked.

And so she did.

Corbin still woke at the same time each day. Made the same things for breakfast. Drove his dad to appointments. His publicist and agent still called, and he still responded to them in the usual ways.

He was faking it. He was moving his body through daily routines while trying to accept that Willow was gone and that his dad was dying. It felt as though his true self was looking down on him from far, far away. It felt as though someone else, his shadow self, had hijacked his body.

Willow had been gone for a month now. It was Christmas Day, and he and his dad were sitting at Bradfordwood's dining room table with Nora and John and Britt and Tristan, a few of the Bradford aunts and uncles, and some of their cousins. Willow's sisters and grandmother had done everything possible to take care of his dad since Willow's departure, including inviting them to this meal.

He nodded and pretended to listen to

what one of Willow's relatives was saying to him as his attention panned across the table. His gaze paused on his dad. He'd talked his dad into listening to the same audio version of the Bible that Corbin had listened to, which was the only good thing that had happened lately.

Corbin had excelled at football for most of his life. He wasn't used to failing at things as badly as he'd been failing at explaining Christianity to his father. They were still having their not-productive talks, but now, at least, Corbin had the comfort of knowing that his dad was getting input from the Bible itself.

His vision moved over the remainder of the room. The Bradfords had cooked a huge amount of food. Christmas music played. And everyone here, except him, appeared to be happy.

He felt as happy as an undertaker. Frankly, it sucked to be surrounded by this house and these people when Willow wasn't here. Spending Christmas at Bradfordwood while Willow celebrated in Africa with her parents was the emotional equivalent of getting sacked.

Because of their phone calls, he knew how her days went. He knew what was on her mind and where she was in the world and if she was feeling happy or sad. She encouraged him to continue talking to his dad about God. She listened to his concerns. She sympathized with him. She discussed the pros and cons of the decisions he faced regarding his dad's care.

The sound of her voice always flowed into him like warm, calming water.

Their conversations were his lifeline.

They were also his curse because they weren't nearly enough.

A part of him was still coldly and completely furious with her. He knew it wasn't fair to be angry at Willow for not loving him back, for leaving him.

Even so, he *was* angry.

On top of that, he flat out wasn't doing well without her. His appetite wasn't what it should be. He wasn't sleeping well. The passing of weeks hadn't helped, and he'd started to wonder if he should see his dad's psychologist. For as long as he could remember, being diagnosed with a mental illness had been his worst fear. That wasn't his worst fear anymore. There were a lot of things worse than mental illness. Living without Willow was one of them for him.

He'd been praying desperately for God's help, and still, he was just getting by.

■ ■ ■

"That's it," Corbin said to his dad on the last day of January. They both took a step back to admire the switch plate Joe had just installed. They'd spent the last few weeks doing finishing work on their house. Quarter round. Trim. Paint. Outlet covers. Exterior improvements. As of this moment, they were officially done. Their eight-month-long renovation was complete.

Joe looked across at Corbin and gave him the old grin he used to give Corbin when Corbin brought home an A on a paper, scored touchdowns, or had dinner waiting for his dad when he got home from work.

"Good work, son." His dad extended a hand.

They shook. "Good work, Dad."

That old grin made his dad look ten years younger. Maybe the doctors were wrong. Maybe his dad still had plenty of time left in him. Maybe his dad would recover and his story would become a miracle story.

The next morning Joe wouldn't get out of bed.

His dad's doctor had instructed Corbin to call with any change in condition, so Corbin called. Dr. Benton drove to the house that evening and went upstairs to treat his patient.

Corbin waited downstairs. He sat at the kitchen island in his finished house, turning his coffee mug around and around. His loneliness pressed in on him from every angle, heavier than gravity, as inescapable as chains.

Dr. Benton was a nice man. But when he came downstairs and told Corbin it was time to call in hospice care, Dr. Benton might as well have clubbed him in the head.

After thanking the doctor and showing him out, Corbin stood inside his front door, one hand splayed on the smooth wood, head dipped. It wasn't going to be a miracle story.

He'd known for a long time that it wouldn't be. It's not like this fate had snuck up on him. Even so, he felt stunned by it.

Hospice? No.

He wasn't ready. His heart began to race with panic.

He pulled out his phone and dialed Willow.

"Corbin?"

He exhaled raggedly, thankful that she'd picked up. "I'm sorry to wake you. I know it's the middle of the night in Paris."

"It's okay."

He sat on one of the chairs that guests had sat in to watch football the night he'd hosted a party so that he could see her. Max and Duke lay on the floor at his feet, staring at him with worry as he told her what the doctor had said.

"I'm so sorry." Her voice was slightly husky from sleep.

"Hospice, Willow?" He hated the sound of his own anxiety. "I'm not ready for that."

"I'm not sure a person can ever be ready for what you and your dad are going through."

"He was just working on the house with me *yesterday.* How could he have gone down so quickly?"

"If I had to guess, I'd say that he willed himself to finish the house, regardless of how he was feeling physically. He told me once that completing work on the house was extremely important to him."

"He did?"

"Yes."

"So now that the house is done he's throwing in the towel?"

She hesitated. "I think it's more that his exhaustion has caught up with him, now that he's accomplished what he wanted to accomplish."

He swore. "Sorry," he immediately said.

551

"It's all right."

"I'm not up for this, Willow. I can't take care of my dad as well as he should be taken care of."

"Yes, you can."

"I should have insisted that he meet with a pastor. I can't convince him to believe in God."

"Just you wait and see. God's the one who will convince Joe. Keep trying, and I'll keep praying."

"I can't watch my father die," he said flatly.

She didn't answer. They both knew that he had no choice. He loved his dad, and so he'd remain right here, with his father, until the end.

"Corbin," she said. He loved her voice, the timbre and the clarity of it. "You have a history of responding to hard things by going into a tailspin."

"If that's a pep talk, it needs a little work."

"Hear me out. We discussed what happened to you when I told you I was worried that I might be pregnant. And after we broke up, your dad told me you were in a bad place for a long time."

"True."

"You went into a tailspin again after your shoulder injury."

"Also true."

"Your dad is dying, which is worse than anything that's come before. . . . Yet you haven't gone into a tailspin." She paused. "You said just now that you're not up for this. But don't you see? You've been bearing up under this for months. You *are* bearing up under this."

Surprise froze him for a long moment. "I'm struggling."

"Yes, but that's to be expected, considering your circumstances. God has been giving you enough strength to get through each day. He's steadying you, Corbin."

He was too stunned to speak.

"You might not feel as if you know God well yet, but He knows you very, very well. He's with you, and He's providing for you."

They said good-night a few minutes later. Corbin set the phone aside and went to stand at the empty fireplace.

Willow was right. As heavyhearted as he'd been lately, he hadn't reached for alcohol. He hadn't gotten in his car and driven someplace far, far away. He hadn't done any of the destructive things he'd done in the past when life had sent him reeling.

God had been holding him together.

His shoulders relaxed as the worst of the stress that had gripped him since Dr. Benton mentioned hospice began to loosen.

God was holding him together.

Not so long ago, he'd wanted to believe that Willow had the power to make the loss of football and his shoulder pain and his dad's condition bearable.

Then she'd gone away.

Even without her here, the loss of football and his shoulder pain and his dad's condition *were* bearable. Awful. But bearable. Because God was on his side.

He, his dad, and Willow had all been scarred in ways that made trusting difficult. In the months since he'd asked God to save him, he'd continued to waffle. He'd never been completely certain whether he could trust God.

He stared at the hearth and imagined puzzle pieces locking together in ways he hadn't seen until now.

God had brought him to Shore Pine. God had brought his father here, too, to this place that had been good for his dad. He'd given them work. He'd brought Willow and connected her to Corbin through Charlotte. God had made a way for Corbin to forgive Willow and Willow to forgive Corbin. He'd made a way for the two of them to resist the mistakes that had caused Willow to break up with him the last time. And then, after she'd gone, God had remained. He'd been offering Corbin something better than Willow's presence or his dad's health or football. He'd been offering Corbin Himself.

Gratitude clutched Corbin's heart. God had been showing Himself to be trustworthy for a long time now. He'd been far more faithful to Corbin than Corbin had ever been to Him.

This God of his was a God who was determined to set broken things right.

Corbin was a broken thing.

From now on, he'd let God set him right.

Three days later, Willow unlocked the door of her LA home and pulled her rolling suitcase inside behind her.

She hadn't been here since last spring, so she'd hired a housekeeper to wash sheets and dust so that the house would be pristine when she arrived. Indeed, everything looked immaculate. She'd decorated and stocked this house to the brim. It hit just the right notes. Stylish and relaxing. Cozy and inviting. Gracious.

It also reverberated with silence.

She'd always had a deep hunger for *home.* She'd done her best to fill that need through countless shopping sprees. She'd put time and heart and money into making this house as fabulous as it could possibly be and, even so, this showplace wasn't *home.*

Home was God. *Home* was the people He gave you to love while you were on this earth.

She made her way through the familiar rooms that felt oddly unfamiliar. They hadn't changed. She had.

When she reached her kitchen, she set her purse on the counter and extracted from it the newspaper article she'd been reading on the plane. She stuck it on her refrigerator with a magnet, then took a step back to read it one last time.

The headline proclaimed, *Wife of Missing Man Accuses Senator Foster Holt.*

The photo showed Senator Holt in profile, hurrying into his limo, surrounded by his attorneys.

Washington, D.C. — Richard Reynolds, 55, Senior Analyst at American corporate giant Sierra, Inc., went missing two years ago. Yesterday, his wife, Angela Reynolds, came forward with material he left for her in their safe deposit box before his disappearance.

According to Mrs. Reynolds and substantiated by sources close to her, the safe deposit box contained audio tapes, photographs, and a zip drive of financial documents that implicate Senator Foster Holt.

"Richard grew increasingly anxious in the weeks leading up to his disappearance," Mrs. Reynolds said. "He confessed to me that he'd been funneling money from Sierra to Foster Holt through campaign donations as well as private payments, and he feared that the FEC was growing suspicious. When he informed his superiors at Sierra and Foster Holt that he wanted no part of it any longer, neither would allow him that option. He was afraid for his life, so he began compiling evidence. He told me he wanted me to have it, in case anything happened to him."

When asked why she waited two years to make the material public, Reynolds said, "I was afraid for my own life. Also, Richard was a wonderful man, and I've been reluctant to share his part in all of this. I've dreaded the media frenzy I knew this would cause. But when I met with a team of private investigators last week, and they told me about some of the other things they suspect that Foster Holt has been involved with, I couldn't remain silent any longer. Senator Holt needs to answer for his role in my husband's disappearance."

Local authorities are studying the material that Mrs. Reynolds has supplied and are said to be reopening the missing persons case of Richard Reynolds.

Ross Levy, attorney for Senator Foster Holt, had this to say when asked for a comment: "Senator Holt has been a respected and hardworking public servant for four decades. This so-called evidence was likely manufactured by Mrs. Reynolds and insiders from the opposing political party. These accusations are both false and outrageous."

No, Willow thought. *Not false. Not outrageous.*

It had taken time, but Corbin's team of private investigators had done what they'd set out to do. Corbin had kept her abreast of their investigation, and last week she'd been one of the first to learn that the team had finally found a chink in Senator Holt's armor. Willow had no doubt that an arrest would ensue, followed by months, if not years, of legal battles. But she also believed that, in the end, Senator Holt would experience the sting of justice.

She was sorry for Marjorie Holt and her

children and grandchildren. Yet the truth she'd considered the day she and Corbin had sat together on John's dock — that actions had consequences — kept circling through her mind. The senator had managed to evade the consequences of his actions toward Josephine and Stan Markum and Vickie Goff and others for years. But no longer.

She rustled through the pantry until she found an unopened box of After Eights that she'd bought for a friend's bridal shower long ago. Gazing out her kitchen window, she nibbled on the mint chocolate square.

Yesterday she'd completed her last modeling assignment. She'd fulfilled every single one of her outstanding work obligations, which left her feeling a hundred pounds lighter and also slightly . . . unmoored.

She'd left one destination behind. However, she was stuck in a kind of purgatory, because she'd yet to reach her new destination. She wouldn't be satisfied until she was where she wanted to be: beside Corbin in the storm of his dad's decline. For the time being, her whole focus, her only goal, was to return to him.

Today, she'd write and mail a letter to Joe because this she knew: The road between LA and Shore Pine was blocked by cantan-

kerous Joe Stewart, a man who was the anto-
nym of her biggest fan.

Letter from Willow to Joe:

Joe,

I realize that I'm not your favorite
person. I hope you'll do me the honor
of reading this letter and hearing me out,
anyway.

I'll begin by apologizing. I know you
feel animosity toward me because of
how my relationship with Corbin ended
four years ago. A few months back, I
might have responded to your animosity
by pointing my finger at Corbin and
angrily listing all the things he did
wrong. But my feelings couldn't be more
different now. At this point, when I think
about our breakup, I primarily see before
me the things that I did wrong.

I turned my back on my own beliefs
for a time, which made me anxious.
When Corbin couldn't make me feel
secure, I distanced myself. When he
didn't say the things I wanted to hear in
a TV interview, I distanced myself. When
I was given a reason to feel betrayed by
him, I snatched it. To protect myself, I
ended things with him and refused to

give him the second chance he asked for.

I'm a Christian, which means the gift of grace I've received allows me to live forgiven. However, until recently, I couldn't find it within myself to forgive Corbin. After hanging on to bitterness much, much too long, I finally did forgive him. And I believe that he's forgiven me.

I apologize for hurting your son and for the hurt I caused you, too. I apologize for the pain Corbin went through because of me after our breakup. I apologize for my unforgiving heart.

You see, I came to love Corbin (again) this past fall. In the months since I left Washington, through our phone conversations, I've come to love him more and more and more.

I've fulfilled my modeling contracts and haven't accepted any future assignments because I'm very eager to return to Washington. In all honesty, I can't stand not to be there with Corbin during this time. I don't want to cause you frustration or anger. I just want to be there to support Corbin and do whatever you're comfortable with me doing to support you.

I haven't returned sooner because I've

561

been very cognizant of the promises I
made to you that day, sitting on the
porch outside your house. Will you
please release me from those promises
and allow me to return?

Please?

I'll make you a new promise. I'll promise to love your son wholeheartedly. To
help him find his keys. To make sure he
continues to order chocolate for dessert.
To laugh at his sense of humor. To look
past his charm when he tries to use it as
a smokescreen and dig deeper to discover what's really going on beneath. I
promise to protect him. And if we marry
one day, I promise you that I'll stay true
to my vows all my life.

I'll await your decision.

You can reach me at the following
phone number.

Sincerely, Willow

CHAPTER TWENTY-SIX

Only a week and a half had passed since the day he and his dad had finished renovating the house. In that short amount of time, Corbin had watched the health drain from his dad's body.

Corbin had been working to place his trust in God. And to place his trust in God. And again, to place his trust in God.

In addition to the hospice specialists who checked in with them daily, Corbin had hired round-the-clock nurses. He'd flown in every one of Joe's family members and friends who'd wanted to visit. Whenever Dr. Benton made a house call, Corbin asked him whether his dad was receiving the best possible treatment. The doctor always assured him he was. Even so, concern gnawed at Corbin.

Was his dad in pain? Should he have moved him into a hospice facility for his final days? He hadn't done that because it wasn't what his dad had wanted. His dad had wanted to stay in his bed. In his room.

Should Corbin have forced his dad to participate in a clinical trial? Could that have saved his dad's life? Could Corbin's life ever be good again without his dad in it?

Corbin lowered into the chair positioned nearest his dad's bed. It was still warm from the last occupant, his dad's sister Donna. Corbin had been downstairs in his office just now, hiding from his relatives. Every time he came within ten feet of one of them, they tried to talk to him, and they all looked at him like they pitied him and like they were painfully eager to help. It was suffocating. When Aunt Donna left his dad, she came downstairs to his office door and let him know his dad wanted to see him. So here he was.

His dad gave him a welcoming look that crinkled his eyes with affection. He extended a hand. They'd never been a handholding pair before, the auto worker and the football player. But then, these past few days their relationship had been different in many ways. Corbin gripped his dad's hand. It felt cool and dry and breakable.

His father was turning into a skeleton before his eyes. How much time did his dad have left? Two more weeks? Two more months? He didn't know.

"I'm glad we finished the house," Joe said.

"I am, too."

"It's a good house."

"Yes."

"A good . . . legacy."

"Yes." Grief tightened Corbin's throat.

"Will you live here for a while? Will you keep it?"

"I never plan to sell the house."

"You could marry and raise your family here. This would be a nice place to raise a family."

"It would."

Late afternoon sunlight flowed into the room, illuminating Max, who was curled at the foot of his dad's bed. Duke sat on the floor, his chin resting on the mattress.

"Do you . . . think you might ask Willow to marry you? One day?"

"If she ever gives me a reason to think she wants to marry me, then yes."

His dad frowned as he rested more deeply into his pillows. For several moments, he said nothing. He appeared to need the time to gather strength. "I made a mistake," he finally said. "With Willow."

Corbin furrowed his brow.

"That day," his dad said, "you found us talking together . . . on the side porch? Do you remember?"

"Yes."

"I asked her not to let things get serious between the two of you, and I asked her not to come back to Washington when she left."

Corbin couldn't move. His dad had . . . ? Wait. He thought back to that day and everything that had come after. Growing realization shot an icy chill through the center of him.

"I asked her not to tell you," his dad said.

He . . . he'd known his dad had concerns about Willow, but he'd never dreamed that his dad would go so far as to meddle in their lives. His dad had no right to ask her to leave and not come back.

Willow was kinder than Corbin was. From the first time she'd met his dad, she'd been trying to win him over. The day he'd found Willow and his dad talking on the porch, Willow had known about his dad's worsening condition. He could imagine why she'd agreed to his dad's requests.

Good grief. He'd thought he'd known everything there was to know about his relationship with Willow. But his dad and Willow had known something he hadn't, and he was having a hard time adjusting to the sudden truth.

"I never liked her," his dad said, "after

566

how things ended the last time you dated. I was sure that no good could ever come from your reunion. I wanted you to stay here and finish the house. I wanted you to find happiness with someone else."

"There is no one else for me," Corbin said evenly.

"What about Macy?"

"No."

"I understand. There was only one . . . woman for me, too. Your mother."

Corbin had no interest in going through life alone, the way his dad had after his mother walked out.

"When Willow left I was hoping things would get back to normal for you," his dad said. "But they never did. You haven't been yourself since she went away."

"That's because I love her, Dad. I miss her."

He nodded. "I shouldn't have asked those things of Willow. I thought I was doing what was best for you, but I was wrong. Willow —" He broke off on a rattling cough.

Corbin started to rise to get water, but his dad stilled him with a glance.

"I'm fine," he croaked, then cleared his throat. "Willow kept her promises to me even though that must have been hard. She never told you what I'd asked her to do.

Did she?"

"Never."

"She sent me a letter."

Corbin regarded him with surprise. "I didn't see a letter from her arrive."

"She typed labels for the outside, and she didn't add her name to the return address."

Once again, Corbin was having a hard time adjusting to the sudden truth. "What did she say?"

"She rattled off all of her mistakes. She apologized. And here's the thing. Her honesty and the fact that she really seemed to want my forgiveness . . . it changed . . . something inside me. She's still not someone I love or anything. Don't get your hopes up on that account. But her openness made me like her some. A good little bit."

The woman who'd once insisted she deserved no more than fifteen percent of the blame for the way things had gone down between them had confessed her mistakes to his dad, who resented her for completely unjustified reasons?

"I was awake part of last night, son, thinking about her letter and my reaction to it. I could understand . . . all at once, I could understand why God forgives people who come to Him and admit the stuff they've done wrong, people who are humble enough

568

to ask for forgiveness. So then I had to wonder what was keeping me from admitting my own mistakes to God. If Willow was brave enough to do it with me, then why wasn't I brave enough to do it with Him? I've always liked to . . . think of myself as brave."

"And?"

"I remembered you telling me that people would rather think of themselves as good than face their mistakes."

"I actually said something that impacted you?" Corbin tried to smile.

"Just that *one* thing. Everything else you said was nonsense." His dad chuckled. "That one thing, though — about refusing to face what I've done wrong — that did make sense. It's just . . . when you've messed up as much as I have, it isn't easy."

"I know."

"God and I spent a long time talking about it last night."

"And? What did you think?"

"About God?"

"Yeah."

"That He's forgiving. Plus, I like His book."

Was his dad really saying what Corbin hoped he was saying? "You grumble when I make you listen to His book."

"Well. It's grown on me. A man has a right to change his mind."

"Yes. A man does."

"I just want you to know that I'm all right. With what's to come."

"You told me you believed nothing was to come. Lights out."

"I figure it doesn't hurt to gamble in God's favor and believe His version of things instead. When I get to heaven, I'll do some renovation work and get the place ready for you, all right? Just like I did here."

Moisture rushed to Corbin's eyes because he was so overwhelmingly relieved. "Okay."

Joe's expression turned suspicious. "You're not going to expect me to pray out loud now, right? Or sing hymns? Because I'm still not."

"I know."

A lifetime of memories of his dad streamed through Corbin's brain. Big moments. Small moments. So often over the years, Corbin had seen sorrow or pain tangled in his dad's eyes. Today, all Corbin could see in those brown eyes he'd known all his life was peace.

"I love you, Corbin," his dad said hoarsely.

"I love you, too, Dad."

"I'm sorry for the things I didn't do right. Including with Willow."

"It's all right." And it was. "Thank you for everything you did for me. For all the things you did do right."

Humor creased his dad's cheeks. "There were a few of those."

"There were a lot of those. And I remember them all and always will." His dad was dying, but he was managing to speak more easily than Corbin. Each word Corbin spoke felt like a rusty piece of metal scraping against his constricted chest. "I wish that you'd had more years in South Haven."

"I enjoyed the years in South Haven. But they weren't my best years. My best years were the ones I spent with you in that condo in Detroit when you were growing up. Those . . . were my best years."

Those had been brutal years for his dad financially, mentally. "They were?"

"Yes. Because we were together."

Corbin was too choked up to say more. He bit down hard on his back teeth.

Joe reached toward his bedside table for his cell phone. He checked it, then looked at his watch. "In her letter, Willow asked if I'd release her from her promises to me so that she could come back."

Hope lurched inside Corbin.

"I called her this morning and told her that I would. She got on the first plane to

Seattle and texted me a little while ago to let me know that she's almost here. Which is why I had Donna go and get you. Unless I miss my guess, Willow should be pulling up outside in the next two minutes."

Corbin stared at him.

"Why are you still sitting here with your old dad?"

Corbin stood up so fast that his chair scraped against the carpet. He strode toward the door. His dad's rusty laughter followed Corbin into the hallway.

Corbin banged the front door behind him and shaded his eyes as he made his way across the yard toward the driveway.

A figure came into view.

A woman. In a red coat. Walking toward him.

His breath jerked in.

His dad's estimate of her arrival time must have been slightly off because she'd already parked. Already exited her car.

He dropped his hand and walked toward her on legs that felt weak. He could begin to make out the details of her face now, her smile. Every bit of her was so familiar. The lines of her body. Her blond hair. Her green eyes.

As soon as they were near enough, he clutched her to him.

She said nothing, and he said nothing. He simply held her, his heart pounding with deep, forceful beats. She held him, too, her arms sure and strong, clasping behind his back.

He wasn't alone.

She was here.

She was here, thank God. *Thank God.*

Her body was warm and soft. She smelled like crisp perfume. And he wanted to weep because he was so rocked by thankfulness. For as long as he lived, he wasn't going to be able to go even a week without seeing her. Ever again.

Willow was crying. Happy tears, yes. Even so, she hadn't planned on crying. Corbin was the one who was losing his parent! She'd planned on being a source of comfort. Also, her mascara was going to run.

She couldn't hold the tears back, however, because the reality of him was so mind-blowingly sweet. His body's strength enclosed hers. His jacket smelled faintly of woodsmoke.

Her Corbin. Hers.

"Red Riding Hood," he finally said.

"Corbin."

He clasped her tighter and pressed kisses into her hair. She felt him raise his face and so she leaned back slightly and made a surreptitious attempt to clear the mascara. Her index fingers bore less of it than she'd feared.

"You're crying." Both of his big hands came up to smooth away the rest of the moisture.

"Yes. I'm just so, so glad to see you."

"Not more glad than I am to see you."

"Maybe it's a tie."

"How did you get here so fast? My dad said you guys talked just this morning."

"I quit my job. For more than a week, I've been waiting in LA for the chance to come back here. As soon as Joe gave me that chance, I was on my way to the airport."

"You quit?"

"I quit." She adjusted the collar of his jacket, glorying in the ability to touch him. "All I've wanted since I left here was to come home."

His cheeks held a few days' worth of russet five o'clock shadow. His eyes were one shade darker than she'd remembered. His short hair had grown a fraction longer than he usually kept it.

"My dad just told me about the things he made you promise," Corbin said.

"I couldn't say no to him, Corbin. He was sick, and he wanted what he thought was best for you. At the time, it didn't seem as though the promises would be hard to keep. But the opposite has been true."

"From now on, don't make any promises not to take me seriously or to stay away from me or not to tell me stuff. All right?"

"Well, now that you've specified it so clearly, I won't." She grinned a wobbly grin. "I'm sorry for leaving you and for staying away as long as I have."

He smoothed a lock of hair from her eye. "I forgive you."

"I know it must have seemed like I was abandoning you right when you needed me . . . which is exactly what I accused you of doing to me all those years ago."

"Seemed that way. But I've been determined not to let you go this time."

"Same here." This time, when things had turned rocky, they'd found a way to hang on to each other. "I love you," she said.

He appeared to hold his breath. Then, slowly, like honey dripping from a spoon, a lopsided smile spread across his face. "You love me?"

She laughed. "Yes, Corbin. I love you."

"I love you, Willow. Will you stay here with me?"

"Well, not on this particular spot. We might get cold, and I bet your yard turns creepy at night. But yes, I'm going to stay in Washington with you."

"You're not going to leave me again?"

"Never. Will *you* stay here with me?" she asked, joy bubbling within her.

"Yes. I'm going to stay with you always." She ran her fingers into his hair, and he kissed her.

It was a kiss to end all kisses.

A kiss christened by sunshine.

A kiss seasoned with blessing and loss.

A kiss brimming with the promise of a golden future.

EPILOGUE

His dad's grave site was hushed. And beautiful, in its way.

From where he stood, Corbin could see acres of cemetery lawn and the town of Shore Pine far below. This early April morning smelled of cut grass and damp wood and earth.

His father had died a month ago today.

Despite the grief of that, mornings kept on coming. Sunlight kept on coming. God could still be trusted. And Willow still loved him.

He watched her kneel and place the bouquet of flowers they'd brought on the base of the headstone.

As his dad's physical condition had worsened, his dad's soul had been more and more at rest.

Joe had been accepting. He'd griped about bad football plays he saw on TV or the fact that the curtains let in too much light or the food Corbin brought him. But he'd never second-guessed the fact that he was dying. And he'd never complained about the pain.

Joe had been calm. After a life of over-blown rough patches and good patches, his dad had ended his life in a steady patch. The steady patches were the ones Corbin had always trusted most.

Throughout those final weeks, Willow had been there. Every single day. Every time he needed her. Willow and his dad had made amends, and near the end his dad had even told her that he liked her baked French toast, which was high praise, coming from him.

Corbin helped Willow up, and they stood without words, their hands interlaced.

The day Dr. Benton had told Corbin that it was time to call in hospice, Corbin had reached the conclusion that his dad's story wasn't going to be a miracle story.

He'd been wrong.

His dad's story had turned out to be a miracle story after all.

God had heard Corbin's prayers for himself and for his father. Corbin knew exactly where his dad was now, and he was holding on to the certainty that he'd see him again one day.

At some point Corbin's own body would be lowered into a rectangular plot of ground. It was up to him to make the most of the time he had left between now and then.

He squeezed Willow's hand, and they made their way toward his car. "You know what I'm in the mood for?" Corbin asked.

"Shopping for housewares?"

"No."

"Meeting with the wedding coordinator?"

He'd proposed a week ago, and she'd said yes. "No. I'm in the mood for flourless chocolate cake and whipped cream."

"It's ten o'clock in the morning," she said.

"And yet I'm in the mood for flourless chocolate cake. You?"

". . . Yes, actually."

"Then don't worry, Willow. I will find us a restaurant somewhere in Washington that serves chocolate cake at this hour."

"I don't have a single doubt that you will." She smiled at him so brightly it caused his pulse to skip.

His story with Willow? He knew a secret about it that he hadn't told her yet.

Their story was a miracle story, too.

"For God in all his fullness was pleased to live in Christ, and through him God reconciled everything to himself. He made peace with everything in heaven and on earth by means of Christ's blood on the cross."

COLOSSIANS 1:19–20 NLT

QUESTIONS FOR CONVERSATION

1. Did you relate more to the cautious character of Willow or the determined character of Corbin? Explain why!

2. *Falling for You* is what romance writers call a "reunion romance" because its hero and heroine were in love once before. What do you enjoy about this type of story?

3. The plot of *Falling for You* revolves around the mystery of Josephine Blake's disappearance. Did you enjoy uncovering clues as Willow, Corbin, and Charlotte sought to solve the mystery? If so, why was the mystery engaging? What were some of your early theories about what might have happened to Josephine?

4. During the course of the story, Willow and Corbin both reflect on the fact that

actions and choices have consequences. Describe a time in your life when your action or choice had an unexpectedly large impact on your life, either for better or worse.

5. As we get to know Willow, we learn that she's always longed to view herself as "good." After she made mistakes, she was filled with regret. Believers understand — intellectually — that we're saved by grace. So why do you think it's difficult for so many of us to accept that we have no "goodness" of our own to bring to the table?

6. Becky added epistolary elements to the end of each chapter in the form of letters, articles, text message conversations, and more. Why do you think she chose to do that?

7. Aside from Willow and Corbin, who was your favorite secondary character in this story? Why?

8. The Lord led both Corbin and Willow to move on from very successful careers so that they could embrace the new thing He wanted to do in their lives. When has the Lord asked you to make a change and fol-

low Him into something new? How did it turn out?

9. On a scale of 1–10, how romantic was *Falling for You*?

10. The theme of *Falling for You* is reconciliation. Can you name three reconciliations that happened in this story? Share a time when the Lord enabled you to reconcile with someone. Do you have a strong relationship with that person now?

ABOUT THE AUTHOR

Becky Wade is a native of California who attended Baylor University, met and married a Texan, and moved to Dallas. She published historical romances for the general market, then put her career on hold for several years to care for her children. When God called her back to writing, Becky knew He meant for her to turn her attention to Christian fiction. Her humorous, heart-pounding contemporary romance novels have won the Carol Award, the INSPY Award, and the Inspirational Reader's Choice Award for Romance. Becky lives in Dallas, Texas, with her husband and three children.

To find out more about Becky and her books, visit www.beckywade.com.

The employees of Thorndike Press hope you have enjoyed this Large Print book. All our Thorndike, Wheeler, and Kennebec Large Print titles are designed for easy reading, and all our books are made to last. Other Thorndike Press Large Print books are available at your library, through selected bookstores, or directly from us.

For information about titles, please call:
  (800) 223-1244

or visit our website at:
  gale.com/thorndike

To share your comments, please write:
  Publisher
  Thorndike Press
  10 Water St., Suite 310
  Waterville, ME 04901